HIS LITTLE BALLERINA

SHEVAUN DELUCIA

Words Written, LLC New York

www.shevaundelucia.com

Publisher's Note: This is a work of fiction. Names, characters, places, and incidents are a product of the author's imagination. Locales and public names are sometimes used for atmospheric purposes. Any resemblance to actual people, living or dead, or to businesses, companies, events, institutions, or locales is completely coincidental.

His Little Ballerina/ Shevaun DeLucia/ Print ISBN 978-0-9863951-7-8

His Little Ballerina/ Shevaun DeLucia/ eBook ISBN 978-0-9863951-8-5

To the women that choose alternative lifestyles, you deserve the magical book love too.

CHAPTER 1

My eyes flutter open, blinking and squinting against the bright sliver of sun slicing through my blinds. God, what time is it? It's got to still be the ass crack of dawn. I lift my head up just slightly enough to look at the time on my alarm clock. The red numbers blaring back at me shine 6:47AM.

I close my eyes and groan.

I just laid my head down hours before and here I am awake again. The destruction of my life years ago brought the lovely friend of insomnia into my world and ever since she has been here to stay.

I roll over and kick my covers off, still struggling to completely succumb to the cheery sun blazing back at me. My eyes burn and my head is pounding as I struggle to sit up. Remnants of last night slowly creep in my mind making me wince from a flash of regret slicing through me.

I grab the bottled water on the nightstand beside my bed and chug. Water slips down the sides of my mouth as I gulp like my life depends on it. Being hungover is something I should be used to by now. Drinking is the only thing that gets me through my job and my guilt. It's the one constant in my life that can numb my pain away.

Dragging myself to the bathroom is always a chore. Turning the shower on I let the heated cloud take over my mind as I step in and wash away my sins of the night before. The hot water is magical to my tense muscles, helping dissipate my pounding headache into more of a dull thrum.

I crank the water off, dry off my body, wrap the towel around my hair, and head out of my bathroom. My bedroom door that just moments ago had been closed is now open with a man standing in the doorway.

I quickly jump back. "What the fuck?!" I yell as I attempt to cover my breasts, still leaving the remainder of my body fully exposed to his wandering eyes.

"Get the fuck *out!*" I scream.

Instead of being embarrassed or mortified about walking into a room with a naked scared woman, he cracks a smirk and apologizes, still allowing his eyes to roam with no urgency in removing them or looking the other way.

My heart is banging against my rib cage ready for my fight or flight instincts to kick in.

My eyes dart from him to the hallway past him waiting to see Trevor's face – but nothing.

Even though I wished I could say this is a one-off incident, this isn't the first time this has happened which makes me angry at myself because in my drunken stupor this morning I was clearly careless in not locking my bedroom door behind me.

"I'm sorry. I'm looking for my brother Luke. He left the club last night with a Desire and I haven't heard from him since," he explains.

I immediately grab the towel from my head and wrap it tightly around me. Even though men's ogling eyes are something I'm very used to in my line of work, this happening in my bedroom is not something I'm used to.

He looks down at his phone and holds it up showing me his tracker.

"I tracked him here and a man let me in," he says as he points his thumb over his shoulder. "Your door was the first one I opened in search of him," he says, still eyeing me intently as he rakes them slowly down the length of my body.

Goosebumps break out over my skin. I instantly wrap my arms protectively around myself. I must admit, even with having this strange man standing in my bedroom doorway, those intense hazel eyes are the most beautiful light green I have ever seen. I can't bring myself to look away. The sunrays peeking from my blinds, shining over his face, are giving them an almost golden glow and have me a bit mesmerized.

My eyes drift down his body drinking him in. Black silky slicked back hair, chiseled jawline with a 5 o'clock shadow, creamy caramel skin, broad shoulders with a tiny bit of black hair peeking out of the top of his unbuttoned dress shirt, and sleeves rolled up giving me a glimpse of ink peeking from underneath.

Jesus.

He catches my eye with a knowing smirk. Heat creeps up my face.

Why is this god-like stranger standing in my room? And seriously – where is everyone?

I know I should be screaming or panicking since this man still hasn't left my space, but the chills and butterflies furiously fluttering against my stomach have me a bit speechless.

I clear my throat, and straighten my back. "Clearly, you're in the wrong room. There's no Luke in here as you can see, so if you don't mind, please leave and close the door behind you," I advise, matter-of-factly.

"Desire's room is at the end of the hall to the right. You'll probably find him there," I direct.

Fucking Desire.

3

I'm going to have to have a serious sit down with her on bringing men back to our apartment. I have told her over and over how unsafe this is for us both and how important it is to keep our work and personal lives separate.

She's my best friend and I love her to death, but if she doesn't stop then I might just have to find a place of my own.

He gives me one last look over before saying, "You know, whoever that man is sleeping on the couch shouldn't be just letting anyone in here. Girls like you I'm sure have enough issues with strange men in your space, but where you sleep should be kept sacred and safe," he advises, before turning and walking down the hall.

You're telling me.

I rush to my door slamming it shut while turning the lock. My heart is bursting out of my chest as I lean my back against the door closing my eyes and finally blowing out the breath I've been holding this whole time.

I POUR A STEAMING cup of coffee and take a seat at the kitchen table next to Trevor. I hear rustling and banging coming from Desire's room, she must finally be up.

"Are you going to have another talk with her?" Trevor asks.

Trevor is our flaming gay muscular best friend slash bodyguard. We met him at the club four years ago and the three of us haven't been apart since. At first glance, he's extremely intimidating; bulging biceps and a chest that almost makes the green hulk look insignificant. But, under all this armor he's kind and loving and an extremely protective friend. Though this morning has me questioning that last part.

"Yeah, after this morning, it's definitely time for another talk with her," I reply. "And what were *you* thinking allowing that guy to just walk in though?" I ask him, realizing I'm a little more than just upset with him.

Normally, he wouldn't allow anyone to step foot in here unless they're completely vetted and interrogated thoroughly.

"I mean *girl*, did you see that hot specimen of a man? Who the hell in their right mind would say no to him?" Trevor admits, while fanning his hand in front of his face.

I roll my eyes.

"*Seriously?* He could have been a serial killer! And because he looked good, you let him in?"

Unbelievable.

"You know I wouldn't have let anything happen to either of you. He said he was looking for his brother. I saw Desire sneaking him in this morning and clearly, she thought she was being quiet," he says, shaking his head. "But I didn't think Mr. Hottie was going to start randomly opening doors either."

I can tell he feels guilty, so I won't make him suffer any longer.

"I forgive you, but don't do it again," I scold, shaking my pointer finger at him.

"Did you at least get his number?" he asks with a sly side smile and a twinkle in his eyes.

I shake my head. "You're out of your fucking mind. No, I didn't *give* him my number! You should have given him yours!" I laugh.

Desire walks in catching the last part of our conversation as she opens the cabinet to grab a cup and pours herself some coffee.

"Sorry Trev, both those brothers are strictly *not* dickly." She giggles.

He pouts.

It is time to have this talk with Dez. I'm nervous she's not going to take me seriously, but I really need her to understand that this is it, she needs to make a change and stop thinking with her vagina all the time and be smarter.

"Dez, about this morning..." I start out.

She takes a seat at the table across from me, holds out her palm toward me to stop me, and takes a long sip of her coffee before interrupting me.

"Naomi, I'm sorry. I know you're mad about Gabriele walking in on you. I shouldn't have brought Luke back here. I just got carried away partying too much at the club and didn't want the night to end," she explains.

"Jesus, even Mr. Hottie has a *hot* freaking name!" Trev scoffs.

Dez and I both laugh. "Dez, I just want you to be careful. Work is work but bringing it home to us scares the shit out of me. Most of these guys are no good and look at last year when we had to deal with your stalker. I mean thank God for Trev watching out for us but he's not always going to be here," I remind her. "It took us months to get that guy out of your life; we don't need another replay of that."

"You're right, Nay. I just get too carried away partying too hard sometimes and make bad decisions. But I like Luke. He comes into the club a lot to see me and wanted to see me outside of the club for once, so I brought him back here," she confesses.

My heart breaks a tiny bit for my friend. She hasn't had a great track record with men and the love department, and I know she's just grabbing on to anyone who gives her some attention. She just wants to feel wanted and loved – as do we all.

"And let's just say Mr. Hottie didn't seem too pleased with that idea!" Trev chimes in.

I finish my coffee and head over to the sink to stick the cup in the dishwasher.

"Yeah, Gabriele was pissed when Luke wasn't answering. Guess they had to catch a flight for a business meeting. Luke works for his older brother and from what he's told me, Gabriele has an extremely short fuse and isn't as laid-back as him," Dez informs us.

"He's definitely not the partying type like his brother."

I wonder if Luke looks as intimidatingly sexy as his older brother does. Now that I think of it, makes sense why he was already suited up at 7AM on a Saturday morning.

Most men we see leaving the club in the early hours don't have crisp suits remaining, or a freshly smelling aroma. They reek of partying, alcohol, and bad decisions.

Gabriele on the other hand looked and smelled delicious.

I turn to them both.

"Let's make a deal – no more letting randos in," I look to Trev, then look to Dez, "and you no more bringing randoms home. You want to date, then make them work for it and take you out like a normal girl. You at least deserve that, Dez."

Dez's eyes soften with a tiny smile.

"Deal," they both reply in unison.

"Now, who wants to hit the gym with me? I need to blow off some major steam," I ask.

Trev jumps up. "Thought you'd never ask!"

Dez and I roll our eyes, and we all head out the door.

CHAPTER 2

"*N*ay, you ready?" Dez calls from the living room.

I grab my bag from the chair near the window and head out of my bedroom.

"We're going to be late! And you know how Jerry hates it when we're late. He'll use that against us to make us tip him out more," Dez gripes.

"I know, I can't fucking stand him. He reminds me of my sleezy uncle," I agree as we head to the car.

Jerry's our sleaze bucket boss who thinks he's God's gift to women. He's a middle-aged man, with a six-month pregnant belly, who smells like week old stale cigarettes.

He's perverted and attempts to coerce us into sleeping with him every chance he gets. It's dishonorable and disgusting, but we're used to it.

I make sure to view the surroundings on the way out of our apartment. It's late, our shift starts at 10PM, and you can never be too observant when it comes to creepers and stalkers.

Last year, Dez got herself involved with a stage five clinger who came in every night to watch her at work, followed her home from work, and refused to take no for an answer. It got to the point that Trev ended up living on our couch because the police refused to do anything to help.

As soon as she told them her line of work, they scoffed and brushed her off not taking her serious enough. It took him breaking in and assaulting her when Trev and I ran to the store, before they placed a restraining order on him finally, and took him back to jail for violating parole.

I still get this uneasy feeling when leaving our apartment. The hairs on my neck stand up as though we're being watched. It's extremely unsettling, and I've mentioned it to her on more than one occasion, but Dez just waves it off as me being paranoid.

She forgets too easily.

I haven't though.

That's why I carry a pocketknife and mace in my open purse for easy access.

As soon as we close the car door, we hit the locks.

"Is your boy Luke planning on coming in again tonight?" I ask as she pulls out against the oncoming traffic.

She pulls a joint from her ear and lights it up.

"Not tonight. He won't be back for another week," she answers with slight disappointment in her tone.

I'm curious about his older brother. There's been a couple of moments throughout the day that my heart rate spiked when quickly picturing those light green eyes staring back at me from this morning.

When it comes to men, my body never reacts. I sometimes feel like I may be broken so when I felt the slight tingle pulse between my legs when he stroked my body with his eyes, I could only imagine what his hands would feel like.

Such an odd shameful feeling considering he was some random guy who entered my room without permission. I should be apprehensive, not intrigued.

"I had to have seen him before, right? How many times has he came in, Dez?"

She passes me the joint, but I decline, as I do each time she offers. Drinking is my only nemesis. I can't handle any more bad decisions in my life.

She takes a long drag.

"Do you remember the loud group of guys that came in that one Thursday months ago? I told you it looked like the mob wives' husbands were here?" she asks. My memory is foggy but sounds vaguely familiar.

I shrug. "Well, he was the one buying the round of bottles the whole night and they had to carry him out," she reminds me.

Yes, now I remember.

He was wild, young, and loved throwing money at the girls. I remember I purposefully stayed clear from that table and Dez came home with hundreds that night. She made an impression on him, clearly.

I like dealing with the more reserved quiet type that comes in on their own. I can handle them better, less touchy-feely types. They tend to look more for conversation and small comforts than partying and disrespectful hand grabbing.

"Oh *Dez!* That guy? But why? Can't you just find someone who doesn't come into the club? A normal average Joe who doesn't want to throw dollars and coke up his nose?" I whine.

She snorts and shakes her head. "Nay, stop being so uppity. Look at where we're pulling up to right now to work!" she raises her voice while flailing her arm back and forth at the sign above the building. It says G-String Girls Club. "You really think someone like us is going to meet someone at the grocery store and take us home to meet mom and pops? Come on, Nay! Stop being so naïve."

She puts out her joint in the ashtray, grabs her bag from the back, and slams the car door on her way out. I blow out a deep breath while looking back up to the sign. Some days I don't know how I even got here and other days I feel this is all I deserve in life.

I feel as though I'm stuck in three lives; my past life, my work life, and the life I feel as though I don't deserve but still dream of.

When I was younger, it was just me and my mom. We had a simple life. She worked a lot trying to make ends meet while being a single mother and having a kid young. She had no family support, and my father was never in the picture. Last I knew he was still roaming the streets.

He was older; he should have known better, but he took advantage of my mother being young, naïve, and alone. She ended up with the shit end of the stick.

My grandparents had my mother and her brother, Carl, very late in their years so by the time they were old enough to take care of themselves, my grandparents decided they were done raising them and left my mother and Carl to fend for themselves after the age of sixteen.

Carl was two years older than my mom, Carla. He wasn't the protective, nurturing, older brother type; he was quite the opposite. He bullied her, making her days dreadful, and visited her at night.

Once she hit eighteen, she left and never went back.

Right before my fifteenth birthday my mom was diagnosed with stage four brain cancer. She lived with migraines for years but couldn't afford to seek medical help, so she just learned to live with the pain. Many nights I had to fend for myself while she was suffering in a dark quiet room. I did my best to take up odd jobs to help with the bills.

These times cut my teenage years short. It was one of the hardest things I had to watch.

She ended up passing when I was seventeen. Since I wasn't of legal age to take care of myself, I was sent to live with my grandparents. My uncle also came to stay shortly after that. I knew what he did to my mother; she told me about the terror she lived through as a child because of him, and she also told me how her parents didn't believe her and turned a blind eye.

I knew I wasn't safe there. I knew what I was going to be up against.

I locked my door at night, but I would wake up to the door handle jiggling and foot shadows beneath my door. I knew it was only a matter of time before I was going to end up like my mother.

I pushed coming home as late as possible; finding places to stay until the lights went out – schools, libraries, diners. Eventually, after becoming a regular the workers at the diner near my house would allow me to stay, giving me a safe place to reprieve and a free piece of pie until I was ready to go home.

The owner offered me a job, so I worked long hours to save up money and put off going home. They were kind to me. It was exactly what I needed to get through that time in my life. I wasn't there long enough to make friends and knew I wasn't going to be staying there long enough either.

The night I met Dez was the last night I ever stepped foot into my grandparents' home. This was the night my uncle finally got into my room. He wasn't expecting me to put up a fight as I did, but I was ready. I bought a tiny pocketknife weeks before and kept it under my pillow.

The moment he climbed on top of me I stabbed his thigh with my knife, grabbed my already packed bag I had ready in case of this scenario, and took off running never looking back.

I'd always planned on going back to Arizona eventually where my mother and I lived; I just didn't plan on making the move this soon. I had a little cash that I saved up, so I took a bus from New York to Arizona that night.

I met Dez on the Greyhound. She looked broken and scared; hoodie over her head and remnants of a black eye that was now yellow and green with her arms protectively glued against herself. She looked up at me with pained eyes and a kind smile. I knew at that moment that we were destined to be friends.

Now here we are six years later, not living the dream, but together still.

THE CLUB IS PACKED TONIGHT. The weekends are our biggest money-making nights, but they're also the most exhausting; emotionally and physically. The music is pumping, the lights flashing, and the sounds of men congregating and laughing are flowing through the back.

Dez comes running in the back where all us girls are changing.

"He's here, Nay!" she yells excitedly, jumping up and down.

My brows scrunch together. "Who's here?"

"Luke!" She smiles, throwing her hands in the air, exasperated, like I should have guessed. This week has flown by.

One of the girls, Shae, walks by rolling her eyes. "He's interested in how your ass jiggles, not your brain, Dez."

I agree silently but still give her a dirty look for insulting my girl. "Keep walking, Shae," I advise her. "Not everyone is as shaded as you," I lie. I'm shaded. But my poor girl, Dez, still has her hopes up for Prince Charming.

Doesn't she know he doesn't exist for girls like us?

"Yeah, keep walking, Shae! And stay away from my table!" Dez yells after her.

I shake my head while listening to the other girls grumble behind us. "Just promise me one thing?" I ask.

"I know. Don't bring him home," she replies with a huff.

I laugh. I get up, give myself a last look, and wrap my arm around her shoulder heading out of the dressing room.

I grab drink orders, throwing shots down my throat to

numb myself, and to help create conversation throughout the night; hands roam my body as I dance, with alcohol induced breath whispering grotesque visions in my ears. I'm forced to smile and giggle while inwardly wanting to puke.

I can't help but be jaded in my line of work. Hearing fetishes of married men, and requests from drunk men, makes me think there may be no normal men in this world. From young to old, I'm no longer surprised by what someone may ask of me.

It's hard to keep prying hands at bay when I'm requested for a private dance, but Trev is never far behind, watching over us. I'm thankful for him on these long and rowdy nights.

"Jazz, you're up!" Jerry yells toward me. I use a stage name, never giving out my true name. I'd like to keep one thing to myself that belongs only to me.

He announces my name over the speaker as I walk up the stairs to the stage. The spotlights are bright and help me tune out the lineup of men below. I wouldn't say I'm the best dancer in the club, but I've learned some tricks over the years-enough to make the men go wild and to keep the bills flying.

I begin to move to the music, swaying my hips as I grab onto the pole. I lean my back against the pole while sliding down and closing my eyes pretending it's just me and the music in the room. I've learned over the years how to turn a deaf ear to the crude comments and shouting.

I crack my eyes open, looking out over the crowd, and in the distance sitting alone at one of the dark corner tables is a man. The lights flash over him, blinding me momentarily and concealing him from my view. Electric currents run down the back of my neck, reaching my arms, painting down the rest of my body.

I stretch my neck as I climb up the pole to get a better look. I feel like I've seen that face before, but I can't quite place it through the shadowed darkness. I continue to work the pole getting whistles and shouts, but I keep my eyeline to that table waiting for the lights to flash by again so I can get a clear picture.

My heart speeds up against my chest like the bass to the music. I move upside down and twirl, contracting my core muscles while squeezing my thighs to help keep me up. After a couple of rounds on stage, workouts aren't really needed but help.

I can still see the shadow of the man from the distance. The music slows and I begin to pick up the bills strown across the stage. As I bend, a hand grabs my ankle and pulls. "Let me the fuck go!" I demand, trying to kick him off.

The man grabs hold tighter and tries to run his other hand up my leg toward my ass. "Come on baby, just one more dance. Bend over and give us a good show," he yells over the music.

Trev has his hands on the back of the guy's shirt in an instant dragging him away. I finish collecting my money, heading off the stage, making my first stop at the table of the man who was watching me. I feel confused and let down as I see an empty booth. He's gone. I look around but the jolt I felt just moments ago has now disappeared and I'm left feeling vacant.

The rest of the night goes by uneventful. I'm now sitting in the back room counting my money as Jerry hovers. He takes a seat behind me groping me with his eyes. Jadah walks in taking note.

"Jerry, Jazz is out of your league, go bother Jess," she warns.

Jadah's been here for years and takes care of us all. Makes sure we have everything we need; outfits, shoes, makeup, wigs – you ask, and she makes it happen. She's motherly in her own way.

He stands, walks over, and holds his hand out to me.

"Seriously, Jer? You can't even wait until I'm done counting?" I respond, annoyed.

"You owe me a hundred on top of my cut tonight since you were late – *again*," he demands.

My neck snaps back. "That's fucking ridiculous! Dez and I were no more than twenty minutes late!" I argue.

Jadah interjects. "You know the rules, Jazz. You're late, you pay."

Jerry grins. "Twenty minutes cost us. Unless you would like to pay me another way, then I would be more than happy to oblige and we can take this back into my office," he snickers.

Fucking gross.

My stomach threatens to chuck up my drinks. "I didn't drink enough for that offer," I say as I slap the hundred along with his cut into his hand. He walks off with a growl counting the money.

I look through the girls and realize I haven't seen Dez yet. I grab my jacket and bag to head out into the club. The music has stopped, the dull lights are now on, and there are only a few stragglers left.

My eyes catch Trev, and I lift my arms out in question. He already knows who I'm searching for and snaps his head in her direction. There in the corner of the room are her and Luke talking in deep thought. He has his hand up her thigh and is whispering into her ear. I see her giggle as I walk up and clear my throat.

They both look up. The first thing I notice is familiar hazel eyes staring back at me, though his aren't as golden; more of a dirty green. I can see the similarities to his brother, but my body doesn't fire up the same.

There's no electric current charging through my body, or cyclones of butterflies swirling through my lower belly. There's only a dull annoyance filling me as I look at the two of them. She's never going to learn.

"It's late. Time to go, Dez," I announce.

Luke smiles with a mouth full of pearly white teeth. "I can bring her home," he offers.

I shake my head. "I don't think so. She's coming home with me."

Dez pouts. "Jazz, come on. I'll be fine. I promise."

I'm grateful she didn't give up my name.

I cross my arms over my chest. "No offense, Luke, but I don't have faith in the men that come in this place, who's to say you're any different?" I ask.

"Can I see your phone?" he asks. I look at him in question. "Please? I'm going to put in my address and phone number for you. If I don't have her back safely by tomorrow afternoon, you can come hunt me down."

I reluctantly hand over my phone. Dez gives me a big smile.

"I swear Trev and I will come hunt you down if you don't come home," I warn.

"Deal," Dez agrees.

I head out of the building and follow Trev to his car. He insisted he come stay with me tonight since I am going to be alone.

"Trev, did you see a guy sitting alone in the booth over near the bar tonight?" I ask.

He looks over to me frowning. "No, why? Did he do something?"

I shake my head. "No, but I don't know, I just thought I knew him and when I got off the stage and went to see him, he was gone."

"Maybe you scared him off with your crazy ass shaking." He laughs. I smack his arm.

"Did you see the blond Luke was sitting with?" he inquires.

I try to recall but I must admit I purposely stayed away from his crazy table. The thought of someone's hands touching my skin after knowing my best friend is giddy for him doesn't go over well with me. "No, why?"

He turns into my parking lot. I scan the area as we pull up to my building. Like always, an eerie sense of dread washes over me.

"Mr. Blondie kept giving me the side-eye all night. I first thought I was just seeing things but then I caught him looking me up and down like a scrumptious snack," he explains.

I burst out laughing.

"So, did you end up talking to him?" I question as we get out of the car.

My eyes twitch back and forth over each shadow covered piece of darkness on the way up to my apartment door. Once inside, after locking the door and deadbolt, I breathe out a breath of relief.

"Nope, but he walked by and slipped me his number before leaving," he admits with a wide smile as he pulls out the piece of paper from his pocket and waves it around.

I shake my head with a smirk. Never fails, Trev always attracts the hidden in the closet types. I mean who can blame them? If I was a straight man, I would also go erect after one look at him.

"Are you gonna call him?"

He plops down on the couch and kicks his legs up. "Nah, what's the point? I don't need another straight man to keep me as his side piece while his wife is home barefoot and pregnant."

My heart aches just a little for him. I walk over and kiss him on the forehead. "You deserve better too, Trev. Thanks for staying the night with me."

I walk down the hall to my bedroom and lock the door behind me.

CHAPTER 3

"*I*t's fucking 3PM, Trev, and she's not answering my calls or texts!" I scream, pacing back and forth in my living room.

"Did you try Luke's number?"

I stop, placing my hands on my hips. "Yes, and *nothing!*"

My heart is going to combust with worry. I fucking warned Dez this wasn't a good idea. Now she's gone missing.

"Nay, calm down!" Trev yells, walking over to shake some sense into me. "He gave you his address, right?"

I nod my head. He puts his hand out and I hand over my phone.

He enters the address into his GPS. She's a twenty-five-minute drive away. I began to panic with tears streaming down my face. Trev hugs me tight. "She's going to be fine. Let's go get our girl," he assures me after kissing the top of my head.

WE'RE LED to a tall building in downtown Phoenix. We find a parking space down the street, and head into the foyer. We pass the valet guy, he tilts his head with a polite hello, and I say nothing with only one thought in my mind – finding my best friend.

We walk up to the elevator, and I realize I have no clue what floor to enter. He didn't put an apartment number with his address – *figures.*

"Shit Nay, what do we do now?" Trev asks, worried, looking around us.

I try Lukes's phone one last time before I go to the front desk and lose my shit. It goes to voicemail. I want to throw the fucking thing!

I whip around, grabbing Trev's arm, pulling him with me. "Come on, were going to go make a scene."

Trev laughs knowing shit is about to go down.

I walk up to the counter. "Excuse me," I say, slamming my hand on the counter. The older man, with tan leathered skin turns his attention to me seeming surprised by my aggressiveness. "I need to know which floor and apartment Luke is located on," I inform him, realizing how idiotic I sound not even knowing his last name.

His eyes seem to widen with understanding, and he smiles as though I'm expected. "Ah and are you Miss Jazz?" he inquires.

My brows furrow together, and my head snaps back in shock. How the heck does he know who I am? "Um, yes?" I reply unsure, side-eyeing Trev.

"Mr. Vanucci asked me to supply you with the key to the penthouse when you arrived," he states while slipping the key card into my hand.

I'm speechless. I wasn't expecting the interaction to go this way. I expected more screaming, arguing, and to be ushered out by security.

"Take the private elevator on the right and press the P button." He points in the vicinity he's directing.

I nod my head and smile. "Thanks," I tell him and turn toward the doors. Trev follows behind.

We get in and press the P as directed and wait for the doors to close. We both turn to each other. "How the hell did he know it was me?" I ask Trev, confused.

He shakes his head back and forth. "I have no idea. That was weird as fuck."

We're both weirded out. This just makes no sense. Why not just answer the phone instead of going through all this trouble of leaving us a key? Clearly, he planned this. Does he have a motive for making me come down here? I hope he's not some sex trafficker that is looking for another victim, because that is most definitely not happening.

My pulse is pounding beneath my skin. My brows are turned down and I'm trying hard to breathe the stress away. Trev puts his hand on my forearm. "Relax, Nay. She's fine. It's going to be okay."

The numbers finally click over to the red P after the number 12 and the door opens with a ding announcing our presence.

I'm taken aback; wide-eyed and mouth gaping open. I look over to Trev and he mirrors my reaction. This place is magnificent. We step into a beautiful, open foyer with white marble flooring and high ceilings. Straight ahead in the vast open apartment are floor to ceiling windows looking out to the skyline. All I see is crystal blue skies from here.

I'm nervous to even take another step almost forgetting why I'm even here-*but then I remember*. I begin to step forward like a bull with a red cape in front of it. "Hello? Dez!" I scream.

The place is so big all I can hear is my echo. Trev yells this time as we walk past the foyer and enter the living room. "Dez? Where are you?" I shout again. My heart is thumping so hard I can feel the beat in my ears as though they have their own pulse.

I hear a man clear his throat to the left of us. My head snaps around to the man walking toward us from the grand luxury style kitchen. I see nothing but white cabinets and marble cascading down the center island like a waterfall. Just pure crisp clean beauty. Nothing like I've ever laid eyes on other than the centerfold of a magazine.

Immediately my guard goes up. My mouth runs dry, and I'm almost lost for words. What the fuck? Why is Gabriele here?

My back stiffens and I stand up straighter as he stops in front of me with a wicked grin. He reaches his hand out to Trev, but his eyes remain steady on mine. "Nice to meet you again," he greets him with a shake.

Trev looks to me just as lost as I am and shrugs his shoulders.

Jesus, Trev, get it together.

My body comes alive with a vibrating buzz. He stands closer to me, reaches his hand out and takes mine in his, only he doesn't shake it, he pulls me gently into him, bends down and whispers in my ear. "And nice to finally see you again, *Naomi,*" he says while slowly backing away.

My brows slam up, my breath hitches from the sweet hotness of his breath against my neck, and I gasp quietly. "How do you know my name?"

He doesn't answer. "I assume you both are here looking for your friend?" he asks as he turns and walks toward the kitchen. He then points to the hallway behind us. "She's down the hall in Luke's suite."

I remain still for a moment longer, willing my feet to move. I can't seem to rip myself from his gaze. Just like that one morning in my room, he caresses me from head to toe, and then back up slowly with just one intense survey. Liquid heat pools between my thighs as I bite down on my bottom lip. As soon as his attention switches to my mouth, I turn and bolt down the hallway.

"What the fuck was that?" Trev whispers, wide-eyed. Then he blows out a breath while fanning his face.

I shove his shoulder as we approach the door at the end of the hall. Fuck knocking. I bust into the room ready to go apeshit. We abruptly stop as we see two naked bodies intwined and wrapped around each other knocked out in bed.

I blow out an exaggerated breath. Trev lets out a loud chuckle as I give him the evil eye.

The room reeks of sex, alcohol, and a good time. A ping of jealousy hits me wishing I could be as carefree as my best friend. I wish I could just let my inhibitions fly and consume my careful decisions for once, but I've never been in the vicinity of someone who made me want to do so. Never *wanted* to throw myself to the wind.

He waves his hands over them. "See, you were freaking out for no reason. Clearly, she's fine."

I walk over to Dez's side and shake her. "Dez! Wake the *fuck* up!"

I'm angry for her not answering her phone and having me worried. She can be so careless sometimes. She's all I fucking have in this world other than Trev and I would die if something happened to her. I literally wouldn't survive without her by my side. She's the only one who truly understands me. We've been each other's rock since day one.

Dez and Luke don't budge. I walk over to the window trying to open the curtains, but they won't move. I look around for a cord or a button to press but nothing. Jesus, why can't rich people just keep things simple?

"Errr!" I growl, getting frustrated that I can't open just one freaking curtain. I keep searching until I pause like a statue as a hot body suddenly presses against my back while reaching up to grab a remote on top of the bookshelf above me.

I can't move. His body is hard, his smell is exquisitely

delicious, and my heart is pumping erratically crazy. I can't breathe. If I continue to breathe him in, my legs may falter and there's no doubt he will break my fall with his touch.

He hovers over my ear. "I bet you taste as amazing as you smell," he states so matter-of-factly. I suck my bottom lip in with my teeth. "Keep doing that and it will be me biting that lip."

Shit. I've heard this whispered in my ears many many times throughout my years, but never has it jolted me in this way. I close my eyes to momentarily gather my thoughts and when I open them back up the shades slide to the side blessing me with bright light.

I move to the side, away from him, and clear my throat.

He looks mighty proud of himself. I look at Trev snickering across the room. I give him the finger as I walk back over to Dez. Her eyes flutter open, and she looks confused.

I look around trying to locate her clothes. I find her dress strewn across the floor beside the bed. I grab it and sit it next to her. "Come on, Dez. It's time to go."

She sits up, breasts and stomach on show while a sheet drapes over the bottom of her. She looks around at all of us, Trev heading out the bedroom door already and Gabriele standing with his arms crossed watching. She looks back toward Luke who is now stirring.

She rubs her eyes and yawns. "What's going on Jazz, why are you here?"

I roll my eyes annoyed. "Gig's up. *Somehow*, he knows my name."

"It's 3PM and you haven't answered my calls or texts!" I shriek. I start gathering the rest of her things and piling them up.

I watch as Gabriele walks around the bed to Luke, grabs his pants from the floor, and throws them at his face before he walks out the door.

She starts looking around for her phone. Luke sits up

rubbing the back of his neck. "Hey, Jazz," he says while looking around for his phone too. "Where the fuck's my phone? I'm sorry, did you try calling?" he asks me.

"I can't find my phone either," Dez admits.

Luke stands up butt naked and puts his jeans on. I turn my head trying not to peek but man if Gabriele is anything like his younger brother than some girl is in trouble.

"So, how did the front desk know who I was and to give me a key?" I wonder.

Luke looks at me puzzled trying to think back. Then a smile spreads across his face. All he says is, "Gabriele."

Like I'm supposed to know what that means. Then it hits me, that must be how he knows my name; Dez's phone. "Hurry up and get dressed," I demand as I head for the kitchen leaving them to get dressed in peace.

Gabriele is talking to Trevor in front of the large window looking out to the city with a cup of coffee in their hands. Great. Just great.

Traitor.

They both stop talking and turn to me as I stomp in the room. I scan all the countertops looking for two phones: then bingo! There they sit on the far side of the kitchen counter. I walk over and grab Dez's phone and hold it up.

Gabriele smirks and Trev looks at me quizzingly. "Really? You couldn't even wake Dez up and give her her phone when I was blowing it up?" I question angry.

He chuckles. Trev's now understanding as his eyes bounce back and forth between us. "Did you do this on purpose?" I question, tapping my foot as I wait for an answer.

He begins to stalk toward me. My breath hitches. But before he reaches me, Dez and Luke walk out.

"Oh good! You found it!" Dez exhales, relieved. "You ready?"

Her voice falters as she looks between Gabriele and me. "What's going on, Nay?" she questions, looking nervous.

Luke walks over to the kitchen, shirtless and barefoot, and pours himself a cup of coffee, then leans his butt against the counter to watch things unfold.

"Fuckface over here decided to take it upon himself to use your phone to get us over here," I explain as I lift my chin up his way, aggravated.

Dez finally resonates what I've just revealed to her and bursts out in a laugh. Is she serious? Way to have my back. I smack her on the arm pissed. Trev walks over to drop his empty cup on the kitchen island and says his goodbyes. Then he turns to me grabbing my hand. "Ready?"

He knows I'm about to lose my shit and cause a scene. Seeing the red creeping over my chest to my face, he steps in before that happens. We head to the elevator but before I can get to the doors a hand grabs my upper arm and pulls me back gently.

I look up and I'm immediately pushed up against a wall to a small hallway. Before I have a chance to say a word, Gabriele's lips are mere inches away from mine. His intoxicating aroma of fresh rain, dark roast, and husky arousal glides over my now heightened senses. Every nerve ending in my body has been lit on fire coursing through me, burrowing low in my belly and shooting down to the center of my core.

I unintentionally squeeze my thighs together trying to conceal the ache growing deep within me. I'm thrown off at the sensation he's ignited in me with just one touch, one breath, one look; *how can this be?* I've always been so strong, so self-controlled, and with just one look from this man I'm putty in his hands.

I'm hypnotized by light golden spheres as he leans to my side, brushing his cheek against mine. Searing my skin with just a light touch, he says, "Not so fast. Where do you think you are running to?"

My breathing stops, but immediately all senses come flooding back to reality with that one question. It's no secret that I've heard things like this before. Men love the cat and mouse chase, and the fact that I don't give in makes them want it that much more. I'm sure Gabriele is no different. Most wealthy men get want they want if they throw enough money at it. But the way my body awakens in his presence is the difference that scares me. Makes me want to run full force in the opposite direction.

I place my hands on his chest and push him. He moves back an inch and looks down at me. "I'm sorry but have I enlisted you as my keeper?" I snap back.

He chuckles. Another assault of his scent hits my nostrils. I need to get the fuck away from him. "I want you, little ballerina," he states so direct.

I shake my head and snarl. "Yeah? Well, get in line. You can't pay me enough."

I slide out and feel his hard length brushing against me as I go; the heat is now replaced with cold air, and I can think clearer as I walk away. I make the mistake of looking back. He's standing there with a shit eating grin clearly proud of himself for riling me up.

"I have a lot of money, little ballerina, and I always get what I want," he informs me loudly as he puts his hands in his pockets and watches me walk away.

I give him the finger. His eyes twinkle, and I continue to my friends.

Just as I reach the elevator the door dings open. They both eye me waiting to get into the elevator to assault me with questions. I turn around and he is still there, with a determination set deep within his eyes. It makes my heart rate spike, breathing against my rib cage like an imprisoned wild bird. I exhale the air I've been holding harshly just as the door closes.

. . .

LAST WEEKEND WAS INSANELY BUSY. Dez and I made enough money to stock away for a couple of months. Some days I feel as though I've sold my soul, but who doesn't when it comes to money. Whether it be a lawyer getting paid to represent a rapist or murderer to the average man who's willing to take any job just to put food on the table for his family. We all give up a piece of ourselves somewhere down the line for the green devil.

I just chose to use my body.

This body is sore from the weekend. Though I finally have a day off, I look over to the clock beside my bed and huff- 7:13AM. Why oh why can't I just sleep in for once? I lift my hands over my head and stretch my legs out under my covers with a huge yawn.

I know Dez won't be up for hours, so I might as well hit the gym. She and I decided to have a girls' day later. Maybe some shopping or dinner and drinks later tonight. After the other week, I've decided to take it easy on the drinking. If I'm not careful I may end up in a situation I can't get myself out of. I've worked hard at saving parts of myself that no one has touched, and I don't plan on fucking that up now.

Although, each time my mind wanders it tends to go back to the other day in the hallway with Gabriele. Every night since then I've slipped my finger inside myself thinking of him; his smell, his voice, his heated breath against my neck, until I've brought myself to climax.

I've never made myself come as hard as I have these last couple days and even now as I think of last night I inch my fingers down my stomach, slip them beneath my panties and touch my slick wetness between my folds.

My back lifts and my breath hitches while picturing those blazing golden eyes on me. I dip my finger into my drenched core, then bring it slowly up to my swollen bud; circling it repeatedly as I picture his tongue sliding over his bottom lip while pretending it's me.

A surge of heat swarms over my body as I dip my two fingers deep inside of me again feeling my juices spill over and bring it back to my clit applying more pressure as I stroke myself to oblivion.

Jesus. My chest is heaving. I keep my eyes closed to catch my breath. I'm fucked, I tell myself shaking my head. I need to do everything in my power to stay far away from this man. He's the type that will suck every last drop from me and leave. I can't allow that to happen. I *won't* allow this to happen.

I throw off my covers and head to the shower determined to wash my sin of him away.

"Dez, you ready?" I shout, walking down the hall attempting to get her to hurry up.

She's turning side to side in front of her mirror with a scrunched-up face.

"You think I look fat in this?" she asks, clearly feeling unsure of herself. She has a pink mid skirt on with a white tank bodysuit and cute strappy nude sandals. Natural wavy dirty blonde hair, light blue eyes, pouty lips any girl would pay for, and a body that has all men swooning over.

I walk over to her and wrap my arms around her from behind. "You look beautiful. Stop doubting yourself," I encourage her. "If I liked girls, I'd be dying to lick your pussy right now," I joke.

She laughs finally getting out of her stupor. "Thanks, Nay. You always know just the right things to say," she admits, turning to give me a kiss on the cheek.

I take her hand and start pulling her. "Now come on! I'm freaking *starving!*"

We get dropped off by our Uber in front of the Mexican restaurant on the strip and take a seat at the bar. The place isn't packed but it's busy enough that conversation surrounds us, and heads turn as we sit.

The bartender walks over asking us what we're drinking with a flirty smile. I smile back ordering a margarita for the both of us.

Dez's phone keeps vibrating and every time she looks at it a blush creeps over her smiling face. I roll my eyes. "*Okay, who are you texting?*" I wonder. "You better tell whoever he is that it's girls' night and you're mine tonight," I threaten teasing.

She finishes texting and puts her phone down on the bar. "It's Luke," she admits. "He wants to see me after we're done."

I furrow my brows and squint my eyes. "Okay, tell me what's going on between you two. What's he like?"

I truly need to know. She seems to be getting attached and I need to help her decipher whether he's actually interested in her or just using her. All I've seen of him is the drunk party mode who loves lap dances, surrounding himself with girls, and flashing his power and money around. Nothing new or eccentric from what I've witnessed throughout the years. So, what is it that holds my girl's attention?

I see the schoolgirl twinkle in her eyes. "I know you've only seen his crazy wild side, but when we're alone he's so sweet. His family has been through a lot from what I get, he's a hard worker, his brother's real hard on him, but he really does have a soft side *and* he's sexy as hell. He also has a wicked tongue," she explains with a wink.

"Are you sure he's not just telling you what you want to hear? I mean wasn't it you that just told me girls like us won't find a nice normal guy?" I reiterate her own words back.

"No, I said we won't find that sort of man in a grocery store or a library, but I found one at the club and he's definitely an animal in bed," she sings, grinning in a mocking way.

The bartender comes over and drops off our drinks with chips and salsa. We put in our food order, splitting the enchiladas. "Ha ha. Funny, Dez. You said he works for his brother, what does he do?"

I must admit, this question isn't all for her. I'm curious about Gabriele's line of work too. He wears designer suits and shoes, Rolex watches, and the penthouse they stay in doesn't seem cheap. He looks to be in his late twenties, so how does a man so young get to afford all these luxuries?

She knows me all too well. "If you want to know about Gabriele, all you have to do is ask," she tells me after taking a sip of her margarita.

"He's an ass, Dez. I just hope Luke isn't anything like him. He's clearly full of himself," I snap.

Her brows lift knowingly. "Ut oh," she replies.

My brows turn down. "What do you mean, ut oh?" I question.

She takes a deep breath before she begins. "When's the last time a man got your panties in a bunch?" she asks, waiting for my answer.

"Other than being grabbed when I say no?"

She nods.

"I don't know, never?" I answer wondering where she's going with this.

"And in a matter of only two times of meeting him, he's pissed you off and made you *feel* something other than a dull encounter. He clearly has an interest in you, and from the sight of your flushed face in the elevator, you have interest too," she states, trying to open my eyes.

I take a large gulp of my drink and direct the conversation back to her. "So, what now? Are you guys going to make it exclusive? Is he ok with your line of work?"

It's one thing coming to the club to let off steam, but most men don't want a girlfriend that works there knowing that other men will have access to her.

She takes a moment to think about my questions. The bartender comes over to drop the food off to us and asks us if we need anything else. This conversation is getting too deep to not get another drink. "Honestly, I'm not too sure. He really hasn't talked about anything to do with the future. It's too early for that anyways. I'm not stressing it for now," she answers. "But I'm really *really* enjoying the sex!" She giggles.

Maybe I'm thinking too much into this. She's right, it is too early to get that serious. I would probably be more skeptical if he was already talking about the future with her. I just get too protective of her. Even though she's thinking of this as easy going fun, I can't help but think she may be feeling way more than she's letting on.

I see the yearning in her voice and the light in her eyes when she talks about him. Maybe it's my job for now as her best friend to just listen but keep reminding her to keep things light.

"Okay, well just remember if he hurts you, I'm fucking him up!" I threaten, but this time I'm serious.

As we're still conversating about the club and scarfing down our food, two men walk up to us clearing their throats to get our attention. We turn to them, annoyed, and waiting for one to speak.

"You girls look familiar, have we met before?" the tall brown haired guy asks.

He's slim, but built, more on the petite side with glasses he keeps pushing up with his middle finger. His friend eyes him with a confirmation. This isn't going to go over well. I already have a bad feeling in the pit of my stomach.

I see Dez tense a bit. We're used to the recognition outside of the club. It happens more than we would like but it comes with the job. We're in a fully occupied public place, so I'm not that nervous with what's to come next.

"I don't think so. Are you from around here?" I ask, playing it cool.

The short blond speaks up. "We come in town from time to time for work. At night we like to let off steam. You ladies here with anyone?" he asks.

The tall brown haired guy takes a step to the bar behind me to get the bartender's attention. "Shots for us all," he orders, points to us all, when he acknowledges him.

"Actually, we're just having a girls' night; catching up," I inform him hoping they might get the hint.

Dez still hasn't said a word. I see her texting again. I'm assuming it's Luke again asking if we're almost finished. The bartender starts pouring from the bottles, jerking the shaker, and pouring the white liquid into four little shot glasses.

He pays and begins handing the shots out to us and his friend. I don't mind taking a shot since I know where it came from and watched it being made. Normally I won't take drinks from any stranger.

They hold them up, and we follow suit. "To new friends. If you can't come in her, then come on her," he cheers taking back the shot. *Gross.*

I just shake my head and take back the shot. "So, can we party with you girls tonight?" the blond asks. I don't bother asking names. I'm just hoping they will turn around and leave.

The tall brown haired guy presses his front against my back and puts his hand on the side of my lower waist. Dez looks over and notices beginning to get angry. I see her eyes zone in on where his hand lays.

I remove his hand from my waist. "No, like my friend told you, we're having a *private* night catching up together!" Dez growls.

Mr. Blond reaches in his pocket and pulls out a hundred flashing it in front of us. "We pay good," he announces while still waving it around.

I get the bartender's attention so we can get our check. It's time to get out of here. I jump off the barstool pushing it back hard on purpose so tall man will get the hint to back up. "Keep it. We don't need your money. We were just on our way out anyways."

They both snicker. The one behind me leans in and grabs my hips again. "Come on, we pay good for pussy. How about a little lap dance to start off with?"

I see Dez texting again. The bartender comes over with our check, I grab money out of my purse and throw it down on the bar. I smack the hand gripping tightly at my waist off me and grab Dez's. "Ready?" I ask.

She jumps off her stool. "I see why you pay for pussy. No one in their right mind would give it to you two for free!" she snarls as we walk by.

We make it out the door but before I can go any further, I feel a hand grab my upper arm almost painfully. He's digging hard enough that I may have a bruise left behind. I snap my head around and both men are behind us looking furious. Shit. This is *not* good.

"Get your fucking hand off me!" I scream.

This time it's the blond that has a hold of me. "Listen you little whore, we asked to party, and ..." Before he can even finish, he's dragged backwards by a man and led to the dark shadow against the building.

It's all happening so fast. I look around my shoulder and Dez shrieks as the tall dark-haired man is knocked to the ground with Luke standing over him.

What the fuck?

I look back to the men tussling against the building and realize it's Gabriele. He has his hand wrapped around the man's neck as he's turning shades of purple. I gasp covering my mouth. Gabriele's threatening him, I can't hear what he's growling, but finally he lets go.

The blond is leaning over coughing, gasping for air, as his

friend jumps up from the ground and grabs him to pull him away. Both men look horrified. They stumble away running and disappear into the night.

I see Luke comforting Dez, she looks a bit shaken up, then I turn to Gabriele who looks full of murderous rage. Dez must have told Luke where we were. I rip my eyes from Gabriele and walk over to Dez.

"Hey, you okay?" I ask her, leaning down so she looks at me. Luke has his arm around her protectively. My eyes soften at his hold. He looks concerned; worried even. Not exactly what I was expecting compared to what I just witnessed in his brother.

"Yeah, I'm okay. I guess I'm just a little in shock at how everything escalated so quickly," she admits.

"They shouldn't have followed you girls out and put their hands on you," Luke jumps in. "Guys like that need to be taught a lesson."

I inhale and exhale calmly. "Luke, if we went around teaching guys lessons that do this, everyone would be in the hospital," I confess with a half-smile.

I see Lukes's attention flick behind me. I feel an intense burn slicing into my backside. When I look back, Gabriele is grinding his teeth so hard they might crack; his fists are balled tightly together showing white over his knuckles. He looks ravenous and deadly all in one. Any man would be crazy to attempt to go up against him.

I shiver at the thought. I turn back to Dez. "I'm going to call an Uber. You coming?"

I start to pull the app up on my phone but am interrupted by the voice behind me. "Our driver's here. We'll be taking you home," he advises. There's no question in his voice. Just authoritative demand.

I lift my chin. "We can get ourselves home."

I see a steely glint in his eyes, but before he can respond

Dez chimes in. "Nay, I'm going with Luke. Let Gabriele get you home safely," she begs.

I look between all three of them and it doesn't look like I'm going to get out of this.

"Fine," I give in and then look to Luke. "Make sure you take good care of her, or I'll be coming after you and teaching *you* a lesson," I threaten, pointing my finger in his face.

He chuckles and looks at Gabriele. "I already texted Conner to come grab us. You guys go ahead," Gabriele advises, looking between the two of them.

Luke just nods, not saying a word. The black SUV pulls up. I give Dez a hug then her and Luke climb into the truck and drive away. A heat wave washes over my skin as I turn and look to Gabriele, waiting for him to say something.

He still looks wild, but calmer now. I decide to break the ice. "You really don't need to bring me home. I can just call an Uber."

He walks toward the street and signals his driver. The Black car pulls up in front of us, he opens the door without a word and waits for me to enter. I can tell by his stern face I won't win this battle, so I follow his lead and climb into the car.

Just being this close to him as he climbs in after me ignites my engine to full throttle. Every nerve ending in my body comes alive on full alert.

He sits close to me, his leg leaning against mine. I feel his eyes on me but I'm afraid to look up from my hands. Every-thing in me wants to lift my head up and look but I'm afraid. I'm already lost in those hazel eyes every time I close mine, and I've already imagined what his fingers and tongue can do to me, so having the real thing next to me, his intoxicating smell engulfing me is way too much already. I can't risk giving myself over to him only to have his fill and throw me away.

"Look at me, ballerina," he demands.

I close my eyes, hold my breath and turn. When I reopen them, I see an intense vicious yearning staring back at me. I've never seen anything so invigorating in just one look. There's no doubt in my mind, even though he's already said it; he wants me. It's clear as day. No questions needed. But is that all he wants? Can I survive him?

"What do you want from me?" I ask quietly.

His gaze drifts down to my lips. Liquid pools between my thighs as I look at his long lashes and full soft lips.

"Come home with me," he orders without a question. I don't think anyone has ever once told this man no.

It takes everything in me to rip my gaze from his beautiful godly face and look away. The break in contact gives me a moment of reprieve until he reaches for my chin, bringing my attention back to him, and drops his lips down grazing them ever so lightly over mine. I'm frozen. I halt all breathing and close my eyes taking in the feel of him.

I feel his chest against my shoulder as he caresses his lips over my cheek to my earlobe and bites down then replaces the sting with a lick. I jump, inhale shocked, and release a small moan in pleasure. I don't even recognize myself. Never had I ever had this reaction to a complete stranger.

Before I can respond the car stops and the driver goes around opening the door for me, breaking the moment and snapping me back into reality. I need to get far away from this man, and quick.

"I need to go," I say, lifting myself up, waiting for him to move.

He nods reluctantly and slides out giving me his hand. The spark I feel as my hand slides into his is saturated with a sensation that's unexplainable. Tingles lick at my flesh scattering all the way up my arm. Once I'm out and standing I immediately remove my hand from his.

He looks pleased with himself as though he knows what

I'm feeling and is enjoying this cat and mouse game. It's as though he's just waiting and wanting me to run so he can run after me and trap me. He's relishing in the game, and I'm nothing more than a mere prize for the moment.

"Thank you for the ride."

He begins to walk. "Let me walk you to your door."

I stop him dead in his tracks. "No thank you," I reply very sternly.

He nods, accepting my wish. "I'll see you soon, ballerina," he taunts and walks away getting into the car.

I make a beeline for the door. He doesn't pull off until I'm safely locked inside and sliding down against the door. I'm utterly fucked.

CHAPTER 4

The club isn't quite packed yet. Thursdays don't tend to get busy until much later in the night, and it's only 11PM- an hour into my shift. Dez has off tonight so it's just Trev and me tonight. I take a seat at the bar next to him. He's standing at the door checking IDs. Normally he's next to the stage or near the champagne rooms standing guard, but Donald called off tonight so that left the security a bit short staffed.

"So, did you end up calling that cute guy from last weekend?" I ask him, lifting my brows up and down.

He hands back an ID and the guys walk by grinning wide-eyed as they walk in. They must be some newbies, they look like kids in a candy store. They walk straight to the bar still turning to watch Shae on the stage. Shae's more on the thicker side, voluptuous breasts, tiny hips, and a plump ass which guys seem to die for lately.

My body is more toned, legs long, my breasts are just enough for a handful but nothing extraordinary, and my ass has never been on the huge side. I'm more ordinary than most of the girls here, but there's always a niche for the plain Jane type.

He waits a second making sure no more customers walk through before answering. "No, but I met someone new!" he says excitedly.

I can't help but match his smile. "Really? Where did you meet him?"

"I met him at the gym. The morning you ditched me." He frowns.

"Damn, now I'm mad I did!" I gripe.

Jen offers me a drink from behind the bar and I gladly take it. "From the guys down there." She points. They raise their glasses with boyish smiles. Shit. And my night of fakery begins. I lift my drink and smile back in thanks.

I turn back to Trev. "What's he look like? Is he a muscle head like you?" I ask laughing.

He gives me a small eye roll. "You know I like them built lean with blue eyes. That's my nemesis."

Jerry walks by and smacks my ass. "Time to get to work. You can't make me money just sitting around."

"Fucking prick," Trev says under his breath so only I can hear.

I climb off the stool and suck down my drink before I head out onto the floor. "You can say that again."

THE NIGHT IS FLYING BY. I'm on my second dance on the stage and the crowd of men below me is jam-packed. Money is flowing and unintelligible remarks flying. I get this weird sense that someone is watching me; not that eerie feeling I get when I walk into my house but more of a sensation of warmth that flows through me sending goosebumps over my skin.

I look out above the crowd, and there he is. The same man, sitting in the same place as the other week. I can't make him out from here because of the bright lights, but I know he's watching me. I can *feel* his eyes on me. But just like the other week by the time I get to the table he's gone.

Jerry calls me over toward the rooms in the back. *Shit.* He's going to make me do a private dance. I look over to Trev, but he's slammed at the door. He's the only one I trust to have my back during these things. The other guys couldn't give two shits and always turn a blind eye.

"You got a client in the back star room. He paid premium for you, so make it a good one," he orders and walks away.

I head to the back room giving myself a pep talk the whole way down. I stand at the red curtains that lead down a small hallway to the star room. This is the VIP room; red leather couches, mirrors, three poles, and its own private bar.

I take one last breath and step through. There's just one dark haired man sitting with his back to me, arm hanging over the back of the couch and a bourbon in his other. I straighten my back, wipe my sweaty palms down the sides of my thighs and begin my sexy catwalk around to face him.

I stop in my tracks. It's *him*. The man from the table – Gabriele.

I place my hands on my hips annoyed. "What are you doing in here, Gabriele?" I demand to know.

He smirks as his eyes drift slowly down the length of my body and then slowly back up. "I came for a dance," he answers, then takes a sip of his drink. But instead of enjoying his drink, he's enjoying drinking me in.

"And you chose me?" I question.

While I wait for him to respond I do my own sipping. I take in every last morsel of him. From the hair that falls over his brow, to the dress shirt just unbuttoned enough to see the little black hairs beneath it, to his strong clenched hand wrapped around his drink wishing it was me he was holding, down to the pants that now seem to bulge with restriction, and his black dress shoes with a peek of his sexy ankles showing. Now this is a man chiseled from perfection.

"I told you. I want you," he replies plain and simple.

I guess there's no second-guessing that answer. But he has me now because he paid and it's my job, not because of my own free will.

"Well, you have me for thirty minutes, and your time is already dwindling down," I warn him.

I walk over to the bar, pour myself a shot and throw it back, then reach for the music control and change the tune. I choose Chris Brown "Under The Influence" and turn the lights down. He wants a private dance? I'm going to give him one hell of a dance.

I walk back in his direction, eyeing him like prey until I'm standing at the pole in front him. He has the look of a starved lion. I smirk and grab the rod above my head and start circling until I'm facing him. I bite my lower lip and slowly sway my hips to the music; spreading my legs wide as I slide down the pole, closing my eyes and tilting my head back.

I let the music course through me, guiding me through my next move. I slide back up and kick my legs over my head and begin spinning, twirling, owning the pole with my body while keeping my gaze on his. His self-control is becoming a losing battle as he clenches his teeth so hard his jaw tics. I feel a sense of pride that I'm under his skin. His arousal is swarming thick around us and giving me the surge to keep going.

Theses dances are always just a job, but this time it feels like more of the art of foreplay and I'm enjoying seeing the need burning in his eyes. It's my own personal aphrodisiac.

I glide myself down to the ground, watching him, as I crawl and stalk toward him never disconnecting from him until I'm kneeling between his legs. The fire is consuming his eyes as he stares down at me. He hasn't moved an inch since I've entered the room other than taking sips of his bourbon, but now instead of the controlled and relaxed state he was in earlier, his fists are clenched tight and the protrusion from his pants is standing large.

I place my hands on his upper thighs, digging into them with my grip, and slink my way up so we're now face to face, as I stretch my legs over him and straddle, grinding to the music without pushing down and touching. He remains a complete gentleman; never removing his hands from where they've been. Allowing me to take control. Though I can see this is new to him. He doesn't seem to do well with not having complete control.

Usually, I would remove my top, but there's something to say about leaving something to the imagination even though he's already glimpsed me naked. I'll leave him with only that vision and nothing more.

I continue to move getting as close to his body without touching. "Beautiful," he whispers.

I flip myself over and bend my ass in his face before sitting back between his legs, grinding the air but never touching. I've learned this trick over the years. It takes leg strength to balance but it's always been worth it to at least try and keep the invisible barrier. Not everyone is as controlled as him.

The music slows after it falls off repeat and switches alerting me that his time has come to an end and my job is now done. I leave him and walk to the bar to pour myself another drink. He follows my every move while remaining still. I need space; the sexual energy that's radiating off of him is intense and I feel it spreading down to the junction between my legs.

"Would you like another drink?" I offer.

He clears his throat, adjusts himself, and joins me at the bar. I hand him his drink and sip mine waiting for him to speak next.

"How long have you been working here?" he asks.

I take another sip of my tequila on the rocks. I need

something stronger than what I was drinking earlier. "This club? Three years."

I see the wheels turning in his head. "How old are you, little ballerina?"

No way I'm playing twenty questions. "Are we on a date?" I ask sarcastically. "Because I'm not sure this is part of our arrangement."

He chuckles and sips his bourbon still eyeing me over his glass. "Would you say yes if I asked?"

Now it's my turn to laugh. "Listen, I know what I am. You paid for me, you don't have to swoon me or make me false promises of roses and romance. I have no time for bullshit," I'm direct, laying the truth out. "I'm here to make money, nothing more. Your time's up. I need to go back to the floor," I say as I down my drink, slam my glass down, and walk out.

I ran, I know. But I can't risk having hopes of anything more with this man. The way my body is defying me at every turn when he's in my vicinity is driving me absolutely crazy. Every time I tell myself that I need to stay clear of him, there he is, showing up invading my space. How am I ever going to be rid of him?

The night comes to an end, and I haven't seen Gabriele since I left him in the back room. I finish counting my money and go to hand Jerry his cut. He shakes his head and waves me off. "It's all taken care of."

My brows furrow confused. "What's taken care of?"

"Your VIP client paid for your night of work along with the time for you," he informs while counting the money he's already taken from the other girls.

Jadah whistles. "Sounds like Mr. Baller likes what he saw," she teases with a wink.

"He's just another man with money," I remark as I grab my bag and head out.

Shae and Jess watch me as I walk out with green jealousy

stained across their faces. Great, the last thing I need is for these girls to be riding my ass with envy. That never goes well in our line of work. Competition is huge here, even though most of the time I feel as though I'm no competition at all with trying to blend in as much as I can.

I find Trev with his keys in hand waiting for me. "Hey, stud. Ready?"

He bats his eyes being silly. "Yep! Oh, here," he says, handing me a wad of bills.

I look down at his held-out hand. "What's this for?"

"Gabriele asked me to give this to you before he left."

I count the hundreds and look back up stunned. "There's a thousand dollars here," I tell him. Now I'm pissed. "I'm fucking giving this shit to Dez so she can return it," I announce.

Trev looks at me confused. "Why in the hell would you do that?"

We start walking out toward his car. The parking lot is dim, Jerry doesn't do a good job on the safety aspect. "Because I don't need him thinking I owe him anything. He paid for the private dance already *and* he paid Jerry for my shift. Now this? I know this is my job, but it just feels wrong taking this from him too," I explain.

He unlocks the doors, and we hop in. "Girl, just take the damn money! He clearly has lots of it and he obviously has a thing for you."

I huff. "I'm still returning it," I admit, crossing my arms over my chest.

"You're such a pain in the ass, Nay," he states.

THE WEEK WAS busy and long. It's Sunday and I finally have the day off. I plan to lounge around in my pajamas doing nothing all day. Sleep evaded me like always this morning, so I forced myself to take a nap.

It's now early afternoon and I feel amazing. Dez must not have come home yet or there would be no doubt she would have already woken me up by now. I already gave Dez the money to give back to Gabriele but haven't seen her since.

Trev texted me to see if I'm up for the gym, but I decline today. I did enough dancing last night that I shouldn't have to work out for at least another week. Even though I hate admitting it, I was on high alert searching the club each night for glimpses of Gabriele, but he never showed.

I keep telling myself I need to stay away from him, but I can't help *wanting* to be near him deep down inside. My body comes alive when I'm in his presence and I've just never felt that before, it's kind of addicting. The high of the rush is invigorating but then the lows of it all are frightening.

I text Dez.

"What time are you gonna be home?"

Surprisingly, she texts back quickly.

"I'm on my way now. Luke's driver is bringing me home."

"Fancy. Chinese?"

I ask.

"Yes!"

she responds with a smiley face.

Dez gets out of the shower as soon as the food has arrived. We throw some pillows down and lay the spread out in front of the coffee table. She got the shrimp fried rice and

I got the vegetable low mein. She uses the chopsticks and I stick with a fork.

"So, tell me, what's been going on? I've barely seen you all weekend," I whine, then shove an egg roll in my mouth after dousing it with soy sauce.

She swallows. "Luke leaves for business tomorrow morning, so I won't be seeing him for another two weeks or so." She plucks a shrimp from her container.

That reminds me. "You never told me what he does for work."

"From what he's mentioned, his brother took over his father's company when he passed. But I really don't know anything apart from that," she confesses. "I mean, it has to be a good job with the lifestyle they're able to have." She shrugs.

I take another bite of the low mein thinking while I'm chewing. She looks up at me catching me in thought. "You know you pissed off Gabriele with returning that money, right?" she divulges.

I smile. Good. "I'm sure he'll get over it."

"Luke said he had to stop him from showing up here last night."

I'm mid gulp when she tells me this and swallow hard. "What the fuck was he planning on doing when he got here?"

Was he going to spank me like a child? Or maybe tie me up until I said yes to taking it. *Shit.* Both of those options make my nipples hard as fuck. I bite the side of my inner lip. Makes me wonder what he would actually do when punishing me, and thoughts of purposely being bad enter my mind. If he gets this angry over something so small, then what would I expect when blatantly disobeying him?

I scoff at my own thought. Am I turning fucking crazy? Did I really use the word disobey in my head? And what if he's just a downright woman abuser and wanted to come here to show me who's boss? But then I think back to the dance, how controlled he remained, and how angry he was when that guy had his hands on me, and I relax. He is definitely not that type of man. I just feel it in my bones.

Dez' smile grows as she watches my reaction. My cheeks begin to turn pink. "Oh, you like hearing that, don't you? You're a bad girl, Nay!" she teases. "Miss Nay may actually be blossoming!" She laughs.

I roll my eyes and throw a crispy noodle at her.

"Did Trev tell you he has a date tonight?" I ask, changing the subject.

Her eyebrows lift. "Oh my God, *no!*" she exclaims, eating the noddle I just threw at her. "What's his name?"

"I think it's Adam or Andrew maybe. They decided to meet at that Top Golf place tonight. He said he needs an open public place in case he needs to ditch him," I tell her, grinning.

"*Please*, who's he fooling? I'm sure they will be back at his place by the end of the night," she states.

I agree. "Yup. There's no doubt in my mind about that." We laugh.

Dez picks up the remote and starts channel searching. "Movie?" she asks.

"Sure."

"What was up with Shae the other night?" Dez questions.

I shove more lo mein in my mouth and shrug. "Just good ole jealousy. She saw what Gabriele did for me and now decided I'm going to be the target for the month."

"Yeah? Well, that's not gonna happen. I'll be saying something to her Tuesday when I see her," Dez advises. "Oh! I found one," she says excitedly.

She always makes me feel better. I love that we always have each other's back. When we first arrived in Pheonix, we had nothing. Just enough money for some scummy motels and the backpack on our backs. We had to take odd jobs and pool our money together to save for a decent place to live.

The motels we could afford were full of pimps, prostitutes, and fiends. I don't even know how many times we were approached. Every night we barricaded our room with the dresser and always remained by each other's side coming and going. It was not a safe environment for two young girls.

We tried our hand at waitressing gigs and working at some convenience stores but it was always just enough to get us by. We met some girls at the restaurant one night, they were flashy and buzzing with hype after a night out.

Dez and I gravitated toward them. They looked young, carefree, and happy. Something I craved to feel. Worry and stress was all we knew at the time; making sure we had a place to sleep and food in our bellies. The pay at these places was shit for an eighteen-year-old; we were taken full advantage of in that aspect.

I guess you can say after that night we got recruited into the first club; that's what they call it in the industry. Girls who work at the club are paid a bonus for bringing in fresh meat. We were naïve at that time, but we learned how to hold our own real quick. We had no choice. We had to or we would get eaten alive in this line of work.

We saw what this lifestyle did to girls like us. It tainted them. If you allow it, it can rip your soul right from within you. We're dancing with the devil, in a literal sense. Dez and I held onto each other at every turn, using one another as a life raft every time we were afraid of drifting away.

We kept each other humble and alert; away from the dark side of this job.

THE REST of the night we curl up under the blanket and watch romantic comedy movies together on the couch. I wake up to a buzzing sound on my phone. I rub my eyes looking around and realize we both fell asleep on the couch.

I grab my phone from the coffee table and see a text from a number I don't recognize.

I open the text.

"Answer me one thing, do you touch yourself to me at night, little ballerina?"

My mouth drops open.

How the fuck did he get my number? Oh yeah. Duh. From fucking Dez's phone the other weekend. Damn him. He's starting to consume my thoughts, my work, my phone, and now *my life.*

I begin typing.

"Do you?"

I totally evaded his question.

"Oh yes, and the image of you withering above me while I sink my tongue deep into your cunt as you ride my face drives me crazy,"

he confesses, unshyly.

Jesus. Lord help me. I sit up straight and do my best not to wake Dez up. If she sees my face now, I will never hear the end of it.

"Well, that sounds like a you problem,"

I respond.

I see the bubbles as I wait.

"No. This is an us problem."

There are so many replies forming in my head as I text

them out and then erase them multiple times. But I settle for something simple.

"Goodnight, Gabriele."

"Goodnight, my little ballerina."

I lay back down wide awake, not being able to come close to sleep after those texts.

CHAPTER 5

The week went by and I didn't receive another text from Gabriele. Bummed is a little understated. Dez did what she said Tuesday and put Shae in her place of course not without repercussions- now she has it out for the both of us.

Dez's mom's in town for the weekend. So, I'm working at the club without her while she tries to mend their relationship.

Her mom, Christy, was a serial dater when Dez was growing up and didn't have a good track record of the type of men she brought home. Dez finally had enough when the last one gave her a black eye after trying to get him off her mother. Unfortunately, her mom took his side in the end, and she decided it was time to take off before things got much worse. That's when I came across her on the bus.

Her mother ended up in rehab and now she's working on her steps to make amends with her past and the ones she hurt. I'm happy she reached out to Dez. I know leaving her mom behind has been heavy on her heart for a long time, but who knows where she would have ended up if she didn't.

Her dad left when she was young and ended up having

another family. He lives somewhere in North Carolina. She tried to reach out to him in the past, but he wanted nothing to do with her. Basically, disowned her and said he's moved on, and she should do the same. I'm not even sure his new family even knows she exists.

Both of our lives are full of heartbreaks, but I firmly believe that's why we were brought together; to help heal each other. We're each other's family now.

TONIGHT IS SLAMMED. Jerry asked me to tend the bar since we're overstaffed with dancers and Jen called in. My job tonight is to keep the drinks full so the money flows.

"Jake, I need some more ice and Don Julio!" I yell to the barback as I pour some shots. "Oh, and we're almost out of limes!"

I can barely hear over the group of guys celebrating in front of me. The one buying a round of shots is the best man of the groom. I'm not a fan of bachelor parties. They're loud, grabby, and always end up obnoxiously obliterated by the end of the night. Not a fun combination when you're just a piece of meat to them.

I lay down all the shots on the bar.

"$85.50!" I lean over and shout.

His eyes drift right to my breasts as he licks his lips. He hands me a hundred. "Keep the change, sexy," he tells me. "When's your shift over?"

I take the money and smile inwardly cringing. "Not until you're already home and passed out," I joke.

He laughs. "How about you come home with me, and *you* can make me pass out?"

My right brow lifts. His friends start taking the shots off the bar. "That's a thoughtful offer, but I think I'm gonna have to pass," I say as I walk away toward the cash register.

They all cheer and throw them back. Another customer grabs my attention but before I can tend to their drinks the same asshole interrupts, "What will it cost me for you to get down on your knees and suck me off?"

Jesus. I can already see he's gonna be my first cut off of the night. He's well on his way to intoxication. "Think you're in the wrong place for that. Your gonna have to head outside past the back alley and down to Motel 6 for that."

I walk away and start grabbing the customers' drinks I was working on before I was so rudely interrupted. But once I finish with them, I notice rude boy is still at the bar while his friends are off near the stage. *Just great.*

I try to remain looking busy, pouring drinks and ignoring him as I walk by, but that doesn't seem to stop him. "Hey sexy, I know you're not just a bartender. That chick over there told me you're a dancer here too." He points his thumb over his shoulder. I follow where he's pointing, and I fucking see Shae. Un-fucking-believable. "I'm looking to get a private dance."

"Sorry, you're out of luck. I'm not dancing tonight, just working the bar," I state.

"Well, you're in luck. I requested you and paid already. Bossman said he would have another girl cover for you." He smirks, proud of himself.

I stop dead in my tracks. How the fuck am I going to get out of this one? He reaches to grab my hand, but I pull it back. He slams his hand on the bar angrily. I jump back a bit. Out of the corner of my eye I see a man stalking over and when I give him my full attention, I realize it's Gabriele. He's *here* and his line of sight isn't me, it's the man standing at the bar across from me.

He looks murderous again. *Dangerous* almost. He walks with authority and strength; people part ways as though he's Moses walking the Red Sea. He demands attention with just being. His golden eyes are now a dark smoldering liquid lava;

the tension rolling off him is leaving a trail of uncertainty in his wake.

Ass-face doesn't notice Gabriele now standing next to him at the bar. He leans against it just waiting in his direction. I turn to grab the bottle of bourbon, and when I turn back around to pour Gabriele a drink, he's got his hand tightly gripping his shoulder talking low in his ear.

I can't make out what he's saying but whatever it is has ass-wipe's eyes growing wide as his face scrunches with pain. The next moment he lets go and grabs the drink off the bar I just poured taking a sip, winking at me with a side grin. The man quickly grabs his drink and walks away toward his party.

I'm a little stunned and curious as to what he just said to him. "Everything okay?" I ask.

He takes another sip while eyeing me over the glass. "Everything couldn't be better," he replies with a glint in his eyes.

God, what is it about this man that makes my libido go wild. My palms start sweating and I feel like I'm fumbling around trying to do my best to avoid his intent look. My whole body becomes completely engulfed in sensitivity knowing he hasn't removed his eyes off me; following me possessively as I work. He looks at me differently than other men, not like a plaything, but more like someone who wants to devour, possess, and indulge every inch of me. I reminisce back to his text as I watch him lick his bottom lip right now. I can imagine that tongue diving into my silky folds and drinking every last drop of my juices until his thirst is filled.

I look away, my face turning a shade of pink. He must notice the change. "Thinking of something, ballerina?" he questions with a knowing smile. He's always taunting and calling me out. My body is a constant betrayer when he's around, letting him into my most intimate thoughts with just one look.

Just the sound of his voice, a deep silky-smooth base, makes the heat in between my legs drown in wetness. He speaks and my panties immediately dampen. How am I ever supposed to invoke confidence in his presence? He's clearly experienced and well-versed when it comes to the world. No doubt in my mind he has women throwing themselves at him. I'm sure he gets top pick, so why is he wasting his time in a dance club sitting in front of me?

I have nothing to offer him. No worldly experiences. No education apart from high school which I didn't finish, and no form of sexual encounters past a paid lap dance and being the constant victim of roaming hands on my skin. What man in their right mind would want a girl like me unless it's only for one thing?

Right. I'm just an idiot.

I walk down to the end of the bar to wash the glasses trying to hide my saddened emotions because even though a tiny part of me was hoping he may want me for more, I slam myself back into reality - he just wants to fuck me. That's the reality. He's just taking the long route to the same destination everyone else attempts to land.

THE REST of the night goes by smoothly. Gabriele doesn't end up disappearing, he remains at the bar now talking to Trevor as I close. I'm exhausted. It's been a long, weird night and thanks to Gabriele, that guy never looked my way again.

I'm finally finished, and I see that everyone has left, even Gabriele and Trev. I try calling Trev since he's my ride home, but it goes straight to voicemail. I texted him asking him where he is but no response back. Weird. Maybe he's waiting for me outside, although that's not really like him.

I notice Gabriele also didn't say goodbye. He sat at the bar all night just to walk out and not say a word? He is a total enigma.

I grab my purse from under the bar after I tip out the barback and say my goodnights. I pull up the Uber app in case Trev forgot about me and left. Maybe he got an emergency booty call from the new guy and took off quickly.

I push out the door keeping my purse open for easy access to my pocketknife and mace. I always hate how dim the parking lot is; easy for someone to jump out without noticing. I look around for Trev but see his car is no longer in the parking lot.

Just as I'm about to request a car in the app, a black SUV pulls up in front of me, the window lowers, and Gabriele's face appears. "Get in," he demands.

I hold up my phone. "I already have an Uber on the way," I lie.

"Just get in, Naomi," he orders again, exasperated.

Like always, I realize I'm not going to win this so I might as well give in and get a free ride home. He opens the door for me, and I climb into the back sitting in the seat across from him.

Annoyed, I decide to hold my own and not relinquish my connection first. His gaze is burning right through me, scalding me as he rakes over my body with such a leisurely sweep.

My heartbeat is erratic. My blood is pumping fiercely through me, molding my nipples into tight pebbles while awakening my clit with a swelling pulse. I squeeze my legs together trying to ease the uncomfortableness.

It's clear he's well aware of the sexual tension radiating off me considering the swell in his pants is more prominent as the time passes. I decide to be bold. I'm sick of having only fantasies. I want to know what it's like to be touched. To melt under a man's hands. To have an orgasm so intense that it might break me apart. I'm ready to just feel and be damned with the consequences.

I suck my bottom lip in knowing it's driving him crazy. I spread my legs apart wide enough for him to watch as I glide my hand up my thigh, over my lower belly, and slip my fingers under my skirt and panties.

His breath becomes louder as he watches. I lean back in my seat and close my eyes as my finger finds my swelled tight bud. I rub myself in small circular motions releasing a moan as I go. I hear his breath hitch, and I smile slightly.

When I lift my lids open just enough to look, I can tell he's on his last leg of composure. I circle my clit one last time before dipping my fingers deep into my entrance, which makes him lose it. He immediately gets on his knees, reaches in between my legs and rips my panties from me. The cool air rushes over my sex as I am now completely exposed to him.

He leans back a moment just gazing. "Fucking beautiful," he whispers, pushing my thighs apart even further. "Open for me, little ballerina."

I give him access. He draws one finger over my clit and my back lifts as I let out a light moan. *Holy fuck that feels so much better than my own.* He continues his assault lowering his finger through my drenched folds and circles my entrance. "You're so fucking wet."

He brings his finger to his mouth, closes his eyes, and sucks like he's tasting the sweetest fruit. "You taste amazing; just like I've imagined a million times," he admits.

I've never been so turned on in my life. My pussy is throbbing with need. There are just no words to describe this feeling. He leans down bringing his mouth to my overly sensitive bud and begins licking and sucking gently. A fire ignites building me up quickly as my body starts to overheat. He circles my entrance one last time before pushing in a finger. "Holy fuck, you're so tight," he says, in disbelief, in between licks.

I let out a loud whimper and then groan out loud. "Gabriele," I call out. "Don't stop, *please*," I beg.

He moves his finger slowly in and out of me until he pushes two digits in. I scream with burning pleasure. It feels so intense being this full. My insides burn from the stretch while trying to accommodate the thickness of his fingers. I pant trying to get past the intrusion to get back to the pleasure.

He suddenly looks up at me, brows furrowed, with uncertainty while searching my eyes. "Naomi, have you ever been with a man?" he asks, stilling all motion.

I whimper at the loss of friction and shake my head side to side. I don't have the courage to admit it out loud, nervous he will pull away and judge me for it. But something in his demeanor changes and he becomes ravenous. He leans back down; licking, sucking, and grazing his teeth over my clit while invading me again with only one finger this time; twisting and turning until he reaches a spot that tilts my waves of heat over the edge.

My whole body shakes, and I explode over him. I scream his name over and over as my greedy sex milks his finger, gripping it so tight he may never be released. He keeps licking and suckling, still stroking his finger in and out until I finally come down from my release.

My eyes are glazed over with contentment, and now I'm wondering why I've waited so long to enjoy something like this.

He pulls his finger out of me, his eyes never leaving mine and he licks it clean of all my juices. A blush creeps over me with shyness. Still open and exposed to him he leans down, watching me, and takes a long whiff in.

Once he's had his fill, he looks back up to me with something I don't recognize. I try to move up to adjust myself, but his hands keep me in place.

"Come away with me. Be mine for a moment and let me show you what you've been missing," he offers. Then he drops his head down and gives one long lick up the middle of my core ending at my clit. I jump with sensitivity and try to slam my legs shut. "I don't think I'll ever get enough of the taste of you," he confesses after taking one last taste.

He finally sits back up. I push him back and immediately adjust myself, so I'm fully covered again. He sits back in his seat across from me waiting.

I try to comprehend what he just asked of me. "I don't understand," I admit.

"I'm leaving the country for three weeks on business. I want you to accompany me. I'll reimburse you for your time. I'd like to finish what we've started," he explains.

I think this through for a moment and then begin to get pissed. So, he's asking me to be his paid whore. He wants to whisk me away on the illusion that he can show me more when really, he wants to just show me a good fuck. I laugh to myself. I don't need to be swept away for that, and I don't need a prince charming to show me what I've been missing. I'm not that clueless when it comes to the act. My friends have kept me very informed.

The truck comes to a stop and there is a knock at the window notifying us we're at my apartment. "Thanks for tonight," I tell him. He glares at me waiting for what's to come next. "I'm not a prostitute. I don't have sex for money. I work at the club because I chose to do so and then I go home and leave it behind me. I don't bring it outside of that building. I'm sorry I gave you the wrong impression tonight, but I was clearly wrong in my choice. So, if you'll please excuse me, it's late and I need to get to bed," I deny him, coldly.

Before I step completely out of the truck he grabs my

wrist. "I don't think of you as a whore. I never have and I never will. Please, reconsider?" he pleads.

"Goodnight, Gabriele," I reply as he lets go of my wrist and I shut the door behind me. Just like before, he waits until I'm locked inside before pulling off.

I CRACK my eyes open to Dez sitting on the edge of my bed with a cup of coffee in hand for me. "Wakey, wakey, sleepy head."

"Ugh, Dez, what time is it?" I gripe.

She gets up and opens the curtains on me. Bright light spills over the room. "It's ten o'clock! I got worried when I woke up before you."

I snap up. "Holy shit. I haven't slept this long since my mom was alive," I say in shock.

I stretch my arms over my head and take a sip of my coffee. This is just what I need. "So, how was work?" she asks.

I shake my head. "No way, we're not talking about work until you tell me how the time with your mom was," I insist.

Dez looks happy. "Honestly, it went really well. It started out rocky and a little awkward, but we talked things through. I mean, we have a lot of work to do still, but this was a good step in the right direction."

My heart is full of joy for her. I embrace her in huge hug. "That's amazing, Dez! Seriously, I'm so glad she's sober and ready to take accountability for her part in all this. How much longer is she here for?"

"She left this morning to head back. She has more meetings and must get back to work. She wants me to come visit soon, so I thought maybe you would want to come with me?" she invites.

I bounce up and down. "Girls' trip!" I yell and we both laugh. "Of course I'll come."

She claps. "Okay, so tell me about work. Did Shae bother you?" she worries.

I think back to last night and immediately heat runs over my skin in the bright shade of pink. Her eyes go wide almost popping out of head. "Okay, forget about Shae. You're hiding something from me! I can see it all over your face, Nay!" She discovers by my body's betrayal.

She sits up straight and scoots her butt closer to me waiting. I lean my hand on my forehead giving in. "Okay, Gabriele came into the club last night. Scared a customer away and sat at the bar the whole time while I worked like my own personal bodyguard."

She squeals like an excited child. "Then Trev ditched me and left," I tell her. Now that I think of it, I need to call him and give him a piece of my mind for leaving me without a word. "So, Gabriele ended up bringing me home."

She knows I'm not telling her the whole story. "*And?*"

I hide my face in my hands, then she pulls them away. "And he went down on me giving me the best orgasm of my life and dropped me off."

She looks conflicted. "Wait, no sex? No losing your virginity? Does he know you haven't had sex?"

I think back to the moment he found out with his fingers deep inside of me. My inner walls clench with just the memory.

"He figured it out but didn't push any further. But he asked me to leave with him for three weeks while he travels for work," I inform her.

"Wait, are you serious?" she asks, shocked.

At this point she's barely sitting down. She stands up and starts pacing the room. "Did you say yes?"

"No."

She stops pacing and I look down messing with the cuticles on my nail ashamed. She walks over to me, stopping in front of me and lifts my chin. "What's going on, Nay?" she demands to know.

She knows me all too well and can see what I'm attempting to hide.

"He told me he would pay for my time," I confess. Saying it out loud makes it sound even worse.

"Jesus Christ."

I can't tell if she's angry or speechless.

She continues to walk back and forth again thinking. Then she abruptly stops like a light went off. "Nay, he clearly is into you. And you clearly are into him, so why not go, get your experience, use him for orgasms and get paid while doing it. Don't think of it as being an escort. Just think of it as a friend helping you out," she explains. "He's not the only one getting anything out of this. If anything, you're the one coming out on top."

I exhale loudly. "But what if I get feelings? I've never slept with anyone before. What if my heart gets attached?"

She sits back down in front of me. "Just think of it more like a job. A business transaction of losing your virginity; no cuddling after. No sleeping together in the same bed. Tell him you need your own room so when you're done you can leave. Make rules between the two of you that he has to agree to before you accept his offer and stick to them."

I stare back at her contemplating hard. It takes me a moment and then I nod my head agreeing.

Maybe I can do this.

She stands up and starts jumping up and down like a psycho. I can't help but laugh with her. She makes everything better. And just like that, a decision is made.

CHAPTER 6

"If I'm to accept your offer, we need to create some rules between us,"

I text Gabriele.
I put the phone down, while folding my laundry, waiting.
I see the text bubbles.

"I'm game. Drinks tonight to discuss?"

he replies.
Shit. Not the answer I was hoping for.

"Fine. Jackson's at 7PM. I'll meet you there."

"Wear a skirt,"

he demands.
I throw the phone on my bed.

I WALK INTO THE BAR. I chose the one within walking distance from my apartment so getting into his car won't be an option this time around. I need to keep this more formal. I need to create boundaries between us to protect my heart. A sort of contract of words if you may.

I also chose this dive bar because I'm curious to see what Gabriele chooses to wear. I have yet to see him in casual laid-back clothing and wonder if he can even be comfortable in this type of place.

I see him standing at the bar; casual and laid-back as can be like he's a regular in this place. He has on a fitted black tee, faded formfitting denim jeans, and black boots. He has a sexy confident, bad boy aura radiating off him. The tatts on display up the ante that much more.

I already see curious eager eyes roaming all over his body from other women in the bar. I'm around beautiful women all the time at my job, but this feels different. I feel inferior to these women as though I shouldn't even be a consideration to him. I'm still not sure why he's chosen me to travel with him. I'm sure any woman with a decent job, money, or status would be a better option than me.

He turns as though he feels my presence and cracks a side smile when he takes in what I'm wearing. I shouldn't have, but I put on a flowery flowing short skirt and black tank top with flat strappy sandals.

He gets the bartender's attention with just one nod and he's already standing in front of us by the time I step up. Gabriele kisses me on the cheek but before he lets me go, he whispers in my ear, "You smell just as good as you taste." His breath tickles against my skin sending goosebumps all the way down to my toes.

He smells like fresh rain and woody forest. I want to inhale him and hold his smell to my memory for later use. He releases me and asks me what I'm having to drink. I order a tequila on the rocks with extra lime.

"Come on, let's go over to the table in the corner," he directs as he takes our drinks with him. I follow.

He waits until I enter the booth first and then he slides in after me. I should have taken the seat across from him so I could think better. Being this close to him jumbles my mind into useless mush. My brain immediately halts, and my vagina takes control full force.

He slides over my drink, and I take a sip while he watches. "I'm impressed how you take your tequila. Most girls like fruity drinks. Has this always been your drink of choice?" he wonders.

I ponder the question for a moment thinking back. I guess I started out with whatever I could get my hands on to numb my inner conscience when I started my line of work, but as I got older, I narrowed things down to a drink of choice-something with a kick but with a smooth rich tang that I've learned to appreciate.

His eyes are drifting over my face. I can see him trying to figure me out, learning me as I think. "I think over time, after trying many brands of liquors, wines, and beers, I finally settled on tequila. I think I've tried every brand of tequila out there, but my all-time favorite is Don Julio Reposado. It just seems wrong to add sugary crap to such an already perfect creation," I answer, but also leave out the fact that good ole Don has helped me comatose myself on more than one occasion.

I see a twinkle in his eyes. "You never fail to surprise me, ballerina."

I look out to the crowd seeing daggers thrown my way. It's clear the girls in here don't see me on his level. Probably wondering why me and not them.

He follows my line of sight, and his eyes soften. "You know they can't compare to you, right?"

"Don't say things like that," I scold him. "In fact, we're here to discuss our terms for the rules on this trip."

He looks back at me, looking over my face. "Okay, I'll bite, and I can promise on this trip I'll bite too." He smirks.

Fucking ass.

I slide back just a foot to get some space between us. "First rule – I want separate rooms," I inform him.

He thinks for a moment then nods his head in agreement. "Second rule – once we fuck, there's no cuddling or intimate gestures."

He looks a little caught off guard but eventually agrees. "And third rule – after this trip, you never contact me again," I say so matter-of-factly.

He downs his bourbon in one gulp then turns to me. "Are you sure this is what you want?"

"Those are my terms."

"Okay, well I have some terms of my own," he counters.

I wasn't prepared for him wanting any terms of his own. "Okay"

I'd have to admit, I'm a little nervous to hear his demands.

He places his hand beneath my skirt on my bare thigh under the table. The scorch of his heat against me leaves me frozen. "First – I want you to give yourself over to me completely, without question or hesitation for the three weeks you are with me," he requests as he slides his hand slowly and intentionally up my thigh.

My breath falters as I look over the crowd to see if anyone notices while his fingers reach the heat in between the junction of my thighs. He runs his finger over the apex of my panties, grazing over my clit, teasing as I let out the smallest moan. His eyes sparkle with triumph. He leans down to my ear, his scent envelops me causing moisture to gather even more. "No one is paying attention, little ballerina."

I gulp. "I will give myself over to you fully, but just for the three weeks."

"Good girl," he praises me.

We lock eyes as his fingers slip under the fabric and delve straight into my sex. "God, you're so fucking wet already. I just want to climb under this table and taste you. I'm unbelievably famished."

Jesus fuck.

This is not turning out how I planned whatsoever. I'm already losing control and this whole thing hasn't even begun. The way he can just make my body sing with just one gaze, one whisper, one touch is frightening and powerful. Somehow, I need to figure out how to gain the upper hand. I've never had the chance to be bold before; not even sure how to do this but it's like my hand has a mind of its own being driven by a magnetic force.

I drag my shaky hand over his thigh, just as he did mine, digging my nails through his jeans until I reach the bulge of his pants and squeeze ever so gently. A growl escapes him which gives me the signal to keep going. I run my palm up his long engorged length, and I almost wish I didn't, the size of him is massive. That's never going to fit inside of me.

He must see my apprehension in my thoughts. "Don't worry, little ballerina, you're going to take every inch of me to the hilt and beg for more," he says as he lifts my hand from his cock and places it on the booth in between us. "This isn't about me, yet."

He slowly moves his finger in and out while his thumb presses against my clit, circling it as my juices become thicker with need. My breathing becomes louder, but I have to remind myself we are in public as I look over the people surrounding us, but with this notion I become far more turned on. The danger of being caught and watched by many is sort of thrilling. It never crossed my mind how turned on this could make me.

Gabriele grins proudly with hooded eyes as he observes me. He continues to move with fast precision. I can hear the gooey sounds coming from my sex as the wetness releases. In just a split second he twists into a new position hooking his finger, reaching the spot that has been dying to be scratched, heat spreads through me creating a light sheen over my skin, and I come undone.

I grab hold of his arm, digging my nails into him, trying to keep my composure. Trying to hold my moans at bay when all I want to do is scream his name. He continues to stroke my clit while still inside of me until I finally slink down into the booth.

I don't care if anyone saw that. I couldn't give two fucks right now if I was the star on the set of a porn. I am completely spent. He removes his hand from underneath my panties and again brings his fingers to his mouth and sucks.

"Fuck, you taste so divine," he says, voice raspy with need.

He moves in the booth to adjust before calling the waitress over for another round of drinks. After that, it's much needed. I excuse myself from the booth so I can take care of myself in the bathroom and when I return, he's back to his composed self.

He gets up so I can slide back in, I hold onto his reached out hand and leave a memento with him. He looks down, golden eyes now glowing with satisfaction as he brings my thong to his nose and takes a deep inhale then tucks it into his pocket. I have to admit, I wasn't expecting that. I grab my drink taking a long pull before bringing my attention back to him. Now that I'm in my right mind I want to finish our terms. "What's your second rule?" I gather the courage to ask.

He looks to me and pushes a fallen strand of my hair behind my ear. "Second rule - that you keep an open mind. I like to push the boundaries. I enjoy things that might make you apprehensive in doing, but I promise, I'll keep you safe, cherished, and completely satisfied."

Prickles run over my body in waves. If only I can fathom what he may mean by this. My brain is unsure what to think of his disclosure. "Just say yes," he pleads, waiting for my answer.

Finally, I nod my head. I've come this far. Why not continue. Something inside me trusts what he's asking, trusts that he will keep me safe and looked after, so I decide to give into my inhibitions and agree to his rules.

"Anything else?" I ask.

"We leave Tuesday. Bring beach attire."

TREV AND DEZ bought champagne and made my favorite appetizers to help me pack for my three-week trip. They're calling it a lose my virginity celebration – I call it count down until I'm stuck with the man that may be the death of me. They should be celebrating my funeral more like it. With all that's happened I forgot I was supposed to ream Trev a new asshole for leaving me that night.

He throws a gift bag on the bed. "It's from the both of us," he announces.

I look up at them with a huge smile. I rummage through it, ripping the tissue paper away and finding multiple sets of lingerie. My mouth hangs open looking at how little fabric there is to these. I look back up to them, they're eyeing me with obnoxious grins.

"Really? Isn't it enough he's seen me at the club wearing things like this?" I tell them.

Trev rolls his eyes. "These are different than what you wear at the club. These are only for his eyes and you're going to drive him mad. Believe me," he explains.

Dez is going through my closet picking out things for me to pack. She has great fashion sense, so I trust her taste.

Though he did say beach attire, so that leaves out most of the things I own other than dresses and bathing suits.

"Okay, but naked is probably cheaper." I laugh.

Trev throws some bras at my head. "By the way, I'm still mad that you ditched me the other night. Did you have a booty call with Andrew?" I ask.

"His name is Adam," Trev corrects me with attitude. "And no, I didn't have a booty call. Mr. Gabriele told me he was taking you home, so I thought you guys already discussed it."

My face scrunches up in disbelief. Dez walks in from the closet. "Oh, *he's good*," she declares.

"I just don't get it. Why me? Has Luke said anything to you?" I question her.

She shoves my skimpiest bathing suits in my suitcase. "He had to leave to take care of some family business, so I really haven't talked to him a lot over the last couple of days. He's texted me to check in, but that's it," she informs. "All he's really said is that his brother is very private when it comes to dating. He's only seen him with one woman."

Trev looks back and forth between us. Instantly, a pain slices through my heart with jealousy. My brows furrow and lips thin with this new information. I wonder who this one woman was to him, and where is she now? She clearly must have been extremely important to him if that was the only one Luke had seen him with.

"Well, that's an interesting revelation. I'm going to put his name in google and see if anything pops up," Trev says as he types in his phone. Trev brows lift. "Oh shit, I found something!"

Dez and I run over to the chair he's sitting in and lean over to see what he's looking at. It's a picture of him and a brown haired blue eyed beautiful woman with his arm around the back of her waist. The writing under the picture says – Gabriele Vanucci and his fiancée, Rosetta Lorito. The article then goes on to talk about how he's heir to the

Vanucci empire once his father, Vincenzo Vanucci, passes away.

"Wow, Luke definitely didn't mention she was his fiancée," Dez admits, surprised.

I can't stop looking at her. She's supermodel material. She looks absolutely flawless, and here I am a plain Jane dancer with brown hair and dark brown eyes. The way he's holding onto her is so possessively protective and makes me envious that she gets to be beside him in that picture; that she almost had a forever life with him and here I am getting three paid weeks.

Dez can see me free falling down the self-pity rabbit hole. She walks over to me giving me a big hug. Trev joins in hugging the both of us. "Nay, fuck that girl. He's not with her anymore and there clearly has gotta be a good reason for it," Dez says, trying to make me feel better.

"Yeah, I know men and this guy has a thing for you. I've seen how he looks at you and watches you. He's clearly been obsessed with you since the moment he met you, and not in that creeper scary way. More in the I can't think of anyone else type of way," Trev explains.

I squeeze them both tightly before letting go. "You guys are the best. Now let's go finish our bubbly."

THE BUZZ of my doorbell echoes through the apartment, and a car is waiting downstairs to pick me up. I give Dez and Trev kisses goodbye and they make me promise to text when I land and every day from there on out to make sure I'm okay. I love that they're so protective of me.

My mind is jumbled and full of nerves. The driver opens the door for me then takes my suitcase. I climb in and the back is empty – no Gabriele. I don't know whether to be relieved to have a little more time with my thoughts or more anxious because this is just dragging out our initial contact since Sunday night.

We pull up to a private airport, must be some place outside of Phoenix. I'm not privy to these sorts of places since money is actually an object for me. I look out the window and see a private charter plane with stairs down on the runway.

The driver opens my door and holds out his hand to help me out of the car. "Thank you."

"You're welcome, Miss Veil. Mr. Vanucci is waiting for you in the plane." He nods his head in the direction of the stairs. Of course, he knows my last name. Gabriele seems to know a lot about me before I've even had the chance to tell him.

I hold the railing, so I don't trip with my nerves on high alert. My heartbeat is thunderous and pulsing through my ears. I bend my head going into the cabin and am greeted by the stewardess. "Good morning, Miss Veil."

"Good morning."

"May I get you something to drink before we take off?" she asks.

I shake my head. "No thanks."

"Well then, please let me know if you change your mind," she says as she allows me to pass.

Once I'm past her, I see Gabriele sitting on the seat facing me, one leg crossed over the other in navy blue dress pants and a white dress shirt deep in a conversation on the phone.

I take a seat across from him, placing my purse on the seat next to me, and pull out my phone. I need to busy myself while he finishes his phone call. I followed his direction and wore beach attire, a long flowing light-yellow sundress and brown heeled wedges. I curled my hair in beach waves and kept my makeup natural.

He drinks me in as he speaks in the phone. Smoldering heat spreads across my skin initiating flutters in my lower tummy. I don't have any social media accounts, it's better that I not let anyone into my personal life for safety reasons and privacy. So, I pull up the book I'm reading while I wait.

I must have gotten too immersed because I hear him clear his throat to gain my attention. I look up. "Whatever has your attention must be good. I'm a little envious," he says grinning.

I look up smiling and turn my phone off. "Yes, I started a book the other night. Guess, I got caught up at the good part," I admit shyly.

"What genre do you enjoy reading?" he asks curiously.

He looks so calm and relaxed with his leg leisurely crossed over his other and arm resting over the seat beside him. How does he remain so confident, so sure of himself? Here I am used to being watched on a nightly basis by many eyes, but when it comes to his scrutiny, I melt like butter unable to complete a normal thought.

"Erotic romance."

Embarrassment now floods my face with a light shade of pink. His eyes light up with mischief as he cracks a smile.

"And what's your favorite erotic story? Whips, chains, toys? Threesomes? Or being watched?" he wonders completely seeming to be entertained.

I inhale and exhale deeply trying to figure out how to answer that best. "When it comes to fantasy, it's more about what's available at your fingertips that's probably impossible or off-limits in the real world – *the forbidden* so to speak that intrigues me. So, not just the acts itself I like reading about but more of the connection that the main characters have while doing them."

I study him as he thinks about how've I've just answered him. He looks deep in thought, wheels turning, dissecting my response.

"And what if the acts you read about were at your finger-tips in the here and now?"

My brows furrow not sure where's he's going with this line of questioning. I've never really considered any possibilities of real life for these books. It just seems juvenile to even have these thoughts. But I guess if I really had an option then I'm not so sure I would have the courage to take it.

"Honestly, I'm really not too sure. We both know I'm not experienced. I know what I like to read because it's fiction, but I don't know what I'd really like in real life," I answer as best I can without sounding childish.

"And have you ever indulged in watching porn?" he wonders.

The stewardess walks in the cabin, interrupting us. "We're ready for takeoff. Please fasten your seats belts and once we're up in the air, I'll by to see if there's anything you might request."

Gabriele waves her off. "There's no need for that. I'll buzz you if needed," he states without looking at her.

She nods, looking between us both for a slight second and then leaves us again closing the cabin door behind her. We're now back to being alone, and I can't help but feel the thick sexual tension looming over us.

I wait for him, hoping he will have been distracted enough to forget what he had just asked, but no luck. "Answer the question, Naomi."

"Yes."

"And what do you enjoy watching?" he asks. His intense gaze is leaving me no room to evade him.

I gulp. "There's no wrong answer or judgement here. We're going to be getting to know one another on an extremely personal level over these three weeks, so there is no need for embarrassment," he adds.

I lift my chin higher hoping to give myself some courage. "I tend to lean more toward threesomes, with two men on one girl," I confess.

I see a spark of pleasure course through his eyes. Is this something that excites him?

"Anything else?" he asks.

I look away, out the window of the plane. There's nothing but blue skies ahead of me. I feel as though he's trying to turn me inside out, wanting to know my most inner demons.

"I enjoy watching orgies. Maybe not picturing myself participating, but more of the interest of watching them. I don't know, maybe it's the pleasure or the domination I enjoy seeing," I finish.

He adjusts his posture in his seat. He's turned on, there's no doubt about it by the way his pants are now straining between his thighs.

Enough about me. I want to know what he meant by pushing the boundaries. "And what about you?"

He cracks a mischievous side grin. The little lines around his eyes glimmer with promise. "Be patient, little ballerina, all in due time that question will be answered."

We eye each other down for a mere moment until I'm the first to cut the connection. He doesn't offer any more insight or conversation after that. His phone buzzes leaving his concentration elsewhere for the majority of the flight.

I hear him talk about the real estate he's trying to acquire along with negotiations on pricing and terms. I understand some but most of it sounds like a foreign language to me.

I've been studying stocks and doing my research on trading. I can't dance forever. Eventually, younger and more agile girls will come up behind me and I'll be less requested. It's the law of nature. I've been saving every dollar so when I'm ready to make a move to invest, I'll be able to have funds to fall back on with the learning curve.

Gabriele had the stewardess bring fruits, cheeses, and crackers along with champagne to snack on. I've been able to read a majority of the book I've started due to him being pre-occupied.

I look out the window and finally see turquoise blue sea below. The water is breath-taking followed by tiny islands speckled within. I realized I never even asked where our destination was. I've been too busy being on high alert with Gabriele flooding my every thought to worry about where I would be spending my weeks with him.

"Gabriele, where are we going?" I ask now that he's finally off his call.

He looks out the window down at the view.

"We're going to *Fantasia Island – also known as Fantasy Island.* It's a private island I bought off the coast of Belize."

I have so many questions racing through my head right now. "Did you name it?"

He smiles proudly. "I did."

I bite my bottom lip without thinking. He watches me as though he wants to devour my mouth with his. Being so close to him in the cabin this long feels like I'm about to combust with the need for release. I want his head in between my legs and his tongue delving deep into my core. Which comes to my next question.

"Will it just be the two of us on this whole island?" I wonder.

The pilot announces our landing countdown for fifteen minutes.

"I have staff, and some guests already there," he informs.

I feel as though he's being extremely evasive. I can't seem to get a full direct answer from him. I know Luke told Dez his personal life is private but sharing my virginity with someone will be as private as it can get, I hope he's going to open up to me more. Even though we only have a short time together, I want to *know* him. I want to know what makes him tick, what makes him moan, what drives him wild and untamed. I want to hear him laugh – that deep guttural kind of laugh, and know his dreams, and deepest secrets.

Shit, Naomi, get it together.

These are the last things I should be wanting when keeping boundaries and distance. I must keep reminding myself to keep my walls in place, whatever happens, the barrier must not fall. I have to stay strong no matter what.

I snap my belt on as the plane begins to descend.

"What is Fantasia Island exactly?"

"It's an island I created for those who wish to fill out their sexual fantasies consensually with the utmost confidentiality," he answers without evasion this time.

I think about this for a moment feeling as though I'm out of my league right now. "So, it's just for the elite?"

His phone buzzes. He looks down at the number and then silences it. There's a quick change in his demeanor for just a flash of a second before he returns to his calm façade. If I wasn't watching him at that exact moment, then I may have missed it.

"It's by membership only. We have a very extensive vetting process of our members before they are accepted. So, whoever can afford this membership and pass our processes, then they may join," he explains.

I'm actually pretty impressed. This idea is clever and unique – in its own way. I know of many places with this sort of concept but not of this stature of being on its own exclusive private island. Most of these places that I know of are of the walk-in type as well, though I'm sure there are places for the elite underground.

"Is this the business you took over after your father passed?"

He leans his forefinger on his top lip contemplating. Then suddenly leans forward clasping his hands between his legs.

"I know you have many questions circling in that beautiful head of yours and they will all be answered in due time. Be patient, little ballerina," he tells me looking sincere.

I nod, allowing myself to let go – for now.

Looking out the window, there's white sand and wild

bright green brush now zooming in closer until I feel the wheels jolting us as we finally hit the ground. The runway is small and private. There're no airport or people other than a single Jeep waiting as we come to a stop.

The captain thanks us for traveling with him over the speaker as the stewardess opens the exterior door and waits for us to gather our things. She says her goodbyes. I catch a glimpse of hope twinkle in her eyes as Gabriele passes her. Maybe hoping he might return the gesture, but only disappointment is left in its wake as he passes her with only a polite grin.

He had to have noticed that. He must get those looks all the time. But my mind keeps drifting back to what his brother revealed about him – he's only seen him with one woman. So, does that mean he doesn't date ever? Or maybe he doesn't have relationships? Or does he indulge in this island as his very own playground? Everything about him is such a mystery. I'm so eager to learn more.

CHAPTER 7

$\mathcal{W}$e pull up a sand road leading to a tiny beach house nestled under a canopy of palm trees. It's quaint and not what I was expecting. I was expecting something grander and more luxurious. Something that fits Gabriele's lifestyle more.

The sounds of birds surround us and the smell of ocean wafts through the air. I almost smell a hint of Gabriele in the wind. Beads of sweat start to form on the back of my neck and in between my breasts. Gabriele must notice the flush of my skin; he gives me a smoldering once-over as we hop out of the Jeep. I look down feeling a bit self-conscious and on display.

He walks up to me and lifts my chin. "What I wouldn't give to lick the dew off of your skin right now," he says with promise.

Thoughts of that has my core melting with need. I'm stifling hot – but now I'm hot for him. I wiggle out of his hold needing some space before I launch at him right here and now in front of the driver wrapping my legs around him and rubbing my core against him until I come.

I turn to take in the nature encompassing us as I begin to

83

walk toward the house. I notice stairs to the side wrapped in a canopy of brush and mangroves leading downward. Without thinking I begin to descend them until I sink in warm soft sand. I pull my sandals off one by one hanging them off my finger and I continue my investigation.

Beautiful flowers growing in the brush engulf the pathway with purples and pinks. Birds swoop over me as I continue to walk, I hear soft footsteps following close behind me, as I reach blue skies and a gorgeous white sandy private beach.

There's not another soul for miles.

I walk over the beach, feet sinking into the velvety sand with each step I take, a light breeze whips gently through my hair as crystal clear waves glide over my feet like heavenly bath water. I close my eyes and inhale the fresh scent of saltwater and freedom – this seriously can't be my life right now.

I open my eyes back up seeing nothing but vast sea in front of me. I'm standing in the middle of a dream, pictures in magazines don't do this justice. I can see in my peripheral view Gabriele studying me so intensely as though he wants me burned into his memory in case I may fade away. I look over to him, my hair still blowing in the wind, and he closes the distance between us.

He tucks a strand of hair behind my ear as he looks deep into my eyes. It's no longer the sun that is heating my skin, it's Gabriele's gaze on me that's burning me straight to my core. He leans down brushing his lips ever so lightly over mine, light enough that I second-guess if I have just felt him brush over me.

I drop my sandals and lay my hands against his chest. He feels like warm steel against my palms. He reaches his hand behind my neck, grabs a handful of hair, and pulls. My head tilts to him having nowhere to go under his vise grip leaving a faint sting in its wake.

Without another word he smashes his lips against mine, running his tongue along the seam of my lips, coaxing me to open for him. I falter with a moan, opening for him, and he takes full advantage delving into me as our tongues collide fiercely together, dancing a silky warm tango leaving us greedy and panting for more. I can't get enough. I feel desperation take over me as I grip his shirt tightly, bringing him closer, meeting him equally with every taste, swirl, and lick of his tongue against mine.

He snarls as he tastes me, devours me, and completely commands me, demanding my mouth to sink with his. He grips my hair tighter, my scalp now singing with elicit pain that sends tingles shooting over my nipples and straight down to my sex.

God, he tastes like fucking heaven. My first real kiss and it already can't compare to anything I've read. It's magical and already heart breaking all in one.

I drag my hands up his body, dipping my fingers into his hair tugging with the same intensity he's given me. He moans deeply with instant pleasure as he leaves my lips and starts a trail down my neck, licking and nibbling along the way.

I whine in protest of the void he's left, but it's immediately replaced with satisfaction as he lifts my leg and grinds his hard length straight against my sex.

"Fuck I want you so fucking bad," he groans.

He keeps grinding against me, balancing me as his grip is digging under my thigh. He licks my neck, then bites down. I howl with pain but then he licks and kisses it away. I'm starting to see the thin line between pain and pleasure that I've read about. It's thrilling and confusing all at once.

He continues his assault up my neck, licking and nibbling at my ear. His breath against my skin igniting an inferno deep within me. "We have company, little ballerina," he whispers.

I look over his shoulder and see a woman standing at the

top of the beach waiting for us. I unwrap my arms and leg from around him shyly. He kisses the tip of my nose. "To be continued," he promises. Then grabs my hand pulling me to follow.

"Good afternoon, Mr. Vanucci," she greets him, then looks to me. "Miss Veil." She nods. "I'm sorry to bother you but I wanted to let you know everything has been set up exactly as you wished. Is there anything else needed before I leave?" she asks smiling. Her eyes reach mine and they soften. She looks to be in her mid-fifties, hair tied back into a bun, casual clothing due to the heat and extremely kind eyes.

I smile back. Something about her feels calming and motherly. My heart twinges with an ache momentarily at the thought of my own mother. I miss her terribly.

"No Joanna, we're all set. Nothing else will be needed," he replies warmly.

I can see the admiration in his eyes toward her. He must have a soft spot for her. I like seeing this softer side of him. She smiles and turns disappearing up the side stairs.

He turns his attention to me. "Hungry?"

"Famished," I say breathily.

He grins pleased, then opens the sliding door leading me into the house.

I walk in, looking around, taking everything in. The house has a contemporary beachy vibe; white fluffy furniture, light wood accents, high vaulted ceilings with beautiful antique wood beams, and an open airy kitchen looking over the living room. Nothing is formal about this house.

The whole layout is open with sliding doors along the whole back side of the house looking over the beach. He leads me to a door off the side of the living room and allows me to step through first. I walk down a short hallway which opens to a spacious room with vaulted ceilings, sandstone wood floors, and a huge canopy style bed in the middle of the room overlooking the open sliding door to the ocean. Sheer white fabric hangs waving in the breeze over the bed. It's sexy and elegant.

I swallow, needing a drink of ice-cold water to cool my nerves. I walk to the sliding door taking in the view wondering which one of us will be staying here or if he plans on negating my rules all together now that he has me here alone. He must sense my unsettledness. "This room is yours. I'll be taking the one upstairs."

A flash of disappointment slices through me, but I remind myself these are my rules and he's abiding by them graciously.

He takes my hands in his. They're warm, soft, and fit perfectly in mine. "Come, let me show you your bathroom."

The bathroom is off to the side, almost the same size as the bedroom, a large glass shower under skylights, huge vanity, and a two-person clawfoot tub also looking out to the sea. This is all too much, completely breathtaking, and I feel as though I don't belong here. I don't deserve to be graced by these sorts of lavishes.

I catch him observing me through the reflection of the mirror, but I disconnect my gaze as soon as we lock and walk by him out of the bathroom. I need some space; I'm feeling closed in and vulnerable.

He takes me back out to the kitchen to the spread of fruits, stewed chicken, rice and beans, and ceviche all laid out over the counters. My mouth is watering. My stomach growls as the aroma drifts past my nose.

He grabs two plates and loads them with food setting them down on the island counter in front of the stools. "Sit," he directs, pointing to the stools. "Would you like a margarita?" he asks.

I nod. "Yes, that sounds perfect."

He reaches into the fridge and pulls out the pitcher filled with the already made mix, rims the glasses with salt, and pours adding a slice of lime to each drink.

He slides mine in front of me and comes around taking a seat next to me. He raises his glass to mine. "To our next couple of weeks together."

We clink and start digging in. I close my eyes and moan with just my first bite. The flavors burst in my mouth. I've never tasted anything like this.

"I can't wait to have you moaning like that around my cock," he says, watching me eat.

My face flushes with that thought.

"What if I'm no good?" I ask quietly revealing my thoughts.

He stops chewing and swallows. "That's not possible and what you're unsure of, I will teach you."

Now's my chance to ask. "I can see with knowing what I know so far that you're extremely experienced. Does this experience come from past relationships or this place?"

I know I may be stepping over an invisible boundary, but I have to try – I need to know.

He shifts his position toward me, then takes a sip of his drink. "Naomi, I don't do relationships. I'm just not that man. My peculiar tastes are something that run deep within me and not many women can handle that. I am a very high-profiled man, so it's imperative that I'm selective with any women that I am with even just for a night."

Now I'm more confused than ever. "Then why me?"

"Because I know from your line of work you can be discreet. But most of all you intrigue me. The more I spend time with you, the more I want to see," he clarifies.

I'm not too sure how I feel about his answer. I feel as though it's just bullshit. Within these couple of weeks, he's sought me out on numerous occasions, not only acting as my protector and bodyguard but has been attentive as well. I feel there should be more to this answer.

I take a large pull of the margarita, then set the glass

down. "So, no relationships. Does this stem from the breakup with your fiancée?"

His façade breaks and he looks irritated. "The engagement with my fiancée isn't what you think. You can't believe everything you read, Naomi."

I see that this is all I'm going to get out of him on that subject. "Fair enough. So, you play here?"

Suddenly, he lets out a loud bout of laughter. The kind I've been waiting to hear and it's music to my ears. It's contagious as I start giggling as well.

He chuckles in between speaking. "No, I haven't indulged here. This place is newly created. We just started accepting members. I've stayed here but only to oversee the construction and design," he makes clear.

I feel relieved. I don't know why but I'm glad that I don't have to compete with my jealousy. "Did Luke help you with creating this island?"

He stands and starts clearing our plates. "Luke has his own endeavors that he's involved in."

"Here, let me," I say, grabbing the plates from him. The least I can do is clean up after he has gone out of his way to have this meal prepared for us.

He snatches them back from me. "Not a chance. I'll take care of them. Why don't you throw on a bathing suit so we can go for a swim," he suggests.

I look over my shoulder out past the deck, the waves are calm, and the sun is shining bright. I could use a soak and some rays against my skin. I nod, and head to my room.

I GRAB my phone and see a group text from Dez and Trev.

"Umm, we need to know if you made it okay! Text us back!"

I smile as I start replying.

> "I made it! It's beautiful! I wish you both were here,"

I send and add a frown face and throw my phone on the bed.

I begin rummaging through my suitcase looking through all my bathing suits. I hold them up one after another trying to find one with more fabric than a string. *I'm going to kill Dez.* I should have never let her pack for me.

I finally find a blue one that has a little more coverage than the rest. I grab a cover-up and head out toward the beach from my room. Gabriele is already in the water. I walk slowly hoping he doesn't notice me yet as I drink him in.

The water is glistening over his olive skin like diamonds in the sun. His ripples of abs cascade over his stomach like waves of the ocean forming a vee right above his swim shorts.

It's like he's sculpted from a roman God. The tattoos scrolling up his arms meeting his pecs give him a contrast of good verses wickedly dangerous. The ultimate bad boy persona. I'm fucking doomed. Just knowing that I've had his tongue inside of me and his mouth on more than one part of me makes me feel insatiable. He's already a thief of my most inner thoughts and now he's ruling over my body like a king.

He turns running his hand through his wet hair as he finally notices me standing at the edge of the water. The smile that looms across his expression is heavenly and makes my insides melt into a puddle of water.

I remove my cover-up and step into the water to join him. It's now midafternoon and the sun is blazing. I probably should have put some sunscreen on over my virgin sunless kissed skin.

"Hey, beautiful."

Gabriele grabs my hips bringing us skin to skin. "Hey."

He leans down gently grazing his lips against mine as he palms my ass cheeks lifting me up. I wrap my legs around his waist as he brings us deeper into the water.

"Gabriele, this place is heaven," I say, looking around. There's nothing for miles. Just white sand and crystal blue ocean in every direction I turn. "Where do the guests stay?" I wonder.

"They are on the other side of the island. I like my privacy so there's no one for miles. Only a handful of people know about this side of the island," he explains.

"You're actually the first person I've brought here," he professes, looking into my eyes not allowing a doubt to enter my mind.

I feel elated about being the first to experience this all with him. "You're not afraid I'm going to spill your secret?" I joke.

He laughs. "I think you will enjoy it here too much to want to share it with anyone else."

"True."

He twirls us in the water, I glide my hands over the top of the surface. "Can I ask you something?"

I guess it's only fair. "Depends on what you want to ask," I reply nervously.

"Why dancing?"

This is most definitely a loaded question. "Dez and I were young when we left home. There wasn't much out there for uneducated girls that paid decent enough. Wasn't the ideal situation or something we planned. I guess it was more of a choice of survival to get us out of the places we lived in."

He ponders this for a moment while keeping his hands on my hips and circling his thumbs over my skin. It takes me all my strength to concentrate on talking rather than feeling.

"What age were you when you left home?"

"Just under the age of eighteen. I met Dez on the bus ride to Pheonix. She had just turned eighteen," I answer.

He smiles softly. "I'm actually pretty impressed. You took a rough situation and figured out how to survive while keeping your virtue intact. That's a very hard thing to do in the world you're in."

He's right. I've been offered a shit ton of money, enough money that I could sit on comfortably while I figured out my next move, but I wasn't willing to trade myself – *until now of course.*

"Yes, well I never even considered whoring myself out before," I say, ashamed just saying those words. "Though I guess one would say I've finally accepted my fate," I imply, looking away out toward the vast sea trying to hide the disappointment in myself.

He takes hold of my chin directing my attention back to him. "That's not what you're doing here at all. I've told you before that's not how I think of you. Yes, I want you here for my own personal greed, but I also want to show you more. I want to be the one to open you to new experiences," he says, trying his hardest to assure me.

Though, I wonder what happens after these few weeks. Will I be able to walk away? What becomes of us then? I'm too afraid to ask. I'm not ready to be heartbroken already with the answer.

"But in all actuality, you're paying for me."

He kisses my forehead, then my nose before he pulls away to respond. "I'm paying for your time, not the sex. Naomi, you still have a choice. Just because you're here with me doesn't force you to give me something you aren't ready to give. If it all gets too much then you say the word and we stop. If you're unsure or not ready, then we stop. It's simple as that," he assures me. "But, as I asked you before, I'd like you to keep an open mind. There's pleasure in the unknowns. I won't ever do anything to hurt you, and I won't allow anyone to harm you. You're completely safe with me."

I can feel the sun beginning to beat harshly on my shoulders, but I don't want this conversation to end yet. "What kind of unknowns are you talking about?"

"Let's you and I work on getting acquainted more first and once you're fully comfortable with me, then I can introduce you to my world," he finishes.

I nod. He leans down and trails his tongue along my lips. I catch his tongue with my teeth and suck as he grips my bum and squeezes hard. I squeal. "Next time you do that, expect a nice hard spank," he growls.

I fist my hands through his hair and pull him in for a deep kiss. Our mouths move to the perfect beat as I grind myself down on his now hard length. He feels so good in all the right ways. I'm suffocated with pure need right now and no matter how much of him I devour, I can't seem to get enough. He's infected me with his toxin and I'm afraid there may be no antidote.

He begins leaving trails of kisses down the side of my neck ending at my sensitive spot right above my clavicle. I moan as I continue to grind my core against him driving him mad. His hands are everywhere and nowhere all at once.

He lifts me up trying to gain some space in between us. "Patience, little ballerina, unless you're ready for me to slide inside of you," he tells me, barely holding it together.

I rub my lips together feeling bashful as I completely lost control of my own inhibitions. He brings out the reckless side of me. The side that just throws carefree caution to the wind.

Our kisses slow to a still as he places his forehead against mine. "Come on, let's get you out of the sun before you burn."

I already feel the tightness over my shoulders with the

beginning stages of a sunburn, and if I stay in the sun any longer I will definitely be in pain.

There's a gigantic daybed below the deck of the house mimicking the bed inside my room, that he guides us to. Gabriele has towels, lotions, and sunscreen waiting for us along with a pitcher of margaritas set on the small table beside the bed.

This man seems to think of everything.

"Sit," he instructs. He unties my bikini top, and I let it fall to my waist. I'm past the point of being shy about my body, so a little boobage being exposed is the same as wearing the top.

He begins rubbing the sunscreen over my shoulders, massaging it down my back and again up over my shoulders to the front of my breastbone above my chest. He slides his fingers just enough to skim over my nipples, turning them into tight hard pebbles, but never going any further. I moan with pleasure. It feels absolutely amazing as he kneads and rubs all of my muscles into mush.

Once he's done, he pours us each a drink and I lay back onto the daybed topless looking out over the ocean. His eyes brush over every inch of me leaving a burning trail in their wake. After that massage, every nerve ending is on high alert, and anything more will tip me over the edge.

"What's on your mind?" I ask, deciding to be bold.

He smirks and takes a long pull of his drink, still staring at me over his glass. Now it's my turn to run my gaze over him. His swim trunks are hanging extremely low, the light happy trail giving me a direct map to what lies beneath, the small droplets of water cascade down hitting every peak and valley dipping down underneath his trunks making envious wishing it was my tongue.

He puts down his drink and starts to crawl over the bed. "I'm thinking about how much I want to taste you. How bad I want my tongue deep into your little cunt," he says as he lands next to me, reaching over beginning to untie the strings on each side of my bikini bottoms. They drop to the side, and he adjusts himself in between my thighs spreading them wide. My bikini is no longer covering me, leaving me open and exposed to his viewing.

He looks insanely sexy as hell with that devilish smirk stretched across his face as he licks his lips. He looks starved and I'm the filet mignon he's about to destroy. My heart accelerates. I try to close my legs together with the anticipation and the need to simmer the pressure building between them already, but he doesn't allow me to.

Instead, he brings me down to the edge of the daybed, spreads me further, pushing my knees all the way back and inhales. "God, I love the smell of you."

His tongue licks from my ass all the way up my slit to my clit in just one slow swipe. A whimper escapes me not caring how loud I am considering there's no one in the vicinity for miles. He reaches his hand around my leg for more precise access spreading me wider as he circles my clit applying soft firm pressure while running his finger up and down the center of my folds.

I'm already panting, and he's just begun.

I can hear my juices gathering as his finger glides around my entrance, not entering me but teasing as his tongue continues to lather by bud with concentrated strokes. I wiggle grabbing at the sheets, his mouth is dangerous and well-practiced. He knows exactly what he is doing.

He enters one finger inside me, and I scream out. The feel is foreign but so damn good. He moans against my clit after he hears my cry and the vibration sends waves of liquid to my core.

"Fuck, you're soaked and so tight. Your pussy is just wrapping around my finger. I can't wait to have my cock buried inside of you," he groans as he licks and sucks my lips on the way down. He removes his finger replacing it with his tongue. He delves deep inside of me, fucking me over and over as he watches my face falter.

My body is wound tight, an explosion is on the horizon as I moan his name. "Gabriele, don't stop," I beg.

He drags his tongue through my pussy landing back on my clit, twirling and licking tilting me more toward the edge. My body burns for release. It's like I've been placed in the middle of an incinerator, and I'm being scorched alive by a single flame.

As if he can read my body, he slowly inserts two fingers, stroking me and stretching me allowing me to adjust while taking his time learning me and making me squirm under his commands.

"Oh *fuck*, Gabriele!" I drag out in a scream as he penetrates deeper. The burn just on the brink of pain turns to a fiery pleasure as a gush of wetness glides over his fingers as he hits that perfect spot.

"That's right, come for me, little ballerina. Come all over my fingers so I can slurp those juices up," he growls as he ricochets me straight over off the cliff while continuing to devour my pussy.

Droplets of sweat form all over my body with an inferno of heat as I combust all over his fingers and tongue. He doesn't stop until my panting slows into small whines.

"I could watch you fucking come all day long," he confesses.

He slips his fingers out and dips his mouth down over my entrance slurping my juices away. The sound is provocative and fucking sexy as hell as I watch him. His eyes are locked with mine as he swirls his tongue over my sex basking in my flavor. I whimper at the continuous assault over my sensitive flesh.

He finally frees me and crawls up my body bringing me into a deep kiss. I can taste the salty sweetness of my release on his tongue, and I smile thinking back to just a moment ago. This is now orgasm number three and I haven't even returned the favor once.

I guess if I was any normal girl I would have been on my knees by now, and I've watched enough porn to understand what to do, but I'm still hesitant of my capabilities. Gabriele seems to know a woman's body more than I know my own. So, how am I supposed to be so sure of myself in pleasing him the same?

He must feel the hesitation of my thoughts through my kiss as I become distant and robotic while stuck in my thoughts.

He looks down at me. "Hey, what's going on in that pretty little head of yours?"

He kisses the tip of my nose while waiting.

"You're just so good at everything you do," I tell him.

He looks confused. "Is that a bad thing?"

"No, it's an experienced thing," I say, not sure if I'm even making sense. My thoughts tend to get jumbled when I'm nervous or out of my league.

He smiles, understanding what I'm saying. "And I *love* that being experienced is *not* your thing."

I giggle and squirm under him. "Oh yeah? And why's that?"

He takes my wrists and locks them over my head as he begins to kiss down the side of my neck. "Because I quite enjoy knowing that I've been and will be the only man inside of you more than one way," he murmurs as he nips at the delicate skin. "I want to dominate every part of you until you come undone and then still beg for more," he continues between kisses over the peak of my breast.

I can't seem to get enough of this man. Just when I think I'm finally sated, he awakens me all over again. "I want to be the first to take you, then be the first to fuck your tight ass, and also the first to pump my cock into that beautiful mouth of yours spilling my seed down your throat," he reveals before taking a nipple into his mouth, teasing and sucking before he bites down.

My back lifts and I scream with a surprised pain that sizzles all the way down to my sex. My breath hitches as he moves over to my other nipple, still caging me in with his body in between my legs and my wrist locked above my head.

He licks and grazes my nipple with his teeth, no pain this time, only soft pleasure. My bare hips begin to grind against his cock forgetting I'm completely naked still.

"You're such a little minx," he jokes.

His phone buzzes on the table beside the daybed bringing us out of our lust induced stupor. We were probably close to heading down the path of another orgasm for me and I pout at the thought of being interrupted.

He releases my wrist and kisses my neck. "I'm sorry. I need to take this," he explains as he moves off me.

I grab the beach towel and wrap it around me. I mouth to him that I'm going to shower, and he nods as he walks off toward the water.

CHAPTER 8

G abriele had to take care of some business on the other side of the island. I laid down after my shower and ended up falling asleep.

I feel a light touch against my forehead. I stir and my eyes flutter open confused. It's now dark with a light breeze and the moon casting a glowing light through the room. I look up and Gabriele is sitting on the bed beside me.

"Hey."

I stretch and then sit up. "What time is it?" I ask, looking around for a clock or my phone.

"It's after 8PM. You hungry?" he asks.

I nod.

"I had my chef make a pizza. You okay with that?"

"Am I okay with that? It's one of my most favorite food groups," I inform him, scooching off the bed. "I'll meet you out there. I need to freshen up."

He nods and heads out.

I wash my face, brush my teeth, and throw a brush through my hair. My phone has been buzzing off the hinges the last couple of minutes, so I grab it and open the texts I see from Dez.

"Call me. It's an emergency."

This is all the text says. What the fuck? She never sends texts like this. I look at my phone log and she didn't try calling me. Why wouldn't she have just called me if it was such an emergency?

I quickly dial her number and wait as it rings pacing back and forth.

After two rings she finally answers.

"What the fuck, Dez? What happened?" I freak out.

I hear her sniffling. Oh no. My gut drops. "Did someone hurt you?" I question worried.

"Yes, that fucking asshole Luke!" she says angrily.

Shit. I freaking knew it. I knew he was going to fucking hurt her. "What did he do, Dez?"

"Trev and I went out for drinks tonight and we saw him there. He was having dinner and drinks with a woman. When I went up to him, he acted as though he didn't know me, like I must have mistaken him for someone else," she explains still sniffling.

My heart sinks and then anger steps in. "Fuck Dez, I'm so sorry. I know you really liked him but he's not worth your tears. Such a douche move."

"What's wrong with me, Nay?" she asks crying. "Why can't someone just love me?"

I sit down on the edge of my bed. "Dez, you listen to me – *I* fucking love you! He's not worthy of your love, and you *will* find someone worthy of it. It's just not the right time yet. So, please, do me a favor and block him and if he comes to the club then have Trev kick his ass out," I direct her.

I can almost hear her nodding. "I know you just got there, but when will you be home again?" she asks.

"I can come home tomorrow if you need me."

I couldn't care less about the money or about being here

with Gabriele at the moment. If my friend needs me then I'm out of here.

"No, don't be silly. I'll be fine. I'm going to douse myself in some cookie dough ice cream and go to bed early," she says.

I walk over to the glass door and look out to the ocean. The palm tree on the side of the house is swaying in the wind as the waves roll high onto the beach.

"Are you sure? I'm serious, Dez. I can be home tomorrow," I ask again.

I hear her open the top of the tub and grab a spoon out of the drawer. "No, you stay put and call me tomorrow."

"Okay, I love you."

"Love you too," Dez replies before ending the call.

I shoot Trev a quick text to go check on Dez.

I can't go out to Gabriele just yet. I need to cool off. I knew that bastard was no good, and Gabriele would probably end up the same way. The apple doesn't fall far from the tree I'm sure. Luke said sweet things, wanted one on one time, acted as though he cared about her well-being – just to act like he doesn't know her? What a fuck-boy.

And here I am on a beautiful remote island with his brother also telling me sweet nothings while he acts like he cares. When in reality he's already put a time frame on us so when he's ready to walk away, he can tell me he was honest and forthright when it came to what he wanted.

It's just all a good setup. I need to refocus.

It's about the money, Nay. And let's face it, you put the rule in place for him to never contact you again.

I need to keep telling myself this. Your feelings are an illusion – *he* is an illusion. I need to keep the orgasms completely separate from the emotions. Because in all reality, none of this is real to him.

I finally gather myself together enough to yank the wall up. The more time I'm with him, the more stress cracks my wall encounters, and the more time I spend sealing them back up to keep the foundation intact. I can do this. I just need to keep reminding myself to stay strong because boy this is going to be a *long* couple of weeks for me if I can't even handle the first day.

Music fills the living area as I exit my room. The lights are dimmed, and the sliding doors are all open allowing a soft breeze to flow in. Gabriele is sitting on the deck with a glass of bourbon while looking out into the moonlit water.

I notice the music he chose – the Chris Brown song I danced to that night.

"Are you requesting a dance tonight?" I ask as I walk up behind him.

"I like the song, and I like to reminisce while listening to it," he admits while still looking out toward the water.

"Did you eat yet?" I ask.

"No, I've been waiting for you. I went to go get you, but I heard you on the phone. Who were you talking to?" he questions as he stands up from the chair now looking at me.

My brows furrow, a little taken back, as he stalks straight to me. He stops right in front of me, leans his arm on the door over me, and asks again. "Who were you talking to, Naomi?"

I take a step back but only end up back up against the glass door.

"What's it to you?" I ask angrily and confused. How dare he invade my privacy and then demand to know who I was talking to. He has no claims on me.

He leans down closer to my face so I can now feel his breath against my face. "Because I want to know who on the other line was making you so angry. Was it a boyfriend? Or client maybe?"

He looks disheveled and wild.

I slap him hard across the face. He grabs my wrist and

holds it so I can't move. "Fuck you, Gabriele!" I spit out with venom.

I catch just the faintest grin with a twinkle in his eyes before he turns back to his anger. "Tell me, Naomi," he demands, his temper now flaring. "Who the fuck were you talking to?"

I yank my hand back. "I was talking to Dez because of your fuckface of a brother! She was upset and crying. There! Are you fucking happy?" I yell.

"I thought you said you didn't think of me as a whore, Gabriele? But here you are thinking I actually may be on a call with a client while I'm here with you!" I spit as I turn around heading for the kitchen.

I see a flash of pain cross his face. But I'm so pissed, I couldn't give two fucks, because I'm the one he hurt. Regardless, I'm still starving, so I grab two slices of pizza and a bottle of water then head to my room. So much for a great first day. It all just turned to shit.

"Thanks for making me feel small, Gabriele. It's just like I'm back at the club!" I shout before I walk into my room and slam the door.

I TOSSED and turned all night long. My pillowcase is now hardened with dry tears. I know what I am, but the insinuation coming from his mouth just made me feel icky. And to think I almost believed what he said the other day too. It's now clear as ever that I'm his paid toy and he's just biding his time until I give him what he wants.

I feel broken. I don't even care to get out of bed to face him. Normally, Dez would be the first person I reach out to but she's dealing with her own issues, and I don't want to pile mine on her.

I grab my phone and see a text from Trev saying he slept

in my room and Dez cried herself to sleep on his shoulder last night. I smile happy that he's at least there with her since I can't be.

I send him another text saying I love him and to text me when she's awake.

I throw the phone onto the bed and head into the shower to wash the night away. I stand under the hot water long enough for my muscles to ease. I'm a big girl. I've handled much worse before, it just feels different coming from him. I don't know why I care so much; he's grown on me like a flower growing in concrete, and I'm trying so hard to keep him from planting roots in my heart. But I just need to think of him as a client, keep my walls up, and learn what I can from this time.

After dressing, I slowly open the door listening for sounds. The house is quiet other than the sound of waves in the distance.

I tiptoe through the living room looking around, but Gabriele is nowhere in sight. I look out to the deck, and that's empty as well. I see a note lying on the counter surrounded by a variety of breakfast foods.

Dear ballerina,

I have business I need to attend to. I should only be gone a couple of hours. We'll talk when I get back.

-G

I THROW the note down on the counter. I don't want to talk. I would rather shove everything under the rug and pretend he didn't crush me. I'm embarrassed for allowing him to see how much he affected me.

I pour myself a cup of coffee and head out onto the deck. The air is thick with warmth. I immediately get little bursts of heat trickling over my skin. It's going to be a hot one today, but the light wind is a nice contrast.

I dial Trev's number looking at the time and realizing it's still extremely early. Just as I'm about to hang up he answers. He sounds groggy and horse.

"Hey," he says.

"Sorry to wake you," I tell him. "How'd last night go?"

He sighs. "She was a mess. I seriously can't believe that guy. He definitely did a number on her. I didn't realize how much she actually liked him. I thought this was just a phase," he confesses.

"I know. I tried talking to her, tried telling her to take it slow, but you know Dez," I reply before taking a sip of my coffee.

"So, what's the plan for today then? I know she won't be awake for a while," I ask.

He scoffs. "I'm going to make her a huge breakfast and then probably a little retail therapy," he advises coming up with a plan.

"Good."

Two tiny geckos run over the ledge past me. I smile knowing they look carefree and happy. If only life could be that simple.

"How was your first day there with Gabriele?"

I exhale deeply. I really didn't mean to, but it just came out. "What's wrong, Nay?" he questions, now seeming worried.

I give him a run-down of the day and how it ended. He's silent most of the time until I finish and then he finally jumps in. "You want to know what I think?"

I chuckle. "Is there any point to asking that question? I know you're going to tell me regardless."

I can almost hear his eye roll. "I think he has feelings for you, and he doesn't know what to do with them. I think he got overbearingly jealous and made a fool of himself. And I think he's probably kicking himself in the ass right now."

"I don't know, Trev. He was just so angry with the thought I may have been talking to a man while here with him. He made me feel like shit, like he couldn't trust me," I admit.

I mean, could Trev be right? Could he just have lost it thinking of me with another man? That would mean he possibly could actually have feelings for me, and Trev could be right. Or he could just be the jealous type when he's with a woman, and when he's done, doesn't give a fuck.

"Exactly. He's showing emotions. If you were just some paid piece of ass like I know you're thinking, then he wouldn't care. He wouldn't have lost his shit. Believe me," he explains.

He is making sense, but I still have my reservations about it. I still don't know who he really is, and I'm not sure three weeks is going to allow me to even touch the surface.

My stomach starts growling. I head to the kitchen and start piling up my plate of fruits, danishes, and eggs with beans. "Thanks for listening, Trev. I owe you," I tell him as we say our goodbyes.

The rest of the morning went by uneventful. I changed into a bathing suit and went for a dip in the ocean, snacked on food, and made myself a couple of margaritas. The heat was at an all-time high this afternoon, and clearly wreaked havoc on my body as I fell asleep on the daybed.

I wake to the feeling of fingers brushing against my cheek. My eyes flutter open, and Gabriele is sitting beside me. I squint as the sun behind him is blaring.

I lay there as he rubs the back of his fingers along my

neck and over my collarbone. Our eyes are locked on each other, not saying a word. I can almost feel his apology through the guilt in his eyes.

"Noami, I'm sorry for my actions last night. I should have given you the benefit of the doubt and just talked to you. I can be harsh at times when I'm angered. My temper gets the best of me, and you didn't deserve that," he apologizes.

Shit. What am I supposed to say to that? How am I supposed to remain mad when he just practically got down on his knees and groveled? He needs to know he can't just do this continuously and then just apologize either.

I nod as he still skims his fingers along my skin searing a trail of desire along the way. Damn my body. It's such a trader.

"Thank you for the apology. I'm normally more self-controlled when something is said that bothers me, but not with you. Your words hurt me, and it's something I'm trying to understand since I never allow that from anyone," I say, trying to still process everything.

His fingers trail over my lips outlining them as if he's trying to burn the memory of how they feel in his mind. "I understand. You've learned to protect yourself. Can I be honest?" he asks.

"Please."

"I guess we may be more alike on this topic. I also practice control in everything I do, but this feeling is new to me. I got jealous, I can admit, and it made me lose all bearings on my sanity. You also make me feel something I do not understand," he reveals. "I can't promise to never lose my temper, but I can promise to ask before assuming."

I don't know what this all means exactly but what I do know is that we both are feeling something that we are unsure of. Something's growing between us, and we can deny it all we want but our bodies know. There's a pull between us that can't be described. We're a magnetic force that no matter how hard we try to distance ourselves, we keep slamming back together. It's intense and riveting but also dangerous like an atomic bomb that collides with the earth's surface without warning.

"Can we start anew today?" he asks.

I lean up and wrap my arms around his neck pulling him down to my lips. This time I coax his mouth open slipping my tongue in a sweet duet with his. We sink into a slow dance. Tasting each other and taking our time. This kiss isn't as demanding or feverish, it's lazy and drawn out.

He pulls away still waiting for my answer. "Yes," I say breathlessly after that kiss.

He smiles, then pulls me up. "Let's go explore the island. There's somewhere I'd like to show you."

HE PACKS lunch and I change into denim shorts and a white tank. He told me to leave my bathing suit on because where we're going there will still be water. Gabriele has a silver Jeep Wrangler waiting outside for us; top and doors off so we're open to the fresh air.

I feel giddy and excited. The house is nice, but we need a change of atmosphere to clean away yesterday's aches. "Ready?" he questions with a wide grin.

I smile back and nod. "Ready!"

He leans over quickly and gives me a peck on the lips. "That smile is addicting. I want to see more."

Ugh. Why does he have to say things like that? *Hold it together, Naomi. Wall up no matter what,* I keep reminding myself.

We start driving down the dirt road for a while. There's nothing but blue skies and mangroves on either side. "How did you come across this place?"

He turns down a small dirt pathway. The brush seems

thicker and uncultivated the deeper we drive in. The shade from the palm trees gives us a nice reprieve from the blistering hot sun above us. I love seeing the variety of colorful birds flying overhead, groups of them swaying in and out of the trees gliding in the wind.

"I've actually vacationed on another adjacent island in the past. It's populated and more of a touristy vibe, but beautiful all the same. One of the locals told me about an island for sale, so the following day I chartered a plane to see it, and bought it," he says like it's an everyday purchase.

My brows raise in amazement. "Wow, do you make these sort of purchases a lot?"

He turns toward me with a grin, snapping his sunglasses down to look at me. "Only when they will make me a substantial amount of money."

Gabriele looks rugged and untamed as the wind blows through his hair. He seems lighter today, happier, and the excitement in his eyes matches mine. With his olive skin tone and dark glossy hair, he could almost pass as native.

I now have the chance to look over his tattoos peeking out of his white tee in more detail now that he's occupied driving. The designs are intricate and cared for with exact precision. I see intwined vines and prickers with droplets of blood weaved throughout his arm with word scriptures inside. I can't quite read what they say, but it's clear this has meaning to him.

Before I can ask him about his tattoos he points ahead of us. "We're here."

I look in the direction and there's a gigantic waterfall coming into view. We pull off to the side and he parks. I can't see anything else yet. It all seems to still be hidden.

Gabriele grabs the cooler and some blankets. I grab the towels, and follow his lead.

"What is this place?" I ask wide-eyed as we walk over some large boulders and down some rocky steps. Before he can answer we come to a secluded crystal-clear hidden beach under the waterfall. The beach can't be any larger than a couple of Olympic size pools, the green canopy opens up allowing the sun to glisten like a mirror off the water, and the sounds of white noise from the waterfall are soothing and mesmerizing.

"This is my little oasis I found while adventuring around the island trying to find the perfect places to build," he explains.

"Wow, Gabriele. This place seriously has no words. It's just incredible," I say amazed as I stay still just taking it all in.

He comes up behind me and wraps his arms around my waist. "It's even more incredible now that you're here to share it with," he tells me as he leans down raking his tongue along my neck then leaving it with a sweet kiss.

"You have to stop saying things like that," I demand softly.

I wish I could be the girl to allow myself to feel those words and believe them.

He turns me in his arms so I'm eye to eye with him. "Why would you want me to stop?"

"Because after these couple of weeks when I return home to my life and you walk away to yours, I need to be able to do the same with my dignity intact," I confess.

He looks hurt. "I see."

He takes a moment, looking past me in thought, but then takes my hand in his like he has accepted my answer, not digging any further and leads me to the water.

He starts undressing. First, his shirt. The contours of his chest down to his abs as he pulls his shirt over his head has me stuck. I can't rip my eyes from him as I watch. I wish I had my own dollars bills available for this Magic Mike scene unfolding right in front of me. Then, he unbuttons his khaki shorts and slides them down allowing them to fall the remainder of the way. I feel drool almost fall from the side of my mouth.

Now, he's left with only black boxer briefs. I guess he said fuck the swim trunks, but I'm fucking glad he did. I lick my lips hungry; my sex begins to throb craving his attention. I'm ravenous and I haven't even had a taste of him yet. That's going to change tonight.

"You see anything you like?" he asks with a wink.

I'm caught though I wasn't even trying to hide the fact that I was gawking. I enjoyed every single minute of it. This moment will be set on replay in my head for years to come.

I smile unbashful. "Oh yes, I very much like what I saw."

He laughs. "Your turn."

I see the glint of mischief in his eyes. He looks naughty with the thoughts I know are roaming through his mind. I follow his lead and remove my tank, then my shorts until I stand only in my bathing suit, but since there's no one for miles in this secluded place, I go one further and remove my top and throw it.

His eyes grow a smoldering forest green. You can't miss the sexual desire radiating off him now. He's every girl's wet dream, and yet he's here with me. I feel like an extremely lucky girl. I watch him watching me as I deliberately slide my bottoms down my legs and kick them aside. I'm bare and now standing in front of him in just my birthday suit.

I still have yet to see him bare, but I can see the bulge now growing in size as he stands in the water looking like a sexually crazed beast.

Gabriele stalks toward me, I almost back up just seeing the threat of promise with each step he takes. I quiver with the unknown but also vibrate with excitement. In an instant he picks me up by my waist and I immediately wrap my legs around him.

"You're such a dangerous tease. You're going to pay for that, little ballerina," he threatens with a gorgeous wide smile. My legs grip him harder as his hand moves to my ass and squeezes.

I feel nothing but warm water cascading over my body as he inches us into the lagoon.

"And how will you punish me?" I ask taunting.

He dips us down to our shoulders. "Oh, I have some ways, and I plan on using all of them," he says deviously.

The water is a perfect bath temperature, so clear I can see the bottom of sand and tiny tropical fish gliding around us like a small ecosystem. Every time we move, they scatter then form back around us.

"Are you planning on opening this place up to your guests?" I ask.

He nuzzles his nose against my neck. "After what I just witnessed a moment ago, I will absolutely never allow another person to know about this place," he vows. "This will forever be my sanctuary."

"Well then maybe we should really make this place memorable for you," I suggest.

He raises his eyebrow. "Oh yeah? And what do you have in mind?"

I squirm against his gigantic length, if we weren't already soaked, I would have left a huge wet spot. He groans and slips his fingers down the crack of my ass, teasing and testing. I wriggle even more from his touch.

He slides even further down until he reaches the entrance of my sex. My breath hitches with anticipation. He remains still and I become impatient so, I grind my hips to inch his fingers inside of me faster. He shakes his head slowly.

"Tsk, tsk," he sounds. "Not so fast."

I pout and he laughs. "Looks like my little ballerina is turning into a sex crazed vixen," he jokes.

I lean into his neck, take his earlobe between my teeth and bite down. He hisses and this time he grinds into me. I kiss my way down his neck as he inches two fingers inside of me.

"God, please don't stop," I beg between kisses.

He tangles his other hand into the back of my hair and tugs down, so I have no choice but to stop my assault and look at him. He continues to slide his fingers with perfect precision, it feels fucking heavenly.

"Tell me what you want," he demands. I moan. "Say it out loud."

I reach down in between us and grab his shaft. I can't even wrap my hands fully around his thickness. I gulp knowing I'm in big trouble. "I want you in my mouth. I want to taste every inch of you. I want you to teach me what you like," I comply with his demand.

"Fuck," he growls. "What are you doing to me?" he asks, grabbing my hair even tighter. I love the reaction I pull from him.

He immediately starts walking us out of the water toward the beach. He nibbles harshly at my lips, fingers now creeping out of me, I whine in protest as I continue to stroke him. His finger slides up from my entrance now over my ass. I jump with the sensation as he circles my hole.

"This I will also have soon," he vows.

Once we reach the sand, he releases his hold on me, and I unlock my legs from around him and slide down to my knees. I look up at him from under my lashes, his eyes burn with a need I've never witnessed before. I have the urge to press my legs together to ease the pulse shooting right through my core.

I grab the hem of his boxers and begin to pull them down. They're soaking wet which makes me tug harder. His cock springs out, bouncing back against his lower abdomen. I almost gasp at the size. I've never seen one this close in person, but I've also never seen one of this magnitude. I know I'm not experienced in this department, but I've watched enough porn and been flashed enough times at the club to know the difference, and his is beyond normal.

He smirks down at me as if reading my mind. He reaches

down and lifts my chin. "Stop thinking, little ballerina. This will fit inside you perfectly."

Somehow, I have reservations on that statement.

He steps out of his boxer briefs the rest of the way and he's now standing completely naked in front of me. I'm in awe. It's like he's chiseled from stone. I run my hands over his sculpted thighs, up to his hips. He stands extremely still while watching me with blazing heat.

I slide through his meticulously trimmed hair and wrap my hand around the bottom of his shaft. He hisses instantly with my touch pushing himself forward. I glide my hand up and over the crown of his head spreading the little bead of pre-cum over the tip.

"Yes, baby. Just like that," he praises.

I bring him down and lick the moisture off his tip in one little swipe. His hand tangles through my hair again gripping tight. The sting gives me pleasure instead of pain. A burst of salty tang runs over my tongue leaving me thirsty for more.

I swirl my tongue around his head stopping underneath his crown flicking against him. A loud groan rips from his lips. Just hearing he's pleased is forging me forward with encouragement as I drag my tongue down the bottom side of his cock and back up now taking him into my mouth in one swift move.

"*Fuuuuck*," he screams.

I swear the sound of his words echoes through the trees. I suck him in fully as I bring myself back to the tip of his head, licking and swirling until I immediately repeat my process of taking him to the hilt, slamming him to the back of my throat and swallowing trying my hardest not to gag as tears slide down my cheeks.

He holds the side of my face gently with his other hand watching as I slowly bring myself back to the tip. I reach for his balls, squeezing and massaging as I dive back down slowly. The muscles on his thighs and abs are contracted to the max while his toes are curled digging in the sand.

Every breath and deep groan emanating from his body has my inner goddess smiling. My first try at this and I'm succeeding in bringing him to his knees just as he's done with me on multiple occasions.

The slurping sounds engulf us each time I bob up and down his length. I begin to gain more control, and I take him to the back of my throat; this time he holds me there until I almost begin to panic and then he releases his hold with a loud grunt.

I can feel the vein underneath expand as his cock swells even larger and I realize he must be on the verge of an orgasm. I moan at the thought as the vibration spreads all the way down to the base.

"I'm gonna come, baby," he says with warning. I don't care, I want to feel every single drop slide down my throat, so I suck harder.

"Holy fucking *shit!* Yes, take me. Just like that," he directs with a strained voice.

And just like that warm thick liquid squirts down the back of my throat as I swallow every last drop. I close my eyes taking into memory the flavor of him. The salty smokey tang swirls all over my mouth like the clouds from a campfire. He tastes of man and sea.

I reopen my eyes and his never leave mine as he continues to pump in and out of my mouth. "God damn, your mouth is fucking perfect. You took every last drop of my come like a good little girl," he praises with a soft pleased gaze.

He slips out of my mouth and comes down on his knees with me. He massages the sides of my jaw knowing my muscles may be sore. "You're amazing, you know that?"

I lean into his hand staring at him. "You taste amazing," I tell him.

He grins a white teethed grin. "Oh yeah? I bet not as good as you though. I'm not sure I'll be able to handle the thought of you taking another man into your mouth like that," he admits.

"Then don't let me."

He smashes his lips against mine claiming me in a feverish haze. He pours every last drop of himself into this kiss. I feel his need and his desire to dominate me with every thrust of his tongue. It's hot and sexy feeling the jealousy swarm within him from just his imagination.

"You're going to become my sex slaved prisoner and I'm going to keep you here just for my own pleasure, so I don't have to share you with the world," he jokes, cracking a grin.

I peck him on the lips. "Don't promise me with a good time."

He laughs then reaches out to my side and starts tickling me. I howl in laughter since I'm extremely ticklish. He's found my weakness, and I have no doubt he will begin to extort me with it from time to time.

"Oh, you're ticklish, are you? Now I know the perfect threat to always get my way," he gleams.

"Okay, okay. No more," I yell between laughs, sand now in every crevice as we roll around.

He stands and tugs me up to my feet then grabs my thighs and lifts me up over his shoulders. All I see is a tight muscle ass in my view. I grab both his cheeks and squeeze with a giggle like he loves to do with mine.

"Oh, you naughty little ballerina!" he yells as we're now deep into the water.

He smacks my ass hard. I screech in surprise. The sting does something to me, I squirm feeling tingles spread through my core as he spanks the same spot again. Shit, why does this sting feel so good as the heat spreads straight over my sex? It almost feels wrong liking it so much. I've always known this has been a thing for people, but I never knew *I* could actually like this thing.

He dunks us both underwater quickly while still holding my thighs. I kick my feet trying to get him to release me but when we come back up and have all the sand washed away, he spanks my other cheek again, hard. I jolt up again with the shock and just before I say something he runs his fingers through my folds and enters one inside of me.

I gasp and then moan halting my fight. He dips in and out of me. "Spread," he commands, and this is all he says, and I follow without argument. His finger glides down to my clit sparking an immediate scream of pleasure from me.

"That's right, tell me how you like it," he coaches me on.

He circles my swollen bud and then drifts back up to my entrance now slipping two fingers inside.

"Holy fuck!" I yell, dragging it out.

The burn from the stretch feels almost unbearable until he finally reaches this one spot, stroking and building my release as his thumb strokes over my clit at the same time, and I finally reach my pinnacle and detonate.

Waves and waves of intense spasms spread through my core trapping his fingers like a vise grip. "That's right, baby. Fucking come all over my fingers," he coaxes me, and he continues his invasion still bringing me down.

He slips his fingers from me and puts me on my feet in the water while still holding me since my legs are now Jell-O.

"Do you know how beautiful you sound when you come?"

I look down shy. I've had people speak vulgar to me before, so I'm used to things being said, but the way Gabriele says things has me bashful.

"Don't you dare look away from me. You're a fucking queen. You hold your head high. Your sexuality is nothing to be ashamed of," he says, compelling me to look up at him. "There you are," he whispers.

"I've never met someone quite like you, Naomi. You always tend to amaze me," he admits.

"I think I'm just getting overwhelmed by the way my body is taking control. These feelings are just so new to me, and the things my body is reacting to make me question myself," I confess while trying to process it.

"Like what things?"

I dip down into the water so only my head is above as I begin to swim backwards. Gabriele follows. "Like being spanked," I reveal. "I didn't think I would be the type to enjoy that."

He smiles proudly. I roll my eyes. "You can't know what you like or dislike until you try it, Naomi. It's important to allow yourself to be open to new things so you don't miss out on something that may really give you pleasure," he clarifies.

"There should be no judgement in sex or pleasure. Not everything's for all to like and there are things that society may frown upon as well, but that doesn't mean it's wrong as long as things are between consensual adults," he finishes.

The sun has now shifted giving a small shadow of reprieve from the trees. I look up at the waterfall behind Gabriele and realize I've tuned out the white noise this whole time being fully immersed in him.

"So how would you feel if I had fantasies that aren't the norm?" I wonder. I already saw his jealous streak after I had him in my mouth, so I must ask. "What if I also wanted to push the limits?"

His demeanor has now changed to intriguing, but serious. "I'm game for hearing your desires. And if it's something in my power to make happen, I will do my best to try. I am a jealous man, but when it comes to your pleasure, I'm open."

I wrap my body around him, arms around his neck. "And what if I want to fuck two men at the same time while you watch?" I say teasing, waiting for him to renege on his words and lose it.

He looks entertained instead of angered. "Fucking you, no. But pleasuring you with their tongue, fingers, and toys? Then yes."

My brows raise and jaw drops in shock. Did I just really hear him right? He pushes my chin up to close my mouth. "I'm dead serious, Naomi," he answers my thoughts with a smirk.

Damn him. How the fuck does he do that?

"Okay, well just so we're clear. I don't want to watch anyone touching you."

He chuckles. "Are you sure? How would you know if you haven't experienced it?" he asks.

"I just know."

He nods and gives me a quick tickle to my side. "Fair enough. I've never been a man who cares for two women at a time, but I'm not opposed to watching one give my woman pleasure," he admits.

I slowly shake my head in disbelief. Where did this man come from? What I've known of men is their selfish interest in satisfying only their needs, but this man – he's something I've never heard of. A rare species. Something most men could never compare to and here he is with me.

"How did I end up so lucky to have you as my first everything?" I ask in denial.

He looks a little taken back. "Wait, was I also your first kiss?"

I nod. He gleams with astonishment and triumph then crashes his lips to mine again. When he pulls back, I swear I witness something in his eyes, is it admiration possibly? But just as quick as I see it, is as quick as he looks away and clears his throat.

"Are you hungry?

"Starving."

"Come on, let's go have lunch," he says, leading us to the beach.

CHAPTER 9

Yesterday was such an amazing day. After lunch we lounged around on the beach and took a couple more leisurely swims until late afternoon. We went back to the house and showered, having a late dinner around the coffee table on the floor of the living room. This reminded me of times with Dez and Trev. After dinner we both turned in early to our own separate bedrooms.

I feel extremely well rested this morning. I think this place is having a calming effect on me since it's now 9AM and I've actually slept in. I stretch with a huge smile and roll out of bed. I open the slider and let the breeze of the ocean rush over me. I don't think I'll ever get enough of this view and the salty fresh aroma that wafts over my skin with every gush of air.

I hear the low sounds of music coming from the other side of the doors and the smell of bacon. My stomach growls. I rush to the bathroom to freshen up then give Dez a call.

She picks up on the first ring. "Hey, how are you feeling?"

Dez sounds a bit cheerier. "Good. Trev and I are about to

hit the gym. He has another hot date with Adam, so he has to get pumped up for that."

"Did you meet him yet?" I ask excited for him.

"Not yet, he's still on the fringe on whether he wants anything more or not. But you know Trev, picky as fuck," she says.

"I heard that!" I hear him screaming in the background. I laugh.

"So, really Dez, how have you been since the other day? Have you heard from him?"

I hear her sigh. "I blocked him," she says. "I don't ever want to hear from him again."

"Good. Okay, I have to get going. I'll call you later. Love you."

She sounds a little sad with our short conversation. "Love you too, Nay."

GABRIELE IS STANDING at the stove turning the bacon, shirtless and just in gray boxer briefs. He has a whole spread out – eggs, toast, sausage, and beans with some orange juice.

"Be careful of that bacon grease. It can be deadly when it bites back," I tell him sarcastically.

He looks over his shoulder and smiles. "Good morning, little ballerina. How'd you sleep?" he asks.

"Surprisingly great. Everything smells delicious. Do you do a lot of cooking?" I wonder. I love seeing him in the kitchen. He looks so tamed and domesticated.

"When I'm home and not traveling I do. I enjoy it. My mom taught me a lot as a boy and I've picked up a few things as I got older," he uncovers.

I know his father passed but no one has mentioned his mother. "What is your mom like?"

"She was very hands on when Luke and I were younger.

Things were strained with her and my father. He was a very promiscuous man. He had money and women flung to him because of it. She tried to ignore his ways almost until the final years of his death but eventually they divorced, and she's now remarried living in Tuscany, Italy," he explained.

I wonder if watching his father all those years growing up made him the way he is about relationships. I guess that would make sense. Why get into something serious and risk cheating when the next best thing comes about.

"So, is that who your brother, Luke takes after, your father?" I wonder.

He grabs the bacon out of the pan and places the pieces on a plate with napkins to drain the grease, bringing it over to the counter.

"Luke's still young. We're seven years apart. He was mainly raised by the nanny as my mother drank her depression away so, I'm not sure what he's seen growing up. But he understood enough as he got older."

He takes two plates and piles them up with food. I see he enjoys taking care of me and making sure I eat enough. He slides my plate over and brings his over to sit next to me.

"Did you know about what Luke had done to upset Dez?" I ask, searching for truth in his eyes.

He nods and then takes a bite of his eggs. "After that night I spoke with him. He told me what had happened." He doesn't say much else.

I wait for him to finish sipping his orange juice. "And? What does he have to say for himself?"

"I know you're her close friend, but I think it's better if he speaks with her first. It's for them to work out or not work out. I don't get involved with my brother's personal life," he claims.

I guess I can see that since his brother doesn't seem to know a lot about Gabriele's either. I nod with acceptance.

He's right, they need to figure it out. I'm just rooting for Dez to keep his number blocked and move on.

I take a bite of the fresh mango and the juice runs down the side of my mouth. He catches it with his thumb then sucks the juice off. I'm not sure I'll ever get used to that. "So sweet," he informs.

We both clear off our plates. After a long day of swimming and orgasms yesterday, food will be definitely needed for today's bouts.

"I need to take care of some business today. Did you want to come with me?"

My eyes must light up because he laughs. "I would love to!"

"Okay, why don't you go get dressed and meet me back here in twenty. I have some quick calls to make," he directs. I grab our plates and set them in the sink to soak.

I SHOWER and throw on a light pink casual sundress with flats and leave my hair down to air dry. I like the wild untamed look considering that's where we are right now. My skin now has a sun-kissed glow so only mascara and lip gloss are required. I'm pretty sure if I walked out stark naked, he would be happy with that.

Gabriele's waiting for me at the kitchen island, sitting on the barstool while on a call. His hair is still wet and he's in a white button-down shirt with the sleeves rolled up, navy blue shorts, and some casual shoes. My mouth waters. I would like nothing more than to get on my knees in front of him and devour him.

He must see the lust in my eyes as I walk toward him because he cracks a white teethed smile and winks. I pour myself a cup of coffee and walk out to the deck to give him privacy. I could sit here all day long and just take in the view.

The seclusion has been great but I'm ready to see some people. I wonder if he would allow us to travel to one of the other islands to shop or do tourist stuff.

I hear shuffling behind me and then feel arms wrap around me from behind. He grazes my neck with his nose and inhales then places light kisses along my neckline.

"Are you ready?"

I turn my head and give him a peck on the lips. "I am. Are we going to where your guests stay?" I ask.

He takes my hand pulling me up and embraces me in his hold. "We are. There're some things I'd like to show you," he clarifies.

We're beginning to build a nice trust with each other now after our little tiff. So, when he says things like this, I know it's something of importance to him.

"Okay."

We jump into the Jeep and head in the opposite direction as we did yesterday. Today the skies are blue with a few fluffy clouds, the birds are serenading us as we drive down the dirt road. He puts on some beach vibe music while we drive in silence.

Normally, I would feel uncomfortable in silence, but with him, it just feels right. We can just be. No awkwardness, no words needed to fill the space, we are just living in the moment in each other's company.

After about a thirty-minute drive, the road becomes wider, the trees start to lighten, and I see a couple of buildings nestled up ahead. I can see the ocean on my right side through the thickets along with white sandy beaches.

Gabriele points ahead at a large house. "That's the main reception house. Our guests check in, it's private so we never have more than one checking in at the same time, and this is where our private chefs, staff, and tour captains reside when they're requested," he explains.

"Oh, so no one actually lives here?"

We pull up to the house. It's a grand villa, something you would see in the centerfold of a magazine with a rustic beach vibe, so it doesn't look completely out of place. The view is nothing but the beach and ocean just as ours is.

"Only very few reside full-time on the island. The others are flown over when requested. We have an exquisitely discreet handpicked staff for every need on standby.

He parks the Jeep and takes me through the front entrance. The reception area is beautiful, full of white couches and natural woods, an open vibe just like the beach house we're staying in. The receptionist greets Gabriele and then directs her smile toward me, not reaching her eyes. She seems friendly enough but also reserved as she watches Gabriele and I together.

He takes my hand and leads me down the hall. We enter a large office, behind the desk is Mrs. Caine, Joanna. She jumps up as soon as she sees us.

"Mr. Vanucci, Miss Veil, what a pleasant surprise! What brings you over here?" she asks, clapping her hands together with a large smile.

"I have some business to take care of with the staff. I was hoping you could show Miss Veil around for a short while, and then I'd like to show her villa six, so if you can call down and have it ready for me, that would be great," he directs her.

She nods. "Of course." She walks over to the desk and makes a couple of calls while Gabriele tells me he will only be a short while before he heads off.

Mrs. Caine is now off her call. She walks over to me smiling. "You ready for the grand tour, Miss Veil?"

"Please, call me Naomi," I ask.

She nods. "Naomi. Such a beautiful name for a beautiful girl. You remind me a lot of my daughter back home," she states.

She leads me out of the office and through a side door to the outside. "Oh yeah? Where is back home for you?"

"Upstate New York. I fly back to visit every couple of months or Gabriele flies them here for me when I take off. He's really so kind and generous," she reveals.

I beam. "That is really sweet of him. Have you worked for him long?"

She walks us down a small pathway opening to a large infinity swimming pool overlooking the ocean. I can only imagine what it would look like sitting by this pool during sunset.

"I have actually. I was one of his brother's nannies growing up. When Luke outgrew me, Gabriele hired me to run parts of his business he could not directly run himself. He knew I wanted to retire but this opportunity came along, and he gave me a choice to retire at home or to retire here and help run the place. I guess you can say I really didn't retire but working here every day is almost like a non-stop vacation," she explains with a chuckle.

I most definitely agree with that. And now I understand the admiration I saw between the two of them when I first met her.

"How does your daughter feel about you living so far away?"

We stop to look over the balcony. I can see the steps continue down to the beach. Cabanas and beach lounge chairs are laid out for pleasure. I can see a couple far in the distance walking along the beach. Maybe the first sign of guests I've viewed.

"You know, she wasn't too happy at first. But then Gabriele kept his word on us traveling back and forth to visit. So, she's happy that her and my grandbabies have a place to vacation," she answers.

"Come let me show you our hidden sanctuary," she tells me, leading me down the side stairs.

"How many grandkids do you have?"

She beams with love. "Just two. Both girls. You know I always bug Gabriele about kids for himself," she hints.

The stairs are made from rock most likely found around the island. And when we reach the sand, we begin walking the beach. We make it to a cave with an opening toward the water, I may have missed the entrance on my own, but she knows exactly where she's going.

"And you don't think he wants kids?" I pry.

Once we're inside I'm reminded of the lagoon Gabriele and I spent the day yesterday only inside this enormous cave. Again, here I am in awe at the amazing view. A canopy of trees shields the hole above us keeping this sanctuary private and hidden with rays of sunlight slicing down against the water.

Steam lifts off the water like a hot sauna. I take some steps forward and remove my sandals dipping my feet into the water. It feels like I stepped into a manmade jacuzzi tub only here we are in the middle of the ocean on an island. Pretty magical.

"Pretty amazing in here, huh?" she asks.

"Very."

She follows suit and sits down on a large rock dipping her feet in. "You know for a while I didn't think he would have children, but I saw him with you the other day, and I've changed my mind."

I feel a heat of blush creep up my face. "Oh, I don't think we're anything serious. We're just enjoying each other's company for now. He's made it clear he isn't the relationship type," I inform her.

She smiles with understanding. "That's what most of them say, dear, until that one woman comes along and changes everything. I've been alive long enough to know that look, and he has that look when he looks at you."

I decide it's probably best for my heart to change the subject. "Are there rules to who gets to use this place?"

She shakes her head. "No rules other than consent and respect. If someone lacks either of those, then their membership is irrevocably revoked immediately and they're sent off the island," she explains.

"Wow, have you had to enforce that yet?"

She smiles proudly. "Nope, Gabriele is extremely stern and very detailed on the vetting process to make it safe for the staff and everyone involved. I'm sure you've heard stories of the elites and their grotesque islands, but I can assure you, this place is very different and Gabriele does a great job at protecting everyone involved here."

Her cell phone rings. She puts up her finger to me to answer.

"Yes? Okay, I'll bring her," she responds, then hangs up and looks at me. "Gabriele requests your presence."

We both stand up, grab our shoes to carry them with us as the sand sticks to our wet feet. "Is he back at the main house?"

"Nope, he wants me to take you to villa six," she answers.

It's a little funny to think Mrs. Cain is aware of all that goes on in this place. I wonder what she thinks of it all or maybe she just doesn't ask. With her running the place she must see things that most people aren't privy to. I'll have to ask her next time we have more time together. I'm sure we'll run into each other again.

We walk through a jungle-like oasis; stone pathways and wooden signs directing us toward each villa, though she has no need for those. She knows right where she's taking us. There are small creeks beneath the bridges we cross, palm trees, and iguanas lounging on the trees. I feel like I'm walking through a rainforest sanctuary in the zoo.

We finally reach a secluded villa on the side of the pathway. The sign is engraved Villa #6.

"Okay, take the stones to the back and Gabriele is waiting for you," she directs.

"Thank you, and I enjoyed our talk. I hope we can do that again, Mrs. Cain."

She takes my hand and gives it a squeeze. "Please call me Joanna. And yes, I hope so too," she agrees and turns to leave.

I follow the stones as directed and see Gabriele at the door waiting. "Hey, you," he greets me with a hug. "How was your time with Joanna?" he asks.

I wrap my arms around his perfectly sculptured warm body and inhale him in, the perfect combination of woody freshness. "She was perfect. Reminds me of my mother in some ways," I admit.

He pulls away from me. "I'd like to know more about that when we have dinner tonight, but for now I'd like to show you this place."

I follow him in down a hall. It's not bright like the main house, it's dim with the looks of a club or warehouse vibe. He brings me into a private room. There are two black leather couches facing a bed in between. I look over to the far side of the room, it's a wall made of a cage and privacy glass with rectangle cut out holes.

I look back to him and he's standing at the door with his arms crossed allowing me to assess the room while gauging my reaction. I move closer to the caged wall and realize on the other side is an open room full of props, beds, couches, and people. *Holy shit!* There are actual real naked people.

My eyes grow wide as I watch two men and two women together. I back up quickly worried they can see me and look back at Gabriele. "Can they see us?" I ask, panicked.

He walks toward me, comes up behind me putting his hands on my shoulders leading me back to the view. "No, this is a one-way mirror. We can only see them unless I hit that button." He points at a control center. "This control can allow the glass to be changed to a two-way view, or it can slide open all together so you can touch beyond the cage without full interaction."

Wow. I don't even know what to say. I think I'm speechless. This is all beyond what I imagined. I watch them now, feeling more comfortable now I know they can't see me. It's like watching a live porno. So much better than the screen.

The longer I watch the scene unfold, the more turned on I get. Gabriele's chin now leans on my shoulder and wraps his arms around me. My breath picks up as I watch them all lick and fuck each other in different positions. The moans are echoing through the room and my arousal is taking on a form of its own.

Gabriele begins to dig his fingers into my stomach, I cover his hands with mine digging my nails into his. He nibbles and then bites my neck. I hiss at the sting, as he drags his fingers over my chest and to my dress's straps and slides them down my shoulders.

They fall showing the top of my breasts, no bra needed. He tweaks a nipple through the material and my back arches poking my ass against his cock.

The screams of a woman's orgasm hum through the room as I watch the man's face in between her legs. "Does this turn you on, little ballerina?" he whispers in my ear. My knees want to buckle at the feel of his hot breath against my ear.

I nod, and he continues to push the top of my dress down my arms and over my breasts until it's left to hang off my waist. Both of my nipples are puckered into tights beads ready to be played with. He takes the first between his fingers and pinches rolling with immense pressure. I moan and grind me ass over his hard bulge.

"Fuck, you keep doing that, I might just bend you over and take your virginity right here," he threatens with a growl.

I smile with satisfaction. He pushes my dress all the way down to the floor and his eyes darken as he looks at my nude body through the reflection. Yep, I decided not to wear underwear either and I'm so glad I made that decision. He slides his hand behind me dipping his finger inside of me, I'm drenched, and he growls approvingly.

"You like watching them, don't you?" he asks, voice now strained. I nod. "No, Naomi. Use your words. I want to hear you say it," he demands.

He continues to stroke in and out of me then suddenly dips to my clit, circling with the perfect pressure, and I almost falter. He holds me up with his other arm still wrapped around my waist, so I don't fall. I moan in complete bliss while we both continue to watch the bodies slapping together in front of us.

His finger is now drenched with my juices as he slips it back through my folds, past my sex and stops at the puckered entrance at my ass. I push my waist forward at the touch, but he holds me in place. "Just trust me. Take a deep breath and just feel," he guides.

I nod and take a deep breath as he circles my hole, lathering it with my own juices as I watch the woman riding a man while the other grinds into her from behind. My body is singing with every touch. The scene unfolding in front of me and the new feeling on my body is almost too much to handle.

Gabriele uses his other hand and slips down the front to my clit, rubbing and circling my bud of nerves as he slowly slips his finger into my backend. I moan loudly at the pressure, just one finger and I feel so full.

He takes his time slowly easing in and out of me as he continues his strokes around my tiny bundle of nerves. "Do you like this, ballerina? Do you like me fingering your asshole as you watch her get double penetrated?" Gabriele asks, soft voice in my ear.

I nod, but that isn't good enough. "Words, Naomi. Use your words," he demands.

"Yes, I love watching it. Please don't stop. It feels so good," I cry out.

The men swap and take their turns filling the other girl. Every grunt and moan is sending electricity through my body straight down to my core, and my core is so wet I can feel it dripping down my inner legs.

"Bend over and grab the cage," he directs, guiding my shoulders down.

I do as he says. I hear him drop to his knees behind me keeping his steady rhythm until he removes his fingers from my clit and shifts around behind me to the entrance of my sex. He circles my opening getting me ready as I moan almost ready to come undone then he gradually slides two fingers inside me while still penetrating my ass. I feel filled to the brim and I'm ready to erupt like a volcano from the onslaught.

"I want you to come for me. Picture yourself being fucked by two cocks; me coming in your cunt while he comes in your ass," he visions for me, and with just one quick flick over my clit I'm a goner.

My sex contracts and I scream out his name over and over until the waves of pure ecstasy finally crash over me.

"Fuck yes, baby. God, your pussy looks so beautiful with your juices dripping," he grunts.

He gently removes his fingers and takes a soft swipe along my folds for a taste. "Your juices are so sweet. I could have you for dessert every single day." He kisses both of my ass cheeks before he stands helping me up as well.

He heads to the bathroom on the side of the room and brings me a warm washcloth to clean me. I hesitate but he gives me a stern look. "Let me take care of you. I've seen every part of your body up close and personal, so there's nothing to be shy about."

I cover my face with my hands smiling and spread my legs. He laughs and washes me up and then removes my hands from my face. "Are you ready to go home and have some lunch?"

"I could eat an elephant right about now."

Gabriele lets out a loud laugh. "I bet you can, little ballerina. Come on, let's go."

CHAPTER 10

*L*unch was relaxing this afternoon, and I was completely spent. After a quick nap and a long shower, I come out of the bedroom to a yummy aroma that has my stomach growling with hunger. I see Gabriele in the kitchen cutting and dicing with a white towel over his shoulder.

He looks sexy as hell as he dominates the kitchen. I always heard the saying – now wait until you see me cook – but I never really understood it until now. I could watch this man all night long if I had to.

I always figured men with his amount of money would rather just pay people than waste time on mundane work, but Gabriele seems to love to get his hands dirty – *in more ways than one.* I'm beginning to admire this part of him. Keeping my walls up would be so much easier if he was just one of those rich selfish assholes I've come across so many times over the years, but he's far from that – he has depth.

He cares for the people who work for him, he would rather please than take, he apologizes when wrong, and now he cooks. And here I am, I haven't even given myself to him fully, and I'm already looking at him like he's on a pedestal. God, I'm fucked. How will I ever recover after these three weeks?

He looks up at me from under those long lashes, a dazzling glint in those beautiful hazel eyes and I become wordless. "Hey, beautiful. Come take a seat while I finish cooking." He points to the barstool behind the island.

I pull out the stool and sit. "What are you cooking? It smells wonderful."

I see lemons, parsley, chicken, and pasta. "I'm making my famous Chicken French," he reveals. "My mom taught me some like I told you, but I also took some cooking classes as I got older. My thought was someday I may have a family to provide for and would be nice to cook for also."

He just shoots that in as he starts searing the chicken in the pan. I think back to what Joanna said, and maybe she was right, maybe it does take the right woman to come along. I just don't think I'm that woman though. I picture him with someone more sophisticated and on his level to live a life with him and to bear his children.

"Are you still wanting a family? I mean I know you said you're not the relationship type, so I would think a family would be out of the picture for you," I state, repeating his own words to him.

He turns to me, looking me straight on, putting his hands against the counter. I'm feeling a little intimidated by his intense glare.

"You're right. I was all fairytales and dreams when I was younger. My father crushed that and slammed me back into reality. I absolutely do not want any kids. I don't have the need to ever bring one into this cruel world. Therefore, another reason I moved on from the idea of relationships because most women can't accept this fact about me," he declares.

I know I've already heard these words from his mouth,

but this time just seems so final. I've never really thought about wanting kids since my childhood also wasn't ideal, but I'm not closing the door on it either. At this point I don't see it as a deal-breaker for the weeks we're going to spend together, considering we will be parting ways regardless, but I guess I'm a little sad that he's purposely trying to spend the rest of his life alone with meaningless contact.

"I understand. You're entitled to your decisions. I just hope you change your mind because spending life alone seems wasteful," I tell him.

His intense gaze has now softened since he can see I'm not here to demand he change his mind for me. I know what this all is. I will accept it even if it kills me when we walk away from each other.

"And what about you?" he asks as he returns to the stove checking on the chicken and the French sauce.

"What about me?"

"I'm assuming you want children and a husband one day?" he questions without turning around.

"I don't know. It's possible, I guess. I haven't really thought too much about it until this conversation. Dez tends to be a hopeless romantic regardless of how she grew up, and me, I guess I've just been trying to survive each day," I rationalize.

"My mother was a good mother considering having me young and struggling through her own issues. So, I didn't really feel I was missing too much until she passed, and I was left with no one. Clearly, with my career choice, it's probably better if I stay away from relationships until I've moved on. So maybe I'm not relationship material at the moment either," I admit, sadly.

He pours me a tequila on the rocks and adds a lime pushing it over to me, then holds up his drink. "To us not being the relationship types – *at the moment.*"

I clink mine with his and smile a sad smile. Not sure this

is something we should really be celebrating, but I'll keep the peace and follow suit. He finishes cooking and lays the Chicken French over pasta on one large platter spreading more juice over.

My mouth waters.

"Grab both our drinks," he orders me and leads us up the stairs.

I haven't been up here yet, as far as I knew it was just his bedroom, but there's a small office space with a balcony overlooking the ocean. The balcony is right above my room, and now I wonder if he's able to hear my conversations on the phone from here. I would have never known if he was sitting up here listening or not.

He has the table already set up with candles and hanging lights. It looks like a dream up here as the sun begins to set. He planned this dinner perfectly so we could watch the sun setting from up here together. It's really a shame he doesn't want someone in his life because he's extremely good at the amazingly romantic stuff.

"Wow, Gabriele. You have really outdone yourself," I say, astonished.

He winks at me and starts serving the food on my plate. "Did you want some white wine or are you sticking with the tequila?"

"I'll take some white."

He pours me a glass and we begin eating. The flavors of lemon and sherry hit my taste buds with explosion. You can't get this in Arizona, I've tried many Italian places, but for some reason never any French dishes.

I finish my mouthful, triggering old memories to the forefront. "My mom used to take me to this tiny mom-and-pop restaurant where we would split a plate of Chicken French with broccoli and angel hair pasta on special occasions when I was younger. She couldn't afford much but she always tried her best to make moments memorable before she got sick," I disclose, teary-eyed.

He catches my water rimmed eyes. "She sounds like she was a really good mother. It doesn't matter about how much money a parent makes, it's about how they make you feel and that they keep trying to provide even though it's hard and exhausting; they keep pushing because they're selfless. That's a great parent."

A tear now escapes sliding down my cheek, he wipes it with his thumb. "My brother and I were raised with money and everything a child could ask for except for time and attention. So, hold those memories close and cherish them," he says.

I put my hand over his. "I see you, Gabriele."

He looks stunned as he stares at me in silence. I gulp hoping I didn't overstep but it's true, no matter how hard he wants to hide, I see he has so many sides to him.

He leans over and gives me a soft peck on the lips, then licks his own lips. "Damn, my French tastes better off of you," he jokes with a cute grin.

I laugh and smack his chest.

I take some more bites dribbling the sauce down my chin. He looks at me again as though he's ready to lick it off or just plain eat me instead. I rub my thighs together with that quick thought but then hold my hand up stopping him from moving any further and use my napkin.

"So, tell me more about your mother?" he asks.

We spent the rest of dinner talking about my childhood memories and stories of my early teenage years. We watched the sunset while he teased me about my awkward phase I told him about. Every teenager goes through that phase, but his I'm sure was more like the captain of football awkward phase.

After sunset we head over to the outdoor couch for one

last drink. He opens his arm for me to sit down and snuggle in. I lean my head on his shoulder, as he leans his chin on the top of my head. We sit like this for a while listening to the waves crashing against the shore while we sip our wine as though we're already an old married couple.

I turn my head into him more and inhale. He chuckles. "Someone likes my smell, doesn't she?" he teases.

"Just as much as the *other* someone likes mine," I tease back.

He tickles my side, and I convulse with giggles. "I don't just like your smell; I *love* your smell. I stay up at night stroking myself to that smell," he says more seriously now.

"I think I'd like to watch that," I admit, shyly.

His eyes now burn with fire as he tries his best to rein himself in bringing me back into his embrace. "Oh, would you now? That can definitely be arranged," he promises with a devious grin then kisses the top of my head.

"How did you come across your particular desires?" I ask.

He looks down at me. "Do you really want to know?"

I nod. "There's always been something different about me. I've always had a certain urge, but I couldn't put my finger on it, I didn't understand what it was as a teenager. Maybe some would say a darkness, I also thought that for a while, that there was something wrong with me. I like normal sex, but I need more."

"Having a father with status and connections gave me access to things and places the average person wouldn't know about. A secret society full of sex and all kinds of desires. My father's best friend saw himself in me. He knew I was struggling; he recognized the look in my eyes. He's the one that introduced me to my first sex club," he explains.

I turn to get a better look at him. "Wow, how old were you?"

He kisses my forehead. "He waited until my twenty first birthday."

"Can I confess something?" I ask.

His eyes connect with mine intensely. "Anything."

"I think I understand a little of what you were feeling because after today I'm feeling out of sorts, and not in a bad way but in a scared unknown way. I think I enjoyed today a little too much, and that's what scares me, because what's next? How far can I go?" I whisper almost seeming as though I'm talking out loud to myself.

"Naomi, you can go as far as you want as long as you're doing it with someone safe. I won't let you do anything that doesn't feel good to you. And you're only feeling this way because you're used to society's rules of what's wrong and right, but those aren't real. Like I said before, what's wrong and right is how you feel. If it feels good then just go with it, enjoy it, embrace it. You're in control of your life. You're in control of your own decisions. No one else. And if I get to experience these new moments with you than I feel like the luckiest man alive," he finishes.

A tear escapes me again. My heart aches with fullness. Just a moment ago I almost felt ashamed of my unknown feelings but now I'm almost excited to embrace them with him. I'm eager for these next couple days and I'm ready to experience more.

"Thank you for making me feel okay with what I'm feeling."

He squeezes me tight, and we spend the rest of the time in silence enjoying each other with the sound of the waves.

I SNAP UP LOOKING AROUND. I feel confused. I'm in my room, sunlight filters through the sheer curtains, and I'm dressed in a tank top and panties, but how did I get here? The last thing I remember is being on the balcony with Gabriele. I must have fallen asleep, and he must have put me to bed.

I grab my phone, eyes wide as I realize it's now 10AM. *Wow!* This island must be good for my insomnia. I haven't felt so rested in a very long time.

I see a group text from Trev and Dez. I snapped some pics for them yesterday on my walk with Joanna.

"Wow girlfriend! That place looks dreamy! Any chance he has a private jet waiting for us?"

Trev jokes with the heart eye emoji.

"Yeah I could use a ticket out of town right about now. Luke won't get the hint,"

Dez texts.
Well, this is news.

"What do you mean Luke won't get the hint?! I thought you blocked him?"

I text.

"Girl, he's been showing up at the house and the club for Dez. I had to remove him from the club last night,"

Trev replies.

"What does he want?"

I text.
Shit. I hope she doesn't give in to him. She needs to stay strong.

I watch the bubbles waiting with anticipation.

"Idk. He wants to talk. Explain himself,"

she replies.

"Shit. Do you want to hear what he has to say?"

I text.
I wait for the bubbles.

"Idk, Nay. I don't think I'm ready to talk to him yet,"

she replies.
Phew. This is good.

"Okay, then don't,"

I text.

"And Trev, if he comes by the club again, tell him she needs space,"

I direct.

"You got it boss,"

Trev replies.

"Love you both,"

I text. Trev hearts the comment.

"Love you,"

Dez replies.
What can Luke possibly say that can justify what he did?

Why do men think they can treat someone that way and then turn around thinking they can man-splain it away? He better have an extremely good one if I have anything to do with it. I'm ready to douse him with gasoline and light a match.

Still lying in bed, I listen for rustling beyond the door. It's quiet as a mouse out there. I wonder if he left. I slide out of bed with a long stretch and wash up before heading out.

The sliders are wide open with a beautiful breeze gliding through. The palm trees sway back and forth looking like it could be the perfect social media video as the sun sparkles off the water like diamonds; water calm almost glass-like. It looks peaceful for the perfect lounge around beach day.

Gabriele is nowhere in sight. I see a note left on the kitchen counter.

> Ballerina -
> Had to go greet some new clients. I'll be back late afternoon. Relax and get dressed for dinner. I'm taking you off this island.
> - G

I jump with excitement almost not being able to contain myself. I feel like a kid on Christmas just getting the best present. I feel spoiled. Here I thought I was just here to be his sex slave, which maybe that's still the case, but he's also making it memorable for me. He's making sure I enjoy the time here and doing a damn good job of making it seem like we're here for real – just two people enjoying each other's company and not being paid for it. I can almost forget the logistics of it all.

Like every morning, he has a layout of breakfast choices. I opt for the coffee, eggs, refried beans, and a johnny cake. The coffee here is strong. Just how I like it. I bring my plate outside, off the deck, feet into the sand, over to the daybed and lounge out while eating and sipping my coffee.

If only my two best friends were here, I could live on this island. I decide to search Gabriele again on google. I want to look at the picture of him and his ex but when I enter his name nothing pops up anymore. Hmm. That's odd. I wonder if he has a team of people that take things down like most billionaires do? That would make sense since there was only one picture and article that mentioned him, nothing else was available.

I read a lot of things about the rich and famous. I know he's a private person, but I wonder if there is more to it.

No, I'm just thinking too much into it.

If I had the power and status he did, I also would pay to be invisible. People can be ruthless about the elite, and the fact that he likes being out of the limelight also says a lot about him. He still seems to remain human, doesn't act on his superiority.

After breakfast, I head to my room to change into my swimwear. I decide today I'm going to take a little stroll down the beach, get some exercise and venture out a bit. I throw on my red bikini, some denim shorts, lather myself with some sunscreen, and stop at the kitchen for a bottled water.

I head out to the water to dip my feet in and look out to the blue sea. Way out into the distance is the white line of waves crashing against the Great Barrier Reef. It's the second largest reef in the world, something I just learned today. I looked up some tourist areas in Belize and information on the other islands. Nothing mentions this island and I wonder if the internet is purposely cleared of this place as well.

I walk along the water for a couple miles. The beach is massive, stretching as far as I can see and not a villa in sight just as Gabriele said. I reach out to Dez on FaceTime and she answers on the first ring.

"Omg. I fucking miss your face!" she screeches.

I laugh and spin showing her the whole view of the island.

"Oh, you lucky little bitch! And you're so damn tan. I'm jealous, Nay. Come fly back and get me," she says.

"If I was staying any longer, I would demand he fly you here," I tell her pouting.

I take my shorts off and sit into the sand keeping my feet to the water as the waves glide up the sand.

"So, tell me, I mean *really* tell me, how have things been going?" Dez asks.

I have to think for a split second since it's such a simple question with a loaded answer.

"Dez, he's everything I was hoping he wasn't going to be. I'm trying to keep my wall up and he's been following my rules, but he is just so different than I imagined. I don't know how I'm going to walk away unscathed after this," I confess.

"Oh no, Nay. Did you fuck him yet?" she asks.

I play with the sand with my free hand. "No, not yet. Almost everything but."

She blows out a breath of air with her cheeks puffed out. I've seen her do that many times and it means I'm in big trouble. "Nay, I hate to tell you, but you're fucked my dear friend."

I roll my eyes and give her the death stare. "Well, damn Dez. Don't hold anything back. Tell me something I don't know," I say sarcastically.

"Okay, something you don't know – I met Trev's new plaything this morning at the gym," she tells me smiling as she taps her pointer finger against her lips.

She's such an ass knowing damn well that's not what I mean, but now I'm glad I know. "And? Oh my god, what was he like? Was he like the last douche bucket?" I ask.

I see her shake her head back and forth. "I actually liked

him and I think Trev does too, even though he completely refuses to admit it," she explains.

"Tell me an actor he reminds you of?" I ask.

"Hmm – Oh, Ryan Reynolds!" she says excitedly.

My brows lift in shock. "Oh, I know Trev is already bumping uglies with him. There's no way he isn't. He fan girls Ryan Reynolds all the time!" I tell her laughing.

"I know, he's in complete denial. But hey, aren't we all?"

I nod. "I know. We're all fucked. Did you actually see Luke's face when he came by the house?" I ask.

I look at the time and it's now almost noon. I stand up, grab my shorts, and begin walking back toward the house.

"No, I pretended I wasn't home when he was banging on the door yelling my name," she admits.

Man, he has clearly lost his marbles. Our neighbors must think there's something wrong with us with all these stalkers.

"Geez, Dez. Doesn't sound like he's going to be giving up anytime soon."

She takes a deep breath. "I know. I'll have to confront him sooner or later, I'm sure. Okay, so tell me, when the fuck are you going to do the deed?" she demands to know.

I shrug. "I'm not too sure yet. I guess it just hasn't been the right time yet and he hasn't pushed either. Soon though, and you'll be the first to know!"

She grins ear to ear. "Good. Okay, I gotta run. Hair appointment today," she clarifies.

She gives me a phone air kiss and we hang up.

Somehow talking to her and seeing her face makes me feel refreshed. As I walk up toward the house, I see Joanna waiting for me on the deck.

"Hi Joanna, I'm sorry, I went for a walk. Have you been waiting for me long?" I question.

She smiles and stands. "No dear, just got here a little bit ago. Gabriele sent me here to have you pack for the night. He had to head over to the main island early and is going to have you meet him. I'm here to take you to the plane and close up the house," she advises.

Oh shoot. I thought we were just going for dinner. I didn't realize this would be an overnight trip as well. My stomach drops thinking of the sleeping arrangements but then my heart jump starts into overdrive also thinking about it. I remember his words last night and I smile. There's nothing to fear. Excitement begins to flow through my body, and I rush toward my room.

"Okay, let me grab a bag. It will only take a moment," I say as she follows me inside.

"No rush, we can leave whenever. It's Gabriele's plane after all." She laughs.

CHAPTER 11

*T*he plane is ready to go on the runway. I climb up the steps meeting the same stewardess at the top of the stairs. This time since Gabriele is nowhere in sight she's not as friendly.

"If you will please take a seat and buckle up, we will be leaving in just a moment," she states without a smile, and turns to the cockpit.

I knew I saw an envious look in her eyes the last time I saw her. I wonder if this comes from the hope of a possibility on her side or if there's any merit to her actions. I wouldn't think Gabriele would fuck anyone who works for him, but I wouldn't put it past any man, single or not.

I take a seat as directed, buckle up, and whip out my phone. I see a text from Gabriele.

"Miss me yet?"

he texts.

I smile. He must miss me if he's the one texting.

"Maybe, U?"

I reply.

> "Oh, I sure do, and I can't wait to take a deep breath and inhale every inch of you,"

he texts back.

I squeeze my thighs tight with just the thought of his face between my legs. He is wicked with his tongue and his fingers; I can only imagine how he can dominate me with his cock. It excites me just thinking about the possibilities waiting for me.

> "I can't wait,"

I respond with a devil emoji.

> "I'm still dealing with business. When you get to the room, put on what I have laid out and I'll meet you for dinner,"

he texts back.

> "Okay, I was planning on wearing nothing, but maybe next time,"

I reply.

> "That will be later tonight,"

he replies with a side grin.

The flight's extremely quick, only ten minutes long. After we land, I'm driven to a private beach resort which looks to be on an excluded part of the island. I wonder if he owns this place as well.

I'm led to another villa off the main house. The room is large, with tile flooring, a living area, and a massive bed looking over the ocean. This place isn't as large as the house we've been staying in but it's beautiful all the same. Lying on the bed is a large box with a big red bow.

I immediately open the box with a huge teethy smile. I pull out a long black flower printed dress, matching sandals, and a skinny square jewelry box that lies underneath.

Inside the box lies a beautiful gold necklace with a flower pendant engulfed in diamonds. My mouth drops open. Is this for fucking real? I've never seen anything so beautiful. I take it out of the box and hold it up to myself in front of the floor length mirror. I feel as though I've been stuck in a dream, this just doesn't happen to girls like me. I frown as I stare at myself.

No, Nay, this doesn't happen to girls like us, because this isn't actually real. After this he will walk away as if this dream never even happened.

I lay the necklace back in the box and take a step outside onto the sand. I need to ground myself, bring myself back to the reality of what this really is. I have no choice but to keep reminding myself of this, so I don't end up broken beyond repair.

IT'S NOW LATE AFTERNOON, I took a nap on the lounge chair outside. I shower and dress myself in the dress and shoes Gabriele provided. The dress fits perfectly. Not sure how he got the size down just right, but I'm sure he's had lots of practice in purchasing these sorts of things for women.

The excitement from earlier has dwindled and I'm left in more of a somber mood. I decide not to put the necklace on. I have no need to get used to such gifts and I have no need to keep such gift as reminders for when he's gone.

I'm greeted at the door by a young man in a black

uniform. "Mr. Vanucci asked me to escort you to dinner," he informs.

I nod, grabbing my clutch, and closing the door behind me. We hop into a golf cart, driving down the dirt road that turns into stone until we reach the village. The streets become bright with lights, alive with music and people walking the streets. Closed gift shops, restaurants, and nightclubs line the way. There are people in conversations along the street, laughing, smiling, and completely carefree as we pass by. My mood now changes from somber to fascinated and completely captivated by the energy that radiates through me as we drive. This island is not like the other.

We pull up to a restaurant bumping with Caribbean music, colorful lights, and people busy in mid conversation with drinks and laughter along the outside sitting area.

"Mr. Vanucci has a table inside," he directs.

I smile. "Thank you." I open my purse to pull out a tip, but he stops me.

"It's already taken care of, Miss."

I nod and head inside. Of course it is, I shouldn't expect anything less. I see Gabriele at a small table overlooking the band that's playing. His body sways to the music as he takes a sip of his drink. The wind rustles his hair. His skin is now a dark caramel brown and he's wearing a black dress shirt with his beautiful tattoos showing, looking dangerous and sexy as hell. Everything about him screams power, dominance, with a don't fuck with me vibe unless you're a woman who wants to get fucked so hard against the wall.

I smile at the thought as I walk up to him. "Excuse me, sir. Is this seat taken?" I mess around with a devilish smile.

The entertainment in his eyes glows with lust as he slowly drifts his eyes over me.

"I can get used to you calling me sir," he praises, getting up and pulling the chair out for me. "I think that's what you will address me as tonight when you beg for me to be inside of you," he whispers into my ear before I sit down.

I gulp, feeling the rush of heat seize my body. He smirks as he watches me squirm. Then he looks at my neck and frowns.

"You're not wearing your necklace," he points out.

I reach at my empty neck feeling a tad guilty. "I'm sorry. It's an unbelievably gorgeous necklace and I really appreciate the gesture," I stutter.

He's waiting for me to finish to understand. "But?" he asks.

"But it's just too much. I can't accept it. I think in our case, we should just keep things simpler. Just stick to our rules and the physical aspect of our friendship," I recommend.

He chuckles looking a bit insulted. "Friendship? Is that what you call this?"

He looks angry now. I've clearly ruined the mood. "What else would you call it?" I question.

I would really like to know his answer but a part of me also doesn't. I'm scared of what he will or won't say.

He grabs my hand. "What we have doesn't need any labels. Can't we just be? Let us just enjoy each other's time and let the cards fall where they may. I like you, little ballerina. I like you a lot, there's no doubt about that. I want you more than I've ever wanted another soul in my life, and I enjoy spending time with you. Can't you just feel with me? Let go of the rules, just feel," he finishes.

"You scare the shit out of me, Gabriele," I admit.

He brings my hand to his lips. "And you as well, my little ballerina."

"I can only promise that for tonight, I will just feel," I say, giving him my word.

He nods with acceptance and a fire now burning in his eyes. "Good girl."

The waiter comes, we order dinner and drinks while listening to the band. There's a dance floor off to the side that is full of vacationers, partiers, and locals mingling with no qualms about a thing. Dez and I have always loved to just people watch and make up stories of their lives as they pass by.

Our ceviche appetizer comes out with our drinks. "Have I told you how beautiful you look today?" Gabriele asks.

I shake my head no.

"You look gorgeous, Naomi. I love the confidence I'm seeing grow in you each day I spend with you," he confesses.

"You seem to bring it out of me. The girls at the club always looks so perfect, I've always seen myself as more of the plain Jane. I guess that's why the older men are more drawn to me because they say they like my naturalness, but you make me feel like I'm the only girl in the room full of beautiful women, you make me feel like I'm alive," I enlighten.

He leans over and kisses my cheek. "Naomi, those girls have nothing on you. You captivated me the first moment I laid eyes on you in your room. And I don't think you see yourself clearly, because eyes, young and old, follow you whenever you go. You're always the center of attention with any room you walk into, and the fact that your oblivious draws us all to you the more," he divulges.

I look down blushing. He grabs my chin forcing me to look at him. "Don't you look away. You own that compliment. Never look down, you walk into every room with this chin held high, and respect will be granted, doors will open, and the world will bend at your will."

Why does he have to say things like this? *Why?* Why can't he just be the typical billionaire asshole? The waiter interrupts us with our food. It smells delicious, my stomach growls since I haven't eaten since breakfast.

We both got grilled lobster with rice and beans. They're

so large there's no way I'm going to be able to eat this whole thing. I'll pop out of this tight dress. The waiter cuts open the lobster in front of us and deshells it placing it on our plates with lime and lemon wedges.

"Wow, I don't think I've seen a lobster this big," I tell him.

"You're going to be seeing things much bigger than this lobster tonight, so prepare yourself," he jokes with a wink.

My nipples tingle with anticipation as I feel the pressure in my core start to build. It's been more than twenty-four hours since he's touched me and I'm dying, fiending for his touch.

"Do you promise?" I tease.

His eyes light up. "Oh, it's a guarantee."

We finish the rest of our dinner, then sit in silence listening to the band as we finish our drinks. He stands up after a while and holds his hand out to mine. "Dance?"

"Haven't you seen me dance enough?" I tease.

He pulls me close to him wrapping his arm around me. "Not nearly enough. I'd like to have one of those dances with you bare naked."

"And what will you pay me for that dance?" I ask with a devilish smirk, brow raised.

He pulls me into him on the dance floor and we begin moving in sync with the music. "I'll be paying you with my tongue and cock deep in your pussy," he whispers in my ear.

My libido now ignites into overdrive. His body is tight against mine grinding and moving to the sexy rhythm. If sex is anything like dancing with him then I'm in huge trouble. The way he leads, moving just right, fire lighting his gaze, as though we're the only two in the whole entire room.

His hand glides over my back, down my ass making a final stop on my hip as he digs his fingers into me. I'm on fire, my core is burning up and every nerve ending is lit up pulsing through me with every touch he lays upon me, I'm like hot lava in his arms.

I take my fill roaming my hands over his sculpted body, feeling every spectacular muscle of his back all the way down to his rock-hard ass. He nuzzles his nose along my neck while inhaling.

"I don't think I'll ever get enough of your smell. Your scent is like an aphrodisiac to me. The pheromones you put off drive me insane. I want to take you into that bathroom and make you scream my name for everyone to hear," he describes.

"Take me back to the villa," I demand.

He backs up to look me in the eyes. "Are you ready for me, little ballerina?"

"Yes," I answer, voice raspy.

"Are you sure? Are you telling me you're ready to give me all of you?" he clarifies.

I nod. "Yes."

I don't have to say another word before he pulls me out of the restaurant and signals the golf cart driver to pull up.

We get to the villa, and as soon as the door closes behind us, he has me backed against the door, lips on my neck, hands entwined in my hair, and pelvis grinding against me.

Gabriele nibbles up my neck with tiny kisses and bites. My fingers dig into his lower back trying to bring him even closer. My sex is now slick with juices, throbbing and craving an explosion I know is to come. I need him, I need to be close to him in every way possible. I'm dying to know what he feels like to be inside of me, to own me.

He crashes his lips with mine in desperation, our tongues collide together battling for control as he groans into my mouth. I tangle my fingers through his hair, pulling him closer. The wet heat of his tongue dances with mine as though we're back on the dance floor. Every breath against mine has me panting for more. I'm starving and I can't seem to get enough.

He reaches down and grabs my legs to wrap them around

his waist as he walks me toward the bed. He sits me down now standing in front of me, our eyes locked, our chests heaving up and down while the electricity is ricocheting all over the room.

He begins to unbutton his shirt taking his time with each button. I'm ready to lean up and just rip it apart. "Are you on birth control, Naomi?"

"Yes, I'm on the pill," I answer.

His eyes glow with satisfaction as he grins. "Good, because I want to fuck you raw so I can feel every inch of you," he divulges.

I grip my thighs together with the anticipation of his announcement as his shirt slides down his arms. Nothing but chiseled arms, flawless pecs, and rippling abs stare back at me. I lick my lips insatiably hungry. I want to devour him, so I begin to lean forward to reach for his pants, but he grabs my wrist stopping me.

"Not so fast, little ballerina. I need my dessert first," he says.

He stands me up turning me around. His fingers skim my neck, sending goosebumps down my spine as he pushes my hair to the side and begins to unzip the back of my dress, slowly bit by bit. He slides my dress off each side of my shoulders until my dress pools around my feet.

"Beautiful. How did I get so lucky?" He breathes against my skin as I'm standing with my back to him in nothing but a black lacey thong.

He wraps his hands around to my stomach while kissing my neck. I lean back against him opening my neck to him more, feeling his hard bulge against my buttocks. His one hand slides up to cup my left breast kneading and then tweaking my hard nipple sending a jolt straight to my clit. A moan rips out of me as he slides his other hand under my panties gliding over my bundle of nerves.

His finger circles my clit before dipping further between

my wet folds. I pant waiting for what's to come as he slips his finger deep inside me. I whimper with pleasure, reaching my hand behind me to grab his swollen length.

"Fuck me, you're so fucking tight. I can't wait to feel you gripped around my cock," he growls.

I begin to grind on his finger as he pumps in and out of me before reaching back to my clit, rubbing with the perfect precision. He removes his fingers from my panties, slipping them down to my ankles, then turns me around sitting me back onto the bed as he kneels in front of me and spreads me apart.

I watch him lick his lips and consume me with eyes like a hungry lion. "Lean back," he directs.

I feel his hand glide up the inside of my thigh as he follows with light kisses and licks. I squirm with eagerness as I feel his hot breath against my sex. He blows over my clit then gives me one long directed stroke up my folds and over my bud. I buck up and gasp at the feel of his wet hot tongue against me.

"Mmmm," he mumbles.

He traces my entrance, lathering his fingers with my juices as he kneads my clit over and over with his tongue. The teasing is driving me mad. I move my hips urging him on, enticing him. He chuckles and slips two fingers gently inside me, working me and stretching me to get me ready for him. I feel full and the burn of the stretching is uncomfortable, but I know he's doing this to ease the pain when he enters me for the first time.

My breath is held until he hits the spot deep within me, and I scream out his name. "Oh god, Gabriele. Please don't stop," I beg as the burn turns to an intense heat that licks over the inside of my core.

His tongue continues to glide over my flesh as his fingers bend inside of me, stroking me, working me to climax, black dots swarming over my vision, as the walls of my sex begin to tighten around his fingers like a vise grip.

"Yes, come for me, little ballerina. Drench my fingers with your sweet juices," he pleads still working me to the max.

Sweat beads form over my body as I begin to combust in waves of pure explosion. His licks soften and his fingers slow as I come down from breathlessness.

"Holy shit," I manage to get out in between breaths. He smiles up at me proudly.

"Now you owe me that lap dance," he teases. I giggle.

I hear his zipper unzipping and the shuffle of clothing as he slides his pants off his legs before he follows up my body with light kisses. I feel his swollen dick against my stomach as he rubs his nose over mine.

He balances over me on his elbows. "Are you sure you're ready?" he checks again needing reassurance.

"Yes," I speak softly.

He reaches down between us stroking me again. I buck up from the sensitive touch. He works me slowly making sure I'm dripping wet before rubbing the head of his cock up and down my entrance. He hisses at the feeling as he spreads my creaming wetness over his tip.

I feel him begin to gently push into me, opening me for him inch by inch. The burn becomes fiery with intense pressure. I whimper with discomfort, and he stops allowing me to adjust.

"You ok? Do you want me to stop?" he asks, barely getting out between grit teeth. His arms are shaking beside me, and I can tell it's hard for him to control himself.

I shake my head, and he continues to slowly push into me. "God, you feel amazing. So – fucking – tight," he struggles to say in between breaths. "This is going to hurt for a moment, but I promise I will let you adjust before I move again."

I nod again and he kisses me so hard and fiercely as he pushes himself all the way into me with one single push. I scream out with pain, heaving as he halts waiting for my body to accommodate his long, massive girth.

He kisses my forehead, my cheeks, my nose, and drifts down my neck to my sweet spot. I begin to relax as he palms my breasts and brings his mouth over my nipple, grazing with his teeth. I arch at the feel of his mouth and the fullness inside of me. He begins to slowly move out of me and then gently pushes into me again. I moan at the continuous stretch as his tongue laps my tight nipple, pleasure and pain such a thin line.

The pain begins to subside and change to an aching build as he picks up his rhythm. His jaw now clenches tight, his eyes now glazed over with determination as his hips move in circles opening me up more to him.

"You feel like heaven," he groans.

He reaches down between us to my clit; sparks fly through me like embers of a flame as he strokes while adjusting his position now hitting my spot with the tip of his dick. I've heard of multiple orgasms, I never thought I would experience them myself, but here I am digging into his back, toes curled, back arching as my pussy begins convulsing around his dick.

"Fuck yes, baby! I'm about to come. Come with me all over my cock," he commands, picking up his pace while still caressing my clit.

He dives his tongue into my mouth gulping my moans down with his. Our bodies are slick with sweat as they slap together filling the room with the sound of sex and with just one more flick of his hips, I erupt screaming his name as I rip my nails down the skin of his back.

I feel him pump one last time as he spills his warm seed deep within me. "That's right, my little ballerina, milk every last drop from me with this beautiful perfect pussy," he says, still gliding leisurely in and out of me until I finally come down again.

We lay still his weight now heavy on top of me. He lifts up now holding himself up above me while kissing me softly until he finally pulls out of me, and I wince at my soreness.

He kisses my forehead. "I'll be right back," he tells me, and heads to the bathroom.

I smile as I watch his tight ass walk away. Did I really just lose my virginity to this perfect looking human? He not only looks like a god, but he touches everything with perfection. He comes back out of the bathroom in his naked glory with a warm wet cloth.

He pushes my knees open and a blush creeps over my face. Gabriele notices and shakes his head with a grin as he washes me with such gentleness and care. I observe a red smudge as he tosses it on the floor forgetting that happens with the first time; he's unbothered by the blood.

He inches me up toward the pillows and pulls the covers down for me to slip in. My muscles already ache from the act, but this bed feels amazing and now warmer as he slips in behind me.

I freeze momentarily as he wraps his arms around me. "Just feel tonight, Naomi," he whispers in my ear, and I realize he's right. It's what I promised so I relax and ease back into him.

"Thank you for giving me such a gift," he says as he nuzzles his face into the crook of my neck.

CHAPTER 12

*M*y eyes flutter open. I look around almost forgetting where I am until I hear a light snore beside me. I turn and see Gabriele bare chested with his hand laying above his head as though he doesn't have a care in the world. His long lashes fan out over his cheeks, his pink lips full and slightly parted, the light trail of hair is peeking just above the low laying sheet, and his cock is gradually growing by the minute as I continue to glide my eyes over him.

I'm startled as I hear his raspy voice. "If you keep staring at me like that, I'm going to have to roll you over and fuck you from behind," he says.

If I wasn't so sore, I may take him up on that offer. He turns to his side, tucking a fallen piece of hair behind my ear. "How are you feeling?" he asks.

I smile. "Sore, but good," I admit as I stretch my legs and arms out.

"I'm afraid I've failed you a bit," he confesses.

I look confused. "How so?"

He taps my nose with his finger then gets out of the bed and heads to the bathroom. I hear water running and rustling about with the sound of cupboards opening and closing.

Gabriele walks back out with boxer briefs now covering his naked body. I pout. I quite enjoy seeing him walk around with nothing on. He comes over to me and removes the covers off my body, grabs my hand and pulls me up out of bed leading me to the bathroom.

There's a large clawfoot tub filled with bubbles to the max, the smell of lilacs radiates throughout the room, and the large door is wide open to the beach allowing the ocean breeze to flow through. He guides me to the tub, giving me balance as I step one foot in after the other. As soon as I sink down into the steaming hot water all my muscles begin to ease and relax.

I moan with gratitude.

Gabriele takes off his boxers and slips in behind me; I lean back laying my head on his chest and close my eyes enjoying the moment. The water feels marvelous over my sore body.

"Feel better?" he asks as he takes the loofah rubbing over my shoulders and down my chest.

"Mhmm," is all I can seem to get out.

I feel the vibration of his chuckle behind me. "I thought you would like to go into the village and look at the gift shops after breakfast, and maybe do some sightseeing?" he questions.

I lean up and turn to him. "Oh my god, I would love to!" I reply excitedly.

He leans in, skims his lips along mine, then gives me a sweet kiss. I close my eyes wanting to cherish these little moments for just a while. I know I'm going to have to tuck them away doing my best to forget them when we leave but for now, I want to wrap them around me.

"Has anyone ever told you that your enthusiasm is contagious?" he wonders with a glint of keenness cast over his gaze.

I nod laughing. "Dez tells me all the time."

He starts massaging my shoulders. I moan with satisfaction. He sure knows how to spoil a girl, now if only he wanted to douse himself in more than just simple pleasures and give up on his notions of no relationships, then he would really be the perfect man for some lucky girl.

"Do you miss her?"

"I do. We haven't been apart a day since we met, and the fact that she's been struggling because of Luke makes me miss her more. I feel a little guilty for not being there for her," I tell him. "I know you don't want to get involved in your brother's personal affairs, but he's been making it real hard for Dez to move on," I disclose.

"Oh yeah? How so?" he questions, rubbing down my arms trailing his fingers now along my lower belly.

My breathing starts to accelerate as he drifts over my pelvis bone, teasing and petting before reaching my clit. I can't even concentrate on his question now. My body is screaming with erratic currents flowing through me.

"Naomi?" he says my name, bringing me out of my stupor knowing exactly what he's doing.

"Um, Luke's been showing up at the house and the club trying to talk to her."

He dips his finger lower, grazing over my tiny bundle, then moves it back up. I whimper in protest. He laughs.

"So, why doesn't she just talk to him?" he wonders like it's just that simple. And maybe it is for him, but not for someone who has their heart in something like Dez does.

I try to control my breathing, not letting him manipulate me as we talk, but that goes out the window as soon as he strokes my clit in tiny, pressured circles, and I immediately moan out loud.

"What was your question again," I stutter.

He dips his finger inside of me gently while still rubbing my clit with his thumb. I can feel a tiny twinge of tenderness but this feeling outweighs all of it.

"Why doesn't she just talk to him," he repeats himself.

I rip myself from my hazed induced pleasure for a smidgen to answer his question. "Because, she had too many feelings for him already and doesn't want to give in to any outlandish excuses he may throw at her," I finish, just glad to go back to my enjoyment.

With ease he slips a second finger inside of me waiting for my breathing to slow and allowing me a moment to adjust before dipping deep inside of me again. I feel his hard length grow like an engorged rod behind my back and I reach my hand behind me stroking down his dick.

"*Fuck*, Naomi!" he growls, urging me on.

A grin spreads across my face feeling pleased. I enjoy making him feel the way I do. Making a grown experienced man melt at the palm of my hand makes me feels powerful. I add pressure to my hold as I glide up and down his shaft. The more I move, the more he works my sex into a ball of tightened pressure ready to rupture at any moment.

The water sloshes over the tub as we move in unison, stroking and grinding our hands and fingers against one another. The groans and moans sound like a porn as we start bringing each other to climax. My release comes hard and fast, crashing over me wave after wave. His is more of a gradual build up as I can finally turn my body around, straddling him with my knees on each side of him, and stroking him with precise pressure while reaching down and cupping his balls.

His head falls back, and his fingers dig into the sides of my hips sure to leave a mark as he ejaculates his seed all over my chest in large warm spurts. I slow my pumps as he has now fallen all the way down from his peak.

Gabriele's breathing evens out and he now looks over the

art he has just created on my chest and smiles. "Oh, I could get used to this. I wish you could stay like this, so I can claim you in front of the world with my come stained on you," he says vulgarly with smoldering darkened eyes.

I roll my eyes at his savagery. He sounds barbaric with an orgasmic high. He grabs my ass hard and begins tickling my side. Water overflows everywhere as I twist and turn with laughter.

"Wait, no more!" I yell between bits of laughter.

He stops holding his hands in front of me with the threat of another tickle. "Roll your eyes at me again," he warns.

I shake my head while biting my bottom lip trying to stop myself from laughing. I love this fun side of Gabriele. His eyes sparkle with mischief making me almost want to break form just for this side to last a bit longer.

The water is now lukewarm. Gabriele grabs the loofah and washes his come off my chest before lifting me up to stand as he gets up himself stepping out of the tub to grab us both towels. He wraps mine around me first helping me step out then wraps his around his waist.

"Come on, I have breakfast waiting," he tells me, walking out of the bathroom.

I'm not sure when this was set up, but whoever set it up must have gotten an earful.

"Wow, are we having company? That's a hell of a lot of food for just us," I tell him while looking over the many dishes laid out over the table.

He pours us both cups of coffee. "I wasn't sure what you would be in the mood for," he answers, handing me my cup.

I shove eggs and fruit on my plate as he piles up two plates full for himself. He leads us outside to sit on the veranda overlooking the ocean. I sip my coffee as I watch the waves brush against the beach. The palm trees rustle in the gentle wind as little geckos chase one another over the railings of the porch.

My thoughts drift back to last night – our desperate touches, his powerful tongue and magical fingers. The way he was so gentle and worshipful as he slid inside of me, it's what most girls dream of for their first time. Being on this island in the middle of nowhere has been a dream come true, but the connection I feel with him has been so unexpectedly amazing.

I'm glad we have another two weeks together. Even though I'm still trying my best to hold my walls up, I still want these memories so I can tuck them deep inside until I'm okay enough to one day bring them back out.

"What's on your mind over there, little ballerina?" Gabriele asks.

I didn't realize how deep in thought I've been, because he has to chuck a napkin in my direction to get my attention.

I finally looked over at him blushing. "I was thinking of last night," I tell him honestly.

"Oh, don't be ashamed, because last night's been running through my head all morning," he comes clean leaving me a little less embarrassed.

I get up, walking down the stairs, wanting to have the sand between my toes and the sun on my skin. I continue down toward the water dipping my feet in trying to lock this place to memory and all its beauty.

Gabriele yells out to me, motioning that he's going to get dressed. I wave and nod needing just a little bit longer to take in the view. I dial Trev's number needing to hear his crazy voice.

He finally picks up after a couple of rings. "Hey, sleepy-head. Long night?" I ask.

He huffs. I hear a male's groan in the background. "Oh my god, did you spend the night with Adam?" I question, excited.

I'll be right back, he tells him. "Okay, I can talk now. And yes, we fucked. And yes, it was phenomenal," he confesses.

I squeal. "So, Dez was right, you do really like him," I state.

I can almost see him rolling his eyes right now. "Let's just say he's fun – for now."

"Oh, come on! It's ok to like someone, Trev. It's about time you let someone in other than Dez and I," I try to tell him, even though I'm not that great at taking my own advice.

"You know me, Nay. I'll eventually find something wrong with him," he whines.

I exhale. "I know, but no one's perfect *and* the fact that I heard he looks like Ryan Reynolds, isn't that a sign?"

He laughs. "Girl, I couldn't even bang him from behind because it was like I had my own personal Mr. Reynolds in my bed to look at," he admits.

"So, tell me, how's Mr. Billionaire? Has he been behaving himself?" Trev questions. "Do I have to come kick his ass?"

I giggle. "Let's just say he's been extremely good."

"Oh, do tell!" Trev requests.

"I just don't know how to explain him, Trev. Every time I think I may understand him, he shows me another side of him. He's just not what I expected him to be, and I don't know what to do with this," I explain to him.

"Just enjoy it and soak it all in, because once you're home then it's back to reality. Shae has been on Dez's ass since you've been gone. If I was a girl, I would have already knocked her on her ass," Trev informs me.

I start to panic. "Trev, what the fuck. Why didn't Dez tell me?" I freak out.

"She didn't want you to freak out like you're doing now. Anyways, what can you do from all the way over there?" he reminds me.

I exhale. "Ugh. I know. But as soon as I'm back, I'll deal with her. She can't keep acting like this just because she's jealous."

"Alright, I've got to go get ready. Gabriele's expecting me," I tell him.

"Okay, call me tomorrow, Nay. Love you."

"Love you too, Trev."

I HEAD BACK to the villa. Gabriele has his back to me on a call. The linen pants he's wearing hang against his ass perfectly and his lean back wide with muscles looks amazing under his white tee. I walk up behind him wrapping my arms around him nuzzling my face into his back. He smells divine, mouthwatering.

He turns, still on his call, and smiles bringing me into him with his arms now around me. He kisses the top of my head and then shoos me off to get dressed. I giggle as he smacks my ass.

I grab shorts, a black tank, some slip on sandals, and throw my hair up ready for a long day of exploring.

Gabriele is off his call by the time I'm dressed. "Ready?"

"Sure am!" I say, skipping to the door. He laughs and shakes his head.

He opens the door for me. "Like I said – *contagious*."

The same golf cart guy is waiting for us. "Mr. Vanucci," he greets. "Ma'am," he turns to me.

"Please, just call me Naomi," I tell him.

"Yes, well, where are we off to first?" he questions Gabriele.

We hop into the back of the golf cart. Gabriele makes sure to place his hand over my leg. It seems like a possessive sort of action, as though he's peeing on me like a dog does to a tree. I roll my eyes to myself.

"I thought we would head into town first to some of the shops," he directs.

The cart driver pulls off heading the same way as last

night. This time I can see the path we took, last night everything was pitch dark. We pass rows and rows of small colorful Mennonite homes high on stilts while locals continue with their everyday lives. We're vacationing where they live.

We finally reach town, the vibe is calmer than last night, more serene. Tourists speckle the streets, gift shops are jam-packed, and locals are busy offering their goods. We stop in front of the first shop, Gabriele advises the driver he'll reach out when we're ready to be picked up.

Dez and Trev are first on my mind to shop for. I promised to bring them back some souvenirs. We take our time weaving in and out of all the shops, teasing each other with hats and clothing. This almost feels like we're two people on vacation carefree and light just beginning their lives together, though this is far from the truth, it's nice to pretend for the time being.

After some time walking the streets and venturing into the shops we stop for lunch. It's this cute little restaurant tucked away behind a side street. There's only a couple of small tables set under the awning, sand for flooring, and the water just a short distance away. The music is playing softly in the background as the waitress comes up to our table.

I see how she looks at Gabriele, I've seen this look many times before. She dismisses me as though I don't exist barely giving me any mind. Gabriele is polite and smiles but keeps his attention directed at me as he orders us food and drinks dismissing her like I've also seen him do to many.

I feel a moment of pride as I witness this. He looks to me like I'm the only woman he sees. It makes me feel confident, bewitching, and mighty.

"So, where to next?" I ask.

His eyes sparkle a crisp golden green. The little lines around his eyes appear as he gives me a dazzling grin. I mimic his enthusiasm. Just as I'm contagious to him, he's infectious to me. We sit here just lost in each other's wordless thoughts before he finally breaks the silence to answer me.

"I thought we would go snorkeling. There's a little company called Caty's Snorkeling and Tours. Its family owned. I've known the owners for a while now, they are the ones that told me about the sale of the island," he discloses.

"That sounds fun! I've always wanted to go snorkeling. Have you ever been before?"

He shakes his head. "This will be a first for me," he replies, smiling.

I feel giddy inside with another first from him. "Well then, even better."

The waitress comes back around to drop off our drinks and food. Gabriele ordered light this time since we had such a large breakfast. The couple next to us takes selfies and catches us in the background. Gabriele looks irritated and gets up offering to help them in taking the pictures for them. I notice he slides through the recents and deletes the one just taken.

They thank him, and he returns to our table. "What was that about?" I question.

"I don't need that picture ending up on some sleezy tabloid," he says aggravated.

I'm not too sure how to take this. It can be taken two ways, I guess. One – he's worried about his privacy or two – he worried about being seen with me.

"And what would happen if we did end up on a tabloid?" I wonder.

He seems annoyed that I'm asking or annoyed just in general. He finally exhales before he responds. "Your life wouldn't be your own any longer. You would be dissected and torn apart by people who know nothing about you. Anything you wanted kept hidden away in the dark would be brought to the light and spread all over those magazines for strangers to read."

Shit. Explaining it that way makes his reasoning all the clearer. "Is this something you know from experience?"

He takes a long pull from his margarita. "My whole life was under a microscope. When you have a father as well off as mine was, it comes with the territory. My life wasn't mine to control when I was younger. Once my father passed away, I gained the means to gain my control back. I hired the best to wipe me clean off the internet so my life can remain mine," he explains.

This explains why in one moment Trev could find only one picture of him on the internet and in the next it was gone.

"I'm sorry you had to endure that growing up. Must have been extremely difficult living under a microscope. I didn't realize how serious us being spotted together could cause such mayhem. I'm sure you being seen with a dancer wouldn't go over very well in the media either," I agree, though just saying this part out loud punctures my heart.

He brings his face closer to mine, anger radiating off him now. "I couldn't give two fucks what the media thinks. What I care about is you, and how this would affect your life, not mine. I'll be okay. I'm not sure you're built to survive this part of my world."

Ouch. That stings. But maybe he does have a point. I nod understanding. He accepts my silence as moving on.

We finish the rest of our lunch and then head over to the snorkeling hut. We're given a quick lesson on how to secure the goggles and breathe through the tube without sucking water in. The lightness dissipated after lunch between us, and left is now a gray heaviness.

His mind seems elsewhere, but I don't question it. It's probably better to just let things lie for now. This isn't something either of us will have to worry about in the weeks to come anyways.

"You good?" he asks as we sit heading out on the boat.

"Yeah. I'm good."

I'm looking forward to peace of the underwater. No questions, no worries, just serenity and quietness. There's been too much noise in my head lately, I'm on the cusp of a headache and need some reprieve.

We finally reach our destination; the director gives us free rein to jump in and start adventuring. Gabriele and I head in our own direction away from the other passengers. The underwater is marvelous – mystical. The fish are florescent in color, and the coral is full of vibrant shades of the rainbow.

Gabriele grabs my hand in his as we swim side by side through the magical marine life of the ocean. I've never witnessed something so beautiful. I can see him through my goggles watching me as I take in our surroundings, pointing animatedly at the new discoveries in sight.

I feel as though I'm seeing the world for the first time in a different light. It's magnificent, grand, and I'm just one small insignificant speck floating around in it.

After an hour or so, we finish and head back to the island. The golf cart is waiting for us to take us back to our villa.

"We need to pack. I have the plane waiting for us to take us back," he informs.

"Okay."

I can see him studying me from my peripheral vision. He looks as though he has something to say, he opens his mouth, and then closes it without a word said. This seems to be a new phenomenon – Gabriele rendered speechless.

We pass by each other not saying a word as we gather our belongings. This silence feels awkward and weird, not our usual stillness, but more of an unknown territory for us.

I think he's finally had enough because I pass by him one last time before he grabs my arm and pulls me into him. "I can't take this anymore," he confesses before dropping his lips down against mine.

His kiss is soft and leisurely, but quickly turns frantic and passionate as our hands roam urgently on every surface of our flesh, tangling in each other's hair, and gripping every inch as though we're about to fade off into nothingness.

We finally pull apart breathless and disheveled. No matter what mood lies in front of us, just a single kiss or embrace seems to disintegrate it all.

"Much better," he says with a smirk. "Are you ready to head out?"

I reel my hormones in and clear my throat. "I am."

It's late afternoon by the time we arrive at the house. Gabriele had to leave to check on some new clients at the main house, I took a shower and ended up napping for the duration of the time he was gone.

I wake up to music and the smell of the grill. My stomach is growling, mouth drooling as I walk out onto the deck. Gabriele has a beer in one hand while flipping two steaks with the other. He looks rogue and sexy manning the grill. If only he would change his mind on a different future, I can almost visualize what domestication could do for him – wife helping make dinner while their children run around being menaces as he grills and chugs down a beer. He could be happy.

He turns around feeling my presence. "Hey, you sleep good?"

I walk over and take a seat adjacent to him. "I did. The sun must have worn me out."

He hands me a beer. "Thanks."

"I hope you like filet and lobster," he reveals as he takes the steaks off the grill and turns the propane tank off. "Come on, I have everything set up inside."

I follow. "Anything I can help with?"

He grabs plates out of the cupboard. "No. Sit," he directs me to my stool as he reaches into the refrigerator taking out the premade salad.

I stand up and head around the counter. "Here's let me at least dress the salad," I tell him grabbing the oil and vinegar. "I do know my way around the kitchen also, you know," I advise him.

"Oh yeah? Please enlighten me," he replies, grinning as he places our food on each plate.

I finish mixing the salad and dish it out onto our plates before sitting. "Well, I make some banging cutlets and home-made alfredo sauce," I apprise him. "Also, a great meatloaf and mashed potatoes."

His brows raise amused. "Sounds amazing. Looks like dinner is on you tomorrow night," he suggests, eyes shimmering.

"Deal. I'll give you a list of ingredients. They shouldn't be that difficult to supply."

He chuckles. "There's nothing that can't be supplied with just a click of a button in my world."

I roll my eyes not impressed. "Wow, look at you. The big bad billionaire always gets what he wants," I tease.

"Always," he replies with a wink.

I cut into the steak, and it's grilled to perfection. The bite melts in my mouth. I close my eyes and moan with delight; good food has always been a weakness for me. "This steak is grilled perfectly. Is there anything you're bad at?"

He finishes chewing before answering. "I'd like to say no, but I think you and I both know the answer to that question."

Relationships. He's bad at those. Though, I really don't believe that, because I'd like to think this is how it could be in a relationship with him – as easy as breathing. The work between us has been minimal. Our connection isn't forced, it's been genuine. He has a jealous streak, but he also knows how to apologize when he's wrong. If only he could just see how easy it could be with the right person.

I decide to change the subject. "Have your clients been enjoying the island?"

His eyes twinkle with pride. "Oh yes. And I was thinking – I'd like to fulfill another fantasy of yours before we leave," he offers me, waiting for me to reply.

I think of his offer for a moment but decide on something else. "Actually, I was hoping I could learn one of yours."

He seems a little caught off guard as his brows rise in surprise. "Are you sure about this? I've already explained to you that my interests are unique. You may go beyond what you're used to, and I may push you to a point of questioning yourself again," he says, trying to remind me.

"I know."

He takes my hand in his. "I don't want to push you or take you there if you have any doubts. I need you to be one hundred percent ready to experience something that pushes you out of your comfort zone."

"I'm still learning what my limitations are, what I like and what I may not, but I want you to be the one to help me with this. I trust you. I want to experience this with you," I clarify.

He brings my hand to his lips and kisses me lightly. "You're amazing, little ballerina."

"I know."

He chuckles at my confidence. "After we're done eating, I'm going to take you to bed and fuck you from behind," he states.

Heat creeps up my body over my face. His promise sends tingles straight to my core. Even though my soreness is still prominent, I'm ready for more. I press my thighs together to ease the pressure.

"I love when your skin turns flush," he says, stroking my cheek. "Your body's reaction to my words drives me insane," he tells me, standing up, pushing my food out of my reach.

He turns me in my stool now standing between my legs, lifting my chin so I'm looking up at him. "Fuck waiting. I want to bend you over this counter and fuck you right here."

Turned on is an understatement. The butterflies are swarming through my lower belly with anticipation, my flushed skin is now pooling liquid heat between my legs, and his hungered stare is melting right through me like lava.

"So, do it," I entice him, one brow raised daring.

I don't have to say another word before his lips are slammed against mine. His fingers grip my hair pulling me in closer as his tongue delves into my mouth with hard impatient thrusts. I start to unbutton his pants, as he begins to kiss my jawline to my ear, nibbling and licking as he goes.

I unzip his pants, push them down with my bare feet, and reach into his briefs to pull his hard length out. He hisses at my touch and continues his kisses down my neck. I squeeze feeling only a steel rod in my grip, he bites down on my neck making me scream out.

"Fuck yes, ballerina. I love feeling your tiny hands wrapped around my cock," he growls.

I stroke him up and down, rubbing my finger over the drop of pre-cum forming on his tip. Gabriele pumps his hips, fucking my hands while he unties my halter dress and rips it down to my belly now baring my naked chest to him.

He leans down gripping my erect nipple between his teeth and bites down. I buck up as I scream out. He may have just drawn blood, but I don't care. The pain turns to pleasure as he lathers my sensitive peak with his tongue.

His kisses drift over my chest to my other nipple, sucking and nibbling softly this time while I continue my even strokes down his cock. His fingers slide up my thigh reaching the outside of my panties. "Damn, you're fucking soaked," he whispers pleased.

His fingers run along the fabric. I whimper wanting him closer, wanting to feel his fingers inside of me, touching me, skin to skin. He looks up at me smiling, knowing I'm becoming impatient.

"My little ballerina is getting impatient, is she?" he asks, slipping my dress and panties down my legs after I lift my ass for him. I'm now completely exposed and sopping wet for him. He stands back drifting his gaze from my chest gradually down every inch of my body as slow as possible. My breath hitches as he laps his finger around my swollen bud, circling it just enough to have me panting and glistening wet. His fingers drag through my folds until he reaches my entrance, teasing and orbiting around my channel, making me beg for his intrusion.

He finally slips two fingers inside of me. I scream out while he works me, stretches me, waiting for me to beg for more. "Are you ready to have my cock deep inside of you?" he leans in and murmurs in my ear.

"Yes. *Please* fuck me," I beg.

He grabs my hips ripping me off the stool, slides it over with his foot, and bends me over the counter, hands flat, and chest squished onto the cold marble.

I feel the head of his dick rub up and down my sex, lathering himself in my juices, before he gently pushes inside of me. We both groan as inch by inch he fills me to the hilt. I've never felt so full, so consumed as I am right now in this vulnerable position.

He waits for me to adjust. "Are you okay?" he asks, sweetly between gritted teeth. I nod, adapting minute by minute. I wriggle my ass back driving him wild. "Keep doing that and I won't be able to control myself. I'll fuck you so hard, I'll have to ice you later," he threatens.

The thrust starts slow, sliding deep inside me and then pulling out gradually, until I begin to meet him drive for drive, he begins to lose his control, and the pumps become quick and hard.

My hips slam into the counter which no doubt will leave

a bruise in the morning, but I don't care. This position reaches me so deep. Tears begin to escape my eyes at the rush of orgasmic waves initiating through my core.

The sound of his pelvis against my ass fills the room, my moans become louder as he reaches between us, strokes my clit in the same moment adjusting the angle of his dick and I combust, erupting like meteors through the sky, milking his cock as his semen spurts deep within me dripping down my inner thighs as he rides out the last of his orgasm.

"Fucking hell, Naomi!" He groans with one last pump. "I've never in my life felt something so intense," he admits breathlessly.

We stay connected until our pants subside. Gabriele kisses the skin between my shoulder blades before he slips out of me. I wince feeling the soreness flare back. He grabs my hand leading me to my bathroom and turns the shower water on.

He checks the water. "Get in," he instructs.

I step in feeling the hot water cascade down the front of my body and he follows suit behind me. The heat feels amazing and much needed. I turn toward Gabriele leaning my head back into the water.

I watch Gabriele pump shampoo into his hand. "Turn around," he directs.

I do as he says. "Man, you're so bossy," I joke.

He chuckles. "It's the best part of me."

His fingers begin massaging the shampoo through my hair. I groan leaning my head back more. "Feel good?" he asks.

"Mhmm."

After washing my hair, he takes his time washing my body too. "Your turn. Switch spots," I demand, taking my turn to boss him.

"Bossy," he says with a wink before he soaks himself underneath the spray.

I watch the water roll down the contours of his skin. My eyes follow the trail of the drops making me thirsty wanting to lick them up. I take my turn washing him, running my soapy hands all over, and if I continue for any longer then we're going to end up in the middle of round two.

Gabriele gives me a light peck on the forehead before stepping out and grabbing towels for us both. "You need your rest," he says, handing me my towel before placing his around his waist.

"Thanks." I grab the towel, dry my body and wrap it around my head. How far we've come from our first encounter in my room. This time I have no qualms about walking around naked in front of him.

I throw on some undies and a tank, and climb into bed exhausted. Even with a nap, I feel as though I've been run over by a dump truck. I feel the bed adjust down as Gabriele climbs in behind me.

I turn around facing him. "Gabriele, what about the rules we agreed on?" I remind him.

He laughs and pulls me into his chest kissing the top of my head. "Can't we just say fuck the rules? You're the one that made them, you can be the one to break them."

I shake my head. "Come on, Naomi, just feel. Let things just happen. Stop trying to control everything in life," he suggests.

I push on his chest so I'm able to look at him. "I should be saying the same to you."

"Okay, touché. Maybe we need to both let go and stop thinking so much, at least for the remainder of our time together," he recommends.

I lay on my back now frustrated. "That's easy for you to say. I'm trying hard here, Gabriele. Trying hard to keep my feelings at bay. You've made it clear where you stand in your future alone, and I respect that decision, but that doesn't mean walking away will be easy for me. Especially, after our time here together. I'm not as practiced at all this as you are."

He leans on his elbow turned on his side to face me, his fingers tracing the plains of my face. "Do you think any of this is easy for me? And you keep saying you're going to walk away once we land, how do you think that makes me feel?" he questions seeming hurt.

My brows furrow, and nose scrunches feeling lost. "I'm confused. Are you saying you want to see me after this? You've made it clear you don't want strings."

He feathers his lips over mine. "Just because I don't want a relationship, doesn't mean this ends as soon as we land. You were the one that decided that, not me."

I think back through all our conversations, and I guess he is right. He's never once talked about our return and what will become of us. That's always been me that made the decision, but I know I always made that decision to protect myself.

"What about the paparazzi?" I ask.

"I'm good at discreet. And they aren't always on my radar unless they've been tipped off to something," he explains.

Ok, that makes sense, but continuing to spend time together with no future doesn't.

"What about the club?"

His fingers halt. "What about the club?" he questions. I see a flash of anger slip through his façade before returning stoic.

I make sure to keep my eyes locked on his so I don't miss a thing. "Will you still be coming in?"

His jaw muscles flex as he tightens. "No."

Huh. He was so keen on stalking me before and being my protector, so what has changed?

"Why?"

It's his turn to now roll on his back, placing his hands

behind his head and stare at the ceiling. I turn to face him now waiting for him to speak.

"Because I'm not sure I'll be able to control my jealousy. Seeing you dance for another man, or someone touching you will drive me over the edge," he admits.

"But you've watched it before," I remind him.

He exhales. "That was before I touched you. Before I tasted you, and before my cock was deep inside of you," he replies seething.

Ok fair enough. I can't argue with that. But now this opens a new question. "What about the fantasies we discussed? You seem to be okay with another man touching me if I chose."

He now turns his attention to me instead of the ceiling. "Touching you yes, fucking you, no. And that's something that would be consensual for pleasure. You working at the club with douche fucks grabbing at you and treating you like a piece of meat they paid for is an extremely different type of touching."

"But isn't you paying for my time here the same?" I know I shouldn't have asked this question again but it's still front and center in the back of my head every day.

He sits up throwing his covers off and jumps out of bed. "Jesus Christ, Naomi! Haven't we already discussed this?" he yells angrily. "I don't see you as a whore or a piece of meat! I fucking have feelings for you! I *like* you – a lot. And I have no idea what to do with these feelings. I've never wanted to spend time with anyone for more than a night," he finishes, looking out the back doors to the water.

My mind is reeling at his confession, but it still leaves me with another question. "Gabriele, that can't possibly be true. You were engaged. Clearly that meant you were planning on spending the rest of your life with her."

He turns, stalking over to me with tight fists, face red and formidable, I've never seen him so pissed off before. He leans down on the bed, fists now supporting himself as his face is directly in front of mine.

"Do not talk about things you know nothing about, Naomi. Like I said before, just because it was on the internet, does not make it so. I do not lie," he snaps.

Okay, I see I've pushed too hard. This is clearly a subject he's not willing to open up about, so I need to fix this. "Okay, you're right. I'm sorry for bringing it up again. You're right. I only know what you tell me, and I shouldn't have questioned your truth," I say softly.

I run my hands up his forearms attempting to calm him. He hangs his head down in surrender. By the time he looks back up to me, his face is kind and apologetic. He climbs back in bed with me, pulls me against him and we lay silent as we both fall asleep.

CHAPTER 13

The last couple of days with Gabriele have been amazing; relaxing and full of sex. We haven't even left the villa once. I cooked for him, and we've also fallen into a nice sync of cooking dinner together too. I spent a couple lazy afternoons napping on the daybed or reading a book while he worked next to me on his laptop or took calls.

I knew this sacred time in our little bubble would have to end eventually, so I took in every moment, tucking each memory away deep inside. We've spent many hours learning about each other's bodies. He's a quick learner, taking him no time to find out the spots that make me tick and drive me wild. It's hard to even fathom that I may end up with another down the road.

He promised he would help me learn myself, and boy he hasn't disappointed. He's talented, thoughtful, patient, and most of all a selfless lover. How is anyone else supposed to compare. He's given me such a gift of knowing myself while ruining me at the same time. The bricks of my walls are crumbling around me, and I don't know how to stop it.

I hear footsteps behind me as I sip on my coffee in the chair on the deck.

Fingers skim over my neck moving my hair to the side, and the feel of lips touch the crook of my neck. I close my eyes and exhale loudly at the feeling. "You ready?" he asks.

"Mhmm."

He grabs my hand to lift me out of the chair to embrace me in his arms. "How'd you sleep?"

"You've been wearing me out these past couple of nights, I don't even think I've had one dream this whole time," I reply laughing.

He nuzzles into me. "Sex helps with insomnia. That means we must continue to have it daily to ensure you sleep well," he jokes.

I laugh. "No complaints from me there."

WE HEAD out to another part of the island, passing the main house continuing down the road along the beach. There's nothing but palm trees and beach alongside my passenger side view. We finally reach the end of the island and park.

I catch wind of an unusually intriguing looking villa off a long pier surrounded by water. I walk over to the cliff to peek over getting a closer look. I search for a way down but am not able to find one. All I can see are palm trees scattered along the white sand beach below, and crystal blue waters far enough for the eyes to see.

I turn to Gabriele. "How do we get down there?"

He winks and begins walking toward the brush off the side of the road. I feel elated as I quickly follow his footsteps. He pushes some overgrown greenery aside and emerging stone stairs appear in its place. A huge smile spreads across my face as he holds his arm out for me to enter first.

It's like I'm entering a secret garden, only this is leading to a mystical hidden beach. The musical sounds of birds echo overhead as we descend the steps, and the further we go down, the louder the ocean becomes as the water coasts up the sandy shore.

"What is the place, Gabriele?" I asked amazed.

"This place is called – Serenity," he answers. "A place you can come to let go and find your most inner self."

That seems a little vague. We finally reach the bottom of the steps, no more steps or stones or pathways, only sand. "So, like a meditation house?"

He chuckles. "Maybe to some, but more like a safe space to act out your most inner desires."

"Oh," is the only thing I can seem to say.

We reach the pier and head down the path. The breeze whips through my hair as the waves splash against the stilts. My heartbeat accelerates the closer we get to the villa. The house is bathed in glass windows, the exterior shape is large and round giving access to every angle of the ocean still in pure privacy, and the roof is hidden under a hut like rustic material.

I follow him into a private back door. This place is bright and heavenly unlike the other hidden dungeon last week. This private room overlooks a main area with full privacy glass and full access for viewing. The room below has some white lounge chairs broken up into groupings surrounding some strange apparatuses hanging from the ceiling.

"What are those?" I question not taking my eyes off the strange contraptions around the room.

Gabriele comes up and wraps his arms around me from behind. "Actually, I was hoping to show you, if you'd let me?" he asks.

I turn my head toward him. "You want to tie me up in that?"

"Yes."

I had asked Gabriele to allow me to see a glimpse into his world and this is him letting me in. As much as he needs me to trust him, I also need him to be comfortable in trusting me. I *want* this. I *need* this just as much as he does. In some crazy way I feel like this brings us closer, more intimate than just the average lovers. This elevates us to a whole new level of closeness and just the thought brings me excitement and an ache to please deep into my bones.

"Okay, I trust you," I tell him, giving myself to him fully.

He squeezes me tight swaying us back and forth. "Thank you, ballerina."

Gabriele grabs my hand, turning me to him. "Now, take off your clothes," he demands.

I unzip the back of my flowered dress and allow it to slide off, pooling around my feet. Gabriele looks hypnotized as he watches my every move, a hunger in his eyes inching over every crevice of my skin. I stand in only my bra and underwear waiting.

"Take your bra off," he says in a deep husky voice.

Keeping my eyes locked with his, I reach behind my back unhooking my clasp and drag each strap down my arms. My breasts hang like small raindrops while my nipples pucker tightly. Gabriele licks his bottom lip as though he's ready to walk over and ravage me.

"Now your panties."

I tuck my thumbs under each side and drag them down until they fall to my feet. He looks insatiable as he takes in every inch of me. He walks toward me, bends down to pick them up, and brings them to his nose inhaling, then tucks them away in his back pocket.

"I wish I could bottle your scent and keep it forever," he tells me.

Here I am standing completely bare for him, wetness now pooling between my legs, and ready to be ravished waiting for his next move.

He pulls a white silk scarf from his front pocket. "Turn around."

I almost hesitate but decide to follow his order. He covers

my eyes testing it to make sure I have no vision tying it tightly around the back of my head. I'm now surrounded in blackness trying to rely on all my other senses. He takes my hand and begins leading me.

"Just follow my lead. I won't let you fall," he instructs.

My bare feet move along the tile reaching something smoother. I hear doors close and then my stomach falls as we descend. We step out of the elevator continuing forward until we stop.

"Stay here," he commands me.

I reach my hearing out trying to listen. I hear padded footsteps walking along the tile floor. Music begins to play loud surrounding us, drowning out any possibility of noise I was hoping to hear. I begin to feel anxious with only just a few senses left.

I reach out sensing Gabriele in front of me. His chest is now bare. I slide my hands down his chest, over his rippling abs, reaching his rock-hard dick against his stomach. He's now naked. I wrap my hands around him, and though I can't hear him, I know he's affected because he grinds his hips into my hand.

He stops my hands, clasping them together. I hear the faint sound of a chain pulling down from the ceiling. He locks one wrist, then the other and clips them together. I move my wrist around feeling a cushiony soft fabric around my skin.

Gabriele's lips skim over mine, I try to lean into him, but his position moves over my jawline down my neck, and skims over my nipples finally taking one into his mouth and circling it with his tongue before biting down. I scream out as the charge shoots straight down to my sex.

I rub my thighs together as the pressure and need begins to build. His fingers glide over my abdomen, past my lower belly, and straight into my folds. I moan moving my hips wanting to ride his fingers to climax. My wetness coats him the more he plays; teasing, not entering me but floating over my clit and then back to my entrance. I whine in protest, but instead he smashes his lips into mine gulping down my moans as his tongue wrestles with mine ready to dominate.

"Please," I beg, hoping he will just give me an orgasm already.

He smiles against my lips. "Please what?" he whispers into my ear.

"Please just fuck me."

His finger dives deep into my core. My back arches as I belt out. "Oh, I'll be fucking you, just not yet."

A detonation of heat licks over my skin as he pumps his finger in and out of me, stroking my little nub with his thumb each time he enters me. My heart pumps my veins full of liquid fire as it travels through my body scalding every inch on the way.

Fingers slide over my breasts from behind tweaking my nipples. I moan out pushing my chest into them further. Every nerve ending in my body lights up until I freeze realizing there's two sets of hands on my body. *What the fuck?* I begin to freak out. My body turns rigid with fear. I know Gabriele is in front of me, but who the fuck is touching me from behind?

"It's okay, little ballerina. I promise this is for your pleasure only," Gabriele murmurs in my ear, comforting me. "Just feel and let everything else go. Trust me," he says, trying to convince me, and just with his last plea, I do as he asks and let go. Screw it. For that half of a second it felt amazing, and I trust him fully.

I nod, and the feeling continues. Gabriele now slips two fingers inside; I cry out as he penetrates me at the same time my nipples are pinched. The electrifying zing jolts straight down to my clit. Gabriele's hot wet tongue licks over my right nipple as the hand behind me tweaks my other. Lips land on my shoulder and slowly make their way up my neck as Gabriele finally crooks his fingers enough to hit my magic spot inside. I scream out feeling overwhelmed with immense pleasure.

Just as the build begins to surge, Gabriele's fingers and lips withdraw from me and I immediately whimper in protest as my body free falls from its climax that was just about to erupt.

"Kneel," he directs then pulls the chains on my wrist bending me forward over a plush piece of furniture tying them down so I can't move. Hands behind me brush against my inner thighs pushing them apart.

Gabriele's fingers grab onto my chin rubbing the head of his dick over my lips. I immediately open for him allowing him to guide his shaft deep into my mouth. Fingers behind me start circling my clit; rubbing then dipping into my sex gathering my juices and then back up to my bundle of nerves. I moan into Gabriele, vibrating over every inch of him as he pumps into me.

The thought of two men pleasuring me no longer scares me. I'm embracing every delish moment of being the center of their attention. I feel powerful and sexy as I can hear grunts and groans coming from each of them.

Fingers are now replaced with a tongue as he licks over my clit; around and around with perfect pressure bringing me back to my build up that was just deserted moments ago while two fingers slip back into place deep within my cunt. I groan hard over Gabriele's dick, and he starts fucking my mouth hard and fast reaching all the way to the back of my throat, holding my head in place tightly until I almost can't breathe and then he releases again.

Drool and spit run down the sides of my mouth as he grips tightly into my hair, pumping me full of his swollen girth. The pain of my hair being pulled becomes void as my orgasm almost reaches the top of its pinnacle.

With just one more flick of his fingers and stroke of his

tongue I lunge off the cliff free diving into a pool of cosmic orgasms. Gabriele pushes one last time into my mouth before hot wet come spurts down the back of my throat. I swallow trying to keep up as I drink every last drop of him. The man behind me runs his tongue through my folds and into my entrance tasting my juices as I come down from my high. I am completely spent.

Here I am spread eagle, bare to a man I've never even seen before with another that has become so much to me in a short period of time, and I feel shameless, beautiful, and completely appeased. Such an odd feeling to have settle over me. Even with the job I hold, guilt still comes with the territory, but this feels different. I feel safe and protected in the arms of Gabriele. No judgments, just feelings.

My hands are now released, and the cuffs are now removed giving me free rein again. He removes the blindfold helping me stand to my feet. "You're so fucking beautiful," he tells me with admiration in his eyes.

He leads me over to a long flat lounge and lays me down on my back. I now see the man who moments ago had his tongue and fingers inside of me, sitting down on the chair facing us. His legs are spread wide, hard on laying against his stomach, tan golden skin, with sandy blond short hair, blue eyes, and a body that makes GI Joe look inferior. I almost feel guilty from enjoying pleasure from him, and I now feel extremely guilty for the way my body is reacting as he begins to pleasure himself slowly while watching us.

Gabriele gains my attention back by rubbing the tip of his head against my sex. He looks magnificent kneeling before me full of pride, no jealousy or angst, just full-on need.

He gradually pushes inside of me, allowing my walls to stretch with his intrusion. My eyes immediately roll back at the blissful feeling. His hands run up my stomach, over my chest, grabbing a handful as he begins his torturedly slow thrusts into me.

"God damn, every time I sink into you it's like the first time," he growls.

Every inch of my skin is already on stimulation overload. Each touch, every caress against my body ignites the ember that was burning low just a moment ago.

He grazes his thumb over my clit. I rip out a moan from the sensitivity as he continuously strokes me. "That's right, baby, soak my cock with your pussy juices. God, you feel so fucking amazing," he groans as he lifts both of my legs over his shoulders.

"Fuck yeah," he says watching his dick slide in and out of me.

I hear movement beside me. Blondie moves and now kneels by my side while still stroking himself. He's even larger up close and personal, and for just a split moment I wonder what he would feel like filling me to the hilt with that cock, but I immediately erase the thought from my head until Gabriele assures me to let go of any remorse.

"Naomi, your thoughts are safe in here. He's here for your pleasure too," he tells me.

I watch as he slides his thumb over the small wet bead of his tip, rubs his fingers together, and then skims them along my lips coaxing me to open for him. I peek my tongue out licking the tip of his finger, he tastes salty and earthy. I moan as Gabriele still pumps steady into my core as he ravishes my clit with his fingers.

Blondie slides his fingers into my mouth watching as I suck and swirl around them as though it was his cock. His eyes dagger into mine filled with want and wishful need. He groans loudly as he thrusts wildly into his hand while finger fucking my mouth. Gabriele's momentum picks up, balls slapping hard against my ass as he watches the scene in front of him unfold.

My body is overwhelmed with emotions, the walls of my sex begin to tremble as I'm surrounded by touches, groans, and sexy as fuck male bodies. This may be the best porno yet and I'm the fucking star.

Gabriele pushes my legs down so my knees are to the sofa, growling as he furiously fucks me, sounds of wet juices and skin to skin smacking consume the room. I reach over and grab blondie's balls as he fucks himself, and he loses all control.

"Holy *fucking* shit! I'm going to come!" he yells as hot semen squirts all over my chest and stomach. He continuously pumps until every drop is now laid upon me.

Gabriele positions himself lower driving up straight into my sweet spot over and over until my walls convulse around his cock milking him to the death. I push back meeting him blow for blow and we both scream out in unison.

"Fuck yes, baby! Just like that!" he growls out. Blondie reaches over rubbing into my folds, dragging up around my swollen tight bud, and I instantly explode all over Gabriele's cock. I fall into a vortex of blinding ecstasy. My vision leaves me with only tiny stars in my wake as my body falls limp. I'm spent, there's nothing left in me.

Gabriele leans over, still inside, and kisses me tenderly. "Thank you for trusting me, my little ballerina," he whispers in my ear. I look over to my side, to the chair, and he's gone. It's almost as if I just imagined this whole experience.

He slides out of me, then cleans me up with a wet cloth, and picks me up carrying me to the elevator we just came down a while ago. I close my eyes and lean my head against his chest exhausted.

Once we get back to the room he takes me outside to a private deck, he sits me down on a lounge chair and starts to make his way down the steps. The water is a light aqua blue only waist deep on him. The sun twinkles like diamonds off the surface causing him to look like a sexy godlike merman. I smile as I enjoy the scene.

He waves over to me. "Come on! Get in, the water feels amazing," he yells before he dives under.

I get up and make my way down the steps. As soon as the water hits my skin, my muscles begin to relax feeling as though I'm entering bathwater full of Epsom salt. The water reaches me waist high allowing my breasts free access to his gaze. I dip under the water and by the time I come back up Gabriele is standing in front of me.

"Feels good, doesn't it?" he asks, knowing the answer already.

I nod. "It really does. This place is like stepping into a dream."

His eyes gleam with the compliment. "That's what I aimed for. How are you feeling? Any regrets?" he wonders, seeming a bit worried.

"Truth?"

"Always," he replies.

I look away from his penetrated gaze. "It all feels surreal, dreamlike. I haven't had time to process it all or take the experience in yet, but I do know I feel a small bit of guilt enjoying something like that so much," I admit.

He holds my face in his hands, so I have nowhere to look but him. "Please don't feel guilty for me or my feelings. I fucking enjoyed every moment of watching you come undone at the hands of me and him. The way you felt, the way you abandoned all control and allowed your desires to lead you was absolutely the most incredible thing to witness. I'm so glad you allowed me to show you how good letting go can feel," he explains.

How does he do this? How does he make all my worries and internal crisis just fade away. Most men would never say things like this or even care about someone else's wants and desires. Most men would think less of a woman who had thoughts of sexual relationships like this. I mean hell, I only thought this was possible in pornos, never a possibility in real life.

The scary part is that after this, my bricks are crumbling into pieces and my wall is falling. I have no way to save it and now when I look at him my heart pings with restriction because it's his hold that is tightened around me. I can't breathe with this realization. I start to back up holding my chest while gasping for air.

"Naomi! What the fuck? What's wrong?" I hear Gabriele yelling in the far distance.

The ringing in my ears becomes louder as everything begins to fade to a sparkling darkness, and then everything turns black.

My eyes flutter open as I come to. I feel sticky and clammy. I look around confused seeing Gabriele in front of me holding a cold towel against my forehead. I try to sit up but he stops me.

"Just stay put," he directs.

"Wh-what happened?" I question not understanding since I was just standing in front of him in the water.

"You passed out."

My brows furrow trying to remember. "I did?"

"Maybe I didn't feed you enough this morning, I have some lunch being brought here. You scared the shit out of me, Naomi," he says frazzled. "How are you feeling now?"

"Weak. Maybe I'm just dehydrated," I try to reason.

Gabriele stands and walks over to the table grabbing a bottled water. He comes back and sits next to me again, opens the bottle and lifts it to my mouth for me to sip. He's such a good caretaker.

I finish gulping. "Thanks."

"Maybe I pushed you too hard," he wonders, brushing a piece of hair out of my face.

I grab his hand and kiss it. "No, it wasn't anything you

did. Don't blame yourself. I'm fine. Could have been a number of things."

He still looks worried. Just as he's about to say something, there's a buzzing sound. Gabriele looks down at his phone and presses a button. He stands greeting the woman.

"Good afternoon, Mr. Vanucci. I've packed everything you've asked for," she tells him handing over a large basket.

He grabs the basket and sets it aside. "Thank you, Jenny. I appreciate that quick delivery."

She quickly looks over to me and then back to him. Jesus. Not another one. Can he just hire men for all his staff from now on?

"Not a problem. Will you be needing anything else?" she asks with hopeful eyes. Can she be more obvious?

"No, nothing at all," he finishes and directs her to the door. She nods and heads out.

My eyes are vexed as I watched the scene unfold not being able to hide my annoyance. "What?" he questions.

I roll my eyes. "Nothing."

He stalks me, then flings his leg over the lounge and sits right on top of me, pinning me back. "Not nothing. Spill it," he orders.

"Do you not see what you do to every woman who you come across?" I inquire.

He smirks. "Is someone jealous?" he teases.

I huff. "No, not jealous. Just irritated watching you get ogled twenty-four-seven."

He leans into me more. "That sounds a bit like jealousy to me," he states. "And let's not forget I have to endure the same thing wherever I go with you," he points out with one brow raised.

I shake my head. "So not true."

Even though he makes me feel beautiful, I haven't always felt that way with the girls at the club, and let's not even mention my blonde bombshell of a best friend. There's no comparison between us. She outshines me every second of the day done up or in sweats.

"You are so very wrong, little ballerina. That man who had his tongue inside of you is one of the world's largest real estate holders. His money is infinite. He can have any woman he wants, but he wanted you. He saw you walking with Joanna the other day and requested you. I told him you were off-limits, but after you and I had the conversation we did, I changed my mind. He now wants what's mine. He requested you again – *alone*, but that's a hard no for me because I only share on my terms," he discloses.

"So, you see, I am a jealous prick when it comes to things that aren't in my control. And men wanting you, and eye fucking you, drives me absolutely insane. But here's the thing, I'm here with you and you're here with me, so just this little fact eases my mind and should ease yours as well because there is nowhere else I'd rather be."

I wrap my arms around his neck and bring him in for a kiss. I kiss his lips, his nose, each cheek, and back to his lips again. He smiles into me before we both open tangling our tongues with one another in such a slow sensual rhythm. What on god's earth is this man doing to me?

We end with tiny pecks before he changes direction. "I need to feed you," he tells me before getting up and heading to the basket.

He pulls out an array of snacks, fruits, cheeses, meats, and a couple of desserts. My stomach growls immediately without warning. He laughs. "I knew you were hungry."

I shrug. "I guess I've been so busy food never really crossed my mind. I was too distracted being filled with other delicious delights," I joke.

Gabriele laughs out loud. I love the sound of him laughing and carefree. It makes me feel giddy. He piles a shit-load of food on a plate and brings it over for us to share. He stabs a strawberry and brings it to my mouth. "Eat."

I giggle at his bossiness. I chew and swallow and then do the same to him. By the time we finish, I'm stuffed. I'm in need of a major shower to get this saltwater off my skin. It's starting to feel scratchy and irritating.

"You ready to head back to the house?" he asks.

"So ready for a nice hot shower," I reply.

"That sounds wonderful. You soaked with water and suds running down that sexy body – " he starts to say.

I smack his chest. "Okay horn ball. I need a night off to recoup," I tease.

He winks. "I'll try hard to be on my best behavior," he lies. He stands up and holds out his hand for me. "Come on, let's head out."

CHAPTER 14

*G*abriele brought me to the house and jumped into the shower with me before he left. He had some more clients landing that he needed to greet and take care of. He said he tries to personally attend to everyone's arrivals when he's on the island. It gives them a feeling of importance, and he also likes to make sure his investigations and vetting process are spot on for the future members of the island.

This part of the business is new to him since it's the first of its kind that he personally ran and owned. He's heard of others, but their reputations are questionable ones, and he will not allow any ill willed actions to ruin this island's reputation. Anything devious, questionable, or illegal will not be tolerated by him.

I love this honorable part of him. Even though he enjoys the darker side of intimacy he remains completely untouched by that darkness and any other persuasion that might come his way. Money hasn't seemed to change his standards he has for himself and that in itself is swoon worthy. He stands for something. He stands for his beliefs, and he seems to treat people well from what I've seen. It's commendable.

I decide to have dinner ready for him when he gets back. He's always doing for me; I'd like to surprise him for once. I throw on some comfy shorts and a camisole, and head out to the kitchen to see what I can scrounge up.

I'm going to grill some seasoned lime chicken and make a nice salad for a side. Something light for tonight's extravaganzas. Even though my body may need rest, it will say otherwise once he's nearby. I can't help the way I react to him. I lose control as though my sex has a mind of its own.

I season and marinate the chicken as I let the grill heat. I prep the salad and stick it back in the fridge. I grab the bowl of chicken heading back out to the deck and as I walk out of the door Gabriele is heading up the back steps. He sees the grill started, the bowl in my hand, and gives me a huge grin.

"And what do we have here?" he asks, walking toward me trying to get a look into the bowl.

I avoid him and sidestep away. "Not so fast, Mr. You go grab a drink and let me get dinner ready."

He looks impressed by my bossiness and puts his hands up. "Okay, okay, master. I'll do as you say for now."

Once he's inside I place the chicken on the grill hearing that sweet sizzling sound. Music begins to play around me. After another twenty minutes or so, Gabriele comes out with two drinks in hand and sits on the seat next to me while I handle the grill.

"Naomi, if I asked you to stop dancing, would you consider it?"

I freeze and turn around slowly in shock. Did I just hear him correctly? Is he asking me to quit my job?

"Excuse me?"

He takes a sip of his drink. "You heard me."

"Why on earth would you ask me such a thing?" I question needing a sip of my own drink.

Has he lost his ever-loving mind? First, he wants nothing to do with a relationship. Second, he wants no children at all. And now, he's asking this of me? Why on god's green earth would I ever consider this? So, I can depend on a man who will want nothing to do with me in the long run?

"Because I can't stand the thought of you going back to that treacherous place. The thought just rips me apart by the day!" he answers, starting to raise his voice.

Now I'm getting pissed. We have already discussed this, and besides he met me doing this line of work. Why have an issue now, because his ego's crushed?

"*Okay*, and you expect me to quit because you're jealous? And what is it you expect me to do for money? Are you going to support me and become my sugar daddy?" I scoff.

He now shoots daggers directly at me with his eyes. "No, not your *sugar daddy*," he says sarcastically. "But I can help you until you figure out what it is you really want to do with your life."

Oh Jesus. Now he wants to be my lord and savoir. Well, I never asked for one and I sure as hell don't want to owe someone a favor for helping me. I guess he doesn't understand how much I profit in this line of work. He's not the only rich man who came by to see me, like I said, I attract the older gentlemen, some that come from wealth and do actually come in for conversation and to watch a dance or two. These types tip extremely well, and I'm not into fashion as much as Dez is, so I've been stacking my money for years. I'm not frivolous with my earnings. I don't need anyone to help take care of me.

I turn, grab the finished chicken from the grill, and head into the kitchen without saying a word. I hear bare footsteps following behind. My blood is now boiling, and I feel another argument brewing on the cusp.

"Why are you walking away from me?" he demands to know stopping short from where I am.

I grab the already made salad out of the fridge, add the oil and vinegar, and begin mixing it. "Because I will not indulge in your tantrum," I tell him while grabbing two plates from the cupboard.

"*My* tantrum?" he questions taken back, angry.

I start divvying up the food onto our plates. He stops me by pushing the plates out of my way and now I'm livid. I slam the utensils down and turn my attention to him. "Yes, your tantrum. I'm not fucking quitting my job until *I* am ready! I don't need anyone taking care of me!" I yell.

"And just so we're clear, I make good money, and everything I make I save. So, I don't need your charity," I growl, poking my finger against his chest.

I don't budge him a bit. He crosses his arms over his chest. Power and authority surge off him, but I'm not backing down. No way.

"Charity hasn't even crossed my mind. That's not what this is about," he sneers.

I cross my arms too and hold my head high. "Then what is this *really* about?"

Without a moment's notice, he grabs my arms and smashes his lips against mine. Our tongues collide, our hands feverishly grasp each other, his hands drag through my hair pulling me closer. My leg climbs up to his side as he reaches under my thighs and sits me on top of the counter.

Every ounce of anger, aggravation, and white-hot desire is branded in this kiss. Gabriele reaches for the hem of my shorts and panties, lifts my butt up, and rips them down my legs throwing them on the floor.

He kisses down my jaw, to my neck, while he unbuttons his shorts pushing them down his legs. My nails dig down his back and without warning he plunges himself into me. I scream out at the unexpected intrusion, as he groans loudly in bliss.

There's no pause allowing me to adjust as he slams into

me hard and fast, the sounds of our bodies slapping together and my juices slicking around us fill the room. This feels exhilarating and full of pure thirst for one another as though we can't get enough. Desperation consumes every inch of our bodies as we fuck like rabbits on top of this counter.

His eyes are now staring directly into mine as his dick slides deeper inside of me. "*This* is what it's about. You're fucking mine, Naomi," he grunts as he pulls back out and plunges into me again. I moan as his tip reaches my sweet spot. "I want to lock you away so no other man can look upon you or touch you ever again because you're *mine*. Do you understand me?" he questions, stopping all movement while waiting for an answer.

I whine not wanting to fall back down from my building orgasm. "Answer me," he demands. "Tell me you're mine and only mine."

This is it, Naomi. Every brick is now tumbling down. There's no way of mending them back now. I am one hundred percent totally fucked as I look deep into his eyes and answer. "I am yours and yours only."

He smirks, possessiveness and triumph glowing from his gaze as he now thrusts back into me with no remorse, pounding deep into me. Driving his dick with such precision and force I gasp. He swallows my screams and his groans with his mouth over mine, gulping every blissful moan down as if his life depends on it. With one last furious pump inside of me, my walls wither, and my core explodes in currents of rippling ecstasy. Gabriele follows tumbling down spilling his hot seed deep inside of me.

We stay embraced, chests heaving, skin layered in sweat just holding each other. This moment was full of raw emotions. I feel completely open and vulnerable and I'm terrified.

Gabriele rubs his hand down my hair and kisses the tip of my nose. "I'm starving."

I look over to our plates. "Well, good thing chicken salads can be eaten cold."

I grab my clothes and head to the bathroom to freshen up. I see my phone light up from a text and open it.

The message is from Trev. "Dez is staying with me. She didn't want to worry you, but she thinks she's being followed."

My heart sinks into my gut. Panic and bile begin to rise through me. I'm immediately brought back to last year when she was attacked, and ever since then I've still had this unsettling feeling every time I walk into our apartment that we're being watched.

I dial Trev's number. He answers on the second ring. "What the fuck, Trev! Why wouldn't she just tell me?" I ask angry.

He sighs. "Because she knows she hasn't been taking you seriously on your warnings. She thought you were just being paranoid."

I start pacing the room. "Jesus, Trev. What changed her mind now?"

Gabriele enters the room stopping as he takes in my frantic face.

"The last two nights she's been seeing a shadow of a man standing outside her window, and when I brought her home last night, I saw it too, so I brought her back to my place," he explains.

I sit down on the bed. Gabriele leans against the doorjamb, listening. "Fuck. I fucking knew it! I'm going to take the next flight out. Make sure she stays put and tell her she needs to take time off work for now. He could be coming to the club as well. We have to figure out who he is," I tell him.

"No, Nay. Just stay put. She's fine here. I'm gonna have a couple of guys stake out the apartment for the next couple of nights and hopefully we can catch him. But there's no need for you to come back and involve yourself," he replies.

Gabriele must be able to hear Trev on the other end. "He's right. You're safer here. I'll hire some professionals to do some investigating. Tell Trevor to keep an eye on her for now until this is figured out."

My heart melts as I let my breath out relieved. Between the both of them, I know we can keep Dez safe. "Where's she now, Trev?"

"She's taking a nap. I'm going to have her call out tonight when she gets up. I'll have her call you then," he advises.

I nod as if he can see me. "Thanks, Trev. I don't think you know how much we both appreciate you," I tell him.

"Awe, stop, Nay. You're making me blush. I love you too. I'll talk to you later."

"Okay."

Our call ends and I just stare at the phone not moving. I guess I'm still in shock. I should have been more determined to get her to listen to me, and now that my feeling was right, I feel icky and creeped out that someone has been watching us this whole time.

Gabriele walks over and sits down on the bed next to me. "Are you okay?"

I lean my head against his shoulder. "I don't know."

He wraps his arm around me holding me tight. "I'm not going to let anyone hurt you. I swear to that," he promises.

"It's not me I'm worried about. Dez doesn't pay attention. She's oblivious to her surroundings and she's way too trusting. I'm shocked she even noticed now. I feel guilty for being here instead of there with her. I should really be there," I express to him.

He shakes his head. "No, you're where you're supposed to be. You would only be in danger if you went back. I can't risk that and Dez is fine with Trevor. He seems like a good friend and won't let anything happen to her."

"I guess you're both right. But do you promise you're going to investigate it for us? I can't go back to the apartment either knowing this creep is still out there," I tell him stressed.

"I promise," he says giving me his word. "Come on, let's go eat."

I SLEPT in late again this morning clearly exhausted from tossing and turning all night long. My brain wouldn't shut off and I kept having these lucid dreams of being stalked. Even though I know going back won't help anything but put myself in danger as well, I still have this weird feeling that I should. Dez needs me, I can feel it.

I jump into the shower to wake myself up. I'm in dire need of some coffee too, but a shower will at least help my muscles relax a bit from the night's tension. I head out of the bedroom, grab a cup of coffee and step out to the deck where I hear Gabriele on the phone.

"Yes, The Parkland Apartments. I'll send you the exact address, and I'll need a twenty-hour watch until we find him. Yes, correct. Keep me updated," he commands.

It's in this moment that I finally admit to myself that I'm madly in love with this man. He's kept his word on protecting my best friend, my sister, and myself. And now seeing how determined he is to keep us safe makes me feel special and cared for. I know I'm still going to have to let go eventually and it's going to rip me in two, but I can no longer control what my heart is feeling.

I sit down next to him on the couch. "Good morning. How are you feeling?" he asks, brushing his fingers down my cheek.

"Sleep definitely evaded me last night. This coffee tastes magical right now," I exaggerate.

"Yeah, you were extremely restless in your sleep last night. I was getting a little worried to be honest," he reveals.

"I just feel really uneasy. I have this bad feeling that something terrible is going to happen. I can't shake it. I guess it's just making me restless in my sleep, but hopefully everything can go back to normal once we figure out who it is," I tell him hopeful.

He rests his hand on my thigh. "My guys are working on it as we speak, and I talked to Trevor this morning. Desire is safe and sound at his place staying put."

I sit up straighter. "Wait, you talked to Trev this morning?" I question surprised but also impressed. "How did you get his number?"

"That night at the club when I brought you home," he answers, smirking.

Yes, I totally forgot about them talking at the bar that night. But Gabriele already checking in with them is sweet and so very sexy as fuck. I lean over and kiss him on the cheek. "Thank you."

He looks taken back. "And what are you thanking me for?"

"For giving a fuck." I smile.

"Oh, I give a fuck alright. I give a fuck what's under these tiny shorts," he jokes, tickling me, pushing me to my back.

He grabs the coffee cup out of my hand before I dump it all over and continues his assault. He has me laughing like a hyena ready to pee my pants. His teasing quickly turns into need as he runs his tongue along my lips. I reach out meeting his with mine, then nip down on him with my teeth. He jerks back, then grins like I'm about to be in for it.

We kiss possessively and slowly until he takes my bottom lip with his teeth and nibbles. I groan and grind my sex into his already hard bulge. He moans into my mouth. I reach for his waistband but stop at the sound of someone clearing their throat.

We both look up from our frenzied lust induced heat. "Sorry to bother you, Mr. Vanucci, but you weren't answering your calls, and we have a bit of an emergency at the main house," a man in a security uniform informs him.

Gabriele jumps up. "I'll be back," he says sternly, jaw tight with aggravation as he follows the guard down the steps.

Well, that's not a good sign. He and Joanna had said before that there hadn't been any issues as of yet. Hopefully, this one is just a minor one. I decide a swim is necessary to relieve all this added stress. We only have another week and a half left here and I'm sure I'll never have another chance to visit this place since it's members only, so I'm going to soak it all in while I can.

Since the beach is private, I chance it and walk down topless. I brought a towel with me to lay out where the water meets the sand. I want the feel of the water against my skin without fully immersing myself.

My phones rings after thirty minutes or so out here. Gabriele's number is on the screen. *Weird.* He just left. I see Gabriele's charter plane fly overhead. "Hey, is everything okay?"

"Yes. It's handled. I just needed to hear your voice," he advises in a strained voice.

"What happened?"

"There was a difference of opinion with a member, so I revoked his membership and sent him off the island," he tells me. That must be why I saw the plane just now.

The warm water glides over my legs and up the back of my body. I watch the plane get smaller the farther it departs.

"I don't understand. Has this happened before?" I question.

"No. I'm on my way back now though. Johnathan will be staying with us tonight, so make sure you're dressed appropriately," he tells me.

I sit up quickly. "Wait, who's Johnathan?"

"Security. Don't worry, we're not doing a round two tonight," he teases.

I roll my eyes. "See you soon."

TWENTY MINUTES later Gabriele pulls up with the security guy, Johnathan with a duffel bag towed over his shoulder. I stay on the daybed as Gabriele greets me with a kiss and Johnathn nods hello before Gabriele shows him inside.

This is extremely strange. Something unsettling must have happened for Gabriele to require security by our side for the night. He comes back out with a plate filled with varieties of fruit and hands it to me.

"Eat."

"Gabriele, why do we need security?" I ask, taking a bite of a juicy mango.

He sits next to me laying back on the pillow, placing his hands behind his head. "Because sometimes people don't agree with rules, especially those with money. And sometimes threats are made when mad, so just to be on the safe side I have Johnathan here."

I stop chewing. "I don't understand. What kind of threats?"

He leans over and kisses me, then puts his finger on my lips. "Shhh, no more questions. Let's just enjoy the rest of the day."

I think with all the drama that's been going on I didn't realize we never finished our heated discussion on me not working at the club. It seems as if he may have moved on from it, but the issue was never actually resolved. He seems preoccupied with the festivities from earlier and I'm not sure if now is the best time to bring it back up.

"Gabriele?" I look over to him with his eyes closed just enjoying the breeze of the island.

"Hmmm?" he answers without opening his eyes.

He looks so serene and beautiful just lying there. I can't

help but drift my eyes lazily over the whole surface of his body. There's nothing like a man in some casual shorts and an unbuttoned shirt to make your body sing with longing.

"Are you going to ask your question, or just continue to stare?" He chuckles.

I didn't realize I was so obvious. "About last night," I start to say.

"I'm sorry, I got carried away. I don't know what got into me, but my offer still stands. I would love to help you out of this lifestyle. You deserve so much more, Naomi," he says to me now looking at me admiringly.

I feel some guilt over getting so defensive. "Thank you for the offer, but I do have plans of my own. I'm not as naïve and ignorant as I might seem. This job doesn't define me, it's merely a means to an end."

"I know what people think of me when they see me because of what I do, and there are times I feel as though I don't deserve things in this world because of my choice, because I have sold my soul in a way to make fast money. But this won't be me forever. It's just me for now," I justify myself to him.

He slips his fingers through my hair rubbing his thumb along my cheek. "Fuck what people think, and I've never for one second thought of you as weak or anything less because of your dancing. You're fucking one of the strongest women I know, little ballerina. You've overcome a lot, and I admire the fight in you," he tells me.

I close my eyes and lean my cheek into his palm. "Thank you for that. You always know the right words to say."

"Now, tell me, what are these plans you have?" he questions.

I sit up more and cross my legs. "Well, I've been saving up enough for a personal bank of my own. I've been studying stock trading and I've been dabbling in paper trading until I feel comfortable enough to deposit real money in.

"When I told Dez and Trev about it they thought I was a bit crazy so I've kind of kept that idea to myself lately," I say waiting for him to laugh or tell me that I'm crazy as well.

He looks to me stunned. "You think I'm out of my league also, huh?" I ask, feeling a bit self-conscious.

"Not at all. I know a handful of extremely successful traders. And when I say successful, I'm talking hundreds of thousands in profit. This career path comes with many risks but with the potential to have very high rewards. If this is your dream, then I say go for it," he supports.

I scoot myself in between his legs and lay back with my head against his stomach. We stay like this for a while in silence and he runs his fingers through my hair. I feel nothing but complete contentment at this moment. I don't ever want this feeling to end. I wish we could stay like this forever.

CHAPTER 15

*T*he last couple of days have been stressful. Gabriele's guys still haven't been able to find the stalker, which has me extremely worried since Dez is getting antsy about staying at Trev's house any longer. I've been arguing with her about not going back to work. She keeps telling me she'll be fine at work since we always get walked out. But even with Trev walking me out I still always feel uneasy since it's so dim in the parking lot.

Also, Johnathan is still with us staying in Gabriele's room, so we haven't had too much time to ourselves. I'm feeling needy and desperate for his touch. We don't have too much time left together and who knows how things will play out once we're back home. I just need to get my last fill of him in before the newness dies down and he finds something better once we're back to reality.

My feelings for him grow stronger by the day resonating with me more during the nights as he holds me and kisses me before falling asleep. He has such a soft passionate side that completely melts me into a puddle of goo. I am utterly ruined for the next man now. No one will ever compare to him, and I'm not sure my body will ever react to another the same.

I want so badly to tell him my feelings. To tell him that I'm in love with him, to beg him to change his mind and to just take a chance of having a future with me, but then I remember who I am, and who he is, and I'm brought back to reality. If I say these words out loud then they're out there and there's nothing I can do to stop him from crushing me, but if I just hold on to them and hold them close, then maybe, just maybe I will make it out of this okay in the end.

I open the door to the steamy shower, letting myself oogle Gabriele's backside with the water cascading over his skin. His sculptured muscles flex and harden as he moves the soap over his body. I step in closing the distance between us, running my hands over his back, around to his abs, and lower to his stiff cock. He groans leaning his head back.

Slowly, I run my palm up then down in stern hard strokes. He hisses pumping himself further into my hands. I reach his balls with my other hand, squeezing gently and he nearly loses it. He suddenly grabs my hands turning around and pushes my back against the tile wall. His hands slide through my wet hair pulling down, so he has complete access to my neck.

He kisses and nibbles his way up my neck to my lips. I open, allowing his tongue to glide into my mouth tangling with mine. His kiss is full of demanding need, and I swallow every ounce of it up.

"Turn around," he instructs. "Palms on the wall."

I do as he says while he trails kisses down my spine, then grabs a towel placing it under his knees as he kneels behind me. I look over my shoulder feeling a bit self-conscious with his face being so close to my most intimate parts.

"Don't feel embarrassed, little ballerina. Your body is perfectly beautiful," he tells me. "Besides, I've already seen every inch of it," he finishes with a wink.

Heat crawls up my body leaving my face flushed with pinkness. His fingers skate up my calves trailing up my inner thigh and grazing over the apex of my sex. I moan at the feathery feel of his fingertips as I arch my back pushing my sex closer into his view.

He grabs my hips pulling me toward him and forces my legs further apart. "Bend over more." I do as he asks. "Good girl. Now give me your hands and lean your head against the wall," he directs. I reach my hands back and he places them on my ass cheeks.

"Now spread them for me," he says. I hesitate. "Naomi, do as your told."

I spread my cheeks for him and immediately I feel his tongue lick from my clit through my folds and enter my sex. He pushes his tongue deep inside of me while his finger circles my little bud. Sparks ignite through my core as a moan rips out of me.

"Fuck you taste so sweet," he murmurs as he thrusts his tongue back into me over and over.

This whole position, being so open and vulnerable to him, makes it that much more intense. My whole body is singing with the need for release. The pressure builds with the continuous strokes of my clit as his tongue laps around my entrance, through my folds, and now back up to my puckered tight ass.

I jerk my hips forward from the intrusion, but his fingers grip my hips harder bringing me fully back to him. "Don't move. Just let go and feel," he commands me.

His tongue licks over my puckered entrance. The feel is foreign but good. His fingers slide from my clit to my sex as he dips two fingers inside me while probing his tongue into my ass. I let out a deep moan from both sensations.

"I'm going to fuck this tight ass soon. I'm going to be the first to enter every part of you," Gabriele growls between licks.

"I think I'd like that," I tell him shyly. The way he talks is such a stimulating turn on. I could listen to him all day long. He's completely unashamed and unapologetic, and it's the sexiest thing to witness.

Gabriele stands to his feet and shifts my hands to the wall. "Hold on, because I'm going to fuck you hard and fast."

The tip of his dick is now rubbing against my sex and in one fast movement he slams into me taking me by surprise almost knocking me forward. I hold on for dear life as he pummels deep into me repeatedly. The sound of his grunts are wild and animalistic, and I love every minute of it as my walls ripple around him desperately.

I push my hips back, meeting his thrusts allowing him to slam deeper into me. His right hand runs up my side to my breast then tweaks my nipple hard and rolls the peak between his fingertips. I scream out feeling my insides clench harder begging for my release.

"Fuck yes, baby. God, your pussy is so fucking tight," he yells out.

His other hand slaps my ass hard echoing the sound against the shower walls. The vibration from the spank fires up my building orgasm as his finger now rims my ass and slips slowly inside of my tight anus. I scream out from the fullness and the newness of this feeling that now completely engulfs me, sending me over the edge. Waves bulldoze through my system catapulting straight to my core.

"That's right. Come for me, baby. Come all over my cock," Gabriele shouts, now removing his finger and leaning over to reach my swollen clit. All it takes is one lap around and I'm a goner.

My walls grasp around his shaft and my floodgates open as my orgasm rips through me. In the next moment Gabriele slams his hips into my ass, dick to the hilt inside of me, and roars out a loud guttural groan spilling his seed deep within me.

We stay this way attempting to catch our breaths. Every single time with him is like a first time. Sex with us just ebbs and flows like we are made for each other. He slips out of me and helps me stand straight turning me into him and wrapping his arms around me.

"I'm never going to be able to get enough of you," he admits, leaning his forehead against mine. "Just thinking of another man having what's mine makes me crazy."

He grabs my ass cheeks. "You're fucking mine, Naomi. Do you understand me? *Mine.*"

I don't even know what to say to this. Before, when he said this, I shook it off as though we were just in the heat of the moment, but this time something feels different; more real, more intense. And now I'm even more confused than ever.

"Gabriele, you shouldn't say things like this," I scold him.

He grabs the soap and begins washing me. "Why not?"

"Because I've fallen in love with you, and when you say things like this it just gives me false hope," I finally confess.

I didn't mean to. I told myself I wasn't going to say it out loud. I told myself I was going to remain strong, but the words just slipped out. After the sex we just had and hearing his claim on me, my emotions just got the best of me, and now I'm stuck with the aftermath.

As soon as he heard the words leave my mouth he froze. I keep my eyes down on the floor afraid to look up into his. Afraid of what I might see. Scared to death of the rejection I know is coming and I tried so hard to avoid.

Gabriele lifts my chin so I'm now looking deep into his eyes. I want so badly just to look away, but he holds me here tight.

"If I was capable of love, then my feelings would be the same," he informs me then kisses me on the forehead and leaves me standing alone in the shower.

The now hot steaming shower feels cold and desolate. I

stand under the water blank and void of thought or feeling. I'm numb. I confessed my feelings for him, and he just walked away. I guess I could have gotten worse. He told me basically if in a different world he would have felt the same, but it's not the case now. I'm alone in how I feel and even though he feels possessive about me it all comes down to sex. This is what his caveman animalistic jealousy stems from, and nothing more.

I turn off the shower and step out getting dressed. I stop at the bathroom door with my hand on the handle unable to open it. The anxiety I'm feeling is overwhelming. I try to take deep slow breaths but I'm starting to feel like I did the other day in the ocean.

The walls are closing in on me. I step back and sit down on the stool at the makeup counter trying to avoid another episode of passing out. This time I have no one near me to break my fall so I concentrate on my breathing and keeping myself together.

After a couple of moments my breathing falls back to normal and I'm able to stand. *You're strong, Naomi. You can do this,* I say, giving myself a pep talk. I head out into the bedroom and finish getting dressed. Instead of exiting my bedroom door, I head out the sliding door down toward the beach. I just need to ground myself, feeling the sand between my toes, water on my feet, and the breeze against my skin before I see Gabriele again. I'm praying to gather some strength from nature itself.

I decide to call Trev and get some advice from a male perspective. He always knows just what to say to calm me.

"Hey, Nay. What's up?"

"How's Dez?" I ask.

He sighs. "I don't know how much longer I can hold her captive. She's threatening to tie me up so she can escape," he replies laughing, but I still hear some concern in his voice.

"Shit. I thought Gabriele's guys would have caught him by now."

"Yeah, me too. This guy must know they're staking the place out. She's going back to work tonight. I tried to convince her to give it a little more time, but she just won't listen. Maybe we need to give her an intervention," he explains.

I start to walk down the beach. I look over toward the house and see Gabriele watching me from the deck while sipping on a cup of coffee. "That's a good idea. We'll do a FaceTime call this afternoon with her when she's up."

"What else has been going on? How's hot billionaire man treating you?" he asks.

I huff. "Ut oh. Talk to me, Nay."

I go into detail explaining what just happened in the shower, minus the sex details and he just laughs.

"What the fuck are you laughing about?" I demand to know aggravated. Here's another man, one of my best friends, I just poured my heart out to and he's laughing at me like my feeling are no big deal.

"Are you the fucking oblivious, Nay?" Trev replies.

"Trev, if you don't spit it out, I'm going to throat punch you when I see you next!" I growl.

He scoffs. "The man is in love with you too!" he screeches. "He just can't admit it to himself yet, so he sure as hell isn't going to admit it to you."

I roll my eyes. "I know you're trying to make me feel better, and he might care about me, but it's just the sex that's making him act this way."

"Listen, sex always helps in keeping a man around and occupied for a while, but I think he fell for you way before that. Don't ask me how I know, I just know with being a man myself, even though I'm a gay man, I know men the best," he jokes.

"Just give him time to admit this to himself first, then the rest will follow," he finishes.

I sigh. "I still say he's just a jealous heathen, but I'll let it go for now. How's Adam? Have you admitted to yourself that you have feelings yet?" I turn the tables on him now.

"Nay, I'm fucked too. He's been staying here almost every night and I'm getting freaked out because I'm not tired of him yet. And he's been so patient with Dez too. She freaking loves him. I'm ready to tell him we need a break; it's just moving too fast," he explains.

I realize how far I've walked. I look back and can't even see the house any longer, so I turn back around. "Don't you dare, Trev. Don't you ruin it with your nonsense! You deserve this," I shout.

He laughs. "Okay, *mom!* Geez!"

"So, what about Luke? Is he still trying to reach out to Dez?" I wonder. I haven't heard much about him in the past week.

"Girl, he still calls twice a day. She unblocked him, so he's been leaving pleading messages to talk, but she's still not ready yet."

I know her. She unblocked him because she wants to hear his grovels. She wants to hear his voice without actually hearing it face to face, but she's not ready to hear his excuses yet because she knows as soon as she does, she will be a goner and will take him back. I know my friend all too well and how she thinks. Unblocking him was step one of getting closer.

"Ugh, she's totally going to give in soon. I know it," I tell him.

"Yep, she sure is. Shit, she's getting up. Call me around three and we'll have a little chat with her."

"Okay. Love you, Trev."

"Love you too," he replies before hanging up.

I now stand in front of the house. Gabriele is still sitting on the deck waiting for me. *Shit*. I was hoping he had to leave or deal with an issue before I got back, clearly no such luck. He looks to be deep in thought as he watches me walk up the steps.

I don't know whether to walk past him or to say hi. I'm at a loss for words at the moment and trying so hard to get my big girl panties on. The awkward tension is killing me. I decide that coffee is needed so, I smile and attempt my way past him, but no such luck. His arm sticks out blocking my way as he grabs my hip and brings me down on his lap.

"Where do you think you're going?" he questions, moving my hair aside and inhaling the scent at my neck.

My nipples perk up while I wiggle my bum in his lap. I feel him smile against my neck being pleased he is already affecting me again.

"Was just going in for some coffee," I say breathlessly.

He rubs his nose up and down the side of my neck. "Stop thinking so much, just let things be," he says in my ear. "I have a boat waiting for us. I thought you might want to enjoy a day on the water."

I look to him with mixed emotions but decide to heed his advice and tuck it all inside for now.

"Okay."

He kisses my lips softly. "Pack a small bag. We're going to stay overnight."

I must admit this brightens my mood a bit. Even though I still feel out of sorts from earlier he's making it easy to fall back into step with him. He still touches me the same, and he still looks at me as though I'm the only woman in the entire world.

"What about Johnathan?"

He scoots me off his lap. "Johnathan left back to the main house this morning. We no longer require his services."

Confusion takes over my face. "So, everything is fine

now?" I ask, wondering what changed over the past couple of days.

"At the moment, yes. Now go gather your things," he instructs slapping me on the butt.

I head to the bedroom and grab a night's worth of clothes and my charger. I set my phone alarm to three, so I don't forget about the intervention Trev and I have set up for Dez. Gabriele walks in the room, and it's like the air immediately gets sucked out. I'll never get used to the sex appeal this man alludes every time he enters a room.

"You almost ready? The boat just docked."

"Yeah, one second." I grab one last necessity from the bathroom and throw it in my bag. "Okay, ready."

He locks up, grabs my bag for me, and I follow him down toward the water. "Where are we going?" I ask curiously as we walk the opposite way I ventured the other day. I haven't walked this way down the beach yet.

We walk a good five minutes before I see a boat up ahead attached to a long single pier. I look to the palm trees to see if there are any houses nearby, but there's nothing. Why would he have built a pier in the middle of nowhere?

"Gabriele, why is there a pier here?" I question.

"Because I wanted access to a boat but wanted to keep my house private and the view unobstructed so, I built this out of the way but close enough to walk to," he explains.

That makes way more sense than I was trying to put together in my head. "This boat looks amazing. I've never seen one like this before."

"It's called a catamaran. It's more of a lounge boat. I have a chef on there preparing us lunch and then dinner later, but I thought maybe we can catch some rays and go for a swim at one of the sandbanks," he tells me as we begin our way down the pier.

The boat looks even bigger up close. There's three men

waiting for us as we step up the plank, one holding drinks on a tray and the others with large welcoming smiles.

"Good afternoon, Mr. Vanucci." They greet him then nod to me. "Miss Veil."

"Afternoon, Captain Cruz, Mr. Martinez, and Chef Donte. I appreciate the short notice. Is everything ready for sail off?" Gabriele asks the captain.

Chef Donte hands us our drinks. "Thank you," I tell him.

"Yes, everything's in order, sir," Captain Cruz replies. "Mr. Martinez, please bring up the buoy and untie the boat," the captain orders.

"Yes, sir." Mr. Martinez nods heading to the front of the boat.

"Lunch will be served on the deck in thirty minutes," Chef Donte advises Gabriele.

Gabriele nods. "Thank you, men. I appreciate it."

They both take off to their stations. Gabriele leads me down the stairs to the cabin below. The living area is quaint, nicely lit up from the large windows surrounding us, and there's a bedroom at the back. I look around wondering where the other men will be staying.

"Is there another area of the boat? Where will the crew stay tonight?" I ask.

We head to the bedroom; he lays our bags down on the bed. "There are crew quarters where they will stay for the night and a kitchen where the food is prepared. But don't you worry, this cabin is extremely soundproof. I made sure of that." He smirks.

"Wait, do you own this boat too?" I ask, not sure why I would be surprised since he owns everything else.

He grins. "I do. Why do you seem so surprised?"

"I don't know. I guess I'm still not used to all of this. It's a lot," I admit.

He walks over, stands in front of me grabbing my hand

and kissing it. "Well get used to it, because when you're by my side, you will be smothered in luxury."

My eyes roll as I sigh. I'm feeling a bit smothered right now, and luxury is the last thing I want. I want to shut the world out and not think for a moment – *not feel*. That's what I want because I just know as soon as we step back off his plane, the only thing I'll be getting used to is his void.

"You seriously can be infuriating, you know that?" I say annoyed.

He chuckles. "Oh, that I am completely aware of but regardless, I think you quite enjoy it," he brags then runs his lips gently along mine.

Jesus, he knows exactly how to light my body on fire. It never takes much from him, but this isn't fair one bit. My lips blaze from the afterburn of his touch. I feel the boat shift as we take off into the open waters. Gabriele drops to his knees without warning, unties the side of my bikini letting it pool around my feet.

He lifts my leg placing it over his shoulder giving him full access to my sex. He looks up to me from under his long lashes as he takes one large swipe up the center of my core. I moan instantly at the feeling. His tongue strokes my clit in featherlight licks while he soaks his fingers in my juices.

I lean my hand on the dresser next to me for support as he builds me up dipping his fingers inside me adding pressure to my bundle of nerves while still watching me. Our eyes never waiver from one another as he continuously administers soft licks and strokes.

The moment he pushes his fingers deep into me curving just enough to hit my textured spot I scream out and begin to unravel.

"That's right, baby. I want you to come all over my fingers."

The way he commands my body with his voice just does something to me. I can't explain it. It's as though I have no more willpower. I've given myself completely over to him with a fight. Every piece of me is now owned by him. I belong to him.

He sucks me into his mouth, grazing his teeth over my swollen bud while administering precise strokes to my already rippling core. The way he watches me come undone drives me wild. The slurps and the sounds of my wetness as his fingers glide along my walls echo in the room.

I moan out as my body begins to convulse around his fingers. "Come for me, my little ballerina," he commands in between assaults. And I do just that. I come hard and fast all over his tongue and fingers. He doesn't let up until every ounce of me has released and I'm now Jell-O unable to stand.

Gabriele removes his fingers, and they are glistening, drenched in my arousal. He slides my leg off his shoulder, stands, and then sucks every last drop of me off his fingers closing his eyes while savoring every last morsel. God, I love when he does that. I swear I could come just watching his vulgar ways.

"I just had to have my dessert first," he informs me winking.

"You're insatiable."

"Only for you," he responds, kissing me on the nose.

A voice comes over the intercom informing us lunch is ready on the top deck.

"I'll meet you upstairs. I need to change and freshen up," I advise, leaving him while I head to the bathroom.

He enjoyingly watches my naked bum walk away. I look back at him with a grin, knowing he's already ready to pounce on me again, but I shut the door behind me locking him out. If I don't cut him off now, we won't leave this room for the rest of the night. Although I wouldn't mind being ravaged for hours, I'd also like to enjoy this experience I may never have again.

After I clean myself up and change, I head upstairs. I grab

onto the railing as the sea is a bit choppy. Mr. Martinez meets me at the top of the stairs.

"Hello, Miss Veil. Mr. Vannuci asked me to escort you to the top deck. If you will follow me," he says as he heads up one more flight of stairs.

Mr. Martinez is an older gentleman with sun-weathered skin, salt and pepper hair, and dark chocolate brown eyes. His accent is that of creole, the native language. He seems shy but experience of life shines in his eyes, wisdom and so much knowledge.

Gabriele comes into view. His phone is up to his ear on a call while he sips a coffee. When he notices me, his eyes twinkle, the smirk causes tiny wrinkles on the corners of his eyes. I keep his eye contact as I walk toward him. There's no mistaking that the sexual tension is always radiating from us. Mr. Martinez clears his throat, noticing it as well.

He smiles between us. "Is there anything else I can assist with?" he asks.

"No, Joel. We're all set for now. Thank you," Gabriele says, sending him on his way.

I pour myself some coffee while I wait for him to finish his business call. I hear bits and pieces before I put two and two together. He's talking with the guy he has hired to find Dez's stalker.

"Yes, well that means he's getting bolder now," Gabriele responds. "She's still directed not to come home," he answers.

I hear the male voice murmur on the other end, though I can't make out what he's saying.

"Okay, I need a report back to me tonight," he demands and puts his hand up.

He sees the question in my eyes. "Yes, that was one of my guys. He saw a man that fit the description last night, but they scared him off. We think he's beginning to become impatient," he explains.

"Shit! I have a call with Trev soon to do an intervention

with Dez. She's freaking out and now refusing to stay put," I tell him. "What if she doesn't listen, Gabriele?" I ask scared.

He wraps his arm around my shoulder. "You have to try your hardest to make her understand. My guys will do what they can, but they really think it's only a matter of days before they are able to catch him. I will send them a text warning them of her possible moves. I have a guy outside of Trevor's apartment as well," he says.

I seriously can't handle a repeat of last year. She got so lucky that nothing worse happened to her, but what if it's the same guy? If that's the case he may be after her for revenge for locking him up.

"Gabriele, what if it's the same guy that attacked her before?"

He's now in thinking mode. "Do you remember his name? I can have someone see if he's still incarcerated."

I shake my head. "I'll have to ask Dez. I can't remember."

Gabriele passes me a plate. "For now, eat," he instructs.

I still can't shake this nagging feeling that something is off – something bad is going to happen. I hate even thinking this way with the thought of putting it out in the air and jinxing the whole situation but no matter which way I try to turn it, I get the same results.

The chef has laid out grilled lobster and fish, ceviche and chips, and an array of fresh fruits. How am I ever supposed to go back to regular eating after being spoiled for so long. Dez doesn't cook. She's the ordering queen, and Trev would rather go out to eat so he can stare at hotties the whole time and people watch.

Other than cooking for myself, this is the most I've had someone cook for me since my mother passed away. I fill my plate with a little bit of everything, then Gabriele fills my plate a little more.

"This is all protein. You need to eat more to keep up your strength because what I have planned for you tonight requires all your stamina," he informs me with a mischievous grin.

I laugh. "Oh boy. You're making me a little nervous."

"No worries, my little ballerina. Only pleasure and fun," he clears up giving me a peck on the cheek.

WE FINISH our lunch and head to the front bow where there's a lounge net allowing us to catch some rays. I must have fallen asleep because I woke up to my phone's alarm going off. Shit. It's time to call Dez. Thank God I put the maximum strength sunscreen on, or I'd be toast right now.

Gabriele is still next to me with his hands behind his head like he doesn't have a care in the world. He stretches when he sees me awake.

"I have to make this call to Dez," I tell him getting up to grab my phone.

He nods and follows so he can listen in on the call.

I FaceTime Trev's number and he answers on the second ring.

"Hey girl, you ready?" he asks seeming nervous.

I nod. "Ready."

I gather all my strength ready to say whatever I need to in order to get her to stay put.

He walks into the living room. "Guess who I have on the phone?" he says overly dramatic.

He turns the phone to show my face. "Hey, Dez! I miss you!" I tell her.

She waves her hand excitedly. "When are you coming home?" Dez demands to know, pouting.

I look over to Gabriele for a split second. "Next week."

"Good cause we need a three amigos night out. I'm dying to get out of the jail cell Trev has me in," she whines.

"Listen Dez, I need you to hang on. I know you're getting

antsy, but Gabriele's men think they saw him last night around the apartment. You have to stay put for just a little bit longer," I explain.

Trev stays quiet letting me do the brunt of the work since he knows she's going to already give him hell once we hang up. "Nay, I'm going to work tonight. I'll be fine once I get there. Gabriele's guys are everywhere right now. No one's getting past them."

I sigh. "They can't watch everything you know. This guy already ran from them once. What if it's the same guy that attacked you last year? What if he's come back to get revenge?" I question.

It looks as though she hadn't thought of that idea. I'm not sure how something like that wouldn't possibly cross her mind, but Dez is Dez, she is just oblivious. It drives me up the wall.

She huffs. "Okay, okay. You both win. I will continue to be Rapunzel in the tower, but only for a few more days and I'm out."

I roll my eyes. "Fine. We'll take it. But promise me you will call when that moment happens. I'm gonna check on you every couple of hours too," I threaten. "I mean it."

She giggles. "Yes, mom."

Trev looks relieved that I got some sense into her. "Oh, and text me the guy's name that attacked you last year. Gabriele's going to have his guys check to make sure he's still incarcerated."

"Okay."

"Love you guys," I tell them both before ending the call.

I lean back in the chair thanking God that went so well. Now I just need to keep on her. She's never been able to stay still for too long, and the way she spends money, she has no choice but to keep up with her habits.

"I'm still going to make sure my guys are extra vigil with her. She didn't convince me," Gabriele advises honestly.

I look over to him, brows furrowed, and curious. "What makes you say that?"

"Let's just say it's a sixth sense I have. I've perfected it over the years in business," he clarifies.

He opens his phone and shoots out a quick text message. I walk over and sit on his lap. "Thank you for everything," I express.

"You know Luke's worried about her too," he tells me.

I feel shocked and a little confused. I thought he didn't want to get involved in his brother's personal affairs. "Did you tell him what has been going on?"

"One of the security guards saw him going to the apartment to try to talk to Desire the other day, so he explained to Luke what was going on and why they were there. That triggered a call to me. He's worried so he's doing what he can to help, and has been on watch as well," Gabriele informs me.

I'm caught off guard with the news. "Wow, I didn't realize he really cares. That's very thoughtful of him."

"I think you'll find that not everything is always what it seems. I think once he speaks with Desire, she may think differently," he tells me.

I'm starting to think he may be right. Maybe she should have just heard him out, but she doesn't have a good track record with men, so I was doing my best to try to help her protect her heart. Maybe I have been actually holding her back from something that could really be good for her.

"Maybe you're right. I've been quick to judge. But in my defense, I've learned it's extremely hard and dangerous to let just anyone in. Trust issues run deep for me, so since Dez is always way more trusting than I am, I always do what I can to try to protect her," I try to clarify.

"You're a good friend, little ballerina. I admire your strength, and your love for your friends. It's an amazing quality to hold in such a shitty world."

"Who are you close with, Gabriele?"

I've never even asked about friends or seen him with anyone other than his brother. I don't know why I never thought to ask. Maybe I've been a little selfish, only worrying about my own friends.

"Unfortunately, I've had to weed out a lot of people that were in my life once my father passed. I was on a downward spiral before then and the crowd I was hanging with during that time I realized were no good. I cleaned myself up and cleaned the toxic out of my life.

"Once I took over my dad's company and his inheritance, people became different. You learn very quickly who you can and can't trust. My world is full of leeching sharks. I got bitten one too many times and learned my lessons the hard way," he explains.

My heart aches for him. I know money and power can bring out the worst in people, I'm just glad Gabriele is humbled and kind. I'm not sure I would have liked meeting the younger version of him.

"I'm sorry, Gabriele. It sounds like your world is tough. I know you've mentioned some things about it, but I didn't think about how horrible some of the people might be. I know from experience men with money think they can do as they please, but I'm glad you don't seem to be like those men," I say with ample appreciation.

"Oh, don't get me wrong, I am also one to use my money to get what I want," he says with a devious smirk. "Money is what gets me things like this, and I quite enjoy being able to get the chance to bring a beautiful girl back here to seduce."

I laugh. He's always so confident and sure of himself. It's cute and boy did he seduce the virginity right out of me.

I smack him on the chest. "You're such an ass."

"But you love my ass," he tries to joke, but instead of it coming off as a joke, it reminds me of this morning and my confession I almost forgot about.

He must catch my face drop as I turn away looking out to

the water. He takes hold of my chin bringing me back to face him. "Hey, what's with the face?"

"Just thinking of Dez," I lie.

He searches my eyes deeply as though reading me but decides to allow me to continue with my lie. "You've done what you can," he says. "Now, let's go for a swim. We've made it to the sandbank."

I stand not even realizing we've anchored. There is a large sand beach in the middle of the crystal-clear waters of the sea. Just water and blue skies every which way I turn to look. Being out here, looking at this beautiful force of nature, makes me feel like such a small insignificant part of this world. I'm just a tiny speck in this mystical place, and then I look over to Gabriele who is staring at me as though I'm his whole world. Funny how that works.

Gabriele puts the phone down on the table, heads down the stairs off the back of the boat and jumps in. He looks like a magical merman glistening in the water. My thighs rub together with just the thought of wrapping them around him and grinding my sex over his shaft in the middle of this ocean. Just us, the sea, the fish, and *fuck* – the crew. Not such a good idea.

"Come on slowpoke!" Gabriele yells.

"So demanding!" I shout back as I head down the stairs to meet him on the sand.

I wade through the water to the sandbank. I jump on Gabriele's back, and he carries me down the beach.

"I could carry you all day long, as long as I got to touch these legs," he says, slapping my thigh hard. I squeal.

I take advantage running my hands over his chest and then down over his abs. I could touch these rock-hard muscles all day long. As a matter of fact, I'm ready to run my tongue over the whole front of him, devouring him to the bone.

"I bet if you slide down further, there's more hard things to fondle," Gabriele jokes.

I smack his arm. He lets me down to my feet and we walk the beach hand in hand.

"So, what do you have planned when we get back to reality?" I ask him.

"I'll have to fly out to New York for some business, but I won't be gone for long. When I come back, I plan on consuming you from head to toe," he teases, bringing my hand to his mouth for a kiss.

He looks like he's ready to indulge on me again as we speak. "Do you have a house out there too?"

"I actually do," he replies. "Oh, look!" he says, pointing out to the sea.

Diving in and out of the water are about five to six dolphins following a speedboat cruising by us. They glide flawlessly through the water. I have a grin ear to ear. Gabriele watches me as I jump up and down like an excited child.

"They like following the boat engines," he tells me.

"Wow, I wish I could see them closer. I've seen video of them underwater. It sounds like they're singing to each other in different high pitches, like a beautiful melody," I explain.

"Who knows, maybe we will get lucky, and we'll have some follow our boat back to the house."

CHAPTER 16

*W*e stayed on the beach for a couple more hours. Gabriele grabbed some chairs and drinks, and we made a beach day of it. It was relaxing with the perfect postcard view. We headed back to the boat for dinner once both of our stomachs started talking to each other.

We took another hour to shower and get ready for dinner due to Gabriele fucking me hard against the shower wall. I'm not sure I can walk now. The way he held me up with his arms while he pounded into me would have definitely been a sight to see, pure caveman porno style. After, Gabriele went up to the deck first to make sure everything was going smoothly with the staff while I finished getting dressed.

I hear my phone continuously ringing and chiming with text message notifications. I didn't realize how many I missed until I picked up my phone and saw tons of notifications piled up across my phone. *What the fuck?*

I look at the first one from Trev and it says Dez is gone. My breath catches in my throat, and I can't breathe putting my hand over my lower neck. I gasp as I continue on reading. The next one says she won't pick up. Then the next one says she's not at the apartment or work. And the last one I read with shaky hands is Trev saying call me, she's in the hospital.

I almost drop the phone hyperventilating. How can this be? She had security on her. How the fuck did she sneak off? I call Trev so fast with tears streaming down my cheeks. My vision is blurry, I can barely see the phone in front of me. I feel so lost, panicked, and full of guilt for not being there.

Trev picks up on the first ring. "Trev! What the fuck? Where is she?" I scream. Gabriele and the staff can probably hear me from the top deck I'm in such turmoil.

"She's in ICU, Nay. I'm sorry. I went to take a shower and when I got out, she was gone," he says in distress.

Gabriele comes running down the stairs to the room with his phone to his ear. He grabs me and pulls me in tight to his chest while I start sobbing. Trev's still on the phone listening.

"Nay, she's going to make it. She's gonna pull through. She *has* to pull through," Trev does his best to comfort me.

Gabriele lets go and walks away yelling on the phone. "How the fuck did you let her slip by you?" he screams. "You were supposed to be watching her!"

"What happened, Trev? Is she going to be okay?" I ask between sobs.

He clears his throat before speaking. "It all happened so fast. She went to go into work, and he caught her in the parking lot. His car was parked in the alley beside the club, and he tried to drag her there, but our girl's a fighter and she fought for her life. He beat her bad, Nay. And he would have taken her if it weren't for Jadah coming in for her shift and heard her screaming," he explains.

"Oh my god, thank god!" Is the only thing that comes out of my mouth in disbelief.

"Jadah ran inside to grab a bouncer and within seconds they chased him away, but Luke was already on his way looking for her and chased the guy down. Nay, you were right though," Trev stalls.

"What Trev? Spit it out! Right about what?" I demand to know.

"You were right. It was the man who attacked her from last year. The things they found in his car were not good. He planned some very evil stuff," he reveals.

Gabriele walks back into the room off the phone now. "She snuck out the basement from the other building that's connected. My guys weren't watching that side of the building," Gabriele informs me.

I turn my attention back to Trev putting him on speaker phone so Gabriele can listen in. "What did they find in his car?"

He exhales loudly. "He had duct tape, rope, some torture devices, a gun on him, and a shovel."

I sit down on the bed no longer able to stand. Jesus Christ. I can't even speak, I'm horrified. Gabriele speaks for me.

"How is she Trevor? What did the doctors say?" Gabriele questions.

I can now hear beeping in the background and shuffling I hadn't noticed a moment ago. "She has some broken ribs, a fractured skull, and she's in a coma right now. They need to wait for the swelling to go down to know anything further."

"Trev, I'm coming. I'm coming back as soon as possible," I tell him panicking.

I need to be there. I can't stay in this fucking place any longer with my best friend fighting for her life.

I look up at Gabriele. "I need to leave now," I demand.

He nods and starts to walk upstairs while dialing his phone. "Pack up. I'll tell the captain we're heading back, and I'll have a charter plane waiting for us to leave."

"Trev, call me if there's any changes. My phone is going to be glued to me," I direct him.

"Okay. I'm not leaving her side."

I start gathering my things and throwing them into my bag. "And Trev?"

"Yeah?"

"None of this is your fault. You have been an amazing friend. So, don't you dare blame yourself."

"Thanks, Nay. Appreciate it."

We hang up and I sway from the motion of the boat moving. We're already heading to the island. My hands are shaking, and the only thing I can do to not break down is to keep moving. I haul my bag over my shoulder and head up to the deck.

Gabriele is on the phone again, but by the time I reach him, he's hung up. He takes the bag from me, drops it on the seating, then wraps me into his embrace. I tuck my head into his chest and weep. He runs his hand through my hair, kissing the top of my head, and keeps hold of me tight just allowing me to let it all out.

"She's going to be okay, little ballerina. I've called ahead and have the best doctors looking over her. We'll be back home before the night ends, and you'll get to be by her side. I promise," he gives me his word.

God, I love this man. I love him even more now with all he's doing to help my best friend. I love him for being so patient, kind, and selfless. How did God create such a man – such a perfect man for me. One that I never thought I needed nor wanted, but here he is imprinting his way into my life. I didn't ask for this, and I sure as hell didn't give a fuck or even believe I was ever going to be in love, but here I am completely utterly madly in love.

I hold on to him tighter. We stay like this for the remainder of the boat ride. He transmits strength and energy from him to me to help me get through the next couple of hours. Finally, we pull up to the pier and dock. Gabriele and I head to the house where Joanna is waiting for us.

She holds her arms out for me and welcomes me into her

embrace. "Oh, my dear, I'm so sorry about your friend. Please, if you ever need anything, reach out to me. I left my number in your bags that I packed for you."

"Thank you for being so kind, Joanna. I'll cherish that more than you know," I tell her.

"Of course, my dear. Anytime," she says, then releases me.

Gabriele comes out with both our suitcases. "Ready?"

I nod and follow him to the Jeep. We take off at high speed to the airstrip. I can't stop fumbling with my hands. My heart is beating a mile a minute. I need to take deep breaths every time I think of my best friend lying in that bed because of that scum. I should have never come here. I should have been there with her. I *would* have been there with her going to work or I would have tied her to me if that's what it took for her to stay safe.

I look over at Gabriele and he looks to be in deep thought or determined. I'm not sure which exactly, but probably a bit of both. I feel a pang of guilt for being upset for saying yes to coming here when he's been nothing but kind.

Gabriele reaches his hand over to my lap and places it on top of my hands for comfort. "I know it's easier said than done, but you need to calm down and stop stressing. There's nothing you can do at the moment even if you were there. She's in good hands with these doctors. I had them move her to a private room," he tells me.

"What about the guy who attacked her. Where is he?"

He squeezes my hands. "He's still in questioning. He'll do time. I'll make sure of it and so will Luke."

I finally come to a realization about his brother. "Luke really cares for her, huh?"

"My fun partying brother doesn't go out of his way for any girl. This is a new side I'm seeing of him as well," he confesses.

God, I hope Dez pulls through okay. She deserves happiness even if it's just for a mere second, and I'm not going to

241

judge or get in her way anymore. She never once tried to stop me from coming here with Gabriele and now I'm realizing sometimes I can be such a tough friend to deal with. I tend to try to control everything around me since I had none when I was growing up, and I know I can take things too far because unfortunately no matter how hard we try to direct something, the world has other ideas in mind for us so we're never actually in control of our own destinations, even though we like to believe we are.

"You both seem more alike than you realize," I tell him.

He looks in my direction, looking over my face without a word and just nods returning his attention back to the road without saying a word. I know he cares for me; I can feel it in the way he looks at me, the way he touches me, and the things he says to me, but I guess Trev is right, he has to admit this to himself first before he'll be able to admit the truth to me.

We pull up to the airstrip and the plane is already waiting for us. Gabriele goes around the back grabbing our luggage and handing it over to the steward. I notice this time there is a man, instead of that woman. I wonder if that was on purpose. I never did mention her rudeness toward me to him.

I follow Gabriele up the stairs to the back cabin taking my seat.

The male steward comes to us. "Mr. Vanucci, Miss Veil, is there anything I can grab you before takeoff?"

"Just two waters please, Karl," Gabriele replies.

I love that he knows everyone by their first names. Even with all the money he holds, he's still a respectful, polite human. I'm not sure I'm ever going to get used to not being in awe of him because of this quality. I'm just waiting for the other shoe to drop still. He has secrets, I know this, because everyone holds secrets. I'm just wondering if I'm going to be around long enough to find out what demons he may hold other than not wanting children or a relationship.

Gabriele hands me a blanket and a small pillow. "You need to get some rest before the hospital. You're going to need all your strength."

I agree taking the blanket and pillow doing my best to try to relax enough to get some rest. I must have dozed off because next thing I know the plane is landing and I'm being jerked around. I wipe the drool off my cheek embarrassed as I look at the window to the night sky.

I sit up. "What time is it?"

"Almost ten," he answers.

"How far away from the hospital are we?"

I start to panic again, heart thrumming out of my rib cage, needing to be there next to her now.

"Ten minutes. My driver is waiting on the tarmac for us."

I continue to look out the window impatiently. Gabriele grabs my hands and pulls me over to his lap. He runs his hand through my hair and down to the base of my neck. "Stop freaking out. You need to breathe or you're going to pass out from a panic attack, and you will be no good to your friend then."

I take a couple of deep breaths. "Good girl," he praises.

The doors to the plane open and I jump out of his lap ready to jump down the stairs.

"Good evening," Karl says goodbye.

I nod and barely smile as I make my way down to the car. The driver opens the door for me and Gabriele. We slide in and as soon as both doors close, we take off. I start biting my nails without thought, stuck in my mind only expecting to see the worst.

The car finally pulls up in front of the hospital doors and I jump out not even waiting for him to open it for us. I take my phone and dial Trev's number.

"Hey," he answers.

"We're here. Where do we go?" I ask as we walk through the emergency room doors and head down the hall.

Trev gives me the directions as we go, finally after many turns and three floors up, I see him talking to me outside her door. I hang the phone up and run to him, smashing into his embrace, sobbing immediately.

He squeezes me tightly. "Hey, Nay."

"Has anything changed?" I ask.

He shakes his head. "No, she's still in a coma."

I sniffle and let go. He looks to Gabriele shaking his hand. "Thanks for getting her back here quickly," Trev says to him.

"Of course."

I stop at the door looking through the blinds. I can't move any further. My whole body begins shaking. My whole world becomes tiny and closed in. I feel as though there's a huge elephant standing on top if my chest stopping me from taking in a breath of air. I don't recognize the noise coming from my mouth as I gasp for air holding my hand to my chest.

"Nay! Calm down! Breath!" Trev screams at me.

Gabriele already has my elbow holding me up. "Get her a chair," he orders Trev.

He leads me to the seat rubbing my back. "Deep breaths, Naomi."

"I – I can't," I can barely get out. "I can't see. Everything is black," I tell them.

"You're having a panic attack. You just have to let it pass. You will be okay," Gabriele says.

A few moments pass. I can barely see Trev pacing in front of me. "Jesus, Nay. You just scared the shit out of me."

The ringing in my ears finally stops and my vision comes back. My whole body feels clammy and sweaty, but my chest feels lighter and the air passes through easier. I sit here for another couple of minutes until I stand. Both men are close by my side ready to catch me if I should fall.

"I'm okay," I inform them both.

They fall back as I push the door open. Immediately, the room fills with beeping noises, the pump of the ventilator whooshing, and my little friend full of wires. I gasp covering my mouth with shaky hands. She looks swollen and bruised. My heart cracks into a million little pieces as I walk toward her.

The guys stand back against the wall watching. I pull the chair next to her closer so I can sit and hold her hand. She needs to know I'm here. I'm praying she can hear me somewhere inside her head.

"Dez, it's Nay. I'm here," I whisper, sniffling trying my best to hold myself together.

"I'm so sorry I wasn't there for you. I should have been there to stop you or help you at least. I'm so sorry," I say through my tears.

Trev comes behind me placing his hands on his shoulder. "Like you told me, this is not your fault, Nay. There was nothing you could have done. Dez does what Dez wants to do."

I nod whipping my eyes to him. "I know."

I look around watching the monitor beep with her heart rate and her chest rise and fall with the ventilator. I'm hoping she won't feel any pain and she's thinking of happy things right now.

"I'm so angry at you too, Dez. You *freaking* promised me. You told me you were going to stay put. Why didn't you stay put?" I ask her knowing I obviously won't get an answer back. I just need to get it out before she wakes.

I look up at Trev. "She's gonna wake, right Trev?"

"You know our girl won't give up that easily. She's a hard head. She is going to wake up and continue being a pain in our asses," Trev says.

"When's the last time the doctor has been in?" Gabriele questions.

"Not for a couple of hours," Trev answers.

Gabriele takes out his phone. "I'm going to make a call," he tells us stepping out into the hall.

Trev takes a seat next to me. "Luke was here with her earlier. He stopped by to see her and then went back to the precinct to make sure her attacker is being dealt with. I think he really cares for her, Nay. He chased that guy down himself. If he didn't, that guy may have gotten away."

"I think you're right," I agree.

I squeeze Dez's hand a bit tighter and rub her arm with my other. I roam my eyes over her face. Her left eye and cheek are bruised and swollen. Her lip was split open and now a butterfly bandage is holding it together and her knuckles are bruised from fighting back.

The right side of her head is shaved under the bandages wrapped around her head and I'm assuming she has staples holding her head together. I know this sounds silly, but I think out of everything, she's going to be upset about her hair, she was always so proud of her long silky hair.

Gabriele comes back into the room. "The doctor is on his way up to talk with us since her immediately family isn't able to be here."

"Do you know if her mother was called?" I ask.

Trev shakes his head no. "I didn't have any of her information."

I look around the room to see if her phone is lying anywhere. "Where's her phone?"

"I think they might have it with her things," Trev replies.

I look to Gabriele. "I'll go talk to the nurses to see if they have it with her things so we can get a hold of her mom."

"Thank you," I tell him.

I lay my head on her gently. "Please wake up, Dez. Please be okay," I beg her.

Trev stands up squeezing my shoulder. "I'm going to go grab us some coffee."

"Okay."

I sit here just being with her surrounded by all the monitors. Gabriele comes in with Trev. Trev hands me my coffee and the doctor walks in after them.

Gabriele shakes his hand. "Thanks for looking after her on such short notice, Doctor Harold. We would appreciate it if you gave it to us straight."

"Of course." He nods to all of us. "Miss Cannon has a closed skull fracture, three broken ribs, and minor scrapes and bruises that will heal. The fracture may take a couple months to fully heal with some pain medication, but she had a huge gashing cut that we had to staple. Most likely, the concussion and the head trauma is what's put her in a coma. Her body needs time to rest and heal. We'll wait for the swelling to come down before we run some more tests. That's all we know for now," he finishes.

"But you think she will come out of the coma, right?" I ask.

"Her body has gone through a terrible ordeal. I'm most hopeful that once she starts healing she will also come to, but there's never any guarantee. All I can tell you to do is keep talking with her, touch is important, and be patient."

Tears roll down my eyes as I look back over to her. Gabriele shakes his hand. "Thanks for the update, Doc."

"Anytime. I'll be back in to check on her tomorrow. Our staff is very thorough and will notify me of any changes," he replies.

Doctor Harold leaves. Gabriele advises me the nurse is grabbing her personal items for us. I barely hear a word of anything as I just continuously watch the monitor. My thoughts are just flying a mile a minute in every direction. The guys allow me some time with her while they talk out in the hall.

Gabriele wakes me not even realizing I must have fallen

asleep. "Hey, come on. Let's get you to a bed. I want you to come stay with me tonight."

I shake my head no. "I'm staying here. I'm not leaving her again," I refuse.

"Nay, there's nothing we can do right now. She needs you rested for when she wakes up," Trev says.

Gabriele softly pulls me out of the chair. "The nurses have my number on standby for any emergency. They will call us. I promise."

I finally give in only because I know I'm not going to win. I lean over and kiss her cheek gently and whisper to her, "I'll be back in the morning. I promise."

It takes me another moment before I'm able to turn away and leave but I finally make it out the door. My heart and my soul feel so heavy right now. I let out a sob as soon as I step out of the door. Gabriele grabs me in his tight embrace right away just holding me and allowing me to get everything out.

"Come on, let's get you out of here," he says softly.

"Nay, I'll see you in the morning. Call me when you wake up," Trev advises, giving me a kiss on the top of my head.

I nod not being able to speak, if I speak, I'll break down again. Gabriele has his driver waiting, as we take off, I watch the hospital pass by my window feeling guilty for being able to leave it behind me.

CHAPTER 17

I think I was so exhausted yesterday that I really was almost sleepwalking by the time I got to Gabriele's penthouse. The blinds are closed almost making it pitch dark besides the tiny sliver of sunlight peeking through a crack revealing morning. I reach to the nightstand and grab my phone to see what time it is. Vacation must be over because it shows 6:45AM.

Welcome back insomnia.

I look around the room. The bed is empty beside me. I feel the sheets and they are warm still which means Gabriele must have just gotten up. His room is basic. Hardwood floors, white walls, low bed with a platform wooden frame, a TV mounted on the wall, and a seating area with two white chairs.

I'm in need of a bathroom so I hop out of bed and head to one of the cracked doors peeking inside. The first door I investigate is a large closet. A waft of Gabriele fills my nostrils with his delicious scent. It's scrumptious and invigorating sending a jolt of hunger straight to my core, but then I quickly scold my body for having those thoughts at this time.

I open the next door across the way, and I find the bathroom. This is also nothing grand. Nothing like the villas he created on the island. There's luxury here, but it's stale, cold, and a bit lonely.

After I'm finished freshening up, I head out of the bedroom. This hall isn't familiar. We must be on the opposite side of the penthouse from where Luke is staying. As I get closer to the kitchen I hear voices. The closer I get, the sounds of them fade as they must realize I'm coming.

I see Gabriele, Luke, and another man in the kitchen whom I've seen on multiple occasions. They all turn their attention to me as I enter. "No need to stop talking because I'm here. I'm assuming you're discussing Dez?" I question.

After being held up with Gabriele for so long on the island, I feel more than comfortable helping myself to a cup of coffee without asking permission. He reaches in the cupboard for me and hands me a mug with a kiss on the cheek.

"How'd you sleep?" he asks quietly.

I shrug. "I think good?"

I really don't remember much from after we left the hospital. I think I was in such a dazed haze that anything could have happened at that point, and I probably wouldn't have even been phased.

"Any news on Dez?" I ask him.

He shakes his head no. "But we do have some news on her attacker."

My brows raise and I look over to Luke and the other man sitting at the kitchen counter. "Well, spill it!" I demand.

They look a little shocked by my outburst as they look to Gabriele before opening their mouths. He nods, giving them permission.

Luke starts first. "His name is Craig. Desire isn't the first girl he's gone after. His ex-girlfriend has been missing for the last three years. Her family suspects him of foul play with her disappearance. There were two other girls that had restraining orders on him as well.

"They're charging him with assault and battery, conspiracy of kidnapping, and a gun charge. He's most definitely doing time. I'm going to make sure of it," Luke says with determination.

Guilt takes over me. "Luke, I want to apologize for being so harsh on you. I can see you really care for Dez and she's lucky to have you fighting so hard for her. Thank you for trying to help protect my friend," I tell him.

He gives me a genuine smile. "I more than care for her Naomi. I just wanted her to give me a chance to explain what she saw, explain it wasn't what it looked like, and there was a reason why I was there with that woman. I want her to give us a chance in finding out what this *more* means to the both of us," he explains. "That's all."

"I understand. I appreciate the honesty, and I know she will too once she recovers."

Gabriele comes behind me wrapping his arms around my waist. If it was any other time, I would feel content with him showing affection in front of others, but right now I just feel numb.

Gabriele introduces me to the other man in the kitchen. "Naomi, this is Conner, he's the head of my security and my driver."

Conner is a large bald headed man. Looks to be in his late forties, serious and seasoned eyes with a no bullshit aura. He looks toward me all business, a little intimidating I might say, but I get the feeling he may just be an onion with layers that may take time to peel.

"Nice to meet you, Miss Veil."

"Nice to meet you too, Conner."

I take a sip of my coffee. Gabriele leans down and kisses the side of my neck. "Why don't you go shower, get dressed, and we'll head over to the hospital as soon as you're ready. I need to finish this conversation."

I can see this is his way of getting me out of the room nicely, but at this point, I couldn't care less. I just want to go see my best friend and make sure I'm there for her when she wakes up.

GABRIELE IS on a business call the whole way to the hospital. This leaves me time to let my mind wander and do my best to prepare myself again for another round of having my heart broken as I walk into Dez's room. My heart is pounding like it's going to burst out of my chest the closer we get. I close my eyes and concentrate on my breathing.

Gabriele puts his hand on my thigh giving me support while he's on his call. All I can think about is the wires, the monitors, the bruises, and my friend looking so weak and little. So opposite from what she always is – vibrant and loud.

The driver pulls up to the main doors. Gabriele raises a finger to give him a moment. I mouth I'm heading up and he places his hand over the speaker telling me he'll be up in a moment.

I take the windy halls, and the elevator up to the third floor. Each step closer feels like an elephant is taking a step on my chest. The air starts to dissipate from my lungs, I slam my hand on the wall to catch my breath and hold myself up.

Trev steps out of Dez's room and finds me in mid panic attack mode.

He rushes to my side. "Hey, hey. Nay, I think you need to sit down. Your face is white as a ghost."

I shake my head while leaning over trying to catch my breath. "No, no. Give me a sec. I'll be okay."

I close my eyes to help me concentrate on my breathing. Slowly inhaling and slowly exhaling until the thrum of my beating heart finally calms to a quiet pitter patter. The ringing in my ear begins to fade, and I wipe my clammy palms on the thighs of my leggings.

I stand up straight, Trev hovers over me making sure I don't fall.

"You good now?" he asks.

I nod. "Yeah. How is she?"

He sighs. "The same. No change."

We start heading to her room. I stop again at the door looking in through the window taking it all in. I push the door open and see a bag of her things on the seat. I walk to the chair and open the bag. I see some of her clothes ripped and bloody. I try to ignore them, so the guilt won't consume me again with not being there when she needed me. I dig further and find her cell phone.

The screen is cracked, and the battery is dead. I grab my charger out of my purse and plug it in. As soon as there's some juice, I need to call her mother and let her know what's going on. If this was months ago, I wouldn't have even considered calling her. But now that they're on good terms, it's only the right thing to do.

Trev and I both take a seat next to her bed. I grab her hand and squeeze. "Hey Dez, I'm here. You can wake up now."

I look up at the monitor and there's a quick spike on the heart monitor. Trev and I look at each other in shock. "I think she just heard you, Nay. Keep talking to her."

"Luke's been really worried about you. I think I was totally wrong about him. He cares for you a lot. I think you sensed something different in him all along, it's me that's the old judgmental hag," I tell her doing my best attempt at a joke.

Trev chuckles too. "Did you hear that, Dez. I think she finally admitted her faults to you. Let that sink in and enjoy it."

"So, I have a problem. I know you both told me to keep my walls up and protect myself, and I tried so damn hard, but I fucked up and fell in love with Gabriele," I say, admitting it out loud face contorted waiting for Trev's reaction.

I look to Dez's monitor to see if anything changes from that, but still the steady beeping of her heart.

Trev huffs. "As if we both didn't already know that, Nay. We called it as soon as you left for that island."

I smack his shoulder. "Seriously? You guys didn't have any faith in me?"

"When it came to Mr. Smooth Operator Billionaire Sexy Man, no we had no faith in you. We knew he was going to sweep you away and we were ready to be here when you landed in case we had to pick up the pieces too, but it looks like he's feeling those same feelings as you are."

I roll my eyes, then hear a notification come from Dez's phone. I get up to grab it and see it's a text from her mother. I run through all the notifications quickly and see most of them are from her. She's clearly worried because she hasn't heard back from her and I'm not sure what Dez has or hasn't told her over the last week.

I press call on her mother's number.

"Oh my god, Desire! Thank god you answered! Where have you been? I've been worried sick about you!" her mom yells.

"Hi Christy, this is Desire's roommate, Naomi."

She takes a moment. "Oh, hello sweetheart. I've heard so much about you. Is everything alright? Where's Desire? Can I speak with her?"

I take a deep breath before having to give her the news. "I'm with Desire right now, but unfortunately, we're in the hospital and she's unable to speak."

Her mother begins freaking out. I do my best to calm her as I explain in detail what has happened. She starts crying on the phone, and I do everything I can to try to assure her Dez is a fighter and is going to pull through. I give her all the information the doctor gave us last night and advise her once he comes back to update us that I will call her. Meanwhile, she's going to be working on catching the first flight out she can.

We hang up and I sit back already exhausted from that phone call. Definitely not a call one enjoys making and not one I ever want to make again in my life. Gabriele walks in with coffee in hand for me and Trev and I thank him before taking a large sip. My eyes roll back; this is heaven and just what I needed.

"What did I miss? You look like you just went through the wringer," he informs me while taking a seat next to the wall.

"She just got off the phone with Dez's mom, Christy. It was a rough phone call to say the least," Trev explains to him.

His face softens completely understanding. "I'm sure that was, but when she wakes up, I'm sure she will be happy you made that call."

We all sit in here for the next couple of hours. Nurses come and go after checking her stats. The doctor still hasn't come by yet and it's now mid-afternoon. Gabriele left for his office to get some work done a while ago but said he would be back later to pick me up. I told him I was going home but he insisted on me waiting for him.

Trev stayed as long as he could before he needed to go home and change for his shift at the club. He promised he would stop by here after he got out of work to check on her in case I wasn't here.

I must have fallen asleep in the chair because I'm woken up by Gabriele's kiss on my cheek. My eyes crack open and I look around confused trying to remember where I am, then I land on Dez, and the beeping of the monitor and the pump of the ventilator comes full force.

"What time is it?" I ask while looking for my phone.

"Almost nine. I tried calling you a couple of times, but you didn't answer."

I look down at my phone and realize it's dead. Shit. I get up and walk over to the charger to plug it in for a moment.

"Did you eat anything?" he questions walking to stand in front of me.

I look up to him. "No, I had lunch, that was about it."

He looks annoyed. He puts his hands on my shoulders. "Naomi, you have to make sure you eat and are taking care of yourself too. Come on, let's go grab some dinner. Luke is on his way here; he'll watch over her for now."

"Okay. Let me say goodbye."

I walk over to the bed and grab Dez's hand. "I'll be back tomorrow. I love you." I lean over and give her a kiss on the top of her head.

Gabriele hands me my phone from the charger. I power it back on and the thing lights up. I see some texts from Trev, one from Dez's mom Christy saying she's on her way and will be landing tomorrow morning, and I have a missed call from a New York number that I don't recognize. I guess I didn't realize how long I'd been sleeping, and how long my phone was shut down.

"Wow, I didn't realize how long I must have knocked out," I tell him.

He kisses the top of my head. "You tossed and turned all last night. Hopefully tonight after a full belly you can get a good night's rest."

"Can we just do some takeout or something? I'm not in the mood to dine anywhere."

"Sure, I'll order something and have it delivered."

I know he wants to go back to his house, but I haven't even been back to my apartment yet. I feel like I need to at least stop by and make sure everything is good and pick up some of my mail.

"Can we stop by my apartment first so I can grab mail

and some more clothes?" I ask as we head out of the hospital and into the back of his SUV.

"Conner, can we please stop at Miss Veil's apartment first?" Gabriele asks his driver.

"Not a problem, Mr. Vanucci."

We stop in front of my place. I grab my keys from my purse, but Gabriele takes them out of my hands. "I'm going in first just in case."

I roll my eyes. "Seriously? It's fine. They caught him."

He steps in front of me opening the door. "You never know. It's just precautionary."

I cross my arms. "Fine."

He opens the door and begins walking through each room in the apartment turning on the lights, checking closets and anything closed. When he's satisfied, he takes a seat in the living room allowing me to go through my mail and gather some things.

The place smells stale and thick with unlived air. You can tell no one has been in here for days. Dust is now layering the tops of the furniture, and my mail is piled up high. I look in the refrigerator and scrunch my nose at the smell of the rotten leftovers still in there from before Dez left.

I start throwing away all the food that has gone bad and empty the garbage, putting it outside the door for now. I adjust the AC, since I know for a fact that Dez and I will be coming home soon and need it cool in here.

Gabriele watches my every move but doesn't say a word. I grab some clothes that are more suitable for a hospital. Most of the things I have in my suitcase at Gabriele's are island wear and are in need of washing. I walk down the hall to Dez's room and stand in the doorway.

A tear escapes the corner of my eye, I wipe it away with my finger as I hear soft footsteps behind me. Gabriele wraps his arms around my waist and brings me tight into his hold. I lean against him taking his strength and warmth in. I miss my best friend. I miss her voice, and her annoying loudness. I miss her daring anyone to hurt me because she will ruin them. I just miss her laugh and her face so much that it hurts and feels like my heart is ripping in two right now.

My stomach growls and I sigh. "Come on, food will be delivered any moment now. We need to get back to the house," Gabriele says.

I take one last look at the apartment before I turn off the lights and lock up. I'm assuming Dez's mom may need a place to stay so I grab her set of keys to give her before leaving the hospital. I've seen pictures of her mom, but I still have yet to meet her, and I'm not looking forward to meeting her like this for the first time either.

We pick up the food at the front desk and head up the elevator to his penthouse. The place is empty, no Luke in sight. "Did Luke go to the hospital?"

"Yes, he's there now," he answers as he places the bag of food on the kitchen island. "I'm going to go get changed. Why don't you grab us some plates."

I start pulling the food out of the bag, then go through each cupboard trying to find plates. I open the containers and immediately the smell of steak, garlic, potatoes, and asparagus glazed in balsamic wafts past my nose making my mouth salivate and my stomach growl like a tiger.

I look at the receipt and the price of this takeout is three hundred and fifty-two dollars. Jesus, that's almost a whole month of groceries for me and Dez. I think back to the time we landed in Arizona off the bus and barely had enough for a thirty dollar a night room for the week between the both of us along with food to eat.

I divvy up the food on our plates just as he comes back out wearing some plaid sweats and a white tee looking sexy as hell. He runs his hand through his hair rustling it up making him imperfectly perfect.

"We ready to eat?" Gabriele asks, sitting down next to me at the island.

I slide over his plate then cut a piece of my steak and sink my teeth into it. The flavors burst into my mouth. It tastes like heaven, and I moan as I savor every last morsel I chew. When I finally come out of my hungered stupor, I realize Gabriele has been watching me this whole time. My face flushes with embarrassment.

"What?"

His brows are raised as he shakes his head. "Nothing. It's just I wish I was that piece of meat right now," he admits. "And I know this is the wrong thing to be thinking about at this moment, but I just can't help it with you."

My body clearly can't help but react to him. My nipples pucker up as my chest starts heaving up and down intensively. I know it's wrong, especially with my best friend lying in a hospital bed but I'm clearly a glutton for punishment – *or guilt,* and my body clearly can't behave.

"I understand, but I think we should stick a pin on it at least until Dez is awake. I'm not sure I can handle anymore guilt. How can I possibly enjoy life with her like this?" I question more to myself than him.

He puts his fork down turning his body to me and puts his hands on top of my thighs turning me into him. "Naomi, you shouldn't feel guilty for wanting to be close to someone during this time. Desire wouldn't fault you for any of that, but I totally understand what you are asking and will respect your wishes," Gabriele tells me before leaning over and giving me a sweet peck on the lips.

I wrap my arms around his neck bringing him back to me before he pulls away. "Thank you."

"There's no reason to thank me."

I have so much to be thankful for when it comes to him. Just in these past couple of weeks he's shown me so much that a man can be for a woman, it's opened my eyes to a different kind of world. A world filled with passion, desires that aren't shameful, and a place where I feel protected again. It just kills me that I'm still waiting for the other shoe to drop. Just waiting for the moment when he's done with me and kicks me to the curb. This place is a lonely place to be.

We continue to eat making small talk until we're both full and exhausted. Gabriele grabs the plates and begins cleaning up. Just as I'm about to offer to help, I hear the elevator door ping open. I look over to the hall and see Luke walk into the living area toward us taking a seat at the counter. He looks tired as well.

"How is she, Luke?" I ask.

He hangs his head low before answering. "The doctor came in to check her vitals. He said he's going to give her time before he orders another scan because everything looks good for now, but other than that, there has been no change. He said we're only on day two, and her body is probably taking a pause to heal itself."

I get up and walk over to the seat next to him taking his hand in mine squeezing it. Gabriele passes him a bourbon on the rocks, and he takes a long pull. We all remain quiet just being in the moment full of thoughts. I squeeze Luke's hand one last time before getting up and walking back toward Gabriele's room. I just need a moment to myself.

I change and lay down on the bed. Gabriele comes after another thirty minutes or so and lays down next to me facing my direction. I continue to stare at the ceiling while he runs his fingers over the contours of my face. I close my eyes feeling him leave soft trails over my skin; it's calming and meditative. I love his touch. It gives me goose bumps, a wave of electricity licks over my body and my breathing starts to pick up.

Doesn't matter what I tell myself, my body has other ideas and when Gabriele is near it takes over and consumes my every thought with him. I turn on my side to now face him too. We stare at each other for a while with no words, just penetrating deep within each other's souls. We don't need words; we're saying enough without them. I love this man, and even though I don't want to, it's radiating from every inch of me.

A tear escapes my eye. He reaches over wiping it with his thumb and then brings it to his mouth tasting it. It's such a personal intimate thing to do. I lean over, running my hand through his hair pulling him into me while running my tongue along his lips, coaxing him to open for me.

He meets mine with his, delving into my mouth deep and avidly, dancing with mine with every stroke. We stay just like this for a long moment, just devouring each other and running our hands all over one another's body.

Little beads of sweat break out all over my skin as I heat up with need. I lift my thigh over his and grind myself on his leg. He squeezes my ass bringing me closer to him as we continue to kiss and dry hump each other.

"Naomi, slow down," he suggests. "I don't want you doing anything you'll regret."

I shake my head. "I can't hold back with you any longer. I want you. I *need* you," I beg as my voice breaks.

That's all it takes for him to move over me on his knees, lift my butt up grabbing at the hem of my shorts and panties ripping them down my legs and throwing them on the floor.

He spreads my legs apart wide moving in between my thighs. He takes a long inhale of my scent while closing his eyes enjoying it before he takes one quick sweep up my inner slit. I scream out completely consumed by the sensitivity and my overwhelming need for more.

He sucks on my clit in hard pulses as he inserts two fingers deep inside of me. My back arches, and I moan, as he finger fucks me spilling my juices all over his digits.

My body is on fire already ready for a quick release. I've been carrying so much stress, my body is tense and wired up that this detonation is the only thing that can help me right now.

"Fuck, my little ballerina, I love how tight and responsive you are. I can't wait to stretch you out with my cock," he taunts as he goes back to circling my clit with precise strokes over and over with his tongue. Just as my build up begins to grow, he removes his fingers and his tongue smashing me right back down.

"*No!* Don't stop," I beg, whimpering.

He removes his sweatpants bringing the tip of his dick to my entrance, rubbing himself along my soaking wet lips. He slowly slides into me, stretching me, while keeping his eyes locked onto mine. This moment is intense with unsaid emotions. I open my mouth slightly letting out a soft moan as he inches his way deeper inside of me. He leans down covering his mouth over mine, drinking in my breath from me.

Gabriele stills as he's deep inside of me to the hilt. "This is mine. Say it," he demands in a whisper.

I grab onto his ass trying to direct him to move as I wiggle under him. He leans back watching me, waiting for me to repeat him. At this point I'll say anything to get him to move so he'll bring me back to the brink of release.

"My pussy is yours," I tell him.

He backs almost completely out of me then slams deep into me, hard. "No one else's," he states, still waiting for me to repeat him.

"I'm yours and only yours," I reply. "Now fuck me, god dammit!" I demand in desperation.

Gabriele leans on his elbows kissing me as he pumps into me. I adjust my hips up so his tip reaches my G-spot lifting my legs higher and wrapping them around his torso. He grabs onto the back of my thigh digging his finger into my skin. There's no pain but I know tomorrow there will be bruises left behind marking me.

"Fuck your pussy feels so damn good. You're so warm, tight, and fucking feel like heaven," Gabriele growls as he thrusts into me, sounds of our bodies slapping together filling the room. "If this is what it's like going to heaven, I would die a thousand times over."

Jesus fuck this man and his words. The more he talks, the more my body ignites with fever, and I find myself overheating with the need to combust.

He reaches down in between us gliding his thumb over my swollen clit causing my inner walls to ripple around him. "Yes, baby, I want you to come. Come all over my cock."

And just like that my orgasm convulses around him. I scream out his name as he pumps with full strength fucking me with everything he has, sending me inching back until his release soars through him while he calls out my name.

His arms are shaking as he slows his thrusts emptying every last drop into me. I run my fingers through his hair while his forehead is lying against mine as we work on slowing down our breathing together.

"I don't think I'm ever going to get enough of you," I whisper.

He chuckles. "I'm already hooked on you. I *crave* you. You're in my every thought, my every need, day and night. I'm without a doubt incredibly addicted."

I smirk at his confession. Who would have ever thought I would get him to be this open with me. His ice-cold heart is melting, and I think Trev was right in giving him time to realize he feels more for me than he's ready to admit.

He leans down kissing the tip of my nose before he slips out of me and heads to the bathroom to clean up. He brings me a warm washcloth when he returns and cleans me up. I rollover to my side exhausted, yawning, ready to sleep. I feel the bed tilt as he climbs in and wraps his arm over my waist pulling my back into him. Our breathing sinks, and I finally fall into a deep darkness.

CHAPTER 18

Gabriele's phone goes off repeatedly waking us up. I jump up out of my sleep knowing deep down it's about Dez. My heart immediately slams against my chest, pounding through my rib cage.

He answers the phone. "Luke? What's wrong? Why are you calling me from your room?"

I sit up on my knees listening. Gabriele listens, nodding as Luke talks. He looks over to me with his brows raised.

"What? What is it?" I ask confused.

He covers the speaker. "Luke couldn't sleep so he went to the hospital."

Now I'm freaking. "And?" I yell.

"She wiggled her finger when he was talking to her," Gabriele says.

I jump out of the bed and start grabbing for my clothes. "What the fuck are you waiting for? Let's go!" I scream.

He talks to Luke on the other end. "Okay, yeah. We're on our way." Then he ends the call.

I jump into my pants and pull my hoodie over my head, rushing to the bathroom to quickly freshen up. Gabriele throws some clothes on and calls his driver as we head to the elevator.

I can't stop shaking my leg as we're driving toward the hospital. Gabriele puts his hand on my thigh to still me. "Breathe, Naomi."

I take some deep breaths. Once we reach the main doors, I jump out not giving the driver enough time to walk around and open the car door for us. As soon as we walk through the sliding doors, antiseptic, bleach, and just plain old hospital smell hits my senses. I follow the same route as each time before making it to her room in record time.

Trev is already on his way. I texted him as soon as we got in the car. He was just getting home from the club, so he answered in record breaking time.

I rush into the room and Luke is sitting by her side still. "Did the doctor come by? Did she move anything else?" I demand to know.

"She opened her eyes briefly but didn't say anything. I think she's drifting in and out. The nurse checked her over and says sometimes it can take some time for people to fully come to," Luke explains.

"What about Dr. Harold, has he been in yet?" Gabriele asks.

I walk over to the other side of the bed and take Dez's hand in mine.

"Not yet. The nurse paged him, so I'm sure he'll be on his way shortly."

I lean over giving Dez a kiss on her cheek. "Dez, I know you can hear me. It's time to wake up now. Can you squeeze my hand and let me know you can hear me?"

I feel the lightest movement in her fingers. I gasp, covering my mouth, with a huge smile spreading across my face. "She did it! She moved her fingers!" I announce loudly.

Each one of us claps in excitement quietly celebrating this small victory. I squeeze her hand. "I knew you weren't going to leave me. I love you, Dez. I told everyone you're a fucking fighter!"

Gabriele brings me over a chair to sit on and leans down giving me a kiss on the cheek. "She's gonna be okay, little ballerina. I told you she would be," he whispers.

I smile at him adoringly. I mouth thank you to him. I look at my phone, it's 4AM, and I know her mom's going to be here in the next couple of hours. I shoot her a text letting her know the good news to help ease her worry some.

Gabriele steps out grabbing us all some coffee and as soon as he's back Doctor Harold walks in. I stand up immediately. He shakes Gabriele's hand.

"Nice to see you Mr. Vanucci," the doctor greets.

He nods to Luke and I. "Hello." He walks over to Dez. "Good morning, Desire. I heard you're finally waking up." He puts his hand in hers. "Are you able to squeeze my hand?" he asks her.

I watch as her fingers move more than they did with mine. I jump up and down a little clapping my hands. Doctor Harold looks up toward me and smiles. "This is a good sign," he tells me.

"Now Desire, are you able to open your eyes?" he asks her. Her eyes flutter open quickly then close. He reaches for the light above her bed turning it off. "Try again, Desire."

She opens them again and this time they stay open. She looks around with her eyes only and they land on Luke. I see the tiniest movement from the corner of her mouth as though she wants to smile. Then she closes her eyes again.

"She seems a bit sensitive to the lighting, so I would keep them off for now until she adjusts. Everything else looks stable for now. I'm going to have a nurse come remove her tubing. It may be hard for her to speak at first, but ice chips should help ease the discomfort. I'll come back this afternoon to see if there have been anymore improvements," Doctor Harold tells us.

"Thanks, Doc," Luke says.

Gabriele and I both thank him as well. I squeal in excitement. Trev comes in disheveled like he just ran a marathon and pauses looking at all our faces. "Whoa, what did I miss? Is she awake?" he screeches, rushing over to Dez.

We explain everything to him and catch him all up to speed. He runs his hand through his hair blowing out a breath. "Wow, this is amazing news."

Trev and I wrap our arms around each other, I lay my head on his chest releasing my breath as though I've been holding it for a lifetime. We just embrace for a long moment then look to Dez who's now watching us. Trev and I laugh in pure joy. The room is now filled with lightness as the dread dissipates away. We all spend the next couple hours talking and laughing as Dez gains more strength.

Her mom finally landed and came straight to the hospital. Everyone leaves the room as I update her on everything. Thank god Dez is still awake. I give them some time alone while we head out to grab something to eat.

Gabriele and Luke head to the office, and Trev and I stop at a dive bar for some food and some celebratory shots. This time instead of numbing the pain we're finally celebrating a triumph. Our Dez is going to heal and be just fine, now the next step is making sure that man stays locked up where he can't reach her anymore.

Trev holds up his tequila, and I hold up mine. "To our Dez, who drives us completely mad, but who we can never live without."

We clink our glasses together. "To Dez," I say before we down our shots. No salt or lime, just a good old stiff drink.

"So, how did her mom take things?"

I take a sip of water. "She's a mess, but obviously glad the moment she walked into the room Dez's eyes were open. She's going to stay at the apartment until Dez is released and then stay to help out until she's on her feet. I guess she took some time off at work."

Trev looks surprised. "Wow, that's a huge step. I'm happy for Dez. I think she's definitely going to need all of us to help during her recovery."

"I agree. I think having her mom here will help. I'm going to have to convince Gabriele to let me go back home. It's like he's holding me hostage," I joke laughing.

Trev rolls his eyes. "Don't act like you haven't been enjoying it girl."

I sigh. "A little too much."

The waitress sets down our food. I dig in grabbing my wrap taking a huge bite. I'm starved. The only thing I've had today was coffee. I think we were so wound up over Dez waking up that food didn't even cross our minds.

My phone starts vibrating. I look down and it's the New York number I don't know. I click my phone off letting it go to voicemail.

"Who's that calling?"

"No idea. Probably the wrong number. Some New York number I've never seen before," I tell him.

"What's going on with Adam?"

He finishes chewing, then takes a sip of his Coke. "Well, I actually told him I had to take a break."

My mouth drops open. "But why?"

"Just with everything going on with Dez I just didn't have time for me and him. I thought it would be best if we took some time off. I didn't want to hold him up from finding someone else," he answers, but I'm just not satisfied with that answer.

"Bullshit, Trev! You're fucking running away and you know it. You're using Dez as an excuse and wait until I tell her too. When she's back to herself she's gonna ream you a new asshole," I scold him.

"Nay, just stop. Seriously. I don't have it in me to fight

about this. I made the decision and it's done," he says adamantly.

"Fine, but if he moves on and leaves your ass in the dust then you're going to regret it."

The waitress comes over with another round of shots. We take them down, leave money on the table for the check, and head back to the hospital.

WHEN WE GET BACK to Dez's room, her mom is still by her side. Dez is now propped up more but she's back to being asleep.

"I have Dez's apartment keys for you. You are more than welcome to stay in Dez's room while she recovers, and we have a pull-out couch for when she comes home," I offer her.

She smiles. "Thank you, Naomi. I really appreciate your kindness. You have been such an amazing friend to my daughter and I'm so glad she's had you while I wasn't there for her."

"There's no need to thank me," I reply. "Christy, this is our close friend Trevor. Trevor, this is Desire's mom, Christy," I introduce them.

They shake hands politely, but I can sense the tension with Trev as he's busy judging her for all the wrongs she has committed against our girl.

I sit down across the bed from her and take Dez's hand in mine. "Has there been any changes?" I ask Christy.

"She's weak but was alert for a long while. She just fell back asleep."

"I can take you back to the apartment if you want some rest," I offer. "Trev can stay here with her until I get back."

She stands and gives Dez a kiss on the cheek. "No, I can call an Uber. You both stay. I'll be back later tonight after I lay down."

I hand her the keys and give her the address for the driver. Once she leaves, Trev immediately gives me a look.

"What?"

"If Dez was my daughter, there would be no way you would get me to leave her side. The nerve of her!" Trev says upset.

Dez stirs at the sound of his voice, her eyes open, she looks around the room to see who's still here or to see if her mother is still here.

"She went back to the apartment to get some rest, Dez. Your mom will be back later," I advise her.

She tries to speak but it's extremely low and raspy. My heart skips a beat at the sound of her voice. I have Trev go see if he can get some ice chips for her, and I work on sitting her up even more. Dez moves her fingers easily and is now working on some arm movements. Things are slowly waking back up and coming back together for her.

Trev comes back with a cup of ice. I grab a piece running it over her lips and letting it melt into her mouth. I give her small chips to lay on her tongue and once she seems more lubricated, she tries to speak again.

"Where's Luke?" she whispers.

I roll my eyes. Seriously. Is this really the first thing she is going to ask me after she almost died and is just now coming to? Trev chuckles knowing that I'm annoyed.

"He's at the office with Gabriele. They will be back soon. He was by your side all night. I'm not even sure how he's at the office right now," I inform her.

She nods her head and cracks the tiniest of smiles. "Dez, are you able to move your toes?" I question worried.

She wiggles them and I instantly calm. Trev and I smile at each other ear to ear. I start telling them both about my trip, trying to keep her awake and her mind off things. After a couple of hours of me talking she closes her eyes and falls back asleep. It's now early evening and Trev heads out so he can get ready for his shift. I grab the extra pillow laying it behind me then closing my eyes for a bit. Exhaustion takes me over quickly and I fade into blackness.

I wake up to low voices around me. I rub my eyes cracking them open while stretching. Luke is talking with Dez and Gabriele. She's now sitting up on her own and they said the doctor came in to run some quick vitals and said everything is looking great. He advised if she keeps this up and can walk, eat some solid foods, and use the bathroom on her own then she can return home shortly.

"How long have I've been sleeping?" I ask them.

"Probably just a couple of hours. We got here about an hour and a half ago," Gabriele says.

I stand up and sit on the bed with Dez. "Hey, how are you feeling? Any pain? Headaches?" I ask her then turn to Luke. "Are they giving her any meds for the pain?"

She nods. "Yes, ribs hurt. Small headache," she answers in small breaths.

"I'm pretty sure they're giving them every couple of hours through her IV but I'll make sure to ask the nurse next time she's in," he replies.

Gabriele stands walking over to me. "Come on, let's get you fed. I'm sure you haven't eaten anything since lunch."

I nod. "Actually, Dez's mom is at the apartment. I need to go check and see if she needs anything. She may need a ride back here. I know she said she wanted to rest and come back."

"Okay, we'll stop at your place first."

I say my goodbyes, and we head over to my place. Gabriele, like always is close behind me as I enter the apartment. I walk down the hall toward Dez's room, the door is open a crack and the lights are on. I knock on the door.

"Christy?"

"Come in!" she yells from the bathroom.

I walk in the room looking around seeing her things

already strewn all over the room. "I came by to see if you needed anything, something to eat or a ride to the hospital?"

She pops her head out of the bathroom. "I actually just called an Uber and will grab something at the hospital café. I appreciate the offer though," she says, walking into the room and grabbing some clothes.

"Okay well, you have my number if you need anything. Please send me a list of groceries and I'll be sure to pick some things up for you tomorrow. I'll be staying at Gabriele's tonight and will be by the hospital again in the morning," I tell her.

"Okay sweetie. I'll see you tomorrow then."

I leave the room and grab another set of clothes from mine. My room smells stale, non-lived in, it definitely needs to be aired out. I need to bring my suitcase home and work on some laundry too, but this will be a tomorrow thing. There's no way Gabriele is letting me go so easily yet.

I head out to the kitchen where Gabriele is sitting waiting. "Ready?" he asks.

"I am."

He stands following me out. "I had my assistant grab some fresh groceries. I figured I'll cook instead of going out to eat tonight. You good with that?"

We walk together to the car. "Assistant huh? Is she a pretty assistant?" I question half joking and half with a bit of jealousy.

He chuckles while opening the door for me. He swats my ass as I climb in the car. I squeal. "She is, but she's also happily married."

I roll my eyes dramatically. "Yeah, like that's ever stopped anyone."

He climbs in sitting extra close to me. "That is true for some, but not all. I have no interest in married women."

I've gotten to know him well enough over the last couple

of weeks to know he's telling the truth. "Is it weird to say I'm already missing the island?"

He wraps his arm around me. "Not at all. The island is freedom. Free from the rules of society, free from ordinary everyday life and responsibilities. A place to adventure and try new things. I really enjoyed those moments where you let go of all your inhibitions and let yourself be free. It was sexy as hell, and we will be going back there very soon."

"You're insatiable."

He rubs his lips against my cheek. "Only for you."

I curl up into his chest and exhale allowing all my tension to fade. We get back to his apartment and I head into his bedroom to change into some lounge clothes. Gabriele is already in the kitchen prepping the food by the time I head out to the kitchen.

"Whatcha making?" I ask as I sit down on the counter stool.

"Thought I'd make some chicken Alfredo," he says cutting up the chicken and stirring the sauce that's simmering.

My stomach growls. "That sounds perfect."

I watch him chef-ing it up with his sleeves rolled up in a light blue dress shirt and his magical strong hands as he cuts the chicken. I'm picturing the last couple of weeks and all the time those hands were manhandling me with perfection.

I squeeze my thighs together as my core begins to pulsate with desire. Why does this man have to be so god damn addicting? I think I would rather devour him for dinner instead of the pasta.

"I could watch you cook all day long," I tell him.

He winks at me with a sexy grin. "Maybe next time I'll just wear a chef's hat and nothing else."

I smirk. "I think I'd like that."

I decide to break my news to him now, since he's in a playful mood, that I'm going to be staying back at my house once Desire comes back home. I'm just hoping he doesn't push back on this. He's been so adamant lately about me staying at his house. I'm not sure if it's because of everything that has gone on with Dez being attacked or that he really just wants me near him.

"So, I'm going to go back to the apartment tomorrow to get things ready for Dez when she gets home. She's going to need my help. Dez and her mom made up, but they are still working on their relationship, so I know she's going to need me there."

He's extremely quiet as he continues to cook the chicken in the pan and takes a moment to taste the Alfredo sauce after seasoning it a bit more. I wait patiently for his response since he seems to be simmering with his thoughts.

Finally, he turns to me. "Why don't you just have them both stay here? There's another room for her mother to stay as well and I know Luke has already been considering this idea."

My mouth gapes open. I'm speechless. Is he really this serious? "Gabriele," I say sternly.

I stop and wait until he finally looks up to me. "Gabriele, that's a very kind offer, but Dez won't go for this. I know her. She's going to want to be in the comfort of her own environment. What's this really about anyways?" I question, knowing he must have an ulterior motive for this idea.

"I just am not ready to have you leave yet. I enjoy having you here and I know Luke wants to be a part of her recovery. Also, we have everything you may need at your fingertips here – a driver, security, a gym, pool, and *me*," he says with a smirk proud of himself.

I can't help but laugh. Sometimes he's just so full of himself. "You, huh?"

"Yes, ma'am," he replies sure of himself as he puts the pasta in the boiling water.

"Can I think about it? I need to talk with Dez tomorrow when I go up to the hospital," I tell him.

He reaches into the cupboard grabbing two plates out. The elevator dings open as he sets them on the counter. Luke walks into the kitchen and takes a seat at the counter.

"That smells great. I'm freaking starved," Luke comments.

"Did her mom show up?"

He nods. "Yeah, I figured I'd give them some time together. She just woke up from another nap before she came in."

Gabriele stirs the pasta. "I just offered to have them all come stay with us while she recovers," he informs Luke.

Luke's eyes light up like a little kid with a smile ear to ear. "Yeah?" he asks his brother in disbelief. "I see Miss Naomi has gotten my brother to soften himself just a bit," he teases.

I giggle. "I think he's more bark than bite."

"Oh, don't let him fool you, he definitely bites, but clearly just not with you. You're changing my big bro, Nay," he admits almost thankful.

Gabriele turns, throwing a towel at Luke's face. "Enough."

Luke puts his hands up in surrender. Gabriele drains the pasta then makes all three of our plates. The flavors burst in my mouth as I take the first bite. I didn't realize how starved I was until the food hit my tongue.

"You never cease to amaze me at how everything you touch turns into perfection," I tell him.

He walks around the counter to sit next to me with his plate. "You're just now learning this?"

Luke huffs exasperated. "Just hype him up even more why don't you? His head is big enough."

I turn my attention toward Luke. "So, Luke, tell me a story about your brother over here."

He gives me an evil smirk. Gabriele smacks his lips annoyed. "Okay, I have one for you," he says. "When Gabriele was about sixteen, he was upset with our father, and to get him back he decided to pee on his favorite large plant in his office. He then blamed it on me who was about nine at the time. Lucky for me, my dad had cameras in the office and Gabriele had a lot of explaining to do."

I laugh so hard I snort and immediately cover my mouth embarrassed. Gabriele rolls his eyes as he takes a bite of his Alfredo.

"Thanks for that little reminder," Gabriele says after he finishes chewing.

Luke looks proud of himself. "You're welcome. I have many more stored, but we'll save those for another time," he threatens with a light tease.

Their banter is keeping my mind off Dez, the hospital, and having to decide if I'll be staying here a while longer or not. Everything has been happening at such a rapid pace, I feel like I need a moment to myself to make it all slow down. I can't make good clear decisions when Gabriele is consuming my every thought and when I'm stressed about my best friend.

"Yes, I would love to hear some more at another time," I tell him. I turn my attention to Gabriele, "So, did you get in trouble after that?"

He nods. "My father took my allowance away for a month. Mind you that was his only form of love."

Luke scoffs. "You got that right. Five thousand a month at sixteen was lots of love." Luke snickers with a bit of resentment.

I almost spit out my drink. "Five thousand a month was your allowance?" I repeat loudly in disbelief.

Gabriele finishes his last bite off his plate then walks over to the sink with his back toward us beginning to clean and load the dishwasher. Five minutes has already passed before he says another word. Once he's done cleaning, he turns to answer my question.

"My father threw money at us to keep us happy from his void while he lived his life. Instead of teaching Luke and I the fundamentals of hard work ethics, business strategies, and family dynamics, he taught us how to shove our feelings down and suppress our anger," Gabriele explains.

"You need to give yourself credit Gabriele because whether you had him to look up to or not, you figured it out. You have succeeded and clearly overachieved. I think that's even better that he can't take the credit for that," I say.

I see Luke smiling like a goof at our interaction. "I think she may be right brother. I think we turned out just fine."

Gabriele shakes his head. "Speak for yourself."

I try to hold in my laughter. "Yeah, well this self is exhausted and going to bed. Dinner was great. Now take care of my dishes for me, thanks," he orders him then walks away.

Gabriele exhales, annoyed. "I should have known he would do that. That was a move he did as a kid. It used to drive me nuts."

"He's spunky and witty like Dez. I now see why they get along so well."

He takes mine and Lukes's plates finishing the cleanup then comes over and grabs my hand. "Come on, I'm going to make us a nice hot bath."

I follow him down the hall with my hand in his. As soon as we get to his room, he closes the door and smashes me against it with his body hard on mine. He holds both of my hands over my head with his as he leans down and presses his lips against mine.

I instantly melt against him, allowing him to take control and lead me into a swarm of desire. His fingers entwine through mine gripping me tight as his tongue glides with my tongue in a slow rhythmic dance. There is so much passion and emotion in this kiss that a tear escapes the corner of my eye.

He tilts his head back, takes his thumb and wipes the tear away. He kisses both of my eyes, releases my hands and leads me into the bathroom where he runs the hot water and puts some bubbles in.

Gabriele has me sit on the stool and begins undressing me from head to toe before doing the same for himself. He tests the water with his hand, and turns it off, before helping me in then steps in himself sinking down behind me.

My muscles begin to melt under the blanket of heat as I lean my head back on Gabriele's chest. He pours some soap on a large sponge and begins running it over my arms and chest.

"This feels amazing," I murmur, the exhaustion beginning to consume me.

He starts massaging my shoulders gently. "Can I ask you something?"

"Sure," I assure him.

He pauses for a moment contemplating. "Did you have any past boyfriends?"

"No, never."

He starts rubbing the sponge down my arm again. "Why is that?" Gabriele asks.

I go into detail about my mother, then my grandparents and uncle. I explain in deeper detail about Dez's and our time trying to make ends meet when we first arrived in Pheonix and the things we encountered. By the time I'm finished, his arms are wrapped around me tight, and the water is now lukewarm.

"So, you see, sex and boyfriends have always been the last on my mind. My mother didn't want me to become a young mother like her. She didn't want me to struggle, but little does she know, I still did just that even without a child on my hip." I chuckle to myself.

Gabriele drains the tub then stands us both up and steps out wrapping a towel around his waist then hands me one to dry off with.

I step out of the tub drying off and wrap the towel around my body. Gabriele comes up behind me, wrapping his arms around my waist while watching us through the mirror.

"I'm so glad you waited for me."

I turn to face him wrapping my arms around his neck. "And what makes you think I waited for you?" I question with sass.

I can tell he enjoys our banter. "Because sometimes it only takes that right person to come along to make you lose all your inhibitions. It almost feels like our souls know each other from another lifetime ago, like mine recognized yours, because the moment I laid eyes on you, I knew I had to know you more."

Here he goes again making my blood boil. "How can you keep saying things like this, then turn around and tell me that you're incapable of love?" I demand to know, removing my arms and now crossing them over my chest defensively.

He reaches up to my face gliding his fingers down my cheek. His beautiful golden eyes mesmerize me. "I feel something for you too, little ballerina, love is something I just cannot allow myself to give. But I also can't give you up either. I'm addicted to you."

"I just don't understand. You basically are asking me to stay with you full time, you can't let me go, and you care about me – you refuse to let yourself love me, then what's the point to all this anymore? You got what you wanted with me already, so maybe you should let me go. Why drag this on even more if I'm just going to be the one heartbroken in the end?" I insist on knowing.

He leans in to kiss me, but I back up and storm out of the bathroom, pissed. I untie my towel letting it drop to the floor as I stomp around his room naked. Gabriele leans against the bathroom doorframe with his arms crossed, an amused smirk on his face, watching me.

"I'm not letting you go. You're mine, ballerina and I don't think I'll ever be done with you sweetheart," Gabriele warns.

"Yeah? Well maybe I'm just going to have to let you go," I

snarl as I put shorts and a tank top on and throw the covers back to climb into bed.

He stalks over to me, grabs my wrist pushing me down on my back holding my arms in place above my head as he climbs over me.

He leans down so he's mere inches from my face. "You don't mean that, Naomi." He runs his tongue over the seam of my lips coaxing me to open for him. I refuse though, angry and stubborn.

"Tell me you don't mean that," he whispers in my ear as he grinds his hard length against my core. I shake my head unable to speak, determined not to indulge in him even though my body is on fire with need. I can't help but follow his lead and grind myself back on him. My body has a mind of its own.

He crawls down my body, leans up on his knees, and removes my shorts. His hands trail up my inner thighs until he strokes over my clit. I buck up moaning. His finger coasts over me in small circles, forcing my head back and my mouth open in pleasure.

"Tell me, little ballerina," he requests as he drags his fingers through my sopping wet slit then circles my entrance. I still refuse. He pushes two fingers deep inside and I scream out.

"Oh god, yes. Fuck!" I yell.

His fingers retract then push forward again. My toes curl, waves of heat rush over my skin as he bends his fingers just right to itch my perfect spot.

"Look at me, baby," he asks. "Look at me," he demands.

He continues to fuck me with his fingers but starts to slow down. I meet his eyes looking deep into the window of his soul. I see nothing but pure lust glimmering inside. He takes my hand directing me to rub my own clit while he looks down and watches.

"Tell me you're mine and you're not leaving."

His fingers are in sync with mine. The sound of my juices echo in the room as the walls of my sex begin to convulse sparking an orgasm from deep within me.

"I'm yours."

"Tell me you're staying."

"I'm staying."

He pulls his fingers from inside of me just as I'm about to plumet over the edge.

"No! *Please* don't stop," I cry out.

His towel is already off, his shaft is stone hard, and with just one swift movement he penetrates deep inside of me.

We both scream out as he begins to pump hard and fast bringing me right back to the hilt of my orgasm.

"Fuck yes, just like that," I direct.

Every pump brings me closer to the brink, and just as I think it can't get any better, he adjusts himself to reach upward and deeper making me lose control. My body starts shaking, tears run down the sides of my face as my sex grips tightly around him like a vise grip.

"Jesus fucking Christ, baby. I'm about to come!" he growls, and just like that we both dive over the edge into the deep dark abyss. We free fall until we withdraw every last drop from each other now laying in a heap of sweat.

Our breaths are ragged; Gabriele kisses me slowly and softly while running his fingers through my hair.

"How can my thoughts not be consumed of you after knowing I'm the only one who's been inside of you feeling these mind-blowing orgasms? This pussy is all mine."

I roll my eyes. He grabs a chunk of my hair pulling me gently but forcefully for his attention. "Mine."

I giggle. "Yours."

He smiles satisfied with my reply and gets up to head to the bathroom. I follow to clean myself up. Once we're both done, we slide into bed wrapped in each other's arms until the calm darkness takes over.

CHAPTER 19

The next week went by fast. I spent every day in the hospital with Dez taking turns with her mom and Luke. She's making amazing strides each day, now walking slowly on her own with little help, eating solids, and her concussion has healed with no brain injuries. She still has a way to go with healing and surprisingly she hasn't freaked out yet about her hair.

Her mother has been patient in building a relationship with her, and allowing me to step in when Dez has her moments of breakdown. Luke has surprised me in more ways than one with how attentive he has been to her.

We decided to go back to our apartment, neither Luke nor Gabriele were happy about the decision, but they respect it because it's what Dez has decided. She wants to be comfortable and home. Gabriele has asked me more than once to please reconsider at least myself, but I refused to leave Dez's side again.

He's been testy and short with me on a couple different occasions because he's not getting his way. Dez comes home tomorrow, and I've been busy getting the apartment ready for her. Christy will be sleeping on the couch. I've cleaned every nook and cranny, and have the refrigerator fully stocked. It's been two nights apart after weeks of sleeping together.

I'll be going back to work after I get Dez settled in since her mom will be here to help during the hours I'm gone. They still need some time alone to get to know each other, it will be good for them. I already know Gabriele is going to have a problem with this, but we're nothing more than fuck buddies at this point as he made clear that he refuses to allow himself to love or be in a relationship, so he has no say in the matter.

I hear my cell phone ringing in my bedroom. I run to the room to grab it thinking it may be Dez, but it's Gabriele's number across the phone.

I click answer. "Hey."

"Hey," he replies. "I grabbed some Chinese food; I figured you have been so busy you probably haven't eaten yet. You hungry?"

He's right, I haven't even thought about food. "Starving."

He chuckles. "Open the door."

Shit. I didn't realize he was already here. I haven't even showered yet today I've been so busy running around. I smell my armpits quickly and throw up my hair before answering the door.

Gabriele walks in looking sexy as hell in his suit, tie loose around his neck, smelling better than the food. He gives me a quick kiss on the cheek hello before walking into the kitchen and laying the food out on the counter.

He starts looking through my cupboards to find some plates and silverware. "Go sit down. I'll bring it over to you," he directs.

I put some pillows down around the coffee table just as Dez and I always do. He brings over the containers and plates, taking a seat on the pillow next to me.

He grabs my chin running his thumb over my lips. "I've missed you. My nights haven't been the same without you next to me in my bed," he confesses.

I smile. "I've missed you too," I reply. "How was work? Buy any islands today?" I tease.

He offers me some lo mein, but I take the fried rice instead. We skip the plates and begin eating right out of the cartons. "Not anytime soon," he responds with a grin after he swallows.

"When will Desire's mother get back? Has she been there long?" he questions.

I take a sip of my water to wash down the salty soy sauce and rice. "She left about two hours ago. She said once Luke got there, she would head back. Trev's added some hours at the club, so he's been stopping by to check on her in the early mornings."

I pop a dumpling in my mouth closing my eyes, enjoying the flavors. When I re-open them, Gabriele is still watching me.

"I love watching the way you savor every bit of your food. This might turn into a new fetish of mine," he jokes.

I smack his shoulder. "I've heard of worse ones before."

He stops chewing, looking a bit angry. "I can only imagine the things you've heard at that place, and the fact that you were a virgin working there, you should have never had to be exposed to those sorts of things."

"You tend to learn how to drown it out. It becomes noise in the background, and we just get used to it. Nothing surprises us after a while. Most who come there are harmless and just trying to have a good time anyways," I try to explain.

It doesn't look like he's buying it. "Well, regardless, I'm glad you're not there. I told Trevor I would help him with getting a legit security job so he can get out of that place as well."

I haven't really thought about Trev not working security

there. I mean, I think it would be good for him to try for a real career doing it, and nice of Gabriele to offer, but I've always had him there to depend on. With Dez not being there and Trev possibly moving on, I really need to get a move on with my studies. I just need to make some more money to hold me down after I've already been out of work all these weeks.

"That's really sweet of you, Gabriele. Though, I'm going to miss having him there working with me, but I won't be there forever either," I tell him.

He slams his food down dropping his fork on the coffee table. "What the fuck are you talking about, Naomi?"

Oh boy. I've seen this fury before. "I'll be going back to work as soon as Dez gets settled in."

"The fuck you are!" he growls, raising his voice.

Now I set my food down, looking him square in the eyes. "Gabriele, I'm going back to work, and you have no say in the matter. I need to make money. I need to save a bit more before I can move on to something else. We've talked about this more than once now."

His eyes have darkened, and he looks as though smoke is coming out of his nose, he's so angry. "There's no need for you to go back. There will be one hundred thousand dollars transferred into your account tomorrow," he growls.

I scoff and stand up, beginning to pace across the room in pure rage. "Don't you fucking *dare* put that money in my account! I don't want it! I fucking fell in love with you, Gabriele. I'm no longer taking payment for spending time with you. I'm going back to the club to make my own money. I don't need any handouts!" I yell, wanting to pull my hair out.

He stands up now fuming. "Fuck the men and dancing! It's too dangerous, Naomi. Look what just happened to Desire, that could happen to you. Some fucking creep could decide to follow you home or worse. I can't stand by and let that happen!" he argues, standing his ground.

I sigh loudly. "Gabriele, if you're so worried then why don't you quit your job and be my personal bodyguard," I say sarcastically.

"Funny."

I walk toward him grabbing his wrists. "Trev is still there for now. I'll make sure to only take the shifts when he's working. You don't have to worry about me. I can take care of myself. I'm not as careless as Dez is."

He drops his forehead to mine. "I don't know what I would do if something happened to you," he admits, grabbing the side of my neck and rubbing his thumb along my cheek.

"I'll be fine. Now can we finish eating?"

He's still upset but he nods, giving in and heads back to the cushion he was sitting on. We finish our food and look for a movie to watch. After about an hour snuggled up on the couch, we both fall asleep.

Keys and a door closing wake us both up. Dez's mother walks in from the hospital. I sit up wiping the sleepies from my eyes.

"I'm sorry, I didn't mean to wake you both," her mom says.

Gabriele stretches sitting up on the couch. "How is she? Is she ready for tomorrow?" I ask her.

Christy yawns. "If she could, she would have left tonight."

I laugh. "I bet."

"Are you hungry? There's some Chinese food in the kitchen. Gabriele brought way too much," I offer.

She walks into the kitchen. "Thank you. I'm starving. I didn't have time to grab anything at the hospital. I'm just going to grab a plate and head to her room, if you don't mind?"

"Of course we don't mind. You must be exhausted. I'm

going to head to the hospital in the morning and wait for her release if you would like to join me?" I ask her.

She finishes scooping the food onto her plate. "Yes, I would love that. Thank you for including me," she says before heading to Dez's room.

"I'll probably be leaving around 8AM. I'll knock on your door."

She smiles and nods then walks down the hall to her room. I turn to Gabriele. "Are you going to stay the night?"

He leans in giving me a soft kiss. "Not tonight. I'm going to go home to get some work done in my office. Some things need my attention."

I pout. I haven't realized how much I've missed falling asleep next to him either and now that he's denied me tonight, I'm sad.

"What's with the face?" he asks, leaning down a bit to look me in the eyes.

"I'm not sure when the next time we'll be able to spend time alone together. Dez will be here and she's going to need me."

He takes my hand kissing it. "Nonsense. Luke will be glued here along with her mother; you're going to be dying to get out of the house. What if the nights Luke stays here, you come stay with me, that way her mom can use your room, and we can have that time alone?"

I ponder his idea for a moment before answering. "Okay."

"Yeah? Okay?" he replies shocked that I finally agree with him.

"Yeah." I smirk at his childish excited face.

He smashes his lips against mine, and I instantly melt to him. I'm ready to rip off his clothes but he pushes away, and I whine in protest.

"Though I would love to, I need to get going and her mom's in the other room," he points out, tilting his head toward Dez's room.

I agree and walk him to the door. "Make sure to lock the door behind me," he instructs kissing me on the head.

THE FOLLOWING morning Christy and I head over to the hospital to pick up Dez. When we get to the room Luke is already there by her side. I smile happy to see him. She looks relieved to be finally leaving but also agitated.

I give her a kiss on the cheek. "What's the look for? What's wrong?" I question them both looking between them.

"I want to go now, and they have me waiting for the doctor to come in. I guess he needs to do his last routine checkup before I leave," She sulks.

I laugh and she looks at me giving me the evil eye. "Well, I see you're feeling back to yourself now. Remember where being impatient got you? It landed you here," I scold.

Now she looks even more pissed, but I'll take it. It's great to finally see her getting back to herself.

I look over to Luke. "Shouldn't you be at work?"

"Nah, I'm not going in today. I wanted to make sure you guys had everything you needed," he answers. Dez looks at him with stars in her eyes.

"How's your ribs feeling?"

She involuntarily puts her hand against them. "Still sore. The doctor said they will take a couple months to heal fully."

I take a seat in the empty seat next to her. "What about your head?"

"Same thing – will heal with time. I'll have to come back and have the staples removed. I've been getting some headaches, but he said that was normal," Dez explains. "I need a drink already," she jokes.

Luke scoffs. "Yeah, that ain't happening. Just worry about getting yourself better because it's my turn to take you on a secluded enchanted island," he says winking.

My face immediately flushes pink. I wonder if Luke realizes or knows what that island was actually created for. I mean, his brother would have told him, right?

"And what are you blushing for, Nay?"

Now I know Dez is back because she never misses a beat.

"Could it have something to do with Luke mentioning that island?" she hints.

I shrug looking down toward the floor. Luke chuckles. Damn him, he knows.

"That island was definitely spectacular. So, listen to the docs so you will heal fast, because that place is something worth experiencing," I tell her.

I look over to her mom, who is just scrolling on her phone trying to pretend not to hear our conversation.

Dez smiles from ear to ear. "Oh, you dirty little dog you! I can't wait to hear the details. Girls' night for us!"

I laugh. I missed my Dez. "Yes, girls' night. Some painkillers, popcorn, and a movie," I tease.

She yawns. Looks like all this excitement has already tired her out. Luke stands up fixing her pillow and adjusting her blanket. "You need some rest. We're going to step out in the hall and see what's going on with the doctor and your release papers," he tells her.

She smiles and nods. "Okay."

We all step out of the room into the hallway.

Luke comes up to me. "Naomi, I was hoping to speak with you for a moment."

"Okay –"

He looks a little nervous. What could this possibly be about? "I was hoping maybe you would allow me to stay with her tonight. I want to be there for her, help her settle in since I couldn't convince her to come home with me."

Immediately I start seeing red. "Oh, so you don't think I can take care of my own best friend?" I snarl, anger setting in.

He rubs the back of his neck. "That's not what I'm saying at all, Naomi," he tries to clarify. "I just want to be there to help, and after everything, I'm trying to prove to her that she can trust me."

I take a deep breath, calming myself, and filling myself with a bit of guilt for being so abrupt with him. "I'm sorry. I'm just a little on edge. I shouldn't have just blown up on you like that. You're right, you should be there for her tonight. She would want you there."

He looks relieved. "Thank you."

I nod, then look past him to the doctor heading our way.

"Good morning," Dr. Harold greets us.

"Hey doc, are you here to release our girl?" Luke asks.

Dr. Harold chuckles. "I am. Please excuse us while I go in and perform the last exam."

Luke and I move out of the way so he can enter the room. As soon as the door opens, I hear Dez's mouth scolding him on why he took so long. I just giggle. Poor Doc is in for it.

My phone begins ringing. My heartbeat spikes up with the thought of Gabriele calling but as soon as I see the number I realize it's that out-of-town New York number. I'm not big on answering numbers I don't know, so I hit end and let it go to voicemail.

My face must show my confusion because Luke asks me if everything is okay. I don't hear him the first time he asks as I stare at my phone but once he puts his hand on my arm to get my attention, I answer.

"Yeah, I'm good. Just an odd number that I don't know that's called a couple times," I respond.

"Maybe you should just answer it," Luke suggests.

I shake my head. "I'll let it go to voicemail and wait to see if they leave a message."

We continue to stand in the hallway against the wall for the next twenty minutes until finally Dr. Harold comes out.

"She's all cleared to go. I'll have the nurse come in with

discharge papers. Good luck, she's a feisty one," he warns with a grin, then heads off after we thank him.

We head in, Christy following right behind us, and see Dez already trying to sit up and get out of bed. I rush over to stop her.

"Dez, relax. Let me help. I'm going to grab your clothes, and Luke can help you change while I grab your things," I instruct her.

She huffs. "Fine."

Luke already has a car waiting to take her home. Christy and I drive back together. I realize she's been extremely quiet this whole time. I don't know her well, but I know when something feels off.

"Christy, is everything alright?" I ask.

She continues to look out the window before answering. "My rent payment is coming up, and flying here drained what I had in my savings. I got a call from my job that if I didn't show up for my next shift, they are going to fire me. I won't be able to pay my bills if I lose this job, but I also don't want to leave Desire," she explains.

I can completely understand her dilemma. I rack my brain trying to come up with a solution. I can help her with rent, but that won't help save her job.

"Is there anything I can do to help? I know once you explain things to Dez she will totally understand. She wouldn't want you to lose your job, and she has Luke and I here to help her. When is your next shift?" I question.

She looks so conflicted. "Friday."

Shit. Today is Wednesday, which means she will need to leave tomorrow.

"I know Dez is grateful for you being here. That right there goes a million miles with her. I know you love her, and I know she knows it too. Just know, Luke and I are here for whatever she needs and you're welcome to come stay with us anytime," I tell her.

She sniffles, wiping a tear from her cheek. "Thank you, Naomi. She's extremely lucky to have you as a friend."

We get to the house and Luke already has Dez settled in her bedroom. I go in to take a seat next to Dez on her bed. Luke is on the phone ordering lunch for us all.

"Happy to be home?" I ask.

She looks relieved, content, and extremely exhausted.

She leans back on her pillow carefully while holding her ribs. "So happy," she replies. "I hope you don't mind that Luke stays here tonight –" she questions.

I smile and grab her hand. "Of course not. I'm glad he's here with you. I think he really cares for you, Dez. He's been so attentive and sweet with you. It's nice to see. You deserve it."

Her face lights up. "I really, really like him, Nay. He explained what happened with the woman I saw him with. It was Gabriele's ex-fiancée."

She waits for my reaction before she continues. "Why was he with Gabriele's ex?" I ask, confused.

She grabs my hand before she continues, "Gabriele only did that for show to protect his mother." Now I'm extremely confused. "That was his dad's mistress. The paparazzi were putting two and two together because they were seen out, so to stop his mother from finding out, he told them she was his fiancée, and they were making plans together for the wedding. That got them off his dad's back and put him in the limelight instead. Meanwhile, they continued their affair behind closed doors," she explains.

"Gabriele hated his father for it. He watched his mom bury herself in alcohol because of him for years and there he was being forced to be a part of his adultery. Luke said it ripped Gabriele in two," Dez says.

This all makes more sense now with as many times as Gabriele has told me things aren't always as they seem and the fact that he's against relationships. His father scared him. But this still doesn't explain why Luke was meeting with her.

"So, why was Luke meeting with her?" I question.

She sighs. "Gabriele was paying her off to keep quiet. She threatened more than once to go to the tabloids about his family, so to keep the peace he had just paid. But recently he's stopped. She's pissed and has threatened to bring him down. So, Luke met with her to try to talk some sense into her. He acted as he if didn't know me because he didn't want her to have ammunition to start digging," she finishes.

This makes sense. If she starts digging around on Dez and Luke, then she's bound to find out about Gabriele and me. This would cause a media frenzy. Exactly what Gabriele didn't want in the first place. Things are starting to make sense now. I just wish I found this information out directly from Gabriele.

"That's good. I'm glad he cleared things up. He seemed extremely upset about the whole situation. I'm just sorry I was so quick to judge him. I just had your best interest at heart," I advise her.

She squeezes my hand. "Gabriele didn't tell you any of this?"

I shake my head back and forth. "No. He didn't seem to want to speak on the subject much so I didn't push him."

She nods understanding.

"So, I was thinking I may stay at Gabriele's tonight. Your mom's here and since Luke's staying here, I figured I would go spend some time with him. He's been acting like a baby for days because I told him I was staying here with you," I inform her.

Dez giggles. "Oh boy, Nay. Gabriele has it bad for you. I don't mind one bit. You go get you some good dick, and ease his tension *and* yours for that matter," she finishes laughing.

I have to admit I have some built up tension that needs some major releasing too.

"Thank you for being by my side through all this, Nay. I feel like the luckiest girl to have met a friend so amazing as you," Dez tells me.

A tear escapes me, and I lean over giving her a soft careful hug. I'm so full of happiness right now. I hear a throat clear from behind us. We both turn and Luke is at the door.

"Sorry to interrupt," Luke says, holding a plate of food. "Lunch is here."

I nod and stand up but falter a bit, feeling lightheaded.

"Nay, are you okay? Sit back down!" Dez orders.

Luke puts the food down on the dresser and quickly walks over to me squatting down.

I swat them away. "I'm fine. I just stood up too fast."

They both look at each other and then back to me. "When's the last time you ate, Nay?" Luke asks.

I shake my head. I had a bagel this morning before I came to the hospital. They both nod. "You need to eat," Dez says.

I stand up again but this time I'm fine. "I'm going to go grab some food now and then go take a nap before heading over to Gabriele's."

Luke hovers over me as I leave. "Luke, I'm fine. Go feed my girl."

He looks skeptical but complies.

I WAKE UP TO A TEXT. I roll over grabbing my phone off my nightstand and see it's Gabriele. I stretch first before responding, enjoying the feel of my own bed. Don't get me wrong, I love sleeping next to Gabriele, but there's something about sleeping back in your very own bed that makes me happy.

I open Gabriele's text.

"I'll be there in thirty minutes to pick you up."

Shit. I need a shower. I sit up but immediately feel my stomach turn. My mouth begins to water, I cover my mouth running to the bathroom and empty my lunch into the toilet bowl.

Tears run down my face as I dry heave the last of it. Finally finished, I push off my knees and sit against the bathroom wall with my head back wiping my mouth. Fuck, I'm now turned off from turkey sandwiches for a very long time. The meat must have been bad. I wonder if anyone else feels this way.

I drag myself up and start the shower. I strip my clothes off and climb in, letting the hot water ease my nauseous body. By the time I'm finished I'm feeling more relieved and back to myself.

I wrap the towel around my hair heading out to my room to get dressed. I stop in my tracks, then smile as I see Gabriele lying on my bed with his hands behind his head, completely naked, looking sexy as fuck. He grins dragging his eyes over my buck-naked body. Feels a little like deja vu.

"Come here, little ballerina."

I walk slowly over to him, body already heated like an inferno stopping at the bed beside him. He removes his hands from behind his head, gaze locked on mine while reaching for my knee and dragging his fingers slowly up my inner thigh. My vagina pulsates with anticipation as he inches closer and closer to my beating apex of need.

He swipes over my sex making me hiss from his touch. He looks ravenous as he watches my need flame to a desperate desire.

"Tell me what you want, little ballerina," Gabriele asks, never taking his eyes off me.

"You. I want you. I want you to make me come."

He smirks, grabs my hips, slides down the bed and pulls

me over him so I'm now directly over his face. I place my hands against the headboard to balance myself while he begins his leisurely assault on my clit.

I grind myself against his tongue, he moans against me making the vibrations do funny things. His fingers drift through my sex entering me slow, stoking and taking his time with his insertion matching his movements with his tongue.

Heat consumes my insides, licking every part of me just like his tongue. I do my best to keep my moans light, so nobody hears us but it's getting harder by the minute.

I lean back grabbing his hard length with my hand, and a moan rips from him.

"Shhh," I shush him with a giggle.

I decide to venture my way down, removing his tongue and fingers from me.

"What are you doing?" he whispers, looking confused until I place myself directly over his cock and sink down.

"*Oh shit*, ballerina," he groans.

Gabriele's mouth opens with a silent moan, eyes rolling back, and leans his head back down on the pillow. His fingers dig into the sides of my hips as I begin to move, grinding myself back and forth with his help.

Our bodies slip and slide as they are locked together; sweat beads covering my skin as I grind over him. His cock is buried to the hilt inside of me and every move I make hits my spot deep within me. I dig my nails into his chest as the feeling of combustion begins to devour me.

I slam my head back allowing the pleasure to consume me as I begin to ride out my orgasm trying my best not to scream out while biting my bottom lip.

"Look at me, ballerina," Gabriele commands in a whisper.

I meet his gaze, and the feeling of love fills me to the core. The way his stare pierces through my soul is almost too much. He opens his mouth as though he's going to say something then slams it shut reaching between us stroking my clit instead, detonating my orgasm into a nuclear explosion.

He falls right after me, spewing his warm gooey seed deep into me. I fall on top of him panting, my face in the crook of his neck. We both lay here heaving trying to catch our breath as he runs his fingers lightly up and down my back.

"That was amazing," he admits.

I smile. "It was. I think I'm going to need another shower," I joke. We both laugh.

We stay like this for awhile longer until eventually my stomach begins to growl. He lifts his head up looking at me.

"When's the last time you ate?"

I sit up. "I had lunch, but it upset my stomach, and I ended up bringing it back up," I tell him.

He looks concerned. "Are you feeling okay now?"

I nod, get up, and head to the bathroom to jump in the shower again and wash my body off quickly. I feel as though I just came home from the gym with all the sweat lathering my body. I hear the shower curtain move and Gabriele's warm body heat radiating behind me.

He grabs the soap from me beginning to wash me down. I turn and do the same for him before we hop out. We wrap ourselves in towels then head out to my room to get dressed.

"What are you in the mood to eat? I can cook or call in some takeout for my place," Gabriele suggests.

I grab a pair of jeans and shirt from my closet. "I'm sort of in the mood for some comfort food. How about some Pho? There's a place down the street we can order from and pick it up on the way to your place," I suggest.

"Perfect," Gabriele agrees as he finishes getting dressed.

"You order. I'm going to go check on Dez before we leave and make sure Christy is all set for the night."

He nods and picks up the phone to call.

I head down the hall and knock on the door quietly. "Come in," Luke says quietly.

Dez is knocked out cold when I enter the room. Luke is on the bed beside her working on his laptop. "Gabriele and I are taking off. How's Dez?"

He looks over to her admiringly. My heart softens. "She knocked out after I gave her some pain meds. She's uncomfortable and exhausted."

"Do you need us to grab anything before we leave?" I ask.

He shakes his head and holds up his phone. "I have everything available with just one push of a button," he boasts childishly.

I shake my head rolling my eyes. "Just like your brother." I chuckle. "Okay, call me if anything changes. I'm going to go check on Christy."

"Night, Nay."

"Night, Luke."

I close the door quietly and head out into the living room. Gabriele is already there in mid conversation with Christy. Christy's eyes are red and swollen from crying. My heart rips in two and I rush over to the couch to comfort her.

"Were you able to speak with Dez yet?" I ask her.

She shakes her head. Gabriele brings me a tissue to give to her.

"I'm sure she will be up early tomorrow morning after all the sleep she's getting tonight. Make sure to go in and speak with her. Luke won't mind at all," I tell her.

"I will. I didn't want to upset her on her first night home."

I grab her hand. "Like I said earlier, Dez will completely understand. Were you able to book a flight?"

She nods wiping her nose. "Yes, my flight leaves tomorrow night. I have to be at the airport by 5PM."

"Okay, I'll be back tomorrow afternoon, and I can bring you."

She looks relieved. "Are you sure? I can take an Uber?"

I swat the air. "Nonsense. I would be more than happy to bring you."

"Thank you, Naomi. I really appreciate all you have done and for making me feel welcome."

I reach over giving her a hug before I head out. "You're part of Dez, which makes you part of this little family we have created too. Now, call me if anything changes or you need anything."

"I will. Have a good night you two," she says.

We say our goodbyes and head out to Gabriele's.

CHAPTER 20

$\mathcal{I}$'ve been spending every other night at Gabriele's so Luke and Dez could get some alone time but also so Gabriele and I could have the same as well. It's been a week since Christy left. Dez was upset that her boss was so cruel to her, but ultimately understood why her mother had to leave. She has plans to save up some money so she can come back and spend some time with Dez in the next couple of months. Little does she know; Gabriele and I already plan on sending her a ticket and some extra cash for bills when that time comes.

Dez has been recovering quickly, quicker than the doctors had expected, but they still want her to take it easy with very minimal activity. She's getting extremely antsy but between us all, we've been able to subdue her during those times.

Tonight, I've decided to head back to work, and I haven't told Gabriele. Even though I've already told him he had no say in this, I've already witnessed his reaction to the idea of me going back, but I'm not ready for his tantrum when I'm actually heading back.

I pop my head into Dez's room, and I hear nothing but

laughter echoing through her room. This just melts my heart seeing Dez so happy. They both look like carefree teenagers.

"Hey, guys."

They both turn not even realizing I am now standing at the end of the bed.

"Hey, Nay," Dez says. "Are you heading out?" she asks.

I really didn't want to announce this in front of Luke, but Dez won't let me evade the question regardless.

"Yeah, I'm heading back to work. Trev is here waiting for me."

Luke looks conflicted with this information.

Dez nods. "Okay, just be careful, Nay. Are you coming back home or are you going to Gabriele's?"

"Trev's bringing me home once the shifts over. Have fun you two!" I yell as I walk out the door.

I can hear Luke voice his concerns as I walk out but Dez puts him in his place advising him to mind his business. I smile silently high-fiving my friend for having my back always.

I take a deep breath as Trev pulls into the parking lot. I look over to the alleyway where Dez was attacked feeling guilt and panic hit me like a tsunami. I grab my chest and immediately lean down as my vision begins to fade. I faintly hear Trev yelling my name as I try hard to take deep breaths while a high-pitched ring floods my ears.

I concentrate on my breaths until finally my panic attack subsides.

"Nay! What the fuck?" Trev yells.

He's now kneeling beside me with the car door open.

I lift my head up shaken up a bit. I need to get these under control.

"Trev, I'm okay. It's passed now," I tell him.

He has his phone pulled out looking as though he's about to dial a number.

"You're lucky, I was just about to call Gabriele," he admits.

I squint aggravated. "Don't you fucking dare call him. The last thing I need is him showing up here making a scene and stopping me from going in there to work."

"Well, in this case I would have agreed with him. I don't think you're ready to go back to work. Look what just happened when you saw the parking lot. You have too much going on and I think you need to figure out how to control these panic attacks, Nay."

Trev helps me as I step out of the car. "Not one word to anyone about this. I'll be fine. Promise me, Trev?"

He looks pissed that I'm putting him in this predicament, but ultimately, he agrees but tells me if it happens again on his watch, he's not keeping his mouth shut. I agree.

The girls were all surprised to see me back to work so soon. They all asked about Dez except for Shae. She rolled her eyes as she walked by me in the dressing room. Jerry without a beat demanded I handle the bachelor party. He says I owe him for being out so long and making him miss out on money.

Fucking asshole.

I head over to the table of rowdy men, Jen's already there entertaining. I see nothing but disrespectful hand grabbing and pulling as they pour drinks down their throats. This is not the first day back I was envisioning.

"Well, well, look what we have here, gentlemen. We have us some fresh meat. Come here beautiful and grind that sexy body on me," one of the men demands.

I smile taking a silent breath, I look over to Trev first to make sure he's in proximity before walking over to him. Trev nods, and I immediately feel a bit better.

The redhead immediately reaches for me, grabbing my hips down, and smacks my ass hard. I snap my head around. "No touching!" I growl.

"Oh, come on, darling. I'm just having a little fun," he slurs.

He smells of cheap bourbon and cigarettes. He now wraps his hand around grabbing a handful of my breast while holding my hip with his other hand so I can't move. I begin to panic and look to Trev. I see him heading my way but before he can even reach me, I'm lifted off the guy and his face is being pummeled by Gabriele's fist.

Blood is now spewing from the man's face as he lies limp against the booth. Trev pulls Gabriele off, but now the other men from the table are coming at them both. Fists and glasses begin flying, and the whole club is now broken out in chaos.

I watch in shock as Jerry comes running over losing his mind. Eventually, security gets the crowd under control, but just a moment too late as the police come barreling through the doors. Jerry runs over trying to minimize the damage by convincing them it was a simple misunderstanding until they see the redhead unconscious and bloodied up laying lifeless on the booth.

The officer tends to the man and calls for medical assistance.

After the officers speak with his friends, they now head over to our direction. Gabriele's busy looking over me, making sure I didn't get hit in the crossfire, not having a care in the world that the officer is now standing in front of him trying to get his attention.

"Gabriele," I say, nodding my head toward the cop.

Gabriele now acknowledges him. He speaks to them on his side of the story, but they aren't buying the whole rescue act for a dancer. I'm not surprised since they're looking at me as I'm beneath them, which pisses Gabriele off even further.

They advise him the friends want to press charges and they need to take him in to book him.

"Wait, are you guys fucking serious?" I yell. "They were breaking the rules. I told them more than once not to touch me and he continued to manhandle me!"

I cop blatantly laughs in my face. "Ma'am, no offense, but do you see where you're working? Isn't that what's expected from this type of environment that pays for those type of services?" he questions sarcastically.

Gabriele's knuckles are white from squeezing his fists as he walks up face to face with the officer, fuming with anger. I grab hold of his upper arm trying to pull him back, but he doesn't budge one bit. The officer takes a step back feeling uneasy.

"Sir, I suggest you take a step back," he warns.

"I'd like to know if this is how they taught you how to treat women in your basic training? I don't give a *fuck* where she has chosen to be employed, she fucking deserves some respect when she's telling you she was being manhandled and assaulted unwillingly by a man. But here you are acting as though she deserved this while being a fucking judgmental fucking prick! This is what's wrong with the wrong people in service. I can promise you, after I am bailed out by my attorney that you my friend will be taken care of. I don't think you know who the fuck you're dealing with!" Gabriele threatens.

At this point the whole club has cleared out and the ones left are now watching this scene unfold. Another colleague comes up and whispers in the officer's ear standing in front of Gabriele, and his eyes widen. My guess he has now been made aware of exactly who he is dealing with.

Gabriele smiles with a knowing grin. "Yes, I am a huge donator that helps fund the police. Gerald, the commissioner, is a great friend of mine and will be well informed on how his police officers are trained and handling victims."

The officer backtracks now. "Listen Mr. Vanucci, I apologize. You're right, I shouldn't have jumped to conclusions so fast," he admits. Then looks to me. "I apologize, ma'am."

Gabriele nods still not pleased. "I still unfortunately must do my job and take you in to book you. These guys over here are adamant about pressing charges," the officers inform.

"I understand."

Gabriele turns to me. "Make sure you leave with Trevor. I'll be by the apartment in a little while. Pack a bag because you're coming to stay with me tonight and I'm not taking no for an answer," he demands.

"Okay, I'll see you soon."

I do my best not to bring any more attention to us by being affectionate, but my co-workers are noticing and whispering already due to Gabriele causing a scene, and Jerry is looking mighty pissed off. I already know he's going to demand my pay due to the fact the club was interrupted and shut down tonight due to my relationship with Gabriele.

Gabriele leaves in cuffs and after the redhead is taken by ambulance the rest of his possie disperses. I head back to the dressing room to get changed.

"Not so fast, Jazz!" Jerry yells, following me.

I don't stop. I continue to grab my things. "Not now, Jerry."

"You owe me for this little stunt that you and your little boyfriend caused tonight. I expect double payment," he demands.

I'm fucking done with him, this place, and his ridiculous demands. "Jerry, I'm not paying you a dime. It's not my fault that you can't control your customers, and you blatantly allow me and every other girl here to be disrespected."

He stands with his arms crossed in front of the doorway blocking my way out. "You leave, you're not allowed back," he threatens.

I throw my makeup in my bag, pull my sweatpants on with a hoodie, and whip my bag over my shoulder squaring up to him as I walk toward the door.

"Fine. I wasn't planning on coming back here. Now move the fuck out of my way!" I growl.

Jadah comes behind him. "Jerry, let the girl go," she tells him.

After a moment of a stare down, he finally moves aside, and I see Trev waiting for me at the door. Trev takes the club security shirt off and throws it down on the bar and we walk out together with our heads held high.

"Fuck that place, Nay. We can both do way better than this dump," Trev says.

I wrap my arms around him as we walk proud of us for both making a stand. "Thanks for having my back, Trev. You're the bestest gay friend a girl could ever have," I say laughing.

"I'm your only gay friend," he replies laughing.

We get into the car, and head out. "Until I meet Adam. You have to call him and tell him you made a mistake. Dez told me how happy you seemed, and I don't want you to regret your decision because of us. Dez has Luke to help, and I have Gabriele up my damn ass, you need someone too."

Trev remains quiet as he thinks and deciphers what he's going to decide in his head. "I think you're both right. I'm going to call him once I drop you off. I really do like him. You know me and commitments; it scared the shit out of me that I enjoyed having him around all the time. I guess I felt like if I let him go before he realizes I wasn't right for him then I could save myself the heartache in the long run," he admits.

I sigh. "I know exactly what you mean, but sometimes we have to just let go and embrace heartbreaks. I guess if I can take anything from my situation with Gabriele, it's to just live in the moment because tomorrow is never promised. All these years I have just walked through life not really *living*; I want to *live*. I want to *feel*. I want to love and be loved and that can't happen if I don't take the chance."

Trev smiles as he pulls up to the apartment. "I think Mr.

Gabriele is having a good impact on you, Nay. Miss Realist is becoming more of a dreamer," Trev teases.

I roll my eyes. "Okay, okay. Don't push it," I tell him as I step out of the car. I do a double check of my surroundings before I completely begin to walk away. "Love you, Trev. Call me in the morning and let me know how it went!" I yell behind me.

GABRIELE SHOWS up at my door in record time. I thought it would have at least been a couple more hours until he was released but I guess people are right, money talks.

He gives me a kiss as he walks in the door. "You ready?" he asks, seeming in a hurry.

"Yeah, give me a minute," I tell him walking toward my room to grab my bag.

It's late, Luke and Dez are sound asleep. I grab a couple extra sets of clothes since I'm not sure how long Gabriele will keep me hostage after he finds out I quit the club.

We lock up and head to his place. I drop my bag in his room and immediately I feel his arms wrap around my waist and lips on my neck.

"I've missed this," he admits, while rubbing lips up my neck leaving a trail of sweet kisses behind. I turn around wrapping my arms around his neck. "What happened after I left?" he questions.

"Trev and I quit."

His brows raise surprised. "Really? So, you're done with that place?"

"I am," I inform him. "Jerry tried to extort me for more money, and I decided enough was enough. I'll figure something else out."

He lifts me up off my feet and swings me around. "I'm so proud of you, little ballerina."

I laugh. "You're just happy you finally got your way."

He puts me down. "Yes, but I'm happier the decision came from you. Now let's go celebrate!" he says, dragging me down the hall to the kitchen like an excited schoolboy.

Gabriele grabs two champagne glasses from the bar and a bottle of champagne from the fridge. He pops the cork pouring us both a nice full glass then hands me mine.

He holds up his glass. "To starting a new chapter and new beginnings."

We clink our glasses and take a sip as we stare each other in the eyes – seven years bad luck if we don't. Now I need to figure out my next move, jobless and bored is not a great combo. I refuse to take any handouts either. I know Gabriele is going to make his offer again, but I just can't take his money now that I've fallen for him. It just doesn't feel right.

"How are you feeling about it all?" he asks.

I sigh feeling relieved and lost all at the same time. "I guess it still hasn't really sunk in yet. I know I need to replace my time fast to keep me busy. I enjoy making money. I just need to figure out my next steps."

He watches me as he thinks. I can see his wheels turning as I take a sip of my champagne. I know he's going to offer me something to piss me off. I wait, preparing for it.

He opens his mouth to speak, and I decide to jump in before we end up in an argument. "Gabriele, please don't try to fix this or offer to save me. I will figure something out, but I need to figure it out on my own."

His eyes glow proudly with a side smile. "I guess you're beginning to know me a little too well." He chuckles. "You're right. You don't need my help. I know you will do just fine without it. You're one of the strongest women I have come across."

Heat creeps in my cheeks as they turn pink. He reaches for me and rubs his thumb along my now painted cheek. I close my eyes and lean into him. It's insane how far we have come in just a couple of weeks. A tiny part of me continues to hold my breath as I wait for him to tire of me. I'm waiting for the inevitable event to occur of him walking out the door. It's a little exhausting to be honest, but I wouldn't trade this feeling for the world.

"How do you always know just the right words to say? You say you're not the relationship type, but here you are acting like you know how to be the perfect boyfriend."

He removes his hand from me, and I immediately shiver from the missing heat. I watch him walk away to the window looking over the city looking to be in deep thought. I allow him a moment to himself. Clearly what I've just said bothered him some, but I've only said what's true. He may not think he wants a relationship but how he's acting with me says the complete opposite.

After a moment, I walk over to him. "Did I say something wrong?"

When he turns to look at me, my breath catches. The smoldering darkness his golden-green eyes hold has so much intensity that he gives me chills. I've never seen this look before. It's almost as if he's drowning in emotions that he's fighting so hard to deny.

I reach out and touch his forearm. "Gabriele?"

Without another thought, he reaches down, grabs my ass, and smashes his lips against mine as I wrap my legs around him. This kiss is full of need and powerful desperation to dominate me as he carries us toward his room. Even though he won't admit it, I can taste his immense feelings of love as it pours into me through this kiss.

I may be confusing love with desire at the moment but whatever it is, this feeling is like being on top of the world; hiking through the thinnest trail knowing one step to the right or left could be the end of your demise. My life has been dulled for so long, he makes me feel alive in a world full of possibilities in an array of bright colors.

Nothing can penetrate this bubble we have created in this moment. It's just him and I against the world and there's nowhere else I'd rather be than in it with him right now.

AFTER A LONG NIGHT of multiple orgasms and extreme cardio, I stretch feeling stiff, muscles sore and achy. Gabriele's arm is still wrapped around me allowing me little wiggle room. His hold is a possessive comfort. His breathing is shallow, pink lips ajar just slightly, and thick lashes fanned against his cheeks. He looks serene and majestically sexy lying next to me.

My phone is showing 9AM. I smile, feeling grateful for the extra hours. I carefully move Gabriele's hold around me, my bladder is full and in dire need of relief. I stand up feeling a bit queasy and lightheaded. I take a seat back down on the bed to gather myself for a moment. I must have stood up too fast.

Gabriele stirs looking over at me, then quickly sits up. "Hey, what's going on? Are you okay?"

I turn to him smiling weakly. "Yeah, I just stood up too fast. Probably some low blood sugar. You worked me to the bone last night. Probably in need of some electrolytes," I joke.

I stand back up heading to the bathroom. Gabriele gets up and follows right behind my feet. I roll my eyes annoyed. I turn in the bathroom to face him. "Seriously? I'm fine. Go make us some breakfast."

He chuckles and kisses me on the forehead. "Good idea. Yell if you need me."

I take a long hot shower that's much needed after the cardio acrobats we did last night. There's no need for the gym today, my body just needs some nourishment and some relaxation after these long couple of weeks. I think I may just finally be wearing down a bit after the whole ordeal with Dez. I haven't had a moment to sit down and just catch up with my own feelings on the whole situation. This may be my body telling me to do just that.

The smell of bacon and coffee wafts down the hall as I head to the kitchen. My stomach growls ready to consume an elephant after the night we had. The positions he took me in were not what I was used to, leaving me as sore as my first time; it felt as though he wanted to possess my body and soul, the passion that transpired between us was like no other time. It was magical and intense with words of sweet nothings mixed with hard core porn talk between us. The perfect combination of a steamy night.

Gabriele turns with a beaming smile as I walk into the kitchen. He pours me a cup of coffee, handing it to me before a kiss.

"So, I need to go into the office, but I can drop you off to your apartment if you want to go spend some time with Desire," he offers, stacking a plate full of eggs, bacon, and toast.

I shove a piece of bacon into my mouth before responding. Then sip my orange juice to wash it all down. "Yeah, that works since Luke probably will be heading to the office as well. I'm going to go grocery shopping too and do some studying with stocks."

Gabriele fills his plate but stays standing across the island from me. His hair is disheveled, his bare caramel chest looks like it's chiseled out of stone while his pajama bottoms hang extremely low. I'm no longer hungry for this plate of food in front of me, but hungry for another round from last night.

"Naomi, I want you to reconsider coming to stay here with me."

My brows furrow with confusion. He doesn't want a relationship but wants me to move in with him. What sense does this even make? How does he not see how misleading his words and actions are? God, he's so extremely frustrating.

But I have a proposal for him too. "Okay, I'll move in with you but only when you're ready for a relationship."

He shakes his head aggravated. "You already know where I stand with that."

I hold my head high. "And now you know where I stand with this."

We sit here at a standstill in the kitchen just staring at each other. He walks around the island not taking his eyes away from mine. He grabs my face leaning his forehead to mine.

"You drive me crazy, you know that?" he whispers.

"And you drive me crazy, in more ways than one."

We finish our breakfast, get dressed, and head out. We don't speak of me moving in with him again. He can't give me what I want so in turn I won't give him what he wants. He already took my virginity and now stole my heart, everything else is mine unless he gives me something of his.

When we reach the ground floor, the elevators open, and the sidewalk is full of paparazzi on the other side of the glass waiting for Gabriele; swarms of people holding cameras just waiting for the moment we exit the doors. The doorman immediately runs up to us advising Gabriele that he moved the driver to the back of the hotel and is waiting for us.

Gabriele immediately gets on a call as we walk to the back of the hotel. "What the *fuck*, Conner! Why didn't you warn me?" he screams into the phone. I've never heard this side of him. He's more than angry, he's fumingly mad. Mad enough that I stop and take a step back.

He stopped for a moment and looks to his phone. *FUCK!* He yells again. I jump, trying to catch up as he walks faster now.

He grabs my hand. "Come on, we have to hurry."

We get to the SUV, jump in, and speed off before the paparazzi realize where we are and follow us.

Gabriele is still busy on his phone texting. I'm almost a little hesitant to interrupt him.

"Gabriele, what's going on?"

He doesn't answer. "Gabriele!" I shout this time trying to get his attention.

He finally looks up to me. "What the fuck is going on?" I question with my arms folded over my chest.

He sighs dramatically. "Remember I told you the paparazzi will only come around when there's a story?"

I nod.

"They caught wind of my arrest last night."

Shit. The whole night runs back through my head. He then shows me the article on his phone. It reads, "Billionaire, Gabriele Vanucci, arrested for assaulting a man to protect his stripper girlfriend working at the G-String girls club."

I feel sick. Immediately I feel as though I can't breathe. I lean over in my seat putting my head into my hands trying hard not to bring on a panic attack. I need to remain calm. This is going to be okay. His team will take care of it and make it all go away. Maybe they won't figure out who I am. Maybe I can stay hidden, and they will move onto something else by tomorrow.

He then pulls up another article, and another. It's all over the internet. "I need to clean up this mess," he tells me then gets back on another phone call.

The car feels as though it's going to close in on me. I feel as though I'm walking down a dark tunnel of aloneness as the light dims behind me the further I go. I roll down the window practically sticking my head out the window to breathe in some fresh air. I close my eyes just inhaling the warm air allowing me to calm myself down.

We finally reach my apartment, and I feel relieved as there is no one parked outside my place. I'm not sure what I would have done if the paparazzi were waiting for us. The last thing I want to do is interrupt Dez's healing process with this drama.

Gabriele ends his call as Connor pulls up to the door.

"Were you able to get this handled?" I ask, almost afraid of what his answer might be.

He gives me a weak smile. "I'm working on it. I think for now we should take some time off. They are relentless and they will make it their mission to try to figure out who you are. If we're together then they will. I don't want you involved in this world."

My heart drops feeling like a knife has just slowly sliced it in two. I knew this day would come when he would push me aside. I mean, who wants to get thrown in the spotlight having connections with a stripper? It's not a good look for him, and I knew this deep down inside. He's now confirming it, what I've known all along. I just was expecting a little more time.

I nod, removing my eye contact from his. If I look at him any longer, I may make a fool of myself and cry.

"I understand," I tell him, then grab the door handle to leave, but he yanks me back catching me off guard, sucking in a breath as his lips press against mine.

This kiss is no longer full of promises and possibilities, but now drenched with emptiness and sad goodbyes. A tear escapes my eye so I pull away before anything more can betray me. My heart is literally ripping into shreds in my rib cage. The pain I'm feeling is like no other.

He wipes my tear away with his thumb. "This isn't goodbye. It's I'll see you soon, okay?"

I nod with a weak smile and head out of the car to my door. I turn for one last look before I reach the door, but he's already gone. No waiting to make sure I get in, no one last glace before he pulls off, he just disappears as if he never existed in the first place.

CHAPTER 21

*T*he slice of sunlight through my blinds wakes me up. I've been tossing and turning all night. I am more than sleep deprived. I'm in a zombie state of mind as I rub the crusties from my eyes. When I pick up my phone, I realize it's barely the ass crack of dawn and my good friend insomnia is clearly back now that I'm Gabriele-less and back in my own bed as if the last couple of months never happened.

Only I know it did because Dez is still healing, and I feel like my heart has been ripped out from my chest and placed into a blender.

It's been a couple of days since I've seen Gabriele or heard from him. He hasn't texted or called. I didn't tell Dez about him wanting space because I know she would kill him, so I've kept my agony buried deep inside, only allowing relief of my tears to escape at night when I'm locked up in the dark by myself.

I find myself screaming into my pillow to relieve the pain. I know he said this wasn't goodbye, but I can't help but feel he lied for my sake and for his. If the thought of possibility was still left in the air, then it doesn't make it so final and absolute, and he wouldn't feel like such a shit bag.

I told Dez that he left on a business trip, but I know Luke is well aware of the situation and seems to be on pins and needles every time I'm around him. He clearly doesn't want Dez to know, because she would automatically know that he's guilty of withholding information from her. He's already learned how that can play out, and I know he's just scared of her kicking him out of her life again. Who can blame him? This isn't his fault.

Luke went back to the penthouse, I'm sure he's on clean-up crew with Gabriele but he told Dez that he needed to go into the office. I've been stalking the articles online, as soon as one is taken down another two pops up in its place. The paparazzi are relentless in following Gabriele and smearing his face all over the internet. He looks downright miserable in every single photo. I just want to reach out to comfort him, I want us to teleport back to the island where it was just us in a protected cocoon of beauty. But here I am being hunted down by these money-hungry savages.

Every article is asking, "Who is the mystery stripper that Gabriele Vanucci saved?"

I would have thought after a couple of days things would have wound down, but nope, they are like sharks out for blood.

I hear a quick knock on my door. "Nay? You up?"

I roll over and see Dez. "Hey, why you up so early?"

I fold my comforter back for her and she walks over climbing in.

"I don't know. It sucks sleeping without Luke. I tossed and turned all morning. I feel like a needy baby wanting him with me all the time," she admits.

I laugh, knowing the exact feeling. "Girl, you're not alone. I feel the same way. It's like those damn brothers put a spell on us," I joke, reaching over and pushing a strand of lose hair behind her ear.

"When's Gabriele coming back? We should do a double date here."

Shit. I'm going to have to lie to her, and she's going to see right through me. I don't lie to Dez. I also never keep things from her. What the fuck am I supposed to tell her?

"I'm not too sure, Dez." This is the only thing I could muster up.

She lifts her head up from the propped-up pillow. "What do you mean you're not sure? You always know, and from the moment he met you he's barely left your side. What aren't you telling me, Nay? And *don't* fucking lie to me or I'll call Luke right now!" she threatens.

"Is this all because of the articles online? Luke told me what happened even though you didn't. I've been waiting for you to come talk to me about it all."

Fucking Luke.

Guilt takes over me for not coming to my best friend sooner. Tears begin to slide down my face.

"Oh Nay! What's going on? Just talk to me," she says, wiping the tears away as they fall.

I take a deep breath ready to finally say this out loud. I guess if I didn't then a little part of me could hold on to the possibility of it not being real. Saying it out loud makes it concrete.

"When he dropped me off after the incident, he told me we needed to take a little break. I haven't heard from him since," I admit then exhale a large breath because it's finally out.

"Okay, so he doesn't want you involved, which is understandable, so maybe he's worried that if he contacts you then he won't be able to stay away until this blows over. There's got to be a good explanation for all this. Do you want me to talk to Luke about it?" she asks.

I immediately shake my head no. "No. Please don't. Just leave him out of this. If Gabriele wants to contact me then he knows how to reach me. I don't want Luke involved. Promise me Dez that you won't involve him?"

She looks torn, but ultimately a promise to me overrides any loyalty to him – for now.

"I promise."

"Thank you," I say, relieved.

"Now, how about you make me some breakfast. I've starving and I won't be able to go back to sleep," Dez demands.

I giggle, so happy my friend is coming back to her old self.

"Sure, come on. Let's call Trev and wake him and Adam up too," I reply, stretching then getting out of bed.

Trev reached out to Adam the night we quit, and they have been inseparable ever since. I still have yet to meet him, but we've all talked on FaceTime, and I can see the light in Trev's eyes when they're together. He deserves this so much and Adam seems to be the perfect ying to his yang.

I head to the door, but my mouth starts to salivate getting that nauseous icky feeling. Stopping to lean my hand against my dresser hoping it will pass, I begin to dry heave covering my mouth running to the bathroom. My whole dinner from last night comes up with a vengeance while tears stream down my face.

"Nay! What the fuck?" Dez screeches behind me in the bathroom.

She runs cold water over a washcloth for me, and hands me a tissue to wipe my mouth after I get everything out. I lean against the tub with the washcloth over my forehead feeling drained.

"What the hell just happened?" Dez questions sitting on the toilet next to me.

I just shake my head not able to speak yet.

"Has this happened before? Are you pregnant?" she asks.

I sit up, not having that thought cross my mind all these times, until now. *Fuck.* Could I be pregnant? I can't be. I just fucking lost my virginity a couple of weeks ago.

Dez sees the panic engulfing my face. "Oh, Nay. Okay. I have a pregnancy test in my bathroom. I'll be right back."

She leaves, and I lean my head against the bathroom wall. This can't be happening. I can't end up a single mother like my mom. I promised myself I wouldn't repeat the cycle. I'm on the fucking pill god dammit! I did my part to protect myself so this wouldn't happen, and now Gabriele and I are nonexistent. This just can't happen.

Dez comes back in with the test in her hand. "You ready?"

I bury my face in my hands shaking my head no. "Nay, it's going to be okay either way. Don't worry. If this ends up being positive then I'll be your baby daddy," she jokes, trying to lighten the mood.

I can't help but laugh. She always knows just the right things to say in the worst moments.

I get up, unwrap the test, follow the directions and pee. I set the stick on the counter, and we set her phone for the time clock.

She holds my hand as I stare at the wall knowing in just a mere couple of minutes my life could change dramatically forever. Every emotion is running through me like a fast forward movie bringing me all the way back to my childhood listening to my mom cry herself to sleep worried about where our next meal would come from.

Dez doesn't say a word allowing me this moment in my head by myself until the alarm goes off ripping me away from my thoughts and memories. We both look at each other and then back to the test.

"You ready?" she questions.

I shake my head no.

"Do you want me to look first?"

I shake my head no.

She hands me the test. I close my eyes, breathe, gather my strength, then look. I just stare at the test numb and word-less. I can't take my eyes off it. Tears escape the corners of my eyes, and from this moment on I know my life will forever be different. This life is no longer mine. It no longer just belongs to me. It now belongs to this little invasion growing inside of me, and that scares the fuck out of me.

Dez reaches for the test taking it out of my hand. Looks, then gasps. She carefully wraps her arms around me as best as she can since she's still healing, and we sit in silence.

It feels as though we've been here forever just sitting on this bathroom floor.

"Nay, it's going to be okay. Whatever you decide, I'm here to support you no matter what. You don't have to feel alone," Dez whispers.

I nod, and move to get up, then help her up. "I can't think right now. Let's just go make some breakfast. I'm starving after up-chucking last night's dinner."

"Okay."

The rest of the day I act as though nothing has happened, numb and probably in denial at this point. I can feel Dez's eyes on me concerned but she keeps the thoughts to herself waiting for me to speak on the situation. I almost feel if I don't talk about it, then it never happened. It's not true. Seems to be an ongoing theme for me lately.

I take a long nap, and by the time I wake up, it's dark out. I look at my phone showing 8PM, and no texts or call notifi-cations. I hear voices down the hall in the living room. After getting freshened up, I walk down the hall into the living room, and I'm immediately greeted by Dez, Trev, and Adam.

Trev's the first one to greet me with a big hug. "Hey, sleepyhead. Dez said you weren't feeling well so we brought over some homemade soup Adam insisted on making," he informs me while rolling his eyes and looking over in Adam's direction.

I smile giving him a squeeze back then let him go and walk over to Adam giving him a hug.

"Thank you. It's so nice to finally meet you," I say to him.

"Of course! Any friend of Trev's is a friend of mine."

We all eat, laugh, and watch movies together. I wasn't ready to tell my news to anyone else. I'm not sure this news has even completely sunk in for me yet regardless. It all feels like a dream. With just one little test my life has done a one-eighty. I went from virgin, to becoming a sex goddess, to alone and pregnant all in a matter of months.

I just silently laugh to myself as I lie here in bed – alone.

A COUPLE of weeks have gone by already. I haven't heard from Gabriele at all. The pain of his void has now been replaced with thoughts of my future with becoming a single mother. I have no plans to tell Gabriele, and I've made Dez promise not to tell Luke. She's apprehensive about my keeping it a secret. She keeps telling me maybe things will change if Gabriele knows he has a child on the way. I keep reminding her that he was very clear that he didn't want a relationship and was very adamant that a child would never be in his future.

This child will know nothing about rejection. I refuse to allow anyone near us that has any doubts of being a part of our lives – even if that means keeping Gabriele far away from us and in the dark.

I finally told Trev and Adam, and they were ecstatic calling themselves aunts already. I just laugh at the memory. It makes me smile knowing no matter what, this baby is going to be surrounded by love. I just don't know how long

I'm going to be able to keep up the charade from Luke because I know eventually, I'll be showing.

I've already had conversations with Dez about moving and getting my own place. She's not happy about this one bit and keeps trying to convince me to reach out to Gabriele because he deserves to at least know and get the option to change his mind on wanting to be a part of this baby's life.

I know she has a point, but I think I'm more scared of the end result, of the denial, of the rejection for us both. I'm a stripper for god's sake. He doesn't want to be associated with me in the press, what makes me think he's going to want anything to do with a stripper as a baby mama? But, on the other hand, it's not about me. It's about this baby and giving Gabriele every option to make the right decision to be in its life, not for me, but for the baby.

I walk out of my room barging into Dez's room. Luke already left for work this morning.

"I'm going to do it," I burst out. She looks at me confused. "I'm going to tell him."

A huge smile appears across her face as she jumps up and down.

"Nay! I'm so proud of you for deciding this!" she screeches, coming over to give me a hug.

She winces as she runs into me too hard. "Careful, geez. We don't want Aunt Dez hurting."

We both laugh. "Aunt Dez. I love that. And I already love this baby!"

"When's your next appointment? If Gabriele doesn't come, then I want to be there," she demands.

I take a seat on her bed, then realize Luke just left and stand back up. No way I'm sitting on their sex-capades sheets. Dez smacks me on the arm laughing.

"Don't worry, we fucked under the sheets, not on top."

I wrinkle my nose, then sigh. "I miss having sex with

Gabriele. Now I'm ruined in more ways than one. I'll probably never have sex again," I say dramatically.

Dez walks over to her closet to change. "Oh, stop being so dramatic, Dez. You're pregnant, not dead. There's more dick in the sea. Besides, some guys have a fetish for pregnant women."

I roll my eyes. "That's disgusting, Dez. No way am I hooking up with some rando while I'm carrying Gabriele's child. Besides, Gabriele has officially ruined it for all men. How is anyone supposed to compete with that?"

She comes over and sits next to me. "I know. I'm sure your first experiences with him will be hard to overcome, but eventually those memories will fade and become just that – good memories, and someone else is going to come along and sweep you off your feet. I promise."

I lean my head against her shoulder and sigh. "I'm sure you're right."

The screeching sound of Dez's phone breaks us out of our moment. Dez lifts her phone. "It's Trev."

"Tell him to meet us at the gym," I shout as I walk out of her room.

I open the news feed I have saved of all the sites posting articles on Gabriele to check what has been written today. In reality, his pictures plastered in these articles are now the only glimpse of him I can get. It keeps him real to me, and the memories I have alive. It's sad, but this is all I have of him now. The only slight glimpse into his life even though I know what they write is only assumptions.

But this time is different than the rest. This time he's blatantly walking down the street for all to see hand in hand with a woman. I gasp, stopping dead in my tracks. The article reads, "The most eligible bachelor, billionaire, Gabriele Vanucci, seen coming from a nightclub with his new love interest, supermodel Katherine Danes."

I get lightheaded as my body is void of air from me

holding my breath for so long. I read the title over and over trying to see through the lines. This can't be real. This can't be happening. It's only been a couple of weeks, and he's already moved on. And not just moved on but moved on with a beautiful supermodel. Moved on with a woman of his equal, a woman every man would dream of having on his arm.

I drop the phone hearing this horrible noise that scares the shit out of me. Dez runs in behind me, grabbing me and wrapping her arms around me. As I stand here in Dez's arms I realize the horrid noise is me, it's coming from me, and she's trying to calm me.

"Nay, calm down. It's going to be okay," she continuously whispers in my ear, and she runs her hand over my hair.

My legs give out causing me to sink to the ground. I hear more footsteps in the distance, then feel hands lifting me up from the floor, scooping me in their arms and bringing me over to my bed. How did I allow everything in my life to get this bad? How could I allow him to bury himself so deep into me in every which way so quickly?

I'm fucking shattered, not broken, shattered into a million little pieces that will never be put back the same ever again. Every inch of my body scorches in pain the only thing I can do is curl up into the tiniest little ball hoping to disappear, begging to be swallowed up into the dark vortex of nothingness.

I can't stop crying and hyperventilating. I feel body heat and hands surrounding me, trying to comfort me, but every touch feels like a hot iron across my skin. I fucked up. I allowed him in, and he's now taken everything from me, leaving me with nothing but humiliating heartache.

I hear voices surrounding me, but my crying keeps tuning them out until finally hours later I fall into a fitful sleep. When I wake, my eyes are almost swollen shut and my body aches like I've just been run over by a semi-truck. Dez is asleep next to me and Trev is sleeping on the chair next to my window.

I slowly sit up. I feel drained and empty. Not just my body feels empty but my soul too. I'm sitting here as a shell of nothingness, numb from all the pain and noise going through my head. Dez must feel me move because she wakes and immediately reaches for me squeezing my hand.

"Hey, how are you feeling?" she asks.

Trev is next to stir, sitting up rubbing his eyes. "Hey, did you just wake up?" he asks.

I can't speak. I just continue to stare at my comforter.

"Trev, why don't you go make her some toast, and I'll get her in the shower," Dez directs.

He nods and leaves the room. Dez gets out of bed walking over to my side. "Come on, Nay."

My body does as she asks but my brain is still screaming slumped on that floor. She undresses me and showers me, then wraps a towel around me after drying me off. I sit down on the closed toilet while she brushes my hair and helps me get dressed.

Normally I would feel loved and cocooned but right now I can't feel a thing. I'm in the darkest depths of the deepest ocean drowning unable to escape for air. Every movement is exhausting, and I just want to sleep again.

I try to head back to my bed, but Dez stops me. "Oh no you don't. You need to eat. If not for yourself then you need to eat for that baby depending on you," she scolds me.

I start crying again. Fuck. Reality comes crashing back. I'm pregnant with Gabriele's child and he's off galivanting with his new supermodel girlfriend. How did my life get so fucked up again? Before him I was thriving. I was doing okay, maybe not really living, but I was happy with my little family Trev, Dez, and I created. I just want to go back and rewind time, and erase Gabriele from my existence.

"It's going to be okay. You are a strong woman who

deserves the world. I know you don't believe it now, but one day, after we put you back together again, you will believe it too."

I cry even harder, letting it all out all over again until I have nothing left. Dez is patient with me, waiting until I'm ready to leave my room. Finally, we head into the living room and Trev has made us all some eggs, bacon, and toast. My stomach growls on command and we all laugh.

"My little niece or nephew is hungry," Trev says in baby talk to my stomach. I swat his hand away and take a seat at the table to eat.

They're both silent waiting for me to make the first move, but clearly Trev can't keep his mouth shut any longer.

"He's a motherfucker, Nay."

"Trev!" Dez yells.

"No fuck that! What he did was cowardly because he couldn't admit to his own feelings. I'm glad he's out of yours and this baby's life. He doesn't deserve either of you!"

I just keep chewing letting it all sink in. Dez's phone rings and she immediately gets up from the table walking into the kitchen. I hear her angrily speaking to him before she hangs up and walks back to the table.

"I told Luke he can't come here right now, and he needs to stay away for a while. Let's just say he didn't take that too well, but I don't care after what his brother did," Dez explains.

Now I begin crying again. The last thing I want is to ruin her relationship over this. I wouldn't forgive myself. "Dez, just don't write him off because of what Gabriele has done. It's not Luke's fault and he cares for you," I tell her.

She takes a sip of her coffee. "I know, but you need some privacy while you heal."

"Anyone up for some horrible comedy movies?" Trev asks, standing to clear off the table.

I nod with a weak smile. We get the blankets, popcorn,

and drinks curling up together on the couch and binging on dumb classics. It was just what I needed to keep my mind from sinking any further.

I slept with Dez every night for the next week and Trev slept on the couch. Adam came over most nights to play board games and watch movies with us or to cook us dinner but then leaves to give us our space. I'm loving him more and more each time I see him, he fits perfectly into our little family.

Trev and Dez came to my doctor's appointment. I'm already six weeks pregnant. Time has been flying and Gabriele and his new girlfriend continue to splash across the tabloids on a daily basis. I know my friends are extremely concerned about me since I'm still a shell of a person walking around.

I haven't been able to leave the apartment, eating and bathing is a chore for me, and sleep has become my best friend. They take turns keeping an eye on me, when really we should all be keeping an eye on Dez still. Some days I feel smothered by them, other days I don't even realize they are there.

I keep getting calls from the New York number, but no message has been left yet up until now. I click over to my voicemail and hit play.

"Hello, I'm looking for Naomi Veil. My name is Gregory Blacknord. I am the attorney regarding your grandparents' estate. Please call me back at 585-625-1394."

I look at the phone bewildered. Does this mean my grandparents have passed away? But why would he be calling me and not my uncle?

I dial the number back.

"Blacknord's office," a female voice answers.

"Hello, my name is Naomi Veil. I just received a message from Mr. Gregory Blacknord."

"Ah yes, Miss Veil, he's been trying to reach you for quite a while now. Please hold while I put you through to him."

The phone immediately switches to a ring. "Miss Veil. So nice to finally hear from you. You are a very hard person to reach," he states.

"I'm sorry, I was out of the country for some time. I just got your message about my grandparents' estate, have they both passed?" I ask.

He sighs. "I'm afraid so. I'm sorry to be the bearer of bad news. They weren't well and passed one shortly after the other."

"And my uncle, we're you not able to reach him?"

There's silence for a moment. "I'm sorry, but your uncle passed a couple years back of an overdose. You are the last of kin alive."

"Oh."

"Anyways, they left you full beneficiary of their will and life insurance policy. I was hoping to meet in person, and have you come into my office to go over everything."

I'm a little shocked. "Um, I actually no longer live in New York. I'm in Arizona now. Is this something we can handle over the phone?"

He seems hesitant. "So, in normal circumstances I would say yes, but in your case, I think it's better in person. Are you able to fly here anytime soon?"

This is not the conversation I thought was going to happen. "I need to look into it. Can I give you a call back?"

I can almost see him nodding through the phone. "Sure, sure. I completely understand. I will text you my office address and let me know what you have decided."

"I will, thank you."

"Goodbye, Miss Veil."

CHAPTER 22

"*D*ez, I'm flying to New York tomorrow," I blurt out as we're sitting on the couch sipping our coffee.

I made my one-way ticket last night after I spoke with Mr. Blacknord on the phone yesterday. I think getting out of here will be good for me even if it isn't in the best of circumstances.

"Wait, what the fuck do you mean you're flying to New York, Nay?"

I take another sip of my coffee. "I got a call that my grandparents died, and I need to handle their estate. I won't be long. Honestly, I think this came at the perfect time for me. I just need to get out of here," I explain.

She looks worried but ultimately changes to understanding. "When are you coming back?"

I grab her hand. "Come with me. Let's book a nice house and get away from here," I try to convince her.

She looks hesitant. "Nay, you know I can't do that right now. I have doctor's appointments I have to get to and Luke's here. He would go crazy if I left right now after everything."

I sigh. "I know. I understand. I was just throwing it out

there. Are you going to be okay if I leave for a while? I don't know what to expect or how long this will take."

She squeezes my hand. "I'll be fine. I have Trev, Adam, and Luke surrounding me. You go handle what you need to handle. But don't take too long or I will come after you and drag you back home!"

I laugh. "I love you, Dez," I tell her, wrapping my arms around her.

THE UBER PULLS UP in front of Gregory Blacknord's building. I look at the address he sent me and it shows the 20th floor. The building is massive and full of businessmen and women strolling through the doors with suits and briefcases. This place is extremely out of my league which makes me wonder how my grandparents were able to afford an attorney that works in a place like this.

They didn't seem well-off. Their house was small and worn down. They couldn't have had much to leave in their will other than that house, which is something I want nothing to do with. Stepping foot back in that place was never on my agenda in life.

I wrap my jacket around me tighter shaking out a chill that runs through me. The weather is colder than I thought it would be this time of year. I know I'm no longer in Arizona, but I don't remember it being this cold here in the middle of September.

I take the elevator up to the 20th floor. When the door slides open, I walk to the large white desk in front of me.

The receptionist greets me. "Miss Veil, so nice to meet you. How were your travels?" she asks.

"Long, but okay. I just arrived this afternoon."

"Good. Mr. Blacknord is waiting for you in his office. Please follow me."

She walks me down a brightly lit hallway. It's exactly the office I expected, the cliche New York City style office you would see in a movie. I wonder why this couldn't be handled over the phone. What was so important that he needed to discuss this will in person?

She directs me into the large office with floor to ceiling windows on each side. Mr. Blacknord immediately stands from behind his desk to greet me.

"Miss Veil, so nice to meet you," he says, walking from behind his desk to come shake my hand. The receptionist leaves closing the door behind us.

"Please have a seat," he directs me to the chair at his table overlooking the city.

He grabs a file on his desk before sitting in front of me.

"I'm sure you're wondering why I asked you to travel all this way rather than do this over the phone."

I nod. "I am."

"I knew your grandparents a very long time. We actually grew up together. Our parents were family friends," he explains.

Now this gives some insight into how they were able to retain such a high-profile lawyer.

"My grandparents didn't seem well-off, Mr. Blacknord. Did you assist them as a favor of knowing them so long?" I question.

He smiles as though I understand. "I did. I actually assisted them with a number of things throughout their lives. One being investments and two being life insurance. I have connections to many different areas which I helped them navigate. I'm not sure why they chose to live the way they did because they had the means to live in luxury," he divulges.

Now I'm extremely confused.

"Your grandparents were multi-millionaires. They each had their own investments that built up well over fifty years.

They only used what they needed to survive on, no more, no less. I told them time and time again that there was no reason for that. They could enjoy life and still have way more than enough left. They were just simple folk though. They also each had a life insurance policy which is a couple million dollars each and the house was paid in full," he tells me, dropping this huge ball on me.

"I'm not sure what shape the house is in, but you have the option to keep it or sell it. It's yours to do what you please. As soon as you were born, they had the will changed so everything would be passed down to you.

"I never asked why, and they never gave me a reason why. I just did as they asked. So now you see why it was important for us to handle this in person?" he questions.

I'm speechless. I don't even know what to say. How am I even supposed to respond to all this?

"I know this is a lot to take in. Can I get you something to drink or eat while you wrap your head around this?" he asks.

I shake my head. "No, I'm fine. Thanks. Please tell me where I go from here."

We spend the next couple of hours going over everything with a fine-tooth comb. He brings in colleagues that would be able to help me navigate through it all in each department regarding the life insurance policy, investment accounts, a will set up for my unborn child, and a multitude of other areas.

Last, he calls down a colleague that deals with real estate. Even though a house this size doesn't need someone this qualified, Mr. Blacknord advised only the best for me.

"Miss Veil, this is Mr. Jordash," he introduces us, but there's no need for introductions. We are very, very well-acquainted. I would know that face anywhere. I could pick out those crystal blue eyes in a packed room of people.

Mr. Jordash has an ear-to-ear grin as he walks toward me

slowly grazing his eyes over my body. I immediately flush with heat.

"No need to introduce us. We're already very well-acquainted," he announces.

Mr. Blacknord looks pleased. "Great! Well then, if you both don't mind. I'll let you get to it while I step out for an early dinner."

I take a sip of my water trying to calm my nerves. The last time I saw him he was standing over me stroking himself and releasing his pleasure all over my stomach.

The twinkle in his eyes as he watches me tells me he's reliving that moment again in his head right now. He takes a seat at the table next to me, grabs my hand, and slowly kisses the top.

I gulp feeling out of place. "I thought I'd never lay eyes on you again after I was revoked from the island."

My brows furrow in confusion. "Revoked?"

"Yes, I demanded to see you again. I wanted one on one time with you. I couldn't get you out of my head, I still haven't been able to. Gabriele was not happy about it, so he pulled rank, revoked my membership, and transferred me off the island," he explains.

Now that day makes sense. He was angry when he left me. I saw the charter plane fly over me while lying on the beach, and he came back with security shortly after. Jealousy clearly was in the forefront in that moment. He told me time and time again that I was his and only his, now here he is throwing me away for another to scoop up while he's strutting around with his supermodel.

"I'm sorry. I wasn't aware of this," I tell him honestly. "He wasn't much for sharing things with me regarding his business."

He leans back in his chair with dominance and authority. "And are you still seeing him?"

I look down at the ground shaking my head. "No."

When I look back up, he looks elated. "Will you have dinner with me tonight?" he asks.

Shit. I wasn't expecting this. "Honestly, Mr. Jordash," I begin to say.

"Please, call me Jason."

I nod in acceptance. "Jason, I'm not in the position to date. Things are – complicated," I try to say without going into detail.

He looks me over not wanting to take no for an answer. "Ok, I can accept that. Then how about a business dinner? We can go over the details of your grandparents' house and what you're looking to do with it."

I sigh. "There's really no need to take the time out of your day to deal with this. I know you must have way bigger projects that need your attention. I'd be more than happy to find a small agent that can help me navigate through this."

He almost looks amused. "Miss Veil," he now begins to say.

"Naomi," I correct him.

"Naomi, please, it would be my pleasure. I think it would be good for us to build a rapport if you ever decide to invest in real estate in the future. I have many connections, and I now consider ourselves as more than just acquaintances, but more like intimate friends. I enjoy helping out close friends. Especially friends who taste and smell as lovely as you," he finishes with a smirk.

Heat creeps up my body coloring my cheeks pink. This whole day has not been what I expected. I'm exhausted and at this point I have nothing left in me, so I agree.

"I'll agree to a business dinner, but that's it. I'd also like to keep things professional. I have no interest in anything further as I am with child and as you can see have a lot that has been dropped upon me lately," I advise.

I can't believe I just opened my mouth about this to him. I barely know him. I begin to panic.

"I'm sorry. I've divulged too much. If you could please be discreet about this and keep it to yourself, it would be much appreciated," I ask almost begging.

He studies me before responding. "You haven't told him, have you?"

"No."

"I'm assuming it's because of the pictures plastered all over the internet?" he wonders.

"Yes and no."

"I see. Well, his loss is another man's gain. I would have never let you go. Clearly, he's not as smart as I gave him credit for. But you have my word, what is said between us, will stay between us. I will also be on my best behavior. You have my word on that as well," he promises.

I let my breath out feeling relieved.

He had his driver drive me over to my hotel to rest and freshen up before dinner. We had nice small talk, and he agreed to pick me up at 8PM. I'm surprised at how comfortable I feel with him after everything. The fact that he's seen every part of me is awkward in itself but then revealing to him my most intimate secret was out of character for me, but he never once made me feel less than from any of it.

After my late-night nap and shower, I have twenty minutes to kill before heading out.

I dial Dez's number.

She picks up on the first ring. "Hey! I'm so glad to see your face!" she screeches.

I laugh. "I'm sorry I didn't call when I landed. Things have been a little hectic around here. Some much to unpack in just one day. How's things over there?"

"Good, Luke's on his way here. I told him you were out of town so he could stop by."

I roll my eyes jokingly. "You just can't go a moment without that boy, huh? My best friend is in love," I tease.

"Stop, Nay. Enough about me, how are you feeling?" she asks, concerned.

I pick at my dress. "You know, I can breathe. Honestly, Dez. I might stay out here a little longer. I have some business I need to tend to which might take longer than I thought. I need to get over to my grandparents and clean out the house to get it up for sale, and there's other things too that I'll explain once I come home."

She looks upset. "How long are you talking, Nay?"

"Maybe until I can face Arizona again. He's there with her, and right now the possibility of running into them together isn't good for me or the baby. I just think being away will help me heal," I admit to her.

She nods, understanding. There's a knock at the door before she can say anything else. "Who's there?"

I look back toward the door.

"Oh, it's just a friend. I need to go; I'm having dinner with him. Love you and I'll call you tomorrow."

Her face looks shocked. "Wait! What friend? Who's him?" I hear her scream as I hang up.

Dez is going to kill me for not filling her in. I'm already prepared for text bombs to start coming through, so I silence my phone.

I open the door, and Jason is waiting with a nice friendly smile. "Hey there, you ready?"

I step out and close the door. "I am."

We begin walking down the hall. "How did you sleep?"

"Good. It was much needed after today and traveling."

He bumps my shoulder a little with his in a teasing way. "Well, you look beautiful and well rested. I bet you and the baby are starving," he suggests.

It feels nice openly talking about the baby with him. Most men would feel uncomfortable bringing it up in our situation. He made it clear that he still wants me, but is being respectful in upholding my wishes, and my dilemma hasn't turned him running the other way.

I smile. "We are famished."

"Good, because the chef is a very good friend of mine and is going to be giving us his special menu of tasting while we discuss this house and any others you may be interested in in the future."

I never thought the possibility of me buying a house let alone multiple houses would be reality for me. The thought of benefiting from my grandparents' death makes me sad, but they did live long lives, not sure they were happy since I barely knew them, but they stayed together all these years so that must say something.

"Wow, that sounds amazing, Jason."

The drive isn't that long. We pull up to this quaint little restaurant tucked out of the way from the main road with twinkling lights and a comforting vibe. Nothing like I expected. I was expecting more of five-star stuffy foreign vibe that makes someone like me feel uncomfortable and out of place.

"Hello, Mr. Jordash, please follow me," the hostess says with a flirty smile. She doesn't even acknowledge me, but I don't take it nearly as personally as I did with Gabriele. No jealousy here.

She takes us back to a private room to a table next to a lit fireplace and dim lighting. If this were a date I would be extremely impressed by the thought and the romantic gesture. Jason pulls out my chair as the hostess waits.

"Is there anything else I can get you?" she asks him.

He takes his seat. "No, that will be all. Thank you."

The waiter now comes to get our drink order and heads off advising us that he will start bringing out the chef's plates one by one shortly.

"Now let's discuss this house. Are you looking to keep it

to reside in or maybe as an investment house or are you looking to sell?"

That's an easy question. "Sell," I answer. "I do need to travel there tomorrow and figure out what needs to be done first. I have no idea what I'm walking into. I haven't been there in years, and when I was, I was only there for a short couple of months."

The waiter drops off our drinks and some bread.

"I take it you weren't close with them then?" he wonders.

I take a sip of my Arnold Palmer. "No, not at all. My family wasn't close, very bad blood involved between everyone. I really didn't know my grandparents at all. How about you? What's your story? Why the island?"

He smirks with a mischievous glow in his eyes probably with my mention of the island. "For starters, the island is for my unique style of pleasure. I, like many, enjoy pushing the envelope. As for my story, I'm a self-made very wealthy businessman. Started all my companies from the ground up. I came from a healthy middle-class family; two brothers and a sister.

"I dropped out of college to pursue my dreams, my parents weren't ecstatic about it, but they still supported me, and I've been working ever since. So, my way of having fun and blowing off steam is what you witnessed. I'm not one for relationships, but I'm also not opposed to them if the right girl came along either," he finishes.

Wow he just gave me a quick earful, but one thing caught my attention. "Why not one for relationships?"

He sips his bourbon first in thought. "I'm a very busy man. Most women enjoy the money and the benefits that come with it, but long term, they ultimately feel lonely wanting me to be more available and present; not something I can do. So, I've found that enjoyable non-committed sexual relationships are more to my liking."

The waiter comes by with our first appetizer, explaining

in detail what he's placed down in front of us before leaving us again.

"I can understand that. It makes sense. But I am glad to hear you're open to one if one deems a good enough fit," I respond.

"Will you be applying?" he asks with a grin. He sees my hesitation. "I'm teasing though open to it as well."

That was subtle, I must admit.

"Can I pry for a moment?" he asks.

"Sure."

"What happened with Gabriele? Were you two not serious? He seemed extremely protective over you to just let you go so easily. I've crossed paths with him over the years many times and he's never once acted that intensely," he states.

I give him a quick lowdown without mentioning too much detail. I explained to him we never labeled ourselves and there was always going to be an expiration date with us. I tell him that I was planning on telling Gabriele about the baby but then I saw his new relationship status, so that steered me away from involving him.

The rest of the night goes by smoothly. We laughed, talked, and ate way too much. His chef friend came out to introduce himself. He was kind and took extreme care of us, so much it felt as though I needed to be rolled out of the restaurant.

I really enjoyed Jason's company and a much-needed distraction from my heartbreak. I haven't looked at my google news feed since I left Arizona and it's been great. Jason walked me to my hotel room door.

"So, I was wondering – how long will you be staying in town?"

"I'm really not too sure. I haven't decided."

He leans against my doorjamb after I unlock the room with my key card.

"Come stay with me. I have plenty of room, and you will

341

mostly have the whole place to yourself while I'm working, you won't have to pay this ridiculous room fee, and I will have a driver at your disposal for travel," he offers.

My mouth opens ready to refuse. "Please, don't respond now. Just think about it. I want to make sure you and the baby are taken care of and protected while you're in town. No strings attached, I promise," he states as he crosses his heart.

I nod with a side smile. "Okay, I'll think about it. Thank you for dinner. It was lovely."

He kisses me on the cheek. "Goodnight, Naomi."

CHAPTER 23

I finally open my phone and turn my volume back on. Immediately, my notifications start dinging insanely and I know exactly who it is. I jump into my night-clothes, throw my hair up and jump into bed before I call Dez back.

She answers on a half of a ring. "What the fuck, Nay! I was about to file a missing persons report!" she yells, dramatically.

I roll my eyes. "Well, welcome to my world with you," I snap back sarcastically.

"Ha. Ha. Why didn't you respond to my text? I was so worried."

I snuggle deep into my covers knowing this is going to be a long phone call.

"I told you I was having dinner with a friend. I actually met him through Gabriele, and I wasn't expecting to see him again until he turned up in the estate lawyer's office. We had dinner to discuss my grandparents' house," I explain.

"So, this guy does business with Gabriele?"

I sigh. "Not exactly. He was a member of Gabriele's island."

I'm praying she doesn't dig any deeper, but of course this is Dez we're talking about. "Wait, Luke told me about the island. How did you meet him though? He said the guests only come in contact when they're in the special villas."

I go into detail about my contact with Jason while on the island, but I don't share any other details of Gabriele and me. I feel like I want to hold those memories locked away for myself. Reliving this memory that Jason was in makes me question the offer he made to me on staying with him. What if our lines become blurry because I'm not in the right state of mind?

"Jesus, Nay. He most definitely has a thing for you. Did you tell him you're not ready for anything and your carrying Gabriele's baby?" she asks stunned.

"Yes, he knows. He offered me to stay at his place while I'm here instead of this hotel," I reveal.

Her brows shot up. "And you told him no, right?"

"I told him I would think about it. This hotel is going to get expensive if things end up taking longer than I expected. We've already been intimately involved somewhat, so at least we got that out of the way," I try to joke.

Dez laughs. "From what you told me, you two barely scratched the surface."

I smack my forehead with my hand. "Okay, maybe you're right. It's probably not a good idea in my state of mind."

She looks relieved. "Thank god you're finally seeing clearer."

"I'm exhausted. I'll give you and Trev a call tomorrow after I go and see my grandparents' house," I tell her.

She nods. "Okay, sleep tight. Love you."

I'M DRAGGING THIS MORNING. Usually, I'm already down three cups of coffee but cutting down to one is a must now. Jason was kind enough to send his driver today to pick me up and take me where I need to go.

We pull up to the house I ran from years ago. It looks different now. My memories are dark, dingy, and gray; something I've pushed deep down for so long never wanting to remember. But the house I'm sitting in front of now is bright, airy, with only remembrance of dirty memories echoing inside from the past.

"Would you like any assistance, Miss Veil?" the driver asks.

I shake my head. "No thank you, Stan. I'll text you when I'm ready to be picked back up."

"No problem."

I head out of the car, up the small rubble sidewalk, and let myself in. Flashbacks of my time here come swirling back to me like a typhoon. I close the door behind me, still holding onto the handle to catch my breath. The air is thick, stale, and full of disgusting secrets from my uncle. This is the place my mom ran from as a teen – broken, scared, and alone. Then years later the cycle repeated with me.

I walk through the living room past the dining room into the kitchen. They were simple people, lived with the basics, nothing extravagant or overindulging. The furniture is over-worn, the recliner still has the outline from where one of them must have sat all these years, and the same old gray box TV was being used.

I head down to the bedrooms, looking in each room until I get to my grandparents' room. I notice on the nightstand a black and white family picture from when my mother and her brother were young; robotic smiles on each face that never seemed to reach the eyes. Kind of sad, making my heart break for my mom. Just more proof that solidifies my mother's childhood stories.

I remove my coat settling in for a long day of walking through a time machine of my family's past. After hours of going through pictures and paperwork, separating them into keep and trash piles, I feel drained.

Just as I'm about to text Stan the driver, I hear footsteps walking down the carpeted hall. I immediately jump up and look for something to protect myself with. The door begins to slowly open as I walk backwards.

"Naomi?" I hear Jason's voice, then his head peeks through the door.

I smack my hand to my chest letting out a breath. "Holy shit! I didn't mean to scare you. Are you okay?" he asks, rushing toward me.

"Yes, yes, I'm fine. You just scared the shit out of me. I thought I locked the door behind me," I tell him relieved.

This house isn't located in the best of neighborhoods. It's not the worst, but I dropped the ball on keeping myself safe. Anyone could have walked in. I'm sure word got around that this house is now vacant.

"It's getting late. My driver said you have been here for quite a while. I wanted to make sure you're doing okay, and I'm sure you're starving by now. I came to see if you wanted to grab something to eat?" he explains.

As if on cue, my stomach growls. I hadn't thought much about food as I've been consumed with the past.

"Yes, I would love that. I'm famished."

A huge grin appears across his face. "Good, let's get out of here. This place is going to get freezing as soon as the sun drops."

We pull up to a tiny pizza shop on the corner of a busy intersection. As soon as we step out, I can smell the sauce and garlic, and my mouth begins to water. Jason puts his hand against my lower back, protectively, leading me in. I swear from the corner of my eye I see a flash, but as soon as I look to my right as we walk through the doors, there's no one there.

"Did you see that?" I ask him.

He looks bewildered. "See what?"

"Never mind." This must be my mind playing tricks on me. I'm just overly tired and hungry.

We spend the rest of the night laughing and getting to know each other over a large margarita pizza. Just within these last twenty-four hours it feels as though we're falling into a nice rhythm of friendship. I'm not used to feeling this way with a man other than Trev.

It doesn't stop my mind from wandering to thoughts of Gabriele. All I have to do is pull up the internet and I'm sure I can get a glimpse of him, but it won't be the *real* him. His smile, his laugh, his smell won't be plastered on there. No, she now gets to see that piece of him. I'm no longer privy to that part of him any longer, and every time I have to remind myself of this in my head, my heart breaks just a little all over again.

Jason's been a nice distraction during the times I would have been sitting in the room on my own. There's no doubt in my mind the attraction is there, and maybe if my situation were different, I might entertain it, but for now his company has been comforting, and the fact that he is respecting my boundaries is extremely appreciated.

IT'S BEEN ALMOST a week since I've been here wrapping everything up with Gregory Blacknord. All my investments have been settled, I have the contacts I need, and a new bank account I have access to. Jason had the house taken care of for me. I took the important papers and pictures I wanted and gave the rest to those in need. He helped me hire a crew to do any important fixes along with sprucing up the place before listing it on the market.

I've already accepted an offer, and closing is set for another couple of weeks. Now I'm trying to decide on my next move. It never even crossed my mind to live apart from Dez and Trev, but the reality is, I'm not sure if I can go back. I'm not sure I'm strong enough to even remain in the same state as Gabriele when carrying his child.

Both of my dear friends have found amazing men, and though I would ask them to move with me in a heartbeat, I just can't. They're happy. Who am I to ask them to leave that?

Luke wants to get a place with Dez, and since I already mentioned moving into one of my own, she told me she was really considering it. Even though our time as roommates may be up and we're finally growing up, I can't help but feel alone and sad.

Then there's Trev, completely inseparable from Adam, and Luke was able to help him secure an amazing job working for a private security company. He's ecstatic and starts his new job next week.

So, now it's my turn to figure things out because it's not just about me anymore. What do I want our life to look like? I always thought my two best friends would always be there right by my side, but maybe it's time I venture on my own for a while.

And this is when I get the brilliant idea of North Carolina, where Dez's mom, Christy lives. Maybe I can start a new life in a house on the coast, then Dez has a reason to come visit between me and her mom.

Just as I'm about to dial Christy's number, Dez's number comes through.

"Hey," I answer.

"Are you sitting down?" she asks.

My brows furrow perplexed. "No," I reply with a nervous laugh.

"Pull up google on your phone and look at the TMZ article that just got posted," she demands.

"Dez, you know I don't want to see his face," I whine.

She sighs annoyed. "No, Nay. It's not about Gabriele. Just fucking pull it up," she insists again.

"Hold on."

I take the phone from my ear and do as she says. As soon as I pull the site up, I gasp. My face and Jason's splattered all over it together. Multiple pictures of us walking closely and having intimate dinners together while laughing, portraying a relationship, are thrust all over it. And the worst part is the title, "Has Real Estate mogul, Jason Jordash, finally settled down with this mystery woman?"

Oh no. Oh fuck no! Are the only words that come out of my mouth as I sit down on my bed needing support before I pass out. What the hell have I done? How could I be so careless? And then I think back to the flash I thought I saw but shook it away as I was just crazy.

These photographers must have been following us and hiding in order to get these sort of close up pictures.

I can hear the muffling far away sound of Dez screaming my name into the phone. I finally put it to my ear. "What the fuck am I going to do? I can't have my face all over! This is sure to link me to Gabriele if someone starts digging!" I screech in panic mode.

"Nay, Gabriele just showed up here. He was fucking losing it. He's absolutely furious. I thought Luke lost his mind when I wouldn't talk to him, but this is a hundred times worse," she informs me.

My heart stammers irradicably. "Shit. He's probably worried about them linking me as a stripper to his name and fucking up his new relationship," I advise her.

"Wait, is that what you think this is about? No Nay, he's furious because you're with Jason. He doesn't care about them finding out who you are. He said he's on his way to the airport, they're fueling up his plane as we speak, and he's going to New York to find you," she says, throwing a bomb at me.

I stand up immediately, beginning to pace my room. "What the fuck are you talking about, Dez? Tell me you're lying! He can't come here. I hope you told him to go back to his god damn supermodel girlfriend!" I scream hysterically now.

My whole body is shaking. How dare this asshole get mad about me being seen with another man, and I'm glad it's Jason too. He deserves it thinking he can barge into my apartment and demand information from my friend like he gives a fuck.

"Nay, he wasn't taking no for an answer. Luke had to calm him down. He's never seen him like this."

I stop dead in my tracks. "Did you tell him where I'm staying?"

She hesitates for a moment, and I close my eyes already knowing the answer. My heart sinks into my gut. I feel betrayed. I can't believe she told him after everything. I would have never done that to her.

"Nay – please don't be mad," she stutters weakly knowing she fucked up.

"I have to go."

I hang up without another word and dial my phone as I begin packing.

Jason picks up on the first ring. "Hello?"

"Jason, I need your help."

"Don't move. I'm coming for you, little ballerina."

MY STOMACH DROPS into the pit of my gut as I continue to stare at the text I just received from Gabriele as Jason and I pull off from the hotel. I watch it grow smaller by the minute in the rearview mirror.

I'm just at a loss with this all. So many mixed emotions are coursing through me, and I don't know who to be more mad at in this moment; Gabriele or my traitor best friend.

Between Dez and Trev my phone has been dinging and ringing off the hook over the last hour. I need time, I need space from this whole debacle, and right now Jason is the only one I feel safe with. I switch my phone to no ring and shove it in my purse.

"Everything okay?" Jason questions looking over at me while driving.

"Yes, no, I don't know?" I say conflicted not really knowing what I'm feeling at the moment.

He chuckles. "That's the most honest answer I've heard in a long time."

"You're welcome."

After another thirty minutes in the car, we finally arrive at Jason's house. I sit up straighter stretching my neck out to see his house in more detail. I feel oddly surprised. I'm not sure exactly what I expected, but it sure wasn't this.

Jason is so refined and sophisticated that I guess I didn't picture him in such a small cozy gingerbread looking house. I pictured something harsh and steel; more like the looks of him. Fitting, since this reminds me of him on both sides on the spectrum.

My face must show a million thoughts. "You didn't expect to see me in a house like this, did you?" he asks entertained.

I gulp. "No, I most definitely did not. But I must admit, it suits you."

He smiles proudly as we enter the garage, then leaves the car walking to the trunk to grab my bags. I climb out of the car following him to the side door. The house is warm, inviting, somewhere I could snuggle with a nice book and let the day pass in serenity.

"Wow, Jason. This house is beautiful. Did you decorate this yourself?"

He chuckles. "I wish I could say I did, but that's not really my forte. I hired an interior designer. I gave her my vision and she gave me this.

"Come on, let's get you settled in. I'm putting you in the guest room next to mine in case you need anything," he says with a smirk.

I smack his arm. "Thanks, but I'm sure I will be fine."

We pass the living room and kitchen to the right, go down a hallway, and he brings me into a gorgeous quaint room, fireplace already lit, soft warm lighting, plush bed with an oversized cream comforter, and a cushiony soft carpet under my feet.

The bouquet of lilies on the nightstand engulfs the room as though I'm cocooned in plush gardens. I turn back to him in excitement as he drops my bags while watching me.

"Whoever your designer is, tell her she's amazing at what she does. She set the room up perfectly. This feels like I'm in the middle of the forest in a cozy sexy cabin," I boast.

He chuckles. "I'll be sure to tell her. The bathroom is through that door," he says, pointing behind me. "I'll leave you to get settled. I'm going to be in my study, I have some business I need to attend to."

Jason turns to leave. "Jason?"

He stops turning to face me.

"Thank you."

He nods with a smile. "My pleasure."

I MUST HAVE FALLEN asleep after I drew myself a hot bubble bath. I snap up out of a fitful sleep to yelling in the distance. I sit for a moment confused, just listening as the murmurs of anger get louder. That's when I realize who the voice of the yelling man is.

I rush out of bed; slam open my door running down the

hallway until I reach the foyer just after the living room. Jason is guarding the doorway entrance as Gabriele is face to face with him. Angry is an understatement. Livid, ready to kill is more like it.

"Where the fuck is she, Jason? I want to see her!" he demands.

He looks wild like a crazed caged animal. Jason has no intentions of backing down either. It's a standoff between these men, and if I don't intervene than someone's going to get hurt or arrested.

I walk up behind Jason, placing my hand on his shoulder. Neither of them noticed me standing here until now. They both slowly turn their attention in my direction. Gabriele's eyes immediately soften until he looks down and only sees me in a T-shirt. His eyes immediately glaze over with rage as he looks to Jason again.

"Gabriele, what are you doing here?" I ask quietly.

It takes everything I have to look at him and speak to him. I'm secretly breaking inside. Every piece I thought I started to glue back together is now melting apart.

"I came here for you, Naomi. I came to explain myself. I came to bring you home," he states so matter-of-factly like I would just take his hand and follow him blindly again.

I wrap my arms around my body protectively. Jason notices and reaches over rubbing my arm to give me strength.

"Get your fucking hands off her, you fuck!" Gabriele growls trying to get around him for closer access to me. Jason pushes him back further outside of the door.

"Back the fuck up, Vanucci, unless you want to be escorted out of here in handcuffs for breaking and entering," he threatens. "And who the fuck are you to tell me I can't touch my own girlfriend!" he adds without consulting me.

Shit. I did not see that one coming. Jason and I both look to each other for a quick moment, he gives me the look of just going with it. I bring my attention back to Gabriele looking stunned, hurt, and pissed.

"I don't believe it," he states never disconnecting his eyes with mine almost as if he's waiting for me to put him out of his misery and deny what Jason has just claimed.

I almost want to. I almost want to tell him it's a lie, that I still love every inch of him, that I'm his forever, he branded my heart for life, and that we're going to have a baby together, but then I remember her. I remember all the pictures I saw of them together right after us. I remember how he abandoned me and threw me away like I was nothing after taking everything from me and sucking me dry.

Instead of remorse and guilt I just felt a moment ago, I feel betrayal and anger. Without even realizing it myself, the words fall out of my mouth. "It's true, Gabriele. You need to leave. I'm with Jason now. I don't think your girlfriend will appreciate you being here," I say as I turn away and begin walking.

"What you see isn't always reality, Naomi. Please, just hear me out!" he screams behind me. I stop for a moment trying to understand his words, almost wanting to turn around to listen to what he may have to say, but then shake my head and continue on leaving him behind and walking into a new life without him.

I hear Jason murmur something low then slam the door. Gabriele is still on the other side banging against it.

I take a seat on the couch shaken up. There's no way I'm falling back asleep. I may never sleep again after this night. I'm shaking from the adrenaline coursing through my veins. Jason hands me a bottled water from the kitchen and a fuzzy warm blanket from off the back of the couch laying it over me.

He takes a seat next to me. "I'm sorry, I should have had security. I didn't think he was crazy enough to show up here."

I curl into the blanket hoping to stop shivering. "It's not your fault. I just don't understand why after cutting me out of his life, he would fly this far when seeing me with you. He moved on."

Jason chuckles. "I guess you don't realize the impact you have on those who come across you. You're not someone that's easily forgettable."

I can see Jason believes this as he looks at me with admiration, but he doesn't truly know me. Not like Gabriele did. I need to rip the band-aid off and tell him who I really am.

"Jason, Gabriele met me dancing at a strip club. I was a stripper before I fell into this life. Men threw dollar bills at my feet. I was a nobody that was there for men's enjoyment. I sold my soul for a dollar. That is who I am," I admit, waiting for him to be disgusted.

He wipes a tear from my cheek. "That's not who you are, Naomi. That's what you did. That was a job, but that doesn't define who you are. You'll go further in life if you remember that. There's no need to feel ashamed. I'm not here to judge your past."

I nod taking a breath I didn't realize I was holding. What did I do to deserve another sweet man in my life? I lean my head on his shoulder as we just sit in silence until I fall asleep.

CHAPTER 24

It's been four months since that awful night. Gabriele tried non-stop to reach me in every way possible, but I dodged and ignored him trying hard to erase him from our lives. Dez and Trev called me for a week straight before I finally answered the phone after feeling betrayed by her.

She groveled and begged for my forgiveness and poor Trev was just an innocent bystander that I took it out on due to my feelings of guilt by association. I finally listened to her apologies forgiving her. Let's face it, I need them both in my life. I need them in our lives as I look down at my growing tummy.

Even though I hate hearing updates, Dez has kept me informed on Gabriele only because she's worried about him. Luke said he's drinking all the time, he barely showers, and the business is faltering which means Luke has had to step in doing double the work to clean up his mess.

Dez said he's working nonstop keeping the business afloat and trying to keep his brother out of the booze. A part of me feels guilty for not giving him the chance to hear him out when he begged. But he made his choice back then to disregard me, so I made my choice to build a non-penetrable fortress around me and this baby. He's not going to knock it down this time.

Every day is a challenge for me. Healing my heart has been a long process, but I've had good friends to lean on during these last couple of months. Jason, to my biggest surprise, has become an extremely close friend. Though at times while staying with him I know he yearns for more, he's been nothing but a supportive patient confidant this whole time. He's kept his emotions in check and has been a complete gentleman.

I'm going to miss our nights of laughing together, and the quiet times where words were not needed as he was working, and I was reading a book. We fell into perfect comfort with each other, but even then, it wasn't enough to stop my thoughts from drifting to Gabriele.

I wondered at times if I could learn to love Jason as I do Gabriele and maybe in time my love for Gabriele would fade. But then I would always look down at my stomach and realize that it's just not possible nor fair. My heart belongs to another fully and irrevocably. It was then I realized it was time to figure out my next move in life.

Where was I to raise this child?

That's when North Carolina's coast came back to mind. I've never been there. I've seen pictures and in those I could close my eyes trying to picture what the sea salt air might smell like. Living on a beach waking up to the sunrise and going to bed watching the sunset every night might heal my soul. Might be just what the good old heart doctor would order for me.

When I told Dez and Trev initially they weren't happy with my decision. They actually freaked out at me demanding I fly home, but when I reminded her I would be close to her mother which would give her a reason to visit then she eased up a bit. She's still not happy about me being so far away but she's settling in with her new life with Luke now that they officially moved in together, Trev is still hesitant about Adam's offer for him to move in with him, but he's wearing him down, and I will have Christy to help me and me to help her. It's a win win for us both.

When I told Jason about the move, he asked me to stay. He offered to be there to help with the baby and set up everything we needed here, but ultimately, I wasn't being fair to him. He's an amazing man, I would just be holding him back from finding something he truly deserved since I couldn't be the one to give it to him.

He finally accepted my reasoning and introduced me to a realtor in the area who helped me locate the perfect rental house right on the beach. I figured this was the best route to go since I'm not familiar with the area, and purchasing a home is not something I'm ready to commit to just yet.

My phone rings. "Hey, you, how was the flight?" Jason asks.

"Uncomfortable," I snort.

He laughs. "Well, I can only imagine with that belly of yours."

"Ugh, it's definitely not getting any smaller or easier," I joke.

There's silence for a moment. Almost like an unspoken word between us of missing one another since he's been my strong shoulder for so long. It feels a bit unnerving with my unknown future ahead of me.

"So, I had some basics delivered there already for you, and I'm flying my interior designer down tomorrow to meet with you. I want to make sure you have everything you need with little effort as possible."

I'm stunned at his thoughtfulness. "Jason, you really didn't have to do this."

"I wanted to. It's already too quiet here without you," he admits.

Guilt slices through me.

"I was thinking once you're settled in, I can fly in for a visit –" he hints.

I pause trying to find the right words to say. "Jason, even though I love the idea, I think it's best if I take this time for myself. I've never been on my own before, and I just need some time to get to know me again."

"I understand, Naomi. I'm here when and if you need me."

"Thank you, Jason. You will never know how grateful I am that you came into my life."

He sighs. "The feeling is extremely mutual, Naomi," he replies.

"Anyways, Crystal is waiting for your arrival. I'm sure you're almost there. So please, don't be a stranger," he tells me sadly.

"Thank you again for everything, Jason. We'll talk soon."

I PULL up to my new house. My realtor, Crystal, is waiting for me in the driveway. The house is perfectly tucked away from the street with beautiful colorful flower bushes surrounding the front. I'm reminded for a mere moment of the island in Belize. I shake my head clearing the thought from my mind – only fresh new memories belong at this house.

"Hi Noami, welcome to Wilmington," Crystal greets, shaking my hand. "Let's do a walkthrough of the house and make sure everything is of your liking."

"Thank you. It's nice to finally meet you."

As soon as she opens the door it instantly feels like home. Even though the house is bare, I feel a connection right away. I think I'm going to be very happy here. Before she can show me anything else, I'm drawn to the wall looking over the ocean. The whole back wall is glass from head to toe; yet another reminder of Gabriele I have to erase from my thoughts.

"Wow, the pictures didn't do this justice," I tell her in awe.

"No, they most definitely don't. You should see the view when the sun is setting."

My grin grows from ear to ear. "I can't wait."

We walk through the remainder of the house before she leaves, and once we say our goodbyes and I close the door behind her, I lean my head against the door and let out a deep breath. This is home, not just any home, but my home.

I've never felt anything like this. Thanks to my grandparents, I get to have the life I've envisioned for so long. Best of all, I get to raise this baby without stress and enjoy every single moment.

My phone rings.

"Hey, did you make it?" Dez questions worried.

I turn the camera around and begin giving her a tour of the house. "Wow, Nay. It's freaking perfect! Do you love it?"

I walk over to the windows overlooking the ocean, watching the waves kiss the beach. "I do, Dez. I really do. I think this is where I am meant to be," I confess.

She smiles sadly. "I'm happy for you. Though, I miss the shit out of you, and I'm sad I'm going to miss the important moments of that baby's life, I'm glad you're happy."

"How's living with Luke? Is he treating you well?"

She giggles. "Oh, he treats me very well every night all night," she reveals. I roll my eyes.

"Gross."

She looks like she has something to say but stops before she says it. I know her all too well.

"Out with it," I demand.

She still looks conflicted.

I sigh. "Just say it, Dez."

"It's just Gabriele stopped by an hour ago. He looked

good. He stopped drinking, and he's finally showering again." She laughs. "But he asked about you."

"Dez – you didn't tell him where I am, did you?" I growl.

"No! I promise I didn't. But I think you should still hear him out. Hear what he has to say for himself. I think you'll find what he has to say surprising actually."

I sigh even louder this time. "You know I can't. I just can't put myself through it all. I want to move on and start fresh."

"But doesn't he deserve to know he has a baby on the way? How am I supposed to continue to keep this from Luke? It's his niece or nephew too you know. How do you think he's going to feel knowing I kept this from him?" she whines.

I know she has a point, but I'm just not ready to accept it. I'm not ready to admit she's right, and I'm sure as hell not ready to speak to him.

"Dez, I'm sorry for putting you in this position. I didn't intend it, but please just give me some more time. I'll figure it out," I beg.

She nods. "Okay. Love you, Nay."

"Love you too."

IT'S BEEN three weeks of craziness. Jason's interior designer finished my house in record breaking time. The place is bright, beachy, and radiantly perfect, but most of all, the baby's room is a dream. She finished it with neutral colors with an ocean theme since I have decided to wait until the baby's born to find out the sex. I've been glued to the sliding rocking chair, just sitting in here, picturing my future – *alone*.

There are moments I sit here overly excited, and then there are moments I'm left in tears because I'm scared of doing this alone. I miss Gabriele. I miss his touch, his smell, the way his arms feel wrapped around me, I just miss him.

At times I can picture us as a family together, kissing each other after his long day of work, reading our son or daughter a bedtime story snuggled up, and then turning in for a night of long passionate love making.

And in these moments, I come so close to dialing his number. So close to telling him about our baby, so close to begging him to come, but then I remember how he was so adamant about not wanting kids nor a family and my bubble bursts all over again.

Today was a good day though, I have Zach Bryan "Something in Orange," blasting through the house as I sit on my back deck watching the sun begin to set with a nice glass of iced tea. The moment is picturesque – serene as the wind gently glides across my face, and then I feel the baby kick.

I smile looking down. "Hey there little guy," I say, rubbing the side of my belly.

Just as I'm about to take another sip of my iced tea, the doorbell rings.

My brows furrow confused. I haven't gotten one visitor here unannounced. Maybe it's the baby onesies I ordered from Amazon.

I walk to the door, slowly opening it with my phone in hand just in case and standing in front of me is Gabriele with a shy sexy smirk. My heart drops into my gut. I gulp.

"Hello, little baller-ina," he finishes with a stutter as he looks down to my stomach.

I wasn't expecting company, so I have a half shirt on, belly sticking out, and boxer shorts on. Not ideal for answering the door.

"What the fuck?" he says, looking back up to me then back down to my belly.

Shit.

I cross my arms over my chest. "What are you doing here, Gabriele? How did you find me?"

He doesn't seem to register my questions as he can't take his eyes off my stomach.

I wave my hands in front of his face until I get his attention again. "Hello? What are you doing here?"

"Is it mine?" he asks softly, curious, no anger.

"Gabriele, I –" I begin to avoid the answer, but he stops me dead in my tracks.

"Is the baby mine, Naomi?" he asks again with authority this time.

I give in and nod.

He takes a deep exhale seeming to be relieved. I'm wordless at this point while I stare at him blankly waiting for him to speak.

"Are you going to invite me in so we can talk?"

I hesitate for a moment, the last thing I wanted to do was talk with him, but I concede then move aside so he can pass me.

He walks in looking around impressed taking the place in.

"Is Jason here?"

I follow him as he walks into the kitchen. "No. It's just me who lives here."

He turns quizzically as he leans against the kitchen counter.

"I don't understand," he says.

I sigh leaning against the counter across from him. "Gabriele, Jason and I were never together. He's just a special friend. Nothing further. He helped me in a time of need, but that's it," I explain.

"Did you fuck him?"

Now my blood begins to boil. Who the fuck is he to question me? At this point I almost wish I had so I could rub it in his face.

"Did I *fuck* him? Are you serious! No, I didn't fuck him! I'm not going to explain myself any further to you either," I screech. "What the fuck are you even doing here, Gabriele? How about you explain that to me?" I demand with my hands on my hips looking like a hippo.

His eyes twinkle entertained as he gives me a crooked smirk, looking between my belly and me.

"I came here for you," he says blatantly, staring deep into my soul. I look away disconnecting from him.

"Naomi, look at me."

I refuse.

"Please?" he begs softly.

I look back up to him.

"Who told you were to find me? Did Dez?" I question.

"I keep track of where you are at all times. I have very good people that work for me," he states.

I feel invaded and a bit stalked, but I should have known. He's an extremely wealthy powerful man, of course he has people. But why now? Why come all this way now?

"Gabriele, we're over. You made that clear when you went prancing around with your new girlfriend as soon as you left me."

The pain rips through me all over again. I place my hand over my belly for support. This is what I've been trying to avoid all these months. I've been mending myself together piece by piece and a setback is not something I can handle right now.

He sighs, then walks toward me. I want to back up, but he now has me trapped against this counter placing his hands on either side of me.

"If you would have heard me out months ago, I would have been able to tell you she was a friend. We were helping each other out," he starts to explain. I scoff rolling my eyes.

"She's not into men, and her parents have been on her about finding a suitable man to bring home or she wouldn't receive her inheritance that was coming to her that month. I needed a distraction to get those sleezy paparazzi to stop trying to search for you."

"I couldn't bear the thought of them smearing your life all over the front page of the tabloids for strangers to read while they destroyed you. I didn't give a fuck what they said about me or even that they associated me with a stripper.

"It was you I was worried about. That's why I stayed away for so long. That's why I invented this fake façade of a relationship. I had to make sure they moved on from any possibility of you. I hated being away from you, every moment was pure torture."

He leans in closer, so close I can smell his minty breath and his mouthwatering aroma I've been dreaming of for so long. I close my eyes and inhale, basking in the moment. Trying to imprint this in my memories before it disappears again.

"So, you see, little ballerina. It's you, it's always been you. I'm fucking in love with you," he finally admits.

I just wish I believed him. I wish I could relish this moment, but I can't. I wish I could jump up and down with joy celebrating our love for one another, but I can't. I push him away getting some distance between us so I can think clearer. He has my brain fogged, confused, and tangled.

"Gabriele, I'm pregnant. You said you didn't want children. You said you didn't want a relationship. You say you now love me, but what does that matter when there's no future for us?" I inquire, throwing his words back in his face. He seemed to have forgotten them.

He stalks toward me; I back up and put the couch in between us. He chuckles.

"To be fair, I didn't know you were pregnant with my baby. But I can promise you, no other man will be raising my child. As I stand here in front of you begging for another chance, I'm also standing here asking for us to be a family.

This is my baby too, Naomi, and I want to be a part of its life.

"I fucked up. I was running from my feelings. I've never loved someone before, and I tried to force those feelings away, but I realized once you left, that I couldn't. I fucking love the shit out of you. It has been tearing me up knowing I couldn't hold you, touch you, hear your voice, smell my favorite smell of you. Everyday I've been dying inside, and I can't bear it anymore. I need you. I need you by my side. I need to wake up next to you every morning for the rest of my life. I need you attached to me in every single way," he discloses as he closes the distance between us and begins to drop to one knee.

My mouth hangs open. My mind is jumbled, confused, and trying to decipher this confession swarming my head. He grabs my hand pulling out a little black box from his pants pocket and opens it. A humongous diamond ring is sparkling in my face.

"Naomi Alexandra Veil, you've stolen my heart, and you've invaded my soul. Every ounce of me belongs to you. I don't want to spend another moment without you, and I promise to spend every day of my life making this all up to you."

He reaches for me, placing his hand over my belly.

"And I promise to be the best damn father to our child. I don't give a fuck what I said before, I want this baby with you, and after this one, I want more. I can't picture another day without you by my side. You are my heart and soul; I can't breathe without you. I can't imagine my life without you. Will you please do me the honor of marrying me and becoming my wife?"

My hand slams over my mouth shocked. My eyes are wide as tears begin to stream down my face, and I'm shaking uncontrollably while he waits for my answer.

I feel like my whole world has just turned upside down in

the most unexpected, exquisite way. I had no inkling or thought of marriage, or a family together could actually be a possibility, I always thought that idea was null and void with him – a fantasy for me, but here he is, pouring his soul out to me on a silver platter for me to take or stomp on, and I'm scared shitless.

But even more than scared, I'm fucking in love with this man, there's no doubt about this. I can't deny it. And even though I'm frightened to take the leap and should run the other way, I've always loved the quote, "When it feels scary to jump in, that's exactly the moment when you jump."

So here I go, placing my faith in his hands, placing faith in love, and jump.

EPILOGUE

THREE YEARS LATER...

"And Trevor Alexander, do you take Adam Sole to be your eternal partner and husband for as long as you both shall live?" the officiant asks.

"Fuck yeah I do!"

We all break out in a laugh. I can't keep my wide smile at bay, my heart is so full today. Everyone I love is here in one place.

"By the state of North Carolina, I now announce you husband and husband. You may kiss your partner."

Adam grabs Trevor and leans him back for a sexy passionate kiss. We all break out in claps and whistles.

"Mommy, Mommy! Are Uncle Trev and Uncle Adam married now?" Lucia asks excitedly, clapping his little hands away.

Gabriele chuckles as he bounces Lucia on his lap. Every time I look at these two together my heart melts. My beautiful son is the spitting image of his father.

"Yes, baby, they are now married, *finally*," I answer.

Trev and Adam finally face us all with their hands tangled in the air. This moment is perfect. Finally, my best friend gets his happily ever after.

"Josie!" Dez screams after our niece as she hops off her lap and runs to her uncles in her frilly pink dress. We all laugh as Trev scoops her up and smothers her with kisses while she giggles her little high-pitched laugh.

I look over to my sexy husband, catching him in the act of watching me. He leans over to my ear and whispers, "Have I told you how fucking beautiful you are, Mrs. Vanucci?"

I bite my bottom lip feeling the heat creep over my skin from his breath against my ear. "You have – multiple times today," I answer him with a sultry look.

"Keep biting that lip in front of me Mrs. Vanucci, I'll whisk you away right now, take you upstairs, bend you over and fill you with my seed," he threatens with a promise while covering Lucia's little ears.

I lean in nibbling his ear; he moans quietly. "Too late, Mr. Vanucci. You already have."

His brows furrow as he leans back confused watching my smile grow. Then it dawns on him. "Wait, are you pregnant?" he questions, smiling from ear to ear.

I nod. "Mhmm."

He smashes his lips to mine, then screams excitedly out loud. "You've made me the happiest man alive. I knew from the moment I laid eyes on you that my life was no longer mine. My heart and soul belonged to you from day one. You own me, Naomi," he confesses with his forehead against mine.

I bring his face to mine with a soft kiss.

"I love you, Gabriele."

"I love you too, my little ballerina."

THE END

ACKNOWLEDGMENTS

It's not easy after eight years to jump back into writing again, but I am so happy I did! This book wouldn't have come to life if it wasn't for multiple people helping me along the way.

First, I'd like to thank my editor, Virginia Carey. You have made me feel at ease and comfortable with sharing my writing after being out of the industry so long. So, thank you. Also, Michele Ficht, who did a quick and thorough job of proofreading, helped me with the finishing touches of making this book perfect.

Second, I'd like to thank Sommer Stein for my beautiful book cover – you always knock it out of the park! Paige Jenkins, my formatter, for making the inside beautiful, and The Next Step PR for all the great promotions over the weeks before publication. You guys are all amazing at what you do!

Third, to my family for putting up with my craziness while writing and cheering me on along the way. You all are my biggest supporters.

And last, thank you to the readers who took a chance on me again. I will be forever grateful.

ABOUT THE AUTHOR

Shevaun DeLucia lives in upstate New York with her husband, and two boys while also enjoying spending time with her two grown children who have already left the nest. As a stay-at-home mom while her children were young, she fell in love with reading. She indulged in the small moments that took her away from the reality of her loud, overly rambunctious household, bringing her into a world of fantasy. When reading wasn't enough to satisfy her, she turned to writing, determined to create the perfect ending of her own.

Visit her on her website at: https://shevaundelucia.com/

facebook.com/AuthorShevaunDeLucia